MY SOUL
CRIES OUT

MY SOUL
CRIES OUT

A *novel*
By Sherri L. Lewis

URBAN
CHRISTIAN

www.urbanchristianonline.net

Urban Books, LLC
10 Brennan Place
Deer Park, NY 11729

ISBN-13: 978-1-60162-996-8
ISBN-10: 1-60162-996-6

First Trade Printing July 2007
First Mass Market Printing November 2009
Printed in the United States of America

10 9 8 7 6 5 4 3 2 1

Distributed by Kensington Publishing Corp.
Submit Wholesale Orders to:
Kensington Publishing Corp.
C/O Penguin Group (USA) Inc.
Attention: Order Processing
405 Murray Hill Parkway
East Rutherford, NJ 07073-2316
Phone: 1-800-526-0275
Fax: 1-800-227-9604

Dedication

In loving memory of Pastor James Leroy
Moore

Thanks for everything you taught me about
worship, intercession, the Holy Spirit and
intimacy with God.
I know you're watching me up there in the cloud
of witnesses!

Acknowledgments

First and foremost, thanks to my God for the gift of writing and the love of story and the opportunity to share it with the world. I hope I heard You right, and if so, I trust that people will be blessed by what I believe You gave me to share.

Thanks to my number one editor and big sis, Joyce, for reading *every* single version and revision of this book—only you know how many there were! Thanks to Daddy for reading the book and for all your suggestions on changes I should make. Thanks to Mommy for motivating me by refusing to read it until it was an actual book. Now you have to read it! Thanks to Kelli for teaching me to be true to the artist in myself and inspiring me to pursue this part of my destiny.

Thanks to my best friend, Yvette, for being the best prayer partner and destiny seeker a girl could ask for. What a compliment for someone who doesn't read novels to read my manuscripts and love them. Hopefully we'll be making movies one day!

Thanks to my best friend, Kathy, for always pushing me and inspiring me and for being there for me through the roughest time ever. I know that I can always count on you for any and everything. You are my bestest dude!

Thanks to my best friend, Allen, for being such a great friend—for always listening, for music and for *always* making me laugh. Thanks for the advice on the dialogue for my male characters. Thanks to you, I think they actually came out sounding like men instead of women with men's names.

To my sistawriterfriends—the women of the Atlanta Black Christian fiction writers critique group. Thanks for the critiques, the love, and encouragement. Who's next??? Special thanks to the bestest writing partner in the whole world, Tia McCollors, for the long hours at Joe's getting this book done and for answering *all* my questions about the publishing and marketing process.

To my fellow Christian fiction authors, especially those that have led the way—Victoria Christopher Murray, Jacquelin Thomas, Patricia Haley, Mary Griffith, Claudia Mair Burney, Kendra Norman Bellamy and so many others.

To Kendra Norman Bellamy—what can I say? There aren't enough words I could say to thank you for presenting me with this opportunity. May God bless you richly and reward you all the days of your life. To my editor, Joylynn—thanks for making my experience with Urban such a pleasant one. To my agent, Sha Shana Crichton of Crichton and Associates—thanks for interpreting the legalese and for being so attentive and available.

Thanks to my dear friend, Troy, for helping to make this story come to life. Love you always! To my dear friend and the bestest nurse ever, Toni—thanks for taking such good care of me and for always keeping me covered with your many prayers.

Thanks to my spiritual father, Apostle Peterson, for refusing to let me end this book without redemption and for provoking me to seek the mind of God for the outcome. This is SUCH a better book because of you. I can't believe I was gonna kill Kevin! Thanks for all your love, prayers, and support through my darkest hour.

Special thanks to Pastor Darryl Foster and his precious wife, Dee, for taking the time to meet with me. I appreciate your being so willing to share your testimony with me and with the world. I pray that this book becomes another instrument in the hand of God to snatch struggling Christians out of the kingdom of darkness and into the Kingdom of light!

And finally, thanks to you, the reader, for supporting me in my pursuit of destiny. May this book be a blessing!

1

The worst day of my life was the day I caught my husband cheating on me.

You know those movies where the wife forgets something important for work and comes home in the middle of the day to get it, only to find her husband in bed with her best friend?

I should have been so lucky.

I had forgotten my good Littman stethoscope and hated the flimsy plastic ones we kept at the nurses' station. I didn't know how any nurse could get a decent blood pressure with those things. Since I was home, I figured I might as well eat. I opened the fridge to get some leftover lasagna before going back to the office.

That's when I heard it . . . the bumping.

Not a regular, foot-shuffling bumping like someone walking around. This bumping had a rhythm to it. A beat.

I stepped into the dining room and stared at the ceiling. The noise came from the master bedroom, directly overhead. Women's intuition rose from my belly to form a lump in my chest that ascended to my throat. The hairs on the back of my neck stood at attention.

I tried to reason away the knowing in my head. My husband, Kevin, usually spent the one Saturday a month I worked playing basketball or writing music. Yeah, that was it. He was pounding out the beat to a new song with his size 13 feet . . . in the bedroom, instead of his studio down the hall where he usually wrote music.

I tiptoed toward the steps, hardly able to breathe. Movie clips of guilty husbands and shocked wives flashed through my mind. Which one of my friends would it be? Or I bet it was Janine, the cutesy little soprano who sang all the leads in the church choir. During every rehearsal, she batted her eyelashes at Kevin and always needed him to stay after to help her get her solo right. I knew she was a skank ho.

I dragged my feet up the steps, fighting to lift them as I got closer to the top. I wasn't sure of the protocol for such a situation. Did I throw the door open and cry, "Aha, I caught you!"? Did I knock on the door and wait for them to get dressed and come out and admit their crime?

Nothing in my life could have ever prepared me for what I saw when I swung the door open and sang out, "Honey, I'm home."

Imagine my surprise when I realized that the *she* I thought she would be was actually . . . a *he*.

I had never fainted before, but then again, I

had never caught my husband of two years cheating with the guy who was supposed to be his closest "friend." They were close all right. Closer than two men should ever be.

When I opened my eyes after a few minutes of unconsciousness, they were both scrambling to pull on some clothes—eyes wide, mouths hanging open. I took a deep breath, made sure I didn't have any life threatening injuries, jumped up and went to swinging.

"Wait, let me explain!" Kevin held up his arms to ward off my blows.

"Explain? What could you possibly explain? I've seen enough to know there's no explanation you could possibly come up with that could begin to *explain* what I just saw."

I searched the room for something to swing or throw. Why hurt my hands? I threw books, hangers, a lamp—one of those big floor ones—anything I could get my hands on. I caught Kevin right above the eye with my alarm clock. I felt triumphant when blood trickled down his cheek.

"And you, Trey! You smile in my face, eat dinner at my house, talk about how happy you are for us and how happy I make Kevin, but all the while you were scheming on how to steal my man."

"It wasn't like that, Monica, I promise. I—"

"Wasn't like that?" I threw one of my high heel shoes, aiming for his eyeball. "Obviously it was, Trey."

I stomped out of the room and disappeared down the steps. They probably thought I had gotten tired or come to my senses. I wasn't anywhere near coming to my senses. I just remembered Kevin's golf clubs in the front closet.

When I came back, the look in Kevin's eyes said he regretted the day he ever became obsessed with being the next Tiger Woods. Trey screamed like a girl and ran out of the room when he saw the driving iron in my hand.

I made a wild swing at Kevin and hit the wall instead. Paint and drywall crumbled to the floor. While I was prying the club out of the wall, Kevin grabbed my arm and wrestled me to the floor.

"Monica, please, calm down and let's talk about this like rational adults."

"Calm down? Rational adults?" I unleashed a spray of curse words—strung them together like a pro. Kevin's eyes widened. He had never heard me curse before. By the time he met me, I'd gotten delivered of the cussing demon I had picked up my freshman year of college.

I twisted a hand free and slapped his face. Hard. Twice.

He grabbed my hand again and tried to pin me down. He was forceful enough to stop my assault against him, but gentle enough not to hurt me.

"Monnie, please." His eyes begged me. Those big, beautiful eyes I had fallen so deeply in love with. Seeing the tears forming in the corners of them took some of the fire out of me. I stopped struggling for a minute.

Kevin looked like he was trying to decide if I was faking him out or if he could trust me enough to loosen his grip. He stared, obviously not knowing what to say. What could he say?

I realized my dream life, my fantasy, had just fallen apart. I let out a wail. "Oh my Gaaaaaa-wwwwwddddd . . ."

"Monnie, I'm sorry. I—"

"You're sorry all right. You sorry son of a . . . You mother-lovin' . . ." Forget it. It was too hard. I unleashed another spray of foul language, knowing no matter how much I cursed or how many times I hit him, I'd never be able to make him hurt as much as he had just made me hurt.

I sure could try, though.

He'd let his guard down, giving me perfect space and time to kick him in the groin. When he fell, I jumped up and kicked him in the side with all the force my leg could muster. I didn't know such violence lived in me. I had to make myself calm down before I really hurt him. Even though he deserved it.

I paced around the bedroom. "Help me, Jesus. Help me not to kill him. Help me not to go down to the kitchen and get a knife and gut him. OhLawd-Jesus, help me. I want to take this golf club and beat him in the head 'til his brains drip out his ears. Jesus, keep me. I need You, Lord, otherwise I'm gonna . . ." My eyes darted around the room, looking for other things I could murder my husband with.

Kevin stood up, holding his side, sheer terror in his eyes. He had only seen me this mad once before—the last time my mother caught my dad with one of his many women.

"Jesus Jesus Jesus Jesus Jesus Jesus Jesus Jesus . . ." I called His name like I was on the tarrying bench, trying to get filled with the Holy Ghost. When Kevin heard me praying in tongues, he scrambled toward the door.

After I heard the front door slam, I screamed from somewhere deeper than I knew my soul went. What had just happened? How long had it been happening?

I started pacing again. I walked up and down the steps, into the kitchen, into the den, into Kevin's music studio, back up the steps, into our bedroom, into the guest room, and into my exercise room I never used. Every time I tried to stop and sit, this wave of anger-bewilderment-shock-sadness-confusion-fear-insanity would come over me, and I'd have to walk again.

After about fifteen minutes of walking, cursing, and praying, I got tired. The initial adrenaline rush wore off and I remembered how out of shape I was. I looked at my watch. My half-hour lunch break was over and I was due back at work. I caught my breath and picked up the phone.

"Greater Washington Family Medicine, how may I help you?"

"Anthony, this is Monica. I need to talk to Dr. Stewart. Is she in with a patient?" I tried to keep my voice from doing that shaky thing it did when I cried.

"What's wrong wit' you, girl?"

"Not now, Anthony. Just get her for me. Please." I hoped the "please" would soften my snippiness. I wasn't in the mood for Anthony to catch an attitude.

"Let me check. Hold on a sec."

I waited for a moment, trying to think of a way

to explain why I wasn't coming back to work. My brain was too fuzzy to come up with a good lie.

"This is Dr. Stewart."

"Hey, it's Monica. An emergency came up. I won't be able to make it back this afternoon. I know Saturdays are bad, but I just can't make it back."

"Oh dear, I hope everything is okay. Let me know if you need anything. See you Monday?"

"Oh yes, of course. Everything will be fine by then," I lied.

I hung up the phone and went straight for the freezer to grab a pint of Tom & Larry's ice cream. Chocolate Walnut Brownie Crunch. My favorite. I plunked down in the middle of the family room floor and stared at the walls, covered with pictures chronicling the last six years of my relationship with Kevin.

Tears fell as I looked at the beautiful black and white engagement picture of us staring into each other's eyes. I should've known it was too good to be true. Kevin was every woman's dream. He was the one man I knew who wasn't afraid to share his feelings. He was my best friend. Closer than any of my girlfriends. I could tell him anything and he could tell me anything.

Or so I thought.

How could he have deceived me? This wasn't something he just tried out. He'd known Trey since childhood. Trey Hunter turned up at our door six months ago after not having seen Kevin in years. Kevin introduced him as his high school friend. I guess high school sweetheart was more like it.

I should've known something wasn't right when

Trey first appeared. Trey was more effeminate than me, and I couldn't think of any of the straight men I knew who were close friends with gay men. But something should have alerted me long before that. I racked my brain searching for clues I might have ignored.

Kevin and I met not too long after I finished college, when I started visiting the church he attended. They had the best choir in the city and sang the latest contemporary music.

I joined Love and Faith Christian Center after attending a few Sundays. As soon as I finished my new members' classes, I joined the choir. I had sung in a choir as long as I could remember. Never sang a solo, but I was one of those solid altos any director could count on to keep everyone else on key. Kevin was the minister of music and I was the section leader, and we hung out after rehearsals to discuss songs or parts or whatever.

One night after practice, we went to IHOP and ended up talking until two in the morning. From then on we were inseparable. After that, we went out after every rehearsal and every church service, sometimes with a big group from the choir, sometimes just us.

The end table held a picture of us and our choir clique at our favorite table at IHOP. Judging from the fatness of my cheeks, my all-black outfit, and the salad instead of pancakes on the table in front of me, I must have been on an upswing of my lifelong weight yo-yo. Kevin had this enamored look on his face and I had this look of total shock like, "He's really with me?"

I scraped the bottom of the ice cream carton.

Where did a whole pint go that quick? Good thing they had a two-for-one sale last week. Or maybe it wasn't such a good thing. Forget it. This was no time to worry about my weight. I needed all the comfort Tom & Larry could offer right now.

I turned to stare at our wedding picture hanging over the fireplace mantle. Kevin was dashing in his tux. I looked at his mocha chocolate skin; tall, muscular body; thick, curly hair, and heartbreaking smile.

Sistas was hatin' on me that day.

I had crash dieted to get into my size 12 wedding dress and looked good if I do say so myself. My classy Halle Berry haircut complemented my heart-shaped face. The dress was perfect for my hourglass figure. That was one thing I had going for me. Even at my largest, I was still well proportioned, and *always* had a waistline.

I knew some of my fellow choir sistas were jealous, and I felt good to be the one that caught the mysterious, elusive Kevin Day. He was charismatic as the minister of music—able to lead the whole church into the highest realms of praise and worship. But he seemed nervous when all the women fawned over him and vied for his attention.

That shoulda let me know something wasn't straight. But then again, what would I know? Kevin was my first and only real love. The only man I ever had a serious relationship with. The only one I'd ever been intimate with. And now . . .

Help me understand this, God. Kevin is . . . gay?

Something in me snapped. I picked up a book and crashed it into the picture. I don't know what broke it, the book or the high-pitched scream I let out as I threw it.

I began picking up pictures of me and Kevin from all over the den. The one from our honeymoon in Negril, I threw against the wall. I sent the previous year's Christmas picture hurling into our engagement picture hanging over the stairs. One by one, I destroyed the evidence of what I thought was our wonderful, God-ordained life together.

As I smashed each picture, my heart shattered with the glass. My throat was raw from screaming. I couldn't stop, though. I had to destroy everything that told the lie I now knew my marriage was.

My mind was spinning. Instinctively, I picked up the phone to call my best friend, Trina. Right after the speed dial finished, I hung up. What would I tell her? "Hey, girl, guess what? I just caught my husband with another man." Too embarrassing.

I started pacing again. "Oh my God. Did that really just happen?" No matter how much I walked, I couldn't escape it. "Okay, Monnie. Get yourself together." I made myself stand still and take ten deep breaths.

The phone rang. Without thinking, I answered it. "Hello?"

"Did you just call me?"

"Trina . . . I . . . yeah, it was . . . I dialed by accident."

"What's wrong?"

"Nothing." I tried to clear my throat and sound normal.

"Monica, stop lying. What's wrong? You sound like you been crying."

I didn't say anything, knowing my voice would betray me.

"Monica?"

Why did I answer the phone? I could have played this off to anyone else but Trina. I choked on the lump in my throat and started crying again.

"I'll be right there."

"No! Don't come over. I'm fine—" Too late. She'd already hung up the phone.

I looked around at the mess. Trina lived only about fifteen minutes away. I knew she'd be speeding to get to me. I grabbed a broom and swept the glass into a pile.

I cut my finger on a long, thin shard. "Ouch!" Blood trickled down my arm. I ran to the bathroom before it dripped onto my plush, off-white carpet.

I ran water over my finger until its red tinge ran clear, then wrapped it in toilet paper. That would have to do for now. I caught a glimpse of myself in the mirror. My eyes were puffy, nose red, and my short bob was flying everywhere. I looked like a crazy woman.

The doorbell rang. I splashed my face with cold water, blew my nose and tried to smooth my hair down. The doorbell rang again.

"I'm coming, doggone it!"

My feeble attempt at fixing my face was lost on Trina. When I opened the door, she gasped. "Oh my God, what happened to you?"

The look of concern on her face was too much for me. I burst into tears again.

"Monnie, what is it?" Trina led me into the family room and sat me down on the couch. She stared at the broken glass, picture frames, and picture fragments. "What happened in here? Did you and Kevin get in a fight?"

I nodded, still crying.

She must have noticed the blood soaking through the tissue on my finger. "Oh my God. What did he do to you? Did Kevin hurt you?"

I shook my head, still crying.

"What happened?" Trina got up and walked into the kitchen. I could hear her rummaging through the cabinets while running water. She came back with a wet dishtowel and a glass of water. She unwrapped my finger and wrapped it in the wet cloth and gave me the water to drink. She went to the bathroom and came back with a roll of toilet paper and handed me a wad to wipe my face. She rubbed my back and waited for me to stop crying.

I finally looked up at her. "I . . . Kevin . . . I . . ." I shook my head and took a deep breath. I rolled off some more tissue and blew my nose. I looked at the floor.

"Monnie, this is me, your girl. Whatever it is, you can tell me."

I had to just spit it out. "I walked in on Kevin and Trey this afternoon."

"What do you mean?"

"I walked in on them in my bed."

Trina's eyebrows furrowed. "What do you mean?"

"What do you mean what do I mean? I walked in on my husband . . ." I sucked in a deep breath, "having sex with another man."

Her mouth flew open and her eyes bugged out. "What do you mean?"

"Trina, I can't say it any clearer than that. Unless you want the graphic version."

She held up her hand as if to say "No, thank you." She stood up and began pacing the den. Every few seconds, she would turn back to me with her mouth wide open, her eyes asking if I said what she thought I said. Each time she did, I nodded. She'd open her mouth like she was about to say something then close it, then open it again and close it, until finally she put her hands on her hips. "What do you mean?"

I rolled my eyes. "Should I say it in French?"

"Sorry, but you gotta give me a minute with this one." She frowned as if she was trying to solve the most difficult Calculus problem. "So you're telling me Kevin was . . . he and Trey were . . . Kevin is . . . oh, my . . ."

I started crying again. Her saying it—or not being able to say it—seemed to make it more real.

Trina pulled herself out of her stupor and came over to hug me. "Oh, Monnie, I don't know what to say. I don't know how to—"

"I'm not asking you to fix this, Trina. You don't have to say anything. Just . . . help me not to lose it." I sobbed in her arms. "You coulda never told me Kevin was . . . I never expected . . ."

"Shhh, I know. Me either. He doesn't seem . . . I mean nothing about him is . . ." Trina shook her head and grimaced as if an image just registered in her brain. "Oh, boy, this is . . ."

We both sat there shaking our heads for a few minutes.

She chuckled. "So you kicked his tail, huh?"

Leave it to Trina to make me laugh at a time like this. "Girl, I had to call on the Lord to keep from killing both of them. I lost control."

"Y'all was tearing up the den?"

"No, the bedroom. I did all this after they left."

"Umm." She looked around at the mess again. "Remind me to never get you mad." We both laughed, then I started to cry.

"Oh, Monnie. I'm sorry, girl." She held me until I stopped crying. "Come on. Let's pack you a bag. You're going with me."

I looked around room. "What about this?"

"Let him clean it up. That is if he's stupid enough to come back."

2

I lay back on the headrest in Trina's car. I was glad I called her. Trina was always there for me, no matter what was going on. What made me think I could have gone through this without her?

Without her . . .

I gasped and sat up. "Oh my God, I forgot."

Trina grimaced. "I wondered when it was gonna hit you."

"You're leaving me. I can't believe it."

Trina was scheduled to leave for a two-year mission trip in Africa in two weeks. She had been planning, dreaming, and talking about it for the past year. Trina was an African studies major in college. After completing a Missions degree at a local Bible college, she became obsessed with the idea of going to Africa. Her dream was finally about to come true.

Trina stopped at a red light and turned to give

me her full attention. With her hand on my arm, she said, "Say the word, Monnie, and I'll cancel my trip."

I wanted nothing more than to tell her not to go. "I can't do that. As important as this is to you? What kind of friend would I be?"

"One that just experienced what will probably be the worst thing that will happen in her life, who shouldn't have to go through it alone."

"Trina, I love you for even suggesting that, but I'd never forgive myself if you didn't go."

I wanted to be selfish and tell her I couldn't handle losing my husband and my best friend at the same time. But she had already taken a sabbatical from her job, rented her house to her younger sister, and had gotten the most beautiful tiny African braids so she wouldn't have to worry about her hair.

Looked like I was gonna have to walk through this alone because there wasn't another soul I could tell.

A tear slid down my cheek. I felt Trina wipe it away.

"Monnie?"

I shook my head. "I was supposed to have you a niece or a nephew by the time you got back from Africa. Remember?"

Trina rubbed my arm.

Kevin and I had decided we wanted two years of marital bliss before we started a family. A few months ago, we had set January as the month I would stop taking birth control. Relief flooded my chest. Thank God I hadn't stopped yet.

I sighed and lay on the headrest with my eyes closed until the car stopped in Trina's driveway.

Just walking into Trina's house made me feel better. The calming earth tones welcomed me like a hug. The foyer led into her living room with beautiful hardwood floors and a deep brown leather couch and love seat. Red accents added unexpected life to the muted browns, and her artwork added even more sophistication to the look. The musky scent of burning incense wafted from the kitchen.

Trina and I met in a young adult Sunday school class at Love and Faith Christian Church. I instantly liked her, while everyone else got frustrated with her asking a million questions. Unlike most of us who had been in church all our lives, Trina had never been saved before and didn't know much about God or the Bible.

After listening to everyone's frustrated sighs after the second class, I introduced myself to Trina. I offered for us to study and pray together. I told her I didn't know everything, but would teach her whatever I could. The first time we got together, we studied the Bible for an hour then talked for four more. We'd been close friends ever since.

Trina soon surpassed me in all things biblical and spiritual. She stayed at Love and Faith for three years, took every class, went to every Bible study, attended every service, and then got restless. Finally, she said she felt like Bishop had taken her as far as she could go. She joined a church across town known for its Bible teaching, and was quite happy there.

Trina plopped my overnight bag down on her couch and sat down next to it. I sat on the chair and took off my shoes. We sat there in a weird silence for a while.

Trina let out a little sigh. "What do you want to do? You feel like talking about it?"

I shrugged. "What is there to say? My husband is . . . gay. My marriage was a lie, and life as I knew it, planned it, and dreamed it is over."

She nodded. "Yeah, I guess that pretty much sums it up. I wish there was something I could do or say to make this better. Want to pray?"

"And say what? God, please help Monica deal with the fact that her husband is a fag?"

Trina winced. "Could you not use that word?"

"What? Fag? What would you prefer me to say? Homo? Gay boy? Punk? Sissy?"

Trina stared at me. "Dag, Monica. That's kinda harsh, don't ya think? Not to mention severely politically incorrect and ungodly."

I clenched my teeth. "Do I look like I care about being politically correct right now?" I purposefully ignored the godly part.

She looked at my face. "I guess not. I never knew you were like that."

"Like what?"

"Homophobic."

"I didn't either. Amazing what catching your husband with another man will do." I shook my head. "I'm not homophobic. Anthony at work is gay. I don't have a problem with him. And my cousin Ricky got a little sugar in his tank, and we get along just fine."

Trina laughed. "You know what you sound

like?" She gave her best white girl imitation. "I'm not prejudiced. Some of my best friends are black."

"Whatever, girl. I don't know how I feel about 'em. I never had to think about it before. I mean, when you really think about what they do? That's nasty. And to see it? And for it to be my husband?" I shook the image from my head. "Anyway, I said I didn't want to talk about it."

Trina looked around the living room. "Do you want to watch a movie or something then? Take your mind off it?"

"Yeah, I guess that's cool."

Trina put a movie in the DVD player and dimmed the lights. The surround sound filled the room and my head enough to squeeze out the thoughts. I sank into Trina's overstuffed armchair and thick pillows. The pulsing light from the television flashing into the darkness was hypnotic, and I would have fallen asleep if not for fear of seeing images of Kevin and Trey in my head.

One movie turned into three. It was a good escape, even if for only a few hours. After we finished the last one, I stretched and yawned. "I'm going to bed."

Trina clicked off the TV. "Wanna go to church with me in the morning?"

"I don't feel like going to church tomorrow. And please save the sermon. I don't want to hear it."

"I wasn't gonna say anything."

"Yeah, right."

"I wasn't. I just figured you wouldn't want to

go to your church tomorrow and wanted to offer an alternative."

I smacked my forehead. "Oh, no. I have to go to Love and Faith tomorrow."

"Why?"

"I have to teach my juniors Sunday school and I have to do the announcements."

"Can't you get somebody else to do it?"

I looked down at my watch. It was almost 11:00. "At this hour, no. I'll be okay. I'll just sit in the balcony, give the announcements and leave."

"I can see it now." Trina held her hands up in a TV screen frame. "Crazed woman attacks large metropolitan church's minister of music. Details at eleven."

I threw a pillow at her. "I'll be fine. I don't even know if he'll show up."

"Girl, please. Kevin don't ever miss church. Remember how mad you were the day after your wedding, when he insisted on going to service first and then leaving for your honeymoon?"

I curled my upper lip. "You're right. Shoot. I shoulda called Glenda. She woulda done it for me."

"Want me to go with you?"

"What?" I put my hand on my chest. "You'd lower yourself to spend a Sunday at Love and Faith Christian Center?"

"Stop trippin'. It ain't even like that."

I thought for a second. "What if he doesn't come? What should I tell Bishop Walker?"

"What do you mean?"

"He's gonna ask me where Kevin is. What should I tell him?"

"The truth. Tell him you don't know where he is."

"Yeah right, Trina. You know Bishop won't let me just say that and leave. He's gonna ask me a bunch of questions."

"Girl, y'all got fifteen thousand members. You ain't even gonna see Bishop, let alone have to talk to him."

"Yeah, you're right." I scratched my head. "Don't you think he should know, though? Kevin's the minister of music at this man's church. He leads us in worship, and he's gay. Don't you think Bishop has a right to know that? Now that I know, aren't I obligated to tell him?"

Trina got up and took *Cry Freedom* out of the DVD player and returned it to its case. "I don't know, Monica. I do see your point—he has Kevin in a place of leadership and should know the truth. Don't you think Kevin should be the one to tell him, though?"

"Has he told him all this time? Did he tell me?"

Trina returned the DVD to its place amidst her massive collection. "Just be careful, Monnie. Kevin has been at that church all his life. Bishop is like a father to him."

"Exactly. He didn't tell his wife or his spiritual father. He's gay *and* he's a liar. Bishop needs to know. He wouldn't want that type of person in charge of his music ministry a second longer."

Trina shook her head slowly. "Maybe you should talk to Kevin and give him a chance to tell Bishop first."

"Tell you what. I'll let God decide. If God wants me to tell him, He'll create an opportunity for me to tell him. If He doesn't, then I won't even see Bishop tomorrow."

"So you're gonna fleece God, huh?"

"Not fleecing. Just letting His perfect will be done."

I climbed the stairs slowly and got ready for bed. It took so much effort to do simple things like brush my teeth and change clothes. It felt like an hour passed before I lay down in Trina's guest bed. As I drifted off to sleep, my mind raced. Where did I miss it? How could I have not realized my husband was gay? I mean, dag, seems like somewhere along the way, something or someone would have tipped me off.

Alaysia . . .

I hadn't talked to her in almost three years because of this. She had predicted this and tried to warn me. Alaysia was my best friend and roommate through college and after we graduated. She had been closer to me than a sister. We had the biggest fight the night after Kevin proposed to me.

When I announced to Alaysia that Kevin finally popped the question and there was no one else who could be my maid of honor, she just sat there. She didn't get excited. She didn't squeal. She barely looked at the ring. She didn't say a word.

"Okay, that's an inappropriate response."

She took a deep breath. "Monnie, you're my best friend, right?"

"Right."

"You know I love you and would never do anything to hurt you, right?"

"Laysia, what? You're scaring me."

"I should have said something before, but I never thought it would get to this point. I never thought he would propose because . . ."

My face turned bright red. "You never thought he would propose? Why? You didn't think someone like Kevin would fall for me? You're used to the men falling all over you and ignoring the fat girl, huh? Well, guess what? This fine, talented man is in love with me and asked me to marry him. I thought you were my friend. I thought you'd be happy for me. I can't believe I asked you to be my maid of honor. I can't believe you—"

"Monnie, Kevin's gay." She said it matter-of-factly, like she was saying "Kevin's black," or "Kevin's a musician," or "Kevin's a nice guy."

I stared at her. "Why would you say something like that? Are you jealous? These men play the hit-it-and-quit-it game with you, but nobody ever asked you to marry them? That's low, Alaysia."

She took a deep breath but didn't say anything.

"What would make you say something like that?"

She shrugged and scrunched her eyebrows like she was trying to figure it out. She finally said, "Let me ask you one question. Has he ever pressured you to have sex?"

"No, but that doesn't mean anything. We're Christians. We're waiting 'til we get married. I don't expect you to understand."

"Has he ever tried, though? Has it ever gotten so close one of you had to run away to keep it from happening? I've dated Christian guys before. Even a man imprisoned by your 'no fornication' rule will slip and get right up close to the edge. Have you guys ever gotten so close he had to walk it off or take a cold shower?"

"No, but that doesn't mean anything. Kevin respects me. He would never let it go that far." My lip quivered. If Alaysia didn't know anything else, she knew men.

"I know this is hard for you to hear, Monnie, but . . . I don't know how I know. I just know. He's gay and you can't marry him. If you do, I can't stand there as your maid of honor and act like I agree with it."

"I'm going to marry Kevin, and I wouldn't want you as my maid of honor if you begged. I don't even want you as my friend. Get out, lose my number, lose my address, and lose my name."

That was Alaysia's favorite speech whenever she kicked one of her many boyfriends to the curb. That's how we ended six and a half years of friendship.

God, was that your way of warning me?

I didn't bother to listen for His answer. I just rolled over, stuffed my face into the pillow, and cried myself to sleep, trying not to think of what might happen in church the next morning.

3

I felt numb the entire time I taught my Sunday school class. After the kids left, I lingered downstairs as long as I could. Would Kevin be there? If he was, what should I do? Put on my robe and sing in the choir, pretending nothing was wrong? Yeah, right. There was no way I could smile in his face, let alone sing, while Kevin-the-hypocrite directed the choir.

After procrastinating as long as I could, I finally walked upstairs to the main floor of the church. Before I got in the sanctuary good, I knew Kevin hadn't come. There was a stiffness in the air, an atmosphere not primed by anointed praise and worship. Love and Faith had never felt so dry.

I sat down in the back. The sanctuary was expansive, with seats on the large main floor and balcony to seat eight thousand. It had all the trappings of a modern day mega church, including several large screens projecting the service, so the people in the back and balcony could see. Even with two services, we were packed to capacity.

The singers on the praise team were half singing and half looking at each other like they were trying to figure out what to do. After they sang a couple more lifeless songs, Cynthia, who had taken over praise and worship for the morning, finally gave up.

"Let's give the Lord one last shout of praise as we take our seats." She looked happy to hand the microphone to Elder Johnson.

He read the scripture then Elder Banks led prayer. The ushers moved to take up an offering and the choir got up to sing. They struggled through an upbeat arrangement of "Jesus is Real." Trey's front row seat in the alto section was empty.

I watched the choir and the congregation. If Kevin could fool me all this time, who else in here was gay? All of a sudden, everybody looked suspect. The way Deacon Bates clapped his hands was a little too cute. Elder Hampton seemed a little too skilled with the tambourine. The head usher seemed to switch when he walked to get the offering plate. And the way half the tenors did their little two-step? Made me think.

Kevin probably wasn't the only one undercover.

I don't know how Bishop Walker spotted me in the back, but halfway through the song, an usher tapped me on the shoulder and passed me a note written in big, agitated scrawl.

Where's Kevin?!!!!!!!

Someone was upset. Kevin must not have even called. I looked up into the pulpit and gave an exaggerated shrug. Bishop frowned. I took the fact that he saw me all the way in the back before I even got up to give the announcements as a sign that God wanted me to talk to him. I jotted back a quick note.

I'll meet you in your office after service.

My legs shook as I walked up the aisle to do the announcements. I did them all the time and it usually never made me nervous, but today was different. The walk from the back of the church seemed so long. I could hear the whispers rising from the pews. When I got to the podium, I looked down at the paper and looked up at the congregation. Everyone's eyes were asking me the same question Bishop had. *Where's Kevin?*

I cleared my throat and bumbled through the announcements and then kept my eyes focused straight ahead as I returned to my seat.

I barely heard a word Bishop Walker preached. I could tell he was getting close to the end when his voice escalated higher and higher and the crowd got more pumped, until he reached *the* point. Some members were standing with their hands lifted. Others clapped and shouted out their encouragement. "You betta preach, Bishop."

He wiped his forehead and looked over at the organ. I saw him realize Greg was sitting there instead of Kevin. Everybody was itching for a good shout, but Bishop knew better than to take it there. Greg was all right on the keys, but he couldn't handle himself on the Hammond. And he definitely couldn't keep up with the shoutin' music. Guess you don't realize how much the minister of music is the backbone of the church until he's not there.

I watched Bishop switch from the shoutin' place to a holy hush. "Let's just humble ourselves before Him. Some of you need to lay prostrate before the Lord and let His presence fall on you. Lord, give us a fresh infilling. Baptize us anew."

Watching him direct the congregation's emotions was like watching a conductor direct the Philharmonic orchestra. Bishop signaled for one of the elders to take over, nodded to me, and headed toward his office.

His assistant signaled for me to wait outside while he changed out of his heavy robe and sweaty clothes.

He opened the door. "Come on in, Monica."

God, I don't feel like having this conversation.

When I walked in, Bishop Walker was already sitting behind his big, mahogany desk. He motioned for me to sit down.

"What's going on? Kevin doesn't show up, doesn't call. You're sitting in the back instead of in the choir stand where you belong. Is something wrong?"

I stared at the pictures of Martin Luther King Jr. and black Jesus on the wall, wishing I could disappear. An over-whelming feeling of embarrassment washed over me. But I asked God that if it was His will for me to tell Bishop . . .

"Monica?"

"I caught Kevin cheating on me."

Bishop Walker leaned back in his chair and let out a low whistle. "Whoa, boy. I was afraid something like this would happen. The way them women gather around him . . . Women are always drawn to musicians. I told that boy to watch out for—"

"I caught him with Trey."

Bishop Walker's mouth hung open for a moment, then he put his face in his hands. He peered at me through his fingers, and then covered his face again, shaking his head.

"Oh, Monica. Oh, Jesus. Oh, Monica. Oh, Jesus." Finally he said, "I knew that boy coming back here was bad news."

All the air left my body. "You . . . knew?"

I had no idea what he said next. His mouth moved and sound came out, but nothing registered in my brain.

"You . . . knew?" I jumped out of my chair and started pacing. "You knew about him and Trey? You knew all along?"

"Monica, please calm down."

"Calm down? Calm down?" *Get yourself together, Monica. Don't disrespect your pastor.* I made myself sit back in the chair.

Bishop folded his hands together. "Back when Kevin and Trey were in high school, I suspected we had a bit of a . . . uh . . . a problem. When Trey left for college, Kevin dedicated himself to the Lord, and that was the end of that. I didn't think—"

"That was the end of that? What? It just went away? I can't believe this. I can't believe you knew."

"I didn't *know*, Monica. I was . . . concerned. But when you joined the church and you and Kevin started spending so much time together, I thought maybe I was suspicious for no reason. When you got married, I didn't think about it anymore."

We sat quiet for a few minutes. I waited for the comforting words. There was nothing better than having a true man of God in my life I could trust and depend on to help me through life's difficulties.

Bishop Walker rubbed his chin and stared off into space. "Why did he have to do this now?"

I frowned. "What do you mean, *now*?"

He shook himself. "Nothing. We'll have to work through this. I'll counsel the two of you once, twice a week—as often as you need. We can make this work." He lowered his voice. "I trust that you understand discretion is of the utmost importance. You wouldn't want everyone to know what's going on in your home." He stroked his goatee. "No, we'll work through this ourselves. Don't worry, Monica. I have faith that you and Kevin will be just fine."

He looked like Bishop Walker, but it couldn't possibly be him.

"What do you mean, we'll be just fine? You actually think I'm going to stay with him? Maybe you didn't hear me right. I caught my husband cheating on me. With a MAN." I didn't mean to pound my fist on the arm of the chair. I counted to ten inside my head.

"Monica, I know things look bad right now, but you've got to trust me and trust God. He's going to see us through this. God is not a God of divorce."

"Yeah, but He's not a God of adulterous marriages either, especially when homosexuality is involved."

Bishop Walker winced when I said the "H" word. "Monica, you're going to have to trust me. All things work together for the good of them who—"

"Are you serious? Are you really quoting scripture at me? Are you really telling me I'm supposed to stay married to a man who sleeps with men?"

"Lower your voice, young lady." He looked at his door as if he was concerned that someone was lingering outside. He went into his authoritative preacher tone. "I'm just saying we need to handle this situation prayerfully and according to the Word of God and not your emotions. If you would only—"

"Thank you for listening, Bishop Walker. Have a good day." I jumped out of my seat and stormed out of his office.

I should've gone out the back entrance because I was ambushed the second I stepped into the sanctuary.

"Good morning, Sister Day. Where's your husband this morning? We sho' missed him in the service." Mother Wallace planted a juicy kiss on my cheek.

"He's a little under the weather. Lord willing, he'll be back next Sunday. I better go so I can check on him." I kissed her back and tried to rush by the seeming hundreds of other people who wanted to know where Kevin was.

A group of choir members were gathered in

their usual gossip spot in the parking lot. I pulled my coat around me tighter to block out the biting January wind and tried to breeze past them.

No such luck.

"Hey, Monica. What happened to Kevin today?" one asked.

"He's sick. *Very* sick. I stopped in for a minute, but I've got to get home to him." If they would just leave me alone. I couldn't hold the tears much longer.

"We should stop by to pray for him. Let him know we're thinking about him."

"NO!" *Calm down, Monica.* "I mean, he's really sick and probably shouldn't have company right now."

"All the more reason for us to stop by."

Okay, see, I didn't want to have to lie in the church parking lot, but . . . "To tell you the truth, he picked up a bad stomach bug. He's got bad diarrhea and is throwing up all over the place. He can't sit still five minutes and he's running to the bathroom again. I told him about eating at that Mexican restaurant." I scrunched up my face. "Mexican the second time around is not a pleasant thing."

The grossed out looks on their faces told me I wouldn't have to worry about anyone dropping by.

As I drove out of the parking lot, I couldn't get Bishop Walker's words out of my mind. What happened in there? Did he hear me say Trey? Did he think I said Tracey or Faye? How could he possibly expect to brush this under the rug like it wasn't a big deal? And what did he mean when he said "Why would he do this now?" It was hard to keep from jumping to conclusions.

Everyone talked about how the church growth exploded when Kevin became the minister of music. Two years after he took over, they expanded to two services and then moved into a much bigger, much better building.

If this got out, obviously Kevin would be sat down as the minister of music. Service this morning showed the effect that would have on the church. Plus, the choir was in the process of preparing to record an album. Everyone said Kevin was going to be the next Kirk Franklin.

Let alone the scandal it would cause. Church folk were fickle. Any little thing and they'd go looking for a reason to leave. I couldn't imagine what this could do to Love and Faith Christian Center, especially with us in the middle of a building project. We were about to build a 15,000-seat auditorium. If this kinda thing got out . . .

That was the devil talking to me. Bishop Walker would never think like that. His foremost concern was probably what this would do to Kevin. Losing his position in the music department would destroy Kevin. It meant everything to him. Was his whole life. Yeah, Bishop Walker was thinking about Kevin.

But where did that leave me?

4

I decided to go home for a while so I wouldn't have to answer Trina's questions about what happened at church. When I pulled into the garage, I was glad to see Kevin's car wasn't there. When I got into the house, I didn't even have time to take my boots off to give my aching feet some relief before the doorbell rang.

"Monnie, it's me. Open the door."

He must have been parked down the street in the cul-de-sac, waiting for me to get home.

"I don't want to see you, Kevin. Go away, move to France, die. I don't care. Just leave me alone."

"Monica, please. I need to talk to you."

"I don't want to hear a word you have to say."

I guess he remembered he had a key because I heard him turn it in the lock. Before he could open the door good, I crashed a vase against the wall, barely missing his head.

"Not this again. Please, just let me talk to you." I could hear the tears in his voice.

I allowed him to open the door without throwing anything else. A part of me wanted to hear what he had to say. I needed him to help me understand. The rest of me still wanted to see his blood flow.

Kevin walked into the foyer slowly, acting like he was afraid he would have to dodge more airborne objects. He looked a mess. His eyes were swollen and puffy, like he hadn't slept since he left. He had on some wrinkled jeans and a not-so-white T-shirt. His comb twists were matted to his head.

"Did you sleep in the park with the homeless people?" I asked.

He tried to smile but tears flowed instead. For the first time, it occurred to me that this might actually be hurting him, too. His eyes were filled with more pain than I imagined any human could keep inside.

"When I was ten, a deacon from the church molested me."

"Save it for Oprah, Kevin." I didn't want to get sucked into feeling sorry for him. I was the victim here, and I wasn't trying to share that spot.

I couldn't take the look in his eyes, though. He needed me to listen. Needed someone to hear what he'd obviously been carrying around for years.

The pang in my heart made me realize love didn't have a switch attached to it that I could turn on and off, no matter how much I was hurting. If I could, I'd turn my love for Kevin to the "off" position and kick him out the door.

But I couldn't. In direct opposition to my mind, my heart still loved him. Even though I was mad enough to douse him in gasoline and strike a match and flick it at him, seeing his face—his eyes—did something to me. I never felt so conflicted in my life.

He stepped closer.

I frowned. "My God, Kevin! Have you bathed since the last time I saw you?"

He smiled that crooked, little-boy grin I had fallen in love with. I hated him for doing that.

"Naw. I guess I'm a little on the tart side."

"Have you eaten?"

He shook his head.

"Well, go bathe and I'll fix something."

He started crying, his whole body heaving. I knew he was grateful I wasn't kicking him out, or cursing him out, or throwing things at him. Grateful that in spite of the fact that he'd hurt me deeper than hurt should hurt, I still cared.

"Thanks, Monnie."

I nodded and made a "you stink" face, stepping aside so he could go upstairs.

I wished this were a regular day. I wished he'd just come home from packing up the instruments and chilling with the band while I cooked Sunday dinner. I wished we were going to eat together then snuggle up on the couch and watch TV, or talk, or just fall asleep.

But it wasn't, and we weren't.

When he came back down, I had heated up some leftover lasagna and garlic bread. I went upstairs to change out of my wool suit and boots while he ate. He must have been starving because by the time I got back, he had finished eating and sat at the table, staring at the wall.

"Hey." He gave me a weak smile

"Hey." I didn't smile back. Seeing him clean, dressed, and normal put the hardness back into my heart. I really needed to pack up some more clothes and head back to Trina's. I decided to give him no more than ten minutes for whatever explanation he thought would help this situation.

I sat down across from him. He reached out to take my hands like he usually did, but I kept mine folded in my lap. He folded his hands in front of him and looked down at the table.

He blew out a long breath. "I don't know what to say."

"Oh, I don't know, Kevin. You could start with, 'Hey honey, did I ever mention that I like to have sex with men?'"

He winced and the tears flowed again like he had sprung a leak.

I softened a bit. "Tell me something that makes this make sense."

He leaned back and wiped his face with his hands. I gave him a napkin and took a deep breath. "Tell me about when you were ten."

He shifted from side to side. I could smell his fear as strong as I could smell the oregano, tomato sauce and cheese that still hung in the air.

"You know Momma was the church secretary when I was growing up. During the summer, I begged to go to work with her every day so I could play the piano." He folded the napkin in small squares. "That's what I wanted to do all day—play the piano and the organ."

He stopped and stared at the wall again, his eyes blinking rapidly. I knew him well enough to know to sit there and wait until he was ready to go on.

He finally turned back to face me. "There was this deacon who did things around the church—mowed the grass, cleaned—that kind of stuff. He would listen to me play and tell me how good I was, and how I was going to be rich and famous, and how my music would bless so many people. He said he knew my father wasn't around and if I ever needed somebody to talk to, I could come to him." Kevin twisted a sprig of his thick Afro. He had washed out his comb twists when he showered.

"Momma was glad to have a male figure taking an interest in me. I think she felt guilty that my dad wasn't around. I spent more and more time with Deacon—well, this deacon. He wasn't that old, so it was like hanging around with a big brother. He took me everywhere—out for pizza, to the movies, the arcade. My mom trusted him."

Kevin bit his lip. "One weekend, she went on a trip with the missionary board and I went to stay with him. And . . . that's when it happened for the first time."

"The first time? It happened more than once?"

Kevin nodded. "He made me promise not to tell. Said if I told, Bishop Walker would be mad at me and wouldn't let me play the organ or piano anymore. Said my mom would think I was a faggot and put me out, and since homosexuality was a sin, I'd get kicked out of the church. In my ten-year-old mind, that would be losing everything, so I didn't tell. Momma thought it was strange that I didn't want to go anywhere with him anymore, but she never asked why."

Kevin stared at his hands. "I was all messed up after that. I thought I was dirty and bad. I thought God hated me. I had nightmares all the time and started peeing the bed. Momma couldn't understand what was wrong with me."

"You never told?"

He shook his head and looked down at the table.

"Kevin, look at me. You never told anybody, not even Bishop Walker?"

He stared straight at me. "No, Monnie, I never told anyone. You're the first person that's ever heard this." Big tears plopped onto the kitchen table.

"Oh, Jesus, Kevin." Instinctively, I wiped his face. When I realized what I was doing, I drew my hand back.

We sat there, quiet for a few minutes, before he continued. "After that, I lived in a constant state of confusion. A door had been opened that should have never been opened, and I didn't know how to close it. Can you imagine what it was like to feel feelings I knew it was a sin to feel? I prayed all the time for God to take it away, but it was still there, inside of me. The boys' locker room after gym class? A nightmare. Boy Scouts sleepover summer camp? A nightmare. And let's not talk about all-night youth lock-ins at the church." He rubbed his face and twisted another sprig of hair.

"I met Trey in the tenth grade. His family had just moved to D.C. from Philadelphia. We became

friends and then ... more than friends. He was
the only person I could talk to about it because he
knew exactly how I felt. Only he didn't struggle
with it. He didn't have the same issues about it
because he didn't grow up in church. I mean, you
know he still had the stigma, but he didn't have
the whole 'you're going to hell if you don't get
delivered' thing on top of it. He even started
going to church with me, but it didn't bother him
a bit."

"What's Trey's story? How'd he end up that
way?"

"That way?" Kevin flinched. "Not every gay or
bisexual man has a 'story.' I know that's what a
lot of Christians think. They think we all had this
event where something traumatic happened to us
and opened the door for the spirit of homosexuality to jump up in us. We were all molested by
somebody or grew up without a father or some
drama, but that's not the case. Trey grew up in a
normal home with a mother and father. Nobody
ever molested him, and he's gay."

I shook my head. "But how? Why?"

"Monnie, I don't know. You think I don't ask
God that every day? Was he born gay? Was *I* born
gay? Is it a demonic spirit? Something in the environment? Family upbringing? Or is it genetic like
they're saying now? I don't know. All I know is I
hate it."

Kevin's eyes blazed. "Do you know how it feels
to think I'm going to hell for something I have no
control over? Think about it. I love God with all
my heart. I've been saved since the age of five. Find
me ten Christians, though, who wouldn't argue

that I'm going straight to the bottom of hell when I die. Find me ten others who wouldn't have me sat down as the minister of music or kicked out of the church if they knew about my past."

I nodded because I knew he was right.

"At the end of my senior year, Bishop Walker called me into his office and said he noticed some things he was sure God wasn't pleased with. He said he knew I'd been struggling for some time, and that it looked like the enemy was winning the fight. He couldn't even look me in the eye while he talked to me. He said I needed to take some time off from playing and directing the choir and settle the issues. That almost killed me."

I could imagine. There was nothing Kevin loved more than his music.

"He told the church I was taking a break from the music ministry so I could focus on college. He also announced the church was giving Trey a full scholarship to go to Temple. Trey had planned to go to Howard with me, but his parents wouldn't let him pass up the money."

My stomach churned. The thoughts I had forced out of my head after my talk with Bishop Walker resurfaced.

"After my junior year of college, Bishop said he was satisfied the music ministry wouldn't distract from my studies and put me back over the choir again. He never mentioned me and Trey again, but I knew he was watching to make sure I 'got it out of my system'."

"How were you supposed to do that?"

Kevin gave me a wry smile. "Since I wasn't over the choir, I visited a lot of other churches and went to every conference I could find. If I had a dollar for every prayer line I ever stood in, for everybody who prayed over me and told me God had taken it away—for every time I laid at the altar, crying out to God to make me straight." He shook his head. "I'd be a very rich man.

"When I was at Howard, I stayed to myself. I didn't hang around the other musicians because . . . I guess I didn't hang around many guys at all. I was afraid that even though I had been told I was delivered, it was still there. I didn't want to give it a chance to rise up again."

Kevin looked at me with those dramatic, deep-set eyes. "Then I met you. And we became friends, and fell in love, then . . . you know the rest of the story."

I grabbed his arm to still his fidgeting. He was driving me crazy, folding that snotty napkin over and over. He looked up at me and smiled weakly, his eyes begging me to understand. To love him in spite of.

No way was I letting him off that easy. I got up and put the foil back over the lasagna and put it back in the refrigerator. "What I don't understand is why I had to find out the way I did. You know everything there is to know about me. Every secret, every embarrassing moment, my fears, my dreams. I thought I knew the same about you. I thought we trusted each other. Why didn't you tell me this before?"

Kevin paused. "If you had known this before, would you still have married me?"

"Well, no. I mean, why would I marry a gay man?"

"Let me ask this, then. Could you marry a man who was 'delivered' from the spirit of homosexuality? Everybody tells us, 'get delivered, trust in the Lord—He can deliver anybody from anything.' But really, how many women would marry a man with my past lifestyle?"

"Not many, because they'd be afraid of exactly what happened to me on Saturday happening to them. It would be like marrying an ex-crack addict or a recovering alcoholic. You never know when they might fall off the wagon."

"So you're telling me I can't love a man, but I'll never find a woman who will marry me?"

"No, well . . . yes, well—"

"So a man who's homosexual for whatever reason—whether he was born like that or got turned out, or whatever the theory of the day is—if God 'delivers' him from homosexuality, he has to spend the rest of his life alone because no woman will have him?"

I didn't bother to answer.

"Right or wrong, I guess that's why I didn't tell you." He dropped his head into his hands. "I thought I had it beat. It was over. In my past. I would never have married you if I ever thought this would happen. It had been since high school."

I took Kevin's dirty plate to the sink, rinsed it off, and then turned to look at him. Thought about things that now made sense. "I thought you never wanted to make love to me because of my weight. You were so affectionate before we got married, but the first time you saw my thunder thighs and dimply butt, you didn't want me anymore."

"Monnie, it wasn't that. I've always told you your weight never bothered me."

"Yeah, but that was until you saw me naked."

Kevin came over and put his arms around me. "No, Monnie, you're the most beautiful woman, the most beautiful person I've ever met." He held me like he always did, but it didn't feel the same. "I'm sorry I ever made you think you weren't desirable or sexy to me. It wasn't you . . . I'm sorry I did this to you."

"Yeah." I pulled away from him. "Me, too."

I could tell that hurt him. I always told him I wanted to spend the rest of my life in his arms.

"See, now that you know, you don't want me to touch you. See—"

"See nothing, Kevin. You know what the real deal is here? You cheated on me. Whether it was with a man or a woman, it was still cheating. The whole gay thing is a separate issue—a huge issue, mind you—but the fact is, you slept with another person while we were married. It would be one thing for me to find out you had been with a man in the past, but you had sex with Trey the day after you had sex with me. In our bed. As sorry as I am for everything that's happened to you, I can't get past that."

"It was only that one time."

"Only that one time?" I laughed sarcastically. "Oh, in that case I forgive you. Let's go back to our life like nothing happened and live happily ever after." I rolled my eyes. "Do you think I can get that picture out of my head? I keep seeing it over and over."

"I'm sorry, Monica. I never meant for you to walk in and see that."

"I would hate to think you planned it."

"That's not what I meant. I don't know how it happened. One minute we were playing music and horsing around and the next thing I know . . . he started rubbing my back and—"

I screamed and covered my ears. "Do you think I want to hear this? Seeing it was bad enough. Now you want me to relive it?"

He held up his hands, terror in his eyes, no doubt remembering yesterday's violence. "Sorry. You don't have to worry. Nothing like that will ever happen again. I promise. Trey will never come over here again."

"He sure won't. He won't have any reason to 'cause you're about to pack your sh—stuff and get out." I turned and walked into the family room. Didn't want to see the look in his eyes when I said that.

"Monica."

"Get out, Kevin. I don't want to hear another word." I sat on the family room couch, pretending to watch a movie while he went upstairs and packed. When he came down with his bag, he walked up and stood over me.

"Monica, I . . ." He looked around the room. "What happened in here?"

"Nothing. Just me letting off a little steam the other day after the . . . incident."

He tried to sit down beside me, but I stretched out my legs. "Just go, Kevin. Please. And do me a favor. Don't come back unless I ask you to."

He started toward the door then turned around to say something. "Monnie—"

I held up my hand. He turned and finished his slow trek to the door. I held my tears until I heard it close behind him.

5

I hardly slept that night. Images of Kevin as a lit-tle boy, Kevin and Trey, and Bishop Walker kept floating through my mind. I finally gave up at six in the morning and slipped out of the bed and onto my knees. I tried to pray like I did every morning, but my prayer didn't come out too good.

God, wasn't there some point in the two years of me and Kevin being best friends, two years of dating, and two years of marriage when You could have tapped me on my shoulder and mentioned something about my friend, boyfriend, husband being gay? I mean really, God, I talk to You every day. You couldn't say anything? I prayed before we took our relationship to the next level and before we got married. Was I so head over heels that I couldn't hear your voice? And if I was, You couldn't speak to my pastor and tell him we were making a mistake?

I knelt there for a while trying to find the right words to pray, but nothing else came out. I finally decided to get up and get dressed. Thank God I didn't have to put much effort into finding something nice to wear to work. I took a hot shower, pulled on some scrubs and stepped into my clogs. I wiped the steam off the mirror and stared at my eyes. They needed some work.

I wandered down to the kitchen and tried to use cucumber slices to get rid of the puffy bags. Hopefully, my coworkers wouldn't notice. If they said so much as a "What's wrong, Monica?" it would send me into a fit of tears.

I pulled up at the office at eight o'clock. I liked to get to work before everyone else to get the rooms stocked with medical supplies and make sure the charts were ready. I was the only RN on staff and supervised two medical assistants. We also had an office manager, and Anthony was the receptionist. Dr Stewart and a nurse practitioner shared the practice.

The other staff members trickled in slowly.

"Hey, baby, how you doin'? Everything all right?" Odessa, one of the medical assistants, was like everybody's grandmother. Everybody was "baby" to her. "What's wrong wit' yo' eyes?"

"Allergies acting up, Miss Odessa." I sniffed.

Tammy, the other medical assistant, stared at me. "Allergies? In the middle of January?"

"Tammy, could you pull the labs off the printer and pull the charts? Dr. Stewart likes to go over test results before she starts seeing patients." I didn't have to tell her that because she was always on top of things. I just wanted her to get out of my face.

"Sure, Monica." She smiled but kept staring at my eyes. I walked over to my desk, determined to ignore her.

Tammy sat at the nurses' station, flipping through lab results. She sucked her teeth. "Oooooh, girl, look. These kids around here sleeping with everybody and wonder why they always catching something. Here. Put this with the abnormals." She held out a piece of paper. I scanned the name and looked at the results.

Tammy kept fussing. "Gonorrhea *and* chlamydia. Girl, I'd kill a man if he gave me a disease. These young girls act like they don't know nothing 'bout condoms. If they . . ."

I stopped hearing her chirpy voice as the thought hit me like a sledgehammer. What if Kevin gave me something? He said he only cheated on me one time, but why should I believe him? Oh my God, I had to get tested for sexually transmitted diseases. Me, Monica Harris-Day, virgin 'til she got married at the age of twenty-six, pure as the driven snow, champion of abstinence and keeping oneself pure for Jesus.

This was one of those times when being a nurse was not a good thing. All I could think of was the women I had told that their boyfriend, husband, or one-night-stand had given them a disease. I thought about all those times of trying to keep the disgust off my face while assisting Dr. Stewart when she froze genital warts, or swabbed multiple genital ulcers to diagnose herpes.

The worst was the woman a few years back whose unexplained chronic yeast infections were finally explained by an HIV test. She had been married for eleven years and had no idea her husband was bisexual and very promiscuous. She'd probably been infected for years and now was sicker than dirt. Skin and bones, hair thin and falling out, sores and rashes everywhere . . . sick. She stayed with him, too. Took care of her husband until he died of AIDS about a year and a half ago. I wish I would take care of a man who gave me AIDS. If I found so much as a bump on me, Kevin was a dead man.

I looked at my watch. It was almost nine o'clock. We'd be seeing patients soon. Obviously, I couldn't get Dr. S. to do my STD tests. I was close with my office staff, but I didn't want them up in my business. I could picture Tammy logging my test results. "Oooooh, girl, look."

I'd have to go to Planned Parenthood or a free clinic. I would just have to tell Dr. Stewart I needed a couple of hours during lunch to finalize some business. I knew I had missed work Saturday, but my top priority right now was making sure I was disease free.

My stomach tightened. *God, please let me be disease free . . .*

6

Just walking into the free clinic made we want to turn around and run. It was packed to the hilt. On one side of the waiting room sat a lot of teenagers and young women with screaming babies. Then there were the Lil' Kim dress-a-likes with ten-inch fingernails, popping their gum. On the other side of the clinic, college students hid behind large textbooks, pretending they weren't getting birth control or an STD check, looking up every once in a while like they were afraid their parents would walk through the door. Then there were the professionally dressed women looking like they were considering the disadvantages of being self-employed or cursing their jobs for not providing them with health care.

There was no way I could get back to the office in a couple of hours. I flipped open my cell phone to call Anthony to let him know I would be away longer than planned.

"Is everything okay, Miss Monica?"

His lisp was overwhelmingly annoying today. "I'm fine, Anthony. Just got some things I need to take care of."

"Well, if you need anything, just let me know. You know I'm here for you, right?"

I know you just want to get in my business. "Of course. I'm fine. See you later."

I closed my cell phone and tried to read a magazine, but between the screaming babies and my screaming thoughts, I couldn't concentrate. After two hours, they finally called my name. When the nurse took my vitals, I wasn't surprised my blood pressure was a little high.

I shivered on the cold exam table with the flimsy paper thing over my naked bottom half. It felt weird to be the patient instead of the nurse. An older white lady came through the door.

"Good afternoon, my name is Kate Lawson. I'm a nurse practitioner. What can I do for you today?"

"I need STD testing done. Everything." My voice cracked. "I need to be tested for everything."

She looked at me over the top of her reading glasses. "Okay, dear. First let me get some history." She clicked her pen. "How long have you been sexually active?"

I took a deep breath. "Just over two years."

"Only two years?" She wrinkled her eyebrows and looked at me for a second, then scribbled on the chart. "And how many partners in that time?"

"One."

"Only one?" She looked at me like I had three heads, as if her asking me that would suddenly jog my memory and I would admit that I—like every other young, black woman who sought care at this kind of clinic—started having sex at the age of thirteen and had slept with at least thirty men since.

"Yes, only one." I tried to keep the edge out of my voice.

"Umm-hmm. Have you ever had an STD before?"

"No. Look, I know the whole drill. I'm a nurse. I don't have any medical problems. The only medicine I'm on is the birth control patch. I don't have any allergies, and I've never had sex with any man other than my husband. Any other questions?"

She nodded slowly as it registered. I wasn't the promiscuous whore. I was the poor, innocent victim of a philandering husband, sneaking off to the free clinic so I wouldn't have to admit this to my regular doctor. She took off her judgmental face and put on her sympathy face.

"I'm sorry, dear. Let's get this over with."

I tried to disappear as she examined me. I stared at several posters on the wall promoting abstinence, safe sex, condom use, and birth control. Mercifully, she finished quickly and left me to get dressed.

The overworked and underpaid-looking nurse came in to do my HIV test. "I'm going to draw your blood to test for antibodies to the HIV virus.

If your test is positive . . ." I knew the whole speech by heart. Had given it numerous times to trembling adolescents, promiscuous young adults, and shell-shocked wives.

I thought about a statistic I had recently read about black women being the fastest growing group of individuals newly infected with HIV. It was in an *Essence* magazine article about sistas dealing with brothers living on the down low, as they termed it. It talked about men dibbling and dabbling in having sex with other men, but not necessarily considering themselves homosexuals, and others who were secretly gay or bisexual. While reading the article, I thought about how lucky I was not to have to worry about that kind of stuff.

God, please don't let me become a statistic.

". . . now, it can take up to six months for antibodies to show up in your blood after an exposure, so if you're concerned about any body fluid exposures in the last six months, you should have a follow-up test six months from now. Until then, try to practice safe sex as much as possible. That means using a condom every time you have intercourse."

Please. I might never have sex again for the rest of my life.

She put a Band-Aid on and indicated for me to hold pressure. "We don't give results over the phone. You can come get them in person as early as next Monday."

"Monday? At my office, these tests only take two days."

"Honey, this isn't a private office. That's the best we can do. Sorry."

Great. I was going to be on pins and needles for a whole week.

I got dressed and got out of there as quickly as I could. As I pulled my car out of the lot, I flipped open my cell phone. I couldn't deal with going back to work, so I called Anthony and told him to let Dr. Stewart know I needed the rest of the afternoon off.

"Monica, is something wrong? If it is, you can tell me. You know you can always talk to me, sister to sister." Anthony gave his signature little giggle.

Any other time that would have been funny. Today it reignited the brewing ember of anger that had been burning in me the last few days. "Thanks, Anthony, but everything's fine. I'll see you tomorrow." I tried to keep the edge out of my voice.

"Well, you ain't got to get snippy. I'm just trying to help." He sucked his teeth.

"Sorry, Aunt Tony." Me and the girls at the office called him that because he always gave us relationship advice on how to keep our men in line. "Just got a lot on my mind. You know I don't mean to hurt your feelings."

"That's okay, honey. I know you a little *skressed* out lately. You can tell Aunt Tony all about it tomorrow. Smooches."

"Smooches." I closed my phone. I was sure Anthony would love to hear that Kevin was gay and available. Every time Kevin came to the office, Anthony would go on and on about how fine he was and how I better not ever mess up because he'd be waiting to pick up the pieces.

I swung by Popeye's on the way home and got

a popcorn shrimp basket with an extra order of fries. By the time I got home, it was already gone. I was gonna have to slow down on my eating . . . right after I got my test results.

7

For the next week, I spent every waking moment with Trina, trying to soak up as much of her as I could before she left.

On Friday evening after leaving work, I dialed her on my cell. "Got any plans tonight?"

"I got movies. Stop at Giant and get some snacks?"

"The usual?"

"You know it."

"A'ight. I'll be there in a few."

Before I got married, when Kevin had his musician rehearsals on Fridays, Trina and I would get a bunch of movies, microwave popcorn, Haagen Dazs Strawberry Cheesecake ice cream, and Butterfinger BB's. We'd binge and watch movies until we passed out.

After we got married, Kevin changed his Friday rehearsals to Saturday afternoons while I ran my errands, so we could have a date night on Friday night. He couldn't do date nights on Saturday because he had to play seven and eleven AM services on Sundays, and had to rest. I either went out with Trina on Saturdays or stayed home and relaxed with Kevin.

Tears flowed down my cheeks as I thought about my marital routine with Kevin. Little things had crossed my mind all week that pricked my heart. Our special little jokes together, how sweet his kisses were against my lips, how I felt completely covered by him as a man of God . . .

Stop it, Monica. It's over.

When I pulled up at Trina's, I rubbed the mascara tracks off my face and put some drops in my eyes to get rid of the redness. Sad. I had started carrying Visine in my purse.

I opened Trina's front door with the key she'd given me, and went to the kitchen. I put the ice cream in the freezer and left the other snacks in the bag on the table.

"Hey. That was quick." Trina popped into the kitchen wearing a pair of sweats and a T-shirt. Her long braids were pulled back in a ponytail. Her dark, smooth skin, high cheekbones, and tall stature made her look like an African princess.

"Hey. How was work?" I asked her.

"Cool. How was work for you?"

"Nothing new." I pushed my hair out of my face.

Trina studied my eyes. "You been crying?"

I let out a sarcastic chuckle. "The question is, when do I not cry?" Fresh tears started to flow.

"Oh, Monnie." She hugged me tight then led me

to the kitchen table and sat me down. She sat across from me. "You know, I been trying to respect your wishes not to talk about it, but at some point, you have to. You can't keep it all inside."

I took the napkin she handed me and wiped my face and blew my nose. "I don't get what you want me to talk about. You been there since it happened. What's there to tell?"

"How you feel."

"How do you think I feel? I feel horrible. I'm mad, angry, hurt, and every other bad emotion you can name. I don't see how talking about it can help."

Trina patted my arm. "Just try it."

I shrugged. "I can't believe it. I keep hoping I'll wake up in my bed and Kevin will be there and everything will be wonderful and normal just like it was. Then I realize that wonderful and normal was a big, fat lie.

"Then my mind gets flooded with all these thoughts. Like when he said he was at musician rehearsal, is that where he really was? I think about the other musicians in the band and wonder if he's been with any of them. He says it was only Trey, but why should I believe him?"

Trina nodded.

"Then I wonder, was I not woman enough for him? Did I not please him? I tell myself that's not it, because if he's gay, even the womanliest woman wouldn't be able to do anything about that, but still, it does something to me."

"It doesn't have anything to do with you being a woman, Monnie."

"My head knows that, but my heart feels like . . ." I looked down at the table. "I can't satisfy my man, so he'd rather be with another man." The tears started flowing again.

Trina passed me another napkin. "I know it's hard to believe, but this has nothing to do with you. I guarantee you this didn't start with Trey in your bedroom that day. This has been something deep down in Kevin for a while."

If she only knew. Maybe I should tell her what Kevin told me.

"I know you're right, Trina. Keep saying it to me over and over again. It's hard not to take it personally."

"I know, girl. God is gonna bring you through this."

Trina got up and took the ice cream out of the freezer and two spoons out of the drawer. She sat back down and handed me a spoon. "You never did tell me what happened at church on Sunday. Did you end up talking to Bishop?"

"Bishop spotted me in the back of the church and had an usher bring me a note. I took it as a sign that God wanted me to talk to him."

Trina rolled her eyes. "You and your signs. You need to learn to hear from the Holy Spirit instead of playing those little sign games all the time. What happened?"

I gave the highlights of my talk with Bishop. Trina's eyes widened the more I told.

"So he knew about this all along? I can't believe that. You were so worried about your obligation to tell him about Kevin, and he knew all along and didn't bother to tell *you*. I wonder if that's why he pushed you guys to get married so fast. He even rushed you guys through your pre-marital counseling." Trina put her hand over her mouth. "I'm sorry. I'm not trying to dog your pastor, but . . ."

I shrugged. "It's not like the same thoughts haven't gone through my mind."

I decided to tell her what Kevin told me after church. "It gets deeper, girl." Halfway through my story, Trina dropped her spoon as if she was sick to her stomach. When I got to the part about Trey's scholarship to Temple, she put her hands over her ears.

"I can't listen to any more. That's sick. Bishop Walker really did know all along. So he figured he could get rid of Kevin's lover and then marry him off to a beautiful woman and poof! All would be well and he could keep his star musician to build his church. If that's his approach, no wonder he has a church full of homosexuals that ain't trying to get their lives right."

My mouth flew open. "What are you talking about?"

Trina rolled her eyes in disgust. "Monnie, please wake up. I never met anybody as blind as you."

"What are you saying?" I stared at her. "Is that why you left?"

"Among other reasons."

"Now who's homophobic?"

"It's not that I'm homophobic. I just have a problem with a pastor who sticks his head in the sand and pretends he doesn't see what's going on in his church. Or maybe even condones it. I don't think Kevin is the only person in a position of leadership that has sexual identity issues."

I had heard rumors about Love and Faith being

D.C.'s "gay church," but I never took them seriously. "Well, it's not Bishop's fault he has a church full of them. It's not like he puts a banner up and tells them all to come there. I guess they enjoy the Word, so they come."

"And he lets them stay in their sin. And word gets around. Here's a church that's 'gay friendly,' so they all flock there."

"So what's he supposed to do? Preach against homosexuality every Sunday?"

"No. I don't think that's the answer either. When I was visiting churches, there was this one pastor who preached this horrible message about homosexuals. How they were all filled with the devil and going to hell, and if he ever found a homosexual in his church, he would throw them out the door. He said all sorts of stuff about limp-wristed sissies and men switching worse than women and gay men singing soprano in the choir. It was so bad I left in the middle of the sermon. I bet he doesn't preach that hard against fornication and adultery."

"So what are you saying? They can't ignore it, but they can't preach against it. What are they supposed to do?"

"I don't know exactly. Honestly, I don't think I've ever seen any church effectively deal with homosexuality." Trina picked up her spoon and dug out a big scoop of ice cream. "That's a deep story. Poor Kevin."

My eyes bugged out. "Poor Kevin? What do you mean?"

"I don't know. His side of the story puts a whole different spin on the situation. He wasn't some blatant homosexual who married a woman to cover him so he could continue his life of sin while he looked straight on the surface. Sounds like he really struggled with it and thought he was through with that lifestyle."

I dropped my spoon. "You're taking his side?"

"It's not about taking sides, Monica. It's about trying to understand why he did what he did. At least it makes more sense now."

"Well, I'm glad it all makes sense to you."

"I'm not saying it *all* makes sense. I'm not justifying what he did. He lied to you, or withheld the truth, and there's no excuse for that. I'm just saying—"

"What?" My nostrils flared.

"Calm down, Monica." She passed me the ice cream and put my spoon back in my hand. "I know what it is to be caught up in sexual sin. I know what it's like to cry out to God for deliverance and think you're okay and then find yourself climbing out of a man's bed to get to Sunday service in time. I know what it is to love God with all your heart, but to have this thing inside of you that you can't control, no matter how hard you try."

"How can you compare your old fornication issue with Kevin being gay? Are you saying that fornication and homosexuality are equal?"

"Aren't they? Sin is sin."

"I don't see it that way. Homosexuality is . . . gross. It's perverted. And plus, they make a lifestyle of sin."

"I'd say I made a lifestyle of fornicating back in the day."

"Yeah, but you got delivered."

"Thank God for that. He led me to a church where they teach the Word, and I was able to grow spiritually to the point where I could resist temptation. God gave me mentors who prayed with me and didn't judge me. They kept loving me until I was able to stop. Has Kevin had that?"

"I can't believe you're taking his side." I glared at her.

"I'm not taking his side." Trina gave an exasperated sigh. "It just sounds like this lifestyle was unfairly forced on Kevin by him being molested as a child. Then he cried out for deliverance. His pastor acted like if he just stayed away from men, that would fix him, so that's what he did. His pastor acted like if he just got married, that would fix him, so that's what he did. He said he thought he was delivered. Who knows? He might have been just as surprised to find himself in bed with Trey as you were. He probably thought that chapter of his life was over, and he was looking forward to a wonderful, happy marriage like you were."

I rolled my eyes. "This is amazing. You're supposed to be my friend."

"I am your friend. If you want me to dog him out and say all sorts of bad stuff about him, you know I'm not gonna do that. I don't believe in condemning people when they're struggling with something."

Why did I even bother to tell her?

Trina got up and put the ice cream back in the freezer. "Remember when I went to the women's group leader at Love and Faith to get help with my sexual issues? She said I could live holy if I wanted to, but I didn't want to. Said I liked giving in to my flesh, and when I stopped liking it, I wouldn't do it anymore. Was she there all those times I cried and felt like I disappointed God? Did she offer me any real help? No, she just said to cry out at the altar to God and then to repent, and I would be delivered. Did that work? No. I was right back in Marcus's bed the next weekend."

"What does that have to do with Kevin?"

"It's the same thing."

"So you're saying I should forgive Kevin and get back together and live happily ever after?"

"I'm not saying that at all. I wouldn't say that if he cheated with a woman. I'm saying in order for you to heal, you need to forgive. And it's easier to forgive if you understand why someone did something. Most people don't hurt us on purpose. It's usually something inside hurting them that makes them hurt us."

I rolled my eyes. "Whatever, Trina."

"If you can have compassion for Kevin, the abused little boy molested by someone he loved and trusted in the church, the teenager struggling with homosexual feelings and not being able to talk to anyone about it, the college-age Kevin getting his beloved choir snatched away from him, then the Kevin that cried out to God and thought he was delivered because his pastor refused to deal with the issue head on . . . if you can pity the little boy on the inside of him that's still hurt and confused and betrayed and violated, then maybe you can forgive him and be free to go on with your life."

"You're right. I forgive Kevin, and all is well." My words dripped with sarcasm. "You make it sound easy, and it's not."

"I know it's not. Just open your heart to God and let Him work healing and forgiveness in you."

Trina had been like this since she started going to her new church. It was impossible to argue with her because she always said what I imagine Jesus would have said in any situation. I knew she was right, but it wasn't what I wanted to hear.

She put our spoons in the dishwasher and gave the table a quick wipe-down. "I know. You'd rather me help you plot and scheme Kevin's death."

"Or at least slashing his tires. I'll get to the forgiveness part later, but can't I just get a little revenge first?"

"Girl, there's nothing you could do to Kevin that could make him hurt any more than he's already hurting right now, and has been hurting since he was ten."

"Dang, Trina. You know I hate you right now, don't you?"

Trina laughed. She put a bag of popcorn in the microwave and picked up the chocolate. "All right. Enough of that. Let's watch some movies."

I grabbed Trina and hugged her. "Thanks, T. What would I do without you?"

"Girl, only God knows." Trina bit her lip.

What would I do without her?

We plopped in our usual seats in her family room and she cued up the first movie. As the opening credits were running, a worried look came over Trina's face. She clicked the remote and paused the movie. "Monnie, this might be hard to think about, but well . . . I know Kevin said he only cheated one time, but just in case it wasn't, do you think . . . I mean, not that I think anything could be wrong, but just to be on the safe side, should you—"

"I already got tested, Trina."

She breathed a sigh of relief. "When?"

"Monday."

"Dag, you didn't waste any time."

"Didn't want to take any chances."

"So everything's cool then?"

"I don't know yet. I can't get my results 'til Monday."

"Oh." A bit of worry crept back into her voice. "Want me to go with you?"

"Naw, I'll be fine. Like you said, it's just a precaution."

Was I fine? What would I do if the nurse told me I was HIV positive? I had done a good job of blocking it out of my mind the whole week. Now that Trina had reminded me, it was going to be a long wait until Monday.

8

Monday lunchtime finally came, and I found myself sitting in a packed waiting room at the county clinic again. Fidgeting. Biting my nails. Hoping. Wishing. Praying.

It only took them ten minutes to call my name this time, but it felt like ten hours. I tried to read the look on the nurse's face. Was she nervous because she was about to tell me my life was over? She still had that uninterested, underpaid, overworked look, so I couldn't get any clues from her.

She sat me in the room and told me the nurse practitioner would be with me in a few minutes. Did they always require the nurse practitioner to give test results, or only when something was wrong?

At a clinic like this, they wouldn't waste the nurse practitioner's time if it wasn't something important. My heart started beating faster. What did I have? I prayed for something treatable like gonorrhea or chlamydia. All I had to do was pop some pills and it would be all gone. Yeah. It was probably chlamydia. Women could have that for years without any symptoms.

Oh God, please let me just have chlamydia.

I had to stop myself. What kind of prayer was that?

After another ten-minute-feeling-like-ten-hours wait, the nurse practitioner walked in, looking down at my chart. She flipped through a few pages. Why did it seem like she was moving in slow motion? Was that a look of pity in her eyes? Was she trying to figure out how to break the bad news? My hands started shaking.

She finally looked up. "The nurse gave me your chart to go over your abnormal results with you."

My heart froze. I could hear my heartbeat in my ears, and her voice started to sound far away.

"It seems as if there's a mild abnormality on your pap smear. It shows—"

"Pap smear!" I exhaled a gush of fear and tension. "I'm not worried about a stupid pap smear. What about the HIV results?"

She jumped at my outburst. "The nurse didn't tell you? All your STD tests, including your HIV test, were negative."

I didn't know whether to hug her or smack her for not saying that first. "Oh, thank God." I took deep breaths to get the oxygen going to my brain again. "Thank you, Jesus."

"I'm sorry, Ms. Day. I thought the nurse told you already. How insensitive of me."

"I'm sorry. I didn't mean to . . . what did my pap show?"

"Your pap smear just has a mild abnormality on it . . ."

I zoned out on the rest of her explanation. What difference did it make? I wasn't HIV positive. I didn't even have chlamydia.

"Nothing worrisome. Just something we'll need to repeat in a few months."

"Can I get a copy of it? I'll need to take it to my doctor." No way in the world I was ever coming back here again.

"Sure. I'll have the nurse copy it for you. Just make sure you follow up."

"I will. Thanks for everything. Really." I said it like she was responsible for my negative results.

I practically danced out to my car. As soon as I got in, I dialed Trina. She didn't answer. I left a message. "Hey, girl! Just wanted to let you know I'm disease free, praise the Lord! I'll see you later tonight."

I greeted Anthony with a big grin when I got back to the office. "Hey, Ant. I'm back. Did you miss me?"

"Always, Miss Beautiful. The sun don't shine when you ain't here." He looked me up and down. "What you so happy about? You musta got you a quickie at lunch. Girl, that's the best kind."

"Shut up, Anthony."

"Well, goodbye, Miss Beautiful and hello Miss Attitude. I guess you didn't get none. Is that what's been wrong with you lately? Kevin ain't takin' care of you?"

He didn't know how close he was to me smacking him upside his big peanut head. "You know what, Anthony? I don't think it's appropriate for you to be all up in my life. I would prefer you to keep our relationship purely professional."

He picked up his telephone. "Yeah, that's what I thought. I'ma have to give Mr. Kevin a call and tell him to handle his business so we can all stop catching attitude around here. Don't worry, sugar. Aunt Tony'll make sure you get what you need." He gave me his big wink and signature giggle.

I had to make myself laugh. My cell phone rang. I looked at the caller ID. Speak of the devil. I walked into the lab so no one could hear me.

"Yes, Kevin?"

"I can't believe you answered the phone."

"What do you want?" It was hard not to be rude.

"Bishop Walker wants to meet with us Sunday after church. He said he wants to talk to us together."

"About what?"

"Uh . . . about . . . uh . . . what's going on." Kevin sounded surprised by my question.

"I don't see what there is to talk about."

"He wants to talk about what's next and how to work this out."

"Work what out? There's nothing to work out." I sat down in the phlebotomy chair and fingered the lavender-, red-, and blue-topped tubes.

"I . . . we . . . okay. I understand you're still angry. Maybe we should give this some time and meet with him next week. Or whenever you're ready."

"What do you think is going to change in a week? I don't understand what it is you want."

"I want . . . I want . . . us. Our marriage. I want us to work this out."

"Are you serious?"

"What do you mean?"

"You think we have a marriage? All we have is a lie. How could you possibly think I would even think about staying married to you?"

Kevin was quiet. I hated to think of the pain my words were causing him. I had to picture the incident to keep enough anger in my heart to stand my ground. One glimpse flashing through my mind was more than enough.

"Please don't call me anymore. We have nothing to talk about."

"Will you come out of respect for Bishop Walker? He is our pastor, and if we're not going to . . . if you don't want to . . . if we're not going to be together, we should at least talk to him before we make that decision."

"I'll think about it." I had never heard of a pastor doing divorce counseling, but I guess if they did pre-marital and marriage counseling, they should. "I have to go. I'll call you and let you know when I'll be available to meet with Bishop Walker, should I decide to."

I had no desire whatsoever to see Kevin again. After our last meeting, I wasn't too excited about seeing Bishop either. And if either one of them mentioned me and Kevin staying married, God was gonna have to help me to make sure Bishop Walker's office didn't end up looking like my living room after the incident.

9

On the Friday night before Trina was sched-uled to leave, she convinced me to go out for a goodbye dinner. We went to one of our favorite hang-out spots. After we got there, I was glad she had twisted my arm to go. It felt good to be out, like everything was normal.

While we were sitting at the bar waiting for our table, I heard a screechy voice calling my name.

"Look who it is! Monnie, over here."

Oh, no. I recognized the voice of my friend, Shavon, from the choir. She walked up with Janae in tow. We should have known not to come here. Janae, Trina, Shavon, and I came here almost every Friday night when Trina used to go to Love and Faith. Even after she left, we still hung out here at least once a month.

"Monnie, it's so good to see you," Janae said. She and Shavon hugged me.

"What's up, girl? You okay? We miss you." Janae's eyes were full of concern.

I hadn't seen or talked to any of my friends from Love and Faith because I knew they'd want to know what was going on with me and Kevin, and I had no idea what to tell them. If Kevin had had the decency to cheat with another woman, I could at least sob to my girlfriends and still have some self-respect.

Shavon gave me the same pitiful look. "You don't have to answer any questions or tell us anything. We just want you to know we love you."

I clenched my teeth together. *I will not cry, I will not cry, I will not cry.*

My eyes disobeyed me.

Shavon's eyes grew big. "Oh, no. I'm sorry. We didn't mean to upset you."

I wiped my eyes. "It's okay. Sorry I haven't returned any—"

"You don't have to apologize, girl." Shavon rubbed my arm. "Just know you can talk to us if you need to."

Janae and Shavon looked up and realized Trina was standing there. They both hugged her. "Oh, my goodness, I thought you had left for Africa," Janae said.

"I leave Sunday morning," Trina said.

"I'm glad we got to see you before you left," Shavon said. "It must have been God that led us all here tonight. Let me see if I can get our usual table."

Before Trina or I could stop her, she was already headed toward the hostess' booth. The hostess came over and led us to our favorite table in the corner.

I sat across from Trina, between Janae and Shavon. I wondered what they knew. Had Kevin given the choir some phony explanation as to why I hadn't been there? The choir was like a big family and everybody was really close, but I knew Kevin hadn't told them the truth. Not knowing what they thought was going on made me wary of talking.

I picked up my menu and perused it as if I didn't know everything on it by heart.

Trina said, "So, Janae, who's the new man in your life this week?"

Janae looked insulted. "Whatever, girl." She smiled. "Okay, so his name is Stevie, and I met him at the Metro station of all places."

We all laughed and relaxed into hearing about Janae's latest relationship adventure. It was great, like old times, until . . .

"Oh my God, that's so disgusting." Janae wrinkled her nose.

We all followed Janae's eyes to one of the TV screens up at the bar. There were two men dressed in tuxes, standing in front of what looked like a minister, who appeared to be exchanging wedding vows. They kissed.

Shavon joined Janae in expressing her disgust. "Oh, gross." She made a face. "I am so tired of this same sex marriage junk. It's on the news almost every day."

Shavon pointed at the TV showing people with rainbow flags, marching with signs that read WE SHALL OVERCOME and others in a circle, holding hands and singing. "I hate when they equate the gay movement with the Civil Rights Movement. Like it can even compare to discrimination against black folks. I was born black. Just 'cause they choose that lifestyle, they should have all these rights now?"

I felt heat rising in my face. Of all the things to be the topic of this evening's discussion. The waitress brought our drinks and we ordered our food.

"It's not safe to watch television anymore. They're everywhere," Janae said.

Shavon nodded. "I know. It's like an epidemic. You got *Will & Grace* and *Queer Eye for the Straight Guy*, and what's that new lesbian show? *The "L" Word*. They even got their own network now. And if they ain't got their own show, they put their issues on our shows. I used to watch *Sistergirls* religiously until they had that episode with the two lesbians having a baby. It was a good show until they took it there."

Trina chuckled and stirred her tea. "Oh, so it didn't bother you when everybody was fornicating with everybody. You only stopped watching it when they put the lesbians on?"

Shavon looked a little miffed. "What's that supposed to mean?"

"It's a show about three young, single, carefree black women who have sex with any and everybody. That didn't bother you, but when they put lesbians on, it offended your Christianity? Why didn't it offend you before?"

Shavon had a look on her face like she knew Trina was right, but didn't want to admit it. "That's different. The sistergirls are normal women. The lesbians, well . . ." She seemed at a loss to defend herself.

Janae laughed. "She got you, girl."

"Naw." Shavon shook her head. "It just ain't the same."

Janae said, "Worst thing about *Will & Grace* is it's actually a good show. Have y'all ever watched it? That junk is hilarious."

Shavon said, "Yeah, but that's all part of the devil's plan."

Trina laughed. "Uh-oh. Here comes another conspiracy theory."

Shavon ignored her. "Think about it. Over the last little while, you see more and more homosexuals sneaking into television, magazines, movies, etc. It's like Satan launched a media campaign to normalize homosexuality. We watch shows about it with characters we really like, and although we can't identify with their homosexuality, we see they're okay people. They're funny, good-looking, and deal with some of the same issues we deal with. Next thing you know, you got this warm, fuzzy feeling about homosexuals. They're okay, so then homosexuality is okay."

Janae shook her head. "That's deep, girl. I never saw it that way. I just know I like the show."

Shavon nodded. "Before you know it, it's the norm. The stigma wears off. More people experiment with it, and it becomes another part of the American melting pot."

Janae looked over at me. "Monnie, are you okay? You're really quiet."

"I'm fine. Just listening." I took a sip of Sprite and tried to laugh off my nervousness.

Trina looked over at me. I smiled to let her know I was okay.

Janae said, "You know what bothers me? The way they're trying to push their way into the school curriculum." Janae taught first grade. "They want us to incorporate this tolerance education junk where homosexuality is a normal part of society. We have to teach that a family doesn't necessarily have to have a mother and father. 'Now, boys and girls, you can have two fathers or two mothers, and it's still a happy family.' Can you imagine someone teaching your six-year-old that? But yet, we can't have prayer in school. Why is it *they* can have freedom of speech but Christians can't?"

Shavon said, "I know, right? It becomes politically incorrect to say anything offensive about homosexuals, but we can't have our Christian views without being called religious bigots. You end up looking like a close-minded Christian for believing God's word."

Trina nodded. "What makes me mad is the ones who try to justify their homosexuality by twisting the Word of God. I feel like, if you want to be gay, that's cool, be gay. But don't be trying to make God down with it, because He's not."

Shavon said, "Girl, I heard this radio interview where they was doing that mess, saying crazy stuff like Jonathan and David were gay, or that God wasn't against homosexuality as long as it was two people in a committed relationship. He's only against it when homosexuals are promiscuous. I even saw this thing on the Internet about gay Pentecostal churches. They believe that because they speak in tongues, the Holy Spirit is proving that homosexuality is okay."

"Girl, that don't mean nothing. I've seen plenty of hellions in our church speaking in tongues," Janae said. "That doesn't mean God is cool with what they do. They can roll right out of their fornication bed and right into church, speaking in more tongues than anybody."

Trina laughed. "I'm a witness."

Shavon and Janae gave Trina a shocked look.

Trina sucked her teeth. "Don't act like y'all virgins 'cause you ain't. And if you haven't fornicated, you've lied, or gossiped, or . . ." she glared at Shavon and peeked under the table, "spent your tithes on some shoes."

Shavon giggled. She had a serious shoe fetish.

"Whether it be homosexuality, fornication, or just having hatred in our heart toward our brother; sin is sin. It's not like God has two different levels of hell. Upper hell is for the regular people and lower hell—where it's hotter—is for the homosexuals."

Trina looked over at me and must have realized I'd had all of this conversation I could take. "So, Shavon, what happened to that cutie you were dating from the choir? Last time we talked, I could hear wedding bells."

Shavon rolled her eyes. "Girl, please. That trifling Negro . . ."

* * *

I was quiet in the car on the way home. Trina turned on the smooth jazz station to fill the silence. The saxophone stylings of Kim Waters took the edge off my nerves.

Trina patted my arm. "Sorry, girl. If I had been thinking, we woulda gone somewhere else."

"It's okay, Trina."

"You don't look like it's okay."

I shrugged. "It's just . . . I guess I know it's not gonna be like that anymore. I mean, it's not like I'm gonna stay at Love and Faith after, you know, me and Kevin get divorced. And you're leaving, so I not only lose my husband, but I lose my church and my friends. I gotta start all over. I liked my life, and now I don't have it anymore."

"So that's what you've decided? That you and Kevin are gonna get a divorce?"

I frowned at her. "What other choice do I have? You can't possibly think I would stay with him."

"I just hadn't heard you use the "D" word, that's all."

"What else am I supposed to do?"

"I don't know."

I sat quiet for a minute. "Kevin called the other day, saying Bishop wanted to talk to us. He seems to think we can work this out and stay married."

"Are you gonna meet with them?" Trina turned into her subdivision.

"What for?"

"I don't know. At least to hear what they're thinking or to see what they're suggesting. You know, you're gonna have to talk to Kevin, even if you do plan to get a divorce. He's not gonna disappear."

"I can't believe you're recommending I talk to Bishop Walker."

"He is your pastor. Plus, it might be safest for you to talk to Kevin with Bishop present." Trina chuckled. "That way he doesn't get hurt."

"Oh, you got jokes, huh?" I playfully smacked her arm.

"I'm serious. You can't sit around the house and pretend it's all gonna go away. Sooner or later, you're gonna have to deal with it."

"I know." I nodded. "I just . . ."

"What?" Trina turned into her driveway and parked the car.

What could I say? She was right. I had to pull my head out of the sand and deal with what was going on in my life. "Nothing. I guess I better call Kevin and schedule that meeting."

10

The Sunday morning I was dreading finally came. I pulled up at the airport with Trina and a car full of luggage. I let out a sigh. "Well, here we are."

"Monnie, it's not too late. Just say the word and I'll cash in my plane ticket and we'll go buy a freezer full of Strawberry Haagen Dazs and a case of Butterfinger BB's and microwave popcorn."

I laughed and shook my head. "Trina, God knew this was gonna happen, and He knew you were leaving. Obviously, He's got some kinda plan lined up for me to make it through this."

"That's a good way of looking at it."

"Come on. Get out and get on the plane. The women of the bush need you." That was the worst part about it. Trina couldn't pick a mission trip in a big, modern African city. Nooooo, she had to go to a remote village with limited access to the phone and Internet. I didn't know when I'd get to hear from her.

After the skycap loaded all her bags, Trina turned to me with tears in her eyes. "I'm gonna miss you so much."

I started crying too. "Nowhere near as much as I'm gonna miss you."

She looked at me. "You're gonna be fine, Monnie. I just feel it in my spirit that in spite of everything, and maybe because of everything, your life is gonna end up being so much better. Like that Scripture, what Satan meant for evil, God is gonna turn around for your good. I don't know when and I don't know how, but I just believe it. Can you believe God for that?"

I nodded. Not because I believed it, but because I wanted her to feel like she could get on the plane and know that I would be okay.

We said our goodbyes, and I watched my best friend walk away for the next two years.

After Trina left, I settled into the business of escaping. It was amazing that a part of me could function on autopilot while the rest of me went to this faraway place to hide from reality. The only problem was that to stay in that faraway place required too much sleep, too many fake smiles, too many hours of television, too many false "I'm fine's", and waaaaay too many pints of Tom & Larry's ice cream. I started venturing out. I used to only eat Chocolate Walnut Brownie Crunch. Now I was discovering the pleasures of Snicker

Bar Sundae, Bananaberry Pecan, and Caramel Rum Raisin. Things might have been okay if it was only the ice cream I binged on, but I had made way too many trips to Popeye's, way too many phone calls to Domino's, and way too many drive-thrus at McDonald's.

Every so often, I would pinch myself, hoping I would wake up and get my wonderful life back. All I got were a bunch of little broken skin marks.

My whole life became working, eating, sleeping, and watching television. Oh, and of course, listening to the dreaded answering machine. I kept the phone's ringer off and let the machine catch the calls. Kevin left messages at least twice a day. He'd be playing the piano or the guitar or singing *a capella*, some song he had written for me. He used to do that when we were dating. One of the many things he had done to steal my heart. I knew he was at his mom's because I recognized the clangy, off-key timbre of her old piano.

I ignored the messages from choir members, asking where I was, asking me to go shopping and to the movies and out to eat and the usual places we used to go. I ignored Bishop Walker's messages, telling me God was with me and he understood if I needed to shut in with the Lord for a while to allow Him to heal my heart.

It was hard to ignore the calls from my mother. She left almost as many messages as Kevin, wondering where I was, why I hadn't come to visit, why I hadn't called. Normally, I called my mother twice a week to check on her.

One night, a message from Mommy got my attention.

Monica, I'm concerned about you. If I don't hear from you soon, I'm coming to visit.

I didn't worry too much. She always threatened to come visit me in order to get me to come visit her. We didn't live too far from one another. She lived in Baltimore. I lived in Silver Spring, right outside of D.C. To my mom, though, it was a major day trip.

A few days passed and I was awakened from my daily after-work nap on the couch by the sound of a key in the front door. I was afraid for a minute, but realized a burglar wouldn't use a key. My heart leaped at the thought of seeing Kevin. I had this confused feeling of love-hate-desire-repulsion— with a little violence sprinkled on top.

I heard footsteps in the hallway, accented by the swish-swash of stockings being rubbed together by thick thighs. *Oh, no.*

"Monnie?" she called out.

"Mommy? What are you doing here?"

"I had to come check on you. I left you a message to say I was coming."

"I know, but I didn't think . . . Did you drive yourself?" I couldn't remember seeing my mom drive anywhere but to work, to church, and to the neighborhood grocery store.

"Chile, you D.C. people drive crazy, almost as crazy as them people in Baltimore, but I had to come check on my baby. Why you sitting in the dark?" She flipped on the light and propped her hands on her wide hips to catch her breath. She wiped beads of sweat from her forehead and fanned herself as if the five steps up to the house placed a major stress on her heart.

"How did you get my house key?"

"Kevin came to visit me. He said I needed to come check on you. What's going on wit' you two? All he said was you was having some problems and was takin' some time apart."

I knew he did it out of concern, but I didn't appreciate him dragging my mother into this.

"That's about right," was all I said.

"But why? One minute y'all in love and now you need time apart? Y'all young people and these new-fangled relationships is a mystery to me. Time apart to what? I never heard—"

"Mommy, please." I rubbed my temples. I got up to throw away the empty pizza box on the floor beside me.

"Look at you. When the last time you got your hair done? And I hope you don't wear that house dress when Kevin is around. You young women got to learn how to keep yourselves for your men."

"Mommy, did you eat dinner? Can I get you something to drink?" The last thing I needed was her advice on how to make a marriage work.

"I'm just saying, men need they women to act like they care. Put on something nice. Cook dinner every once in a while. Get you some lingerie. You gotta keep the romance in the relationship. Even a good man will stray if he sees something better in the street than he has at home."

"Too late, Mommy. He already did."

She didn't look surprised, sorry, sympathetic, angry, or any of the emotions any normal mom would have at such a moment. Like men were supposed to cheat. "See, that's what I'm talking 'bout. Don't worry, honey. We'll get you fixed up. He'll come back."

"Did you ever think I might not want him to come back? I'm not like you."

The strained look on my mother's face made me wish I could get my brain to work faster than my mouth. She smoothed a few gray hairs back from her face.

"What I mean is I need some time to deal with this."

"I understand. Take some time, baby. Y'all be okay in no time."

There was no way I was going to tell my mother what really happened. She'd tell my dad and I'd never hear the end of it. My dad was intensely homophobic. I couldn't count the number of times I'd heard him say "faggot this" and "punk that" and "sissy that" whenever he read something in the newspaper or saw something on television.

Plus, if Mommy rationalized that I should stay with Kevin—for whatever reason, she thought women should stay with men no matter what they did—I would lose the little bit of respect I had left for her.

I got up and wandered into the kitchen. I swore off Tom & Larry's two days ago and had done pretty well. Mommy was getting on my last nerve, though. I would just scoop out a spoonful. Or two.

My mother stared at the trash. Pizza boxes, Popeye's boxes, and empty pints of ice cream spilled over the top. I followed her eyes right to my hips.

"I don't want to hear it."

"I wasn't gon' say nothing. 'Cept you need to watch out. You don't want the Calvin curse."

Calvin was my mom's maiden name. Most of the women in her family had wide hips, thick thighs, and big butts. They also had high blood pressure and diabetes, and died of heart attacks or strokes.

"Too late, Mommy." I patted my butt. "Already got it."

"You don't want to end up like me, Monica."

I closed the freezer. She was right. I wasn't going to eat myself to death because my husband wanted to "find something better in the street than he had at home."

I turned toward her with a snappy reply on my lips. When I saw the years of sadness in her eyes, I swallowed it and put my arms around her. No matter how much I disagreed with the choices she had made in her life, I still loved my mother.

We went back to the living room and sat on the couch.

"Yeah, this might be what you and Kevin need. Remember when you were ten and me and you moved in with Grandma?"

I nodded.

"I had caught your father cheating on me. It was a lady at our job at the post office, so every body knew about it. I had to go to work every day and look in those people's faces, them knowing my husband was dogging me. I wasn't gon' stand for it. That's why we left."

Did she think I didn't know the whole story? From listening to my grandmother and nosy aunts, I probably knew it better than she did. I had heard about all the different times he cheated on her and about all the different women. I knew the full effect of my father's cheating on their marriage.

"Your father did everything he could to get me—us—back. I wasn't gon' take him back, but the Lord stepped in—bless His Holy Name—and He worked a mighty miracle on our behalf—Hallelujah—and for the first time, your father gave his life to the Lord. That's what turned things around for us. Your father was so glad to have Jesus in his life, he gave his all and started truly walking with the Lord. I ain't gon' say he hasn't had some slip-ups from time to time, but his heart is with the Lord. Sometimes a man will stray, but if he's a good man, he'll always come back home."

Was this supposed to make me feel better?

"I hate to bring up your father's unfaithful past, 'cause Lord knows women should never point out a father's faults to his children. But if it helps you at this time in your life, that's why I went through it."

Why did Christians always put stuff on God? Did she really believe God wanted her heart broken a million times just so she could "comfort" me at this moment? That ranked right up there with God giving people cancer to teach them a lesson.

"I appreciate you sharing, Mommy, and I'm glad God worked things out for you and Daddy. Keep praying for me, okay?"

"I will, baby. God'll do it. You'll see. When I think of all the things He's done in my life, my

soul looks back in wonder, yes Lawd, yes Lawd."
She started humming "How I Got Over" in her
thick, Mahalia Jackson voice.

She rubbed my back. I laid my head in her lap
and stretched out on the couch. She went from
humming to singing and smoothed back my hair.
Something about her warm, mothering touch and
the melancholy tinge in her voice hit a painful
spot in me and I started crying. She didn't even
flinch. My pain was familiar to her.

"That's it, baby. Let it out. Momma's got you,"
she whispered.

I cried until I was empty, and then sniffled like
a little kid after a whipping. She kept rubbing me
and singing. God knows He did something special when He created mothers.

I must have fallen asleep because next thing I
knew, she was nudging me. "It's late, baby. You
need to get in the bed so you don't wake up with a
crook in your neck." She tucked me into the guest-
room bed where I had been sleeping since the incident. She kissed me on the forehead like she did
when I was little, then sat down on the bed.

"I didn't mean to upset you, baby."

"You didn't upset me. I'm glad you came. I
should've called you sooner, but I didn't want to
talk to anybody."

"It's not good to keep stuff to yourself, baby.
You gotta get it out, like you did tonight. Have
you met wit' Bishop Walker?"

"Yeah." I wasn't about to elaborate. In Mommy's
eyes, no man of God could do anything wrong.

"Good. You can be sure he's praying for you."
She took a deep breath. "I know Trina's gone and

you feel all alone. Have you thought of calling Alaysia?"

I sat up. "Alaysia? Why would I call her?"

"You two were such good friends. She always seemed to know what to say or do to make you feel better. I still don't understand why you stopped being friends. Too many women get rid of they women friends when a man comes along. It's the women friends you should hold on to because even when the men act up, you can trust your girlfriend to be there."

"That wasn't it. Our personalities went in different directions."

"They was always in different directions. It never bothered y'all before. I hope Kevin didn't turn you against her. Sometimes men can be jealous of—"

"It wasn't that. We just grew apart." My tone let her know to leave it alone.

"Okay, baby. Whatever you say. It wouldn't hurt you to call her, though."

My mom adored Alaysia. When we were in college, Alaysia came home with me a lot of weekends for my mom's home cooking. After a while, she started to call my mom "Mommy."

I had to admit, I had thought of calling Alaysia, but too much had happened and too much time had passed.

Mommy patted my head. "I don't want my baby alone. If you want to, you can come stay at the house awhile."

"No, Mommy." The last person I needed to be around right now was my dad. "I'll be okay, I promise. Now you go get some sleep. I know you got your volunteer work tomorrow."

"Oh, yes, Lawd. I forgot tomorrow was Saturday. All right, baby." She smoothed my hair back one last time and kissed me again.

Saturday. My meeting with Kevin and Bishop Walker was tomorrow. I stiffened.

"What's wrong, baby?" My mother rubbed my back.

"Nothing, Mommy. I love you. Thanks for coming."

"I love you too, baby. Now get some sleep."

That wasn't likely to happen.

11

I arrived at the church a few minutes late for the meeting, hoping Kevin was already there. I didn't want to be alone with Bishop. I tapped on Bishop's office door and stuck my head in.

"Monica, come on in. Kevin should be here in a few minutes." Bishop continued working on whatever he was working on. I thought he'd apologize for how our first meeting went, and say something to make me feel better about him and the whole situation. He didn't.

A few minutes later, Kevin came in. He had on some black slacks and a beige wool sweater. He looked a lot better than he did the last time I saw him. Except for his eyes. They looked hollow and sad. I wanted to hug him. Well, the old him. The him I knew and married, not the one I now knew him to be. Did what I now knew change the essence of who he was? Was he really a different person?

"Kevin, have a seat." Bishop Walker turned away from his computer. "We should have prayer first, especially with the nature of the things we have to discuss today."

We stood in a circle and held hands. Kevin squeezed my hand. The squeeze said so many things. *How are you doing? Please, forgive me. I love you. Do you still love me? Please, still love me.*

I didn't squeeze back.

Bishop Walker boomed in his baritone preacher voice, "Dear Heavenly Father, we come before You today asking for Your help and Your guidance. We've wandered into unchartered waters and we need You to be a compass to help us find our way home. Speak to us today. Give us Your wisdom and reveal Your perfect will for this couple, the choir, the church, and this, Your humble servant. In Jesus' name, amen."

His including the choir and the church in the prayer hinted I wasn't going to enjoy this meeting any more than the first.

We took our seats. I didn't know whether Bishop had purposefully put our chairs close together, but I purposefully scooted mine away from Kevin.

Bishop Walker cleared his throat. "I've met with both of you individually, and now I wanted us to come together to bring some resolution to your, uh . . . situation." He drummed his fingers on his desk. "I've counseled couples for years with this type of, uh . . . situation. Not exactly with your specific . . . uh . . . circumstances, but adultery is an age-old problem. Unfortunately, as long as there are marriages, there will be adultery. The most important thing is how to get through it and move on. God doesn't allow anything to happen to us we can't bear, so I believe He's allowed this situation to make your marriage stronger."

Kevin nodded like it made perfect sense to him. Maybe I was crazy, but to me, this went far beyond the issue of adultery. I decided Bishop would get ten more minutes before I left, so he better start saying something that made sense.

"I mentioned to Monica that I was willing to do counseling with the two of you as often as necessary. It's important for you to begin talking to one another again, and to make preparations for Kevin to move home because this will be very difficult to work out with you in separate locations."

I bristled. His ten minutes decreased to two.

I must have gotten a wild look in my eyes because Bishop addressed me as if Kevin wasn't there. "Monica, I know that's difficult for you to imagine right now. Kevin has betrayed your trust, and it's hard to think of putting the pieces back together. You'll be glad to know Trey is completely out of the picture. I met with him, and he's moving back to Philadelphia. He understands the seriousness of what has occurred, and is committed to doing whatever is necessary to get you and Kevin's marriage back on track."

This was deeper than I thought. How did that conversation go? Leave or else?

Bishop proceeded with his plan. "Kevin, I think at this time it would be prudent for you to step down as the director of the children's and youth choirs. We'll have Levi step in and take over those positions. He's been asking for more responsibility, and I think this is a perfect opportunity for us to see what he's made of."

Kevin sat up in his chair. "Why?" He was blinking fast like he did when he was angry or anxious. I wondered which one it was.

Bishop folded his hands. "I've given it a lot of thought and prayer, and this is what I feel the Lord is saying."

"But why? You think I would do something to the kids? Just because I . . . uh, have a, uh, history doesn't mean I'm a child molester. I would never do anything to hurt any child. How could you—"

"I'm not insinuating anything of the sort. I simply think you'll need all the time and energy you have to work on your marriage and to prepare for the album."

More blinking. I knew Kevin was both angry and anxious.

Bishop Walker was probably afraid of what would happen if this info got leaked and he was asked to explain how he knew about Kevin, but left him in a place of leadership over children. It was deep to see what Bishop was really made of. I looked up at black Jesus on the wall as if to say, "Can you believe this?"

I looked at Bishop. "I don't think I'm ready for Kevin to move back in and for us to work on things. With *my* history, this is hard for me."

"Monica, the way things happened between your parents is no indication of how things will go in your marriage. I've put a lot of marriages back together over the years. You'd be surprised at the number of couples in this church you know personally who sat before me with this same situation."

"So you have a lot of men cheating on their wives with men?"

Bishop shook his head vigorously. "No, not your *specific* situation, but adultery is adultery."

"I don't know why I don't see it that way." What was the deal with the way they were both using words like "situation," "circumstance," "history"? Like the real truth was too hard to speak. They couldn't say it, but they expected me to accept it?

"Monica, I've prayed long and hard, and I know this is what the Lord is saying. You're going to have to trust and obey the voice of God through me." Bishop leaned back in his chair. "Try to see things from a broader standpoint. Because of Kevin's position, you can't think only of yourselves when you make decisions. For things not to work out between the two of you would cause considerable stress on the choir, and on the church as a whole. Your life is not your own, and you have to consider how your actions affect everyone. It's one of the sacrifices of ministry. This is not about you. This is about the work God is doing in this local church and in the body of Christ. Think of the lives we've reached with this ministry. Think of the lives that will be reached with Kevin's album once it's released. This is bigger than your marriage."

Well, well, well. We finally got to the real truth. God had to help me not say what I really thought. "Bishop, I appreciate you spending time before

the Lord to get a plan for us—God knows I do—
and I want nothing more than to be in the will of
God. I guess my flesh won't allow me to. Maybe I
need to strive to walk in the Spirit more. Maybe
the Lord will deal with my heart and I'll stop self-
ishly putting my needs above the needs of the
body of Christ. Until I achieve that level of spiritual maturity, I won't be able to work on putting
this marriage back together."

He nodded slowly. "All right, Monica. I can respect that. As I said before, it is of the utmost importance that we exercise discretion. Most church
folk aren't mature enough to handle this type of
situation. Instead of praying for you, they'd
rather gossip about you. You're both so dear to
my heart, I couldn't stand to see you go through
that. You have my word. None of this will go outside these four walls."

"I appreciate your compassion, Bishop. It's
good to know you care so much for us at such a
difficult time, under such *circumstances*, in such a
situation."

Kevin raised an eyebrow and gritted his teeth
in an unspoken message to me to back off. He was
welcome to go along with Bishop's little game. I
wanted no parts of it. Not that I was about to go
blabbing it to everybody. I didn't want them in
my business any more than Bishop did. I just didn't
appreciate him pretending it was because he cared
about us. I wanted Bishop to be real—he didn't
want his church to split, especially since he was
about to break ground for the new building.

"I'll be praying for the both of you. Monica,
when you're ready, let me know and we can start

the counseling. I hope you'll come back to church, too. You can't expect the Lord to help you through this if you're avoiding Him."

I'm not avoiding Him. I'm avoiding you. I nodded and smiled, picking up my purse to make my exit.

"Sure would like to see you back in the choir. Things aren't the same without you." Bishop smiled.

Kevin chimed in, "Yeah, it isn't the same without you. I'm not the same without you." He reached for my hand.

"Yeah. Whatever." I snatched it out of his reach.

They both rose and started to speak, but their time was up. In our twenty-minute meeting, I had heard nineteen minutes too much. "God be with you both."

12

Things went from bad to worse. I cried myself to sleep every night and functioned like a zombie during the day. I kept forgetting things at home and at work. Even performing regular daily functions was painful.

Once, in the middle of the grocery store, I saw some Crunch Berries, Kevin's favorite cereal, and burst into tears. The other shoppers must have thought I was insane. In the drive-thru at the bank, when the teller said, "Thank you, Mrs. Day," I cried so hard, I had to pull over until I got myself together.

I couldn't listen to the radio in the car anymore. Gospel music reminded me of Kevin, and all the music on the R&B stations was about someone head-over-heels in love or broken-hearted from a relationship gone wrong. Everything on TV seemed to be about being in love or broken-hearted, too.

I was all alone except for my good friends Tom and Larry. Sometimes, I wished the freezer was bigger, so I wouldn't have to restock my ice cream pints so often.

One night, I finally had to cry out to God.

Please, help me. I feel like You've left me. I don't know how to find my way out of this depression, and honestly, God, sometimes I don't even feel like being alive anymore. I need You to help me. Do something, God. Please . . .

A few days later, when I got home from work, I did my answering machine check. I had a message from Kevin, and another from my mother, checking up on me.

The next message was short and strange.

"Hey, Monnie, girl—what's up? Check your email."

Was that Alaysia's voice? Couldn't be. She wouldn't know how to get in touch with me. Sounded just like her, though. No one else I knew had a voice that tinkled with laughter and mischief like that.

I went up to Kevin's music studio and logged on to the Internet. When I opened my e-mail, there were forty-three new messages. At least half of them were from Kevin. A cluster of five, grouped together, caught my eye. They were all from AlaysiaZ@yahoo.com.

So it was Alaysia on my answering machine. I opened the first one.

Monnie, your mother called me this morning. I'll pick you up at the airport. Can't wait to see you.

I scrolled down some. It was an e-ticket . . . to Jamaica . . . for tomorrow morning.

Classic Alaysia. Always coming to my rescue. I hadn't talked to her in almost three years, and her first words to me were "Meet me in Jamaica." What the email didn't say was "I heard your life just fell apart, and I want to help fix it." I wasn't about to jump on a plane and fly across the ocean just to hear her say "I told you so." Plus, I treated her so badly when I had last talked to her. I opened the next email.

Best friends are forever, no matter what. Stop tripping and start packing.

I had to smile. Alaysia always knew what I was thinking. I guess things hadn't changed. What really hadn't changed was her complete and total lack of understanding of how the real world functioned. She'd never had to work, so she didn't understand I couldn't just get on a plane tomorrow and leave work for a week. I clicked on the next email.

By the way, I talked to Dr. Stewart this afternoon. She was more than glad to give you the week off. She's such a dear. Have you started packing yet?

My face cracked into a broad grin. Jamaica? What would I wear? I had a few sundresses and some shorts I hoped would still fit. I hadn't put on a bathing suit in ages. I clicked on message number four.

> *We'll shop when we get there. Just pack what you have and come on. Don't worry, I won't make you buy a thong.* ☺

God, I missed her. I clicked on the last message.

> *I miss you too, girl. Now get your big butt up and pack. You have a plane to catch in the morning!*

What else could I do? I packed.

13

The stewardess escorted me to first class. After I got settled, she came back to ask if I wanted anything. I was almost tempted to opt for the mimosa she offered, just to take the edge off, but got plain orange juice instead. The bouncy Caribbean music playing overhead and the lilt to her Jamaican accent already made me feel far from home. As the plane took off, tears of relief slid down my face. It felt good to be getting away from my life. I had to stop crying, though. I should be salt depleted by now.

I couldn't wait to see Alaysia. I had so many great memories of friendship with her.

We met our freshman year at Howard University. When I arrived at my room in the freshman quad, she was already there, unpacking her stuff.

I brought the standard dorm fare—bed-in-a-bag, trunk full of junk, clothes, and, of course, my Boyz II Men poster. Alaysia was doing some serious decorating. She had an African mud cloth bedspread, several African statues and masks, framed art, and matching mud cloth curtains.

"I hope you don't mind. I took a few liberties in decorating." She held out her hand. "I'm Alaysia, like Malaysia without the 'M'."

"I'm Monica." I looked around the room. "Wow, this looks great. You make my half of the room look bad. I think my baby blue comforter set is gonna clash miserably with your African print. I'll have to see if I can find something in black."

"Not a problem." She went to her closet and pulled out a matching African mud cloth comforter set. "I was hoping you wouldn't mind. If we have to live in the dorm, we might as well live in style."

I went from staring at the room to staring at her. She was beyond gorgeous. I couldn't tell what she was—black mixed with Latino or white or something. She had to be at least five inches taller than my five feet five frame, and had perfectly smooth, peachy cream skin. Her salon perfect hair was straight and long—kind of a russet brown color. Her body was perfectly proportioned, with all the right curves in all the right places.

Great. Fat girl gets to be roommates with supermodel.

"What do you think of this for your side of the room?" She held up what I later appreciated to be a Romare Bearden print.

"Yeah, it's nice. You sure you don't mind?"

"It'd be too cluttered if I hang another picture on my side."

Alaysia moved the pictures, masks, and statues as if she had to get them just right. "Where are you from?"

"Baltimore. Born and raised. What about you?"

"A little bit of everywhere." She looked around for somewhere to place a black and white photo of a beautiful woman who had to be her mother. They had the same face, only her mother was much darker. "My mom was originally from New York, but wanted to be a singer, so she moved to Paris, like Josephine Baker and Nina Simone. She met my dad there. He's from Morocco."

No wonder I couldn't tell what her nationality was. Morocco. Wasn't it in Africa somewhere?

"I lived back and forth between New York, Paris, and Morocco all my life."

I was glad my parents dropped me off in the hall with my stuff and left like I begged them to. I'd hate for them to be going on and on and babying me in front of this worldly girl.

She kept explaining like I had asked for her life story. "My dad was going to college in Toulouse— it's in the South of France—but came up to Paris to 'play' on the weekends. He heard my mom singing in a nightclub and instantly fell in love. They got married when he finished school, and I came along soon after. We lived in Paris for a while, but my mom died when I was twelve."

"Sorry. That must have been terrible."

"It was. She drank herself to death. Her career never took off, and she got real depressed. My dad was never the same. He would stare at me with this sad, ghostly look in his eyes and call me by my mother's name. He brought me home to his family in Morocco, but I was . . . well, black, so that didn't work. He finally shipped me off to my mom's parents in Brooklyn and I lived with them for a while. My grandparents were so cool. They were activists during the Civil Rights Movement. They'd never admit it, but I think they were involved with the Black Panthers."

Alaysia continued organizing the décor while spilling her history. "We were a happy family until my grandmother had a massive stroke. My grandfather couldn't take care of both of us, so when I was fifteen, I got sent off to this all-girls' Christian boarding school run by a bunch of religious fanatics."

I was ashamed as I told my bland story about growing up with both my parents in the same house, with the same set of friends, going to the same church, doing the same things. The only interesting thing was the number of times my parents had split up and gotten back together. Even though she was open about her life, I wasn't about to tell that.

"I guess my life has been pretty boring."

"Boring is not always a bad thing." She brushed her fingers against her mother's picture and stared out the window.

By the time we finished decorating and running our mouths all day, our fifteen-by-fifteen box looked like something out of *Essence* magazine.

Alaysia lived like a queen. I had never seen so many clothes in my life. She filled her whole closet, half of mine, and borrowed an extra standing closet from dorm storage. Every week, she went to a spa to get her "beauty treatments." We couldn't have a car at our dorm, so Alaysia kept her Spider parked at a garage downtown.

She shamefacedly admitted to me, "Daddy never got over abandoning me. Spending massive amounts of money on me is the only cure for his guilt. I couldn't possibly deny him that."

After she spent the first year in the dorm, Alaysia said she was satisfied she had done the college thing, and convinced her father she needed a condo on 16th Street. I wasn't looking forward to losing her as a roommate.

Alaysia was insulted when I made arrangements to live in an upperclassmen dorm. "You're moving in with me. Why do you think I got a two-bedroom?"

After that first year, I had learned not to argue with Alaysia when she wanted to do something nice for me. Money meant absolutely nothing to her, so while free housing in a fabulous condo seemed like more than I could accept, to her, it was no big deal. My parents insisted on paying Alaysia, even when I explained it wasn't necessary. Alaysia saved the money and we used it for spending binges at the mall.

Alaysia taught me how to take care of myself. She convinced me to stop wearing frumpy clothes and get the latest fashions at Lane Bryant. She persuaded me that facials, manicures and pedicures were an essential part of every woman's beauty regimen.

She also exposed me to her worst habits. I got drunk for the first time on Boone's Farm Strawberry

Hill while we smoked Virginia Slims cigarettes. I tried marijuana, and we giggled all night and ate almost everything in the kitchen. All this took place in the privacy of our own home. Alaysia's mother had taught her a lady was never drunk in public.

We were an odd pair. I was initially fascinated with Alaysia's beauty and worldliness. She had traveled the world on what she called yearly "guilt trips" with her father. She had been all over Europe, Africa, and even Japan. As I got to know her better, I came to appreciate her spirit. Nothing scared her, and she was open and honest about everything, never afraid to speak her mind.

I think she liked my stability. She loved to go home with me on weekends and pretend we had grown up as sisters sharing my room.

Sometimes, Alaysia got real sad. She would cry for days about nothing. Those were the times she scared me with her drinking. Then she would swear off alcohol and collect all the liquor in the condo and throw it away, only to restock months later when one of her spells hit her again. Sometimes, she would say she was destined to die early like her mother, only there wouldn't be a child left behind to miss her.

I never thought there would be a time when we wouldn't be friends. We said we'd live in the same city and our husbands would have to be best friends, and we would raise our kids together and take trips together every year. Now, I had no idea where she lived. Mom told me she left D.C. before Kevin and I got married.

I looked forward to catching up with her and laughing. Alaysia always made me laugh. Not just a chuckle, but a roll-on-the-floor, grabbing-my-side, squeezing-my-legs-together-so-I-wouldn't-pee-on-myself kind of laugh. Maybe I'd even get drunk and smoke some pot. I just wanted to have a good time. I wanted to forget.

God would have to forgive me when I got back.

14

When I came out of the airport in Jamaica, it was bright and warm—drastically different from D.C.'s January cold. The tropical sun felt like God kissing me and telling me everything would be all right. I scanned the crowd until I heard my name.

"Monnie!" I turned to see Alaysia waving a big straw hat from a Jeep. "Over here!" She jumped out of the Jeep and made her way toward me.

She wore a white, cropped T-shirt and a pale blue sarong. I was used to seeing her in breast-hugging tops, tight jeans, and three-inch heels. Instead of her usual perfectly made-up face, she was going au natural, with only pearly lip-gloss and eyeliner. Her hair fell in long, natural spirally curls.

"Laysia, look at you!"

"Monnie, you look great!"

"Stop lying, wench." I grinned. Alaysia had always tried to convince me I was pretty.

She gave me a big hug. I was so happy to see her, so relieved to be away from everything, and so glad to be in Jamaica that I started crying. Guess I wasn't out of salt after all.

"Thank you, Alaysia. I missed you so much." The words got choked in my throat. "I'm sorry about everything. I should have—"

She flicked her hand. "Girl, forget about it. Best friends are forever, no matter what. I missed you, too. Don't worry about a thing. We're gonna have the best time."

We hugged for a minute and just like that, everything was okay—like nothing ever happened and it hadn't been three years since we'd talked to or seen each other.

"Girl, wait 'til you see this place." She ushered me to the Jeep and we took off. She told me the trip from Montego Bay to Negril would take about an hour, so I figured we had time to do some catching up.

"Where are you now? Mommy said you left D.C. two years ago." I rolled my window all the way down so I could get the full effect of the wind whipping through my hair.

"Atlanta." Alaysia grinned. "One black Mecca to another."

"You always talked about moving there. You like it?"

"It's Southern—a little slower, which is fine with me. Black folks are doing their thing, and there's a nice cultural scene. It's cool."

"What made you move?"

Alaysia shrugged. "Just needed to get away and start over. Somewhere fresh and new."

I could definitely understand that. "How did Mommy find you?"

"We've kept in touch. I send a card at Christmas and Easter every year, and she calls every once in a while to make sure I'm okay."

Good ol' Mommy. I couldn't blame her. She loved Alaysia. I couldn't blame Alaysia, either. She needed a mother figure in her life.

Alaysia turned to look at me. "Aren't you gonna ask me what I do?"

"Do?" I wrinkled my eyebrows. "What do you mean?"

"Oh, I'm insulted."

"You mean work? You work?" My eyes widened. She couldn't be serious. Alaysia had never worked and, as far as I knew, never planned to. In college, she only took classes that interested her. It was never about needing a degree for a career.

She puffed out her chest. "I'll have you know I'm the successful owner of my own business, Synergeez."

"Synergeez?"

"It's a health business designed to bring people to an optimal state of well being by addressing their emotional, mental, spiritual, nutritional, and physical needs." She said it like she was doing a commercial. "I recently got certified as a massage therapist and yoga instructor. I'm also a certified personal trainer."

"That explains the Angela Bassett arms."

Alaysia flexed a bicep. "I contract myself out to

this huge gym and also do one-on-one sessions at people's houses. I'm also doing some self-study on herbs, homeopathy, and spiritual healing. I'm thinking about becoming a naturopath."

"Naturopath?" I gripped my door handle. The roads were curvy and bumpy, and Alaysia didn't seem the least bit interested in slowing down.

"A doctor of holistic medicine."

"They actually have a degree for that?"

"Yeah, it looks pretty cool. You should look into it. Are you still planning on doing the nurse practitioner thing?"

"I don't know, Laysia."

"What? That's all you used to talk about."

"I don't know about the health thing anymore. It's gotten so routine and empty. Same thing, different day. Doesn't seem like we're really helping anybody. I don't know." Back in college, I had always talked about becoming a nurse practitioner. Kevin had been encouraging me to go back to school since we got married. I'd had the applications for two years, but for some reason, I never filled them out. I enjoyed nursing, but it wasn't as fulfilling as I thought it would be.

"You may want to consider something in natural health. You Western trained people only pass out poison. You should check out alternative medicine."

"I don't know what I want to do."

Alaysia rubbed my arm. "Maybe being here and getting a chance to clear your head will give you some time to think about it."

Figuring out my next career move was not the

foremost thing on my mind. We were silent for a minute, so I figured it was my time for catching up. "I don't know what all Mommy told you, but the true story is worse than I could've imagined."

"Shhhh, don't worry about it right now. That's D.C. We're in Jamaica. Relax yourself and let the tropical air get the city smog out of your system." She did a good imitation of a Jamaican accent. "Sit back, mon, take some deep breaths, and enjoy the sights."

She drove on tiny, winding roads through a lot of little townships. We stopped at a roadside food stand to enjoy some Roti and ginger beer. I watched Alaysia handle the advances of the lusty-eyed Jamaican men with ease. Several women approached us with jewelry to sell. I bought a few shells some children came to sell us.

We got back on the road and talked non-stop the rest of the way to Negril. It was as if we hadn't been apart for three years. We finally pulled up at a large, ranch-style house lined with exotic flowers giving off a thick, tropical aroma.

Alaysia hopped out of the Jeep and motioned for me to follow. "Leave your bags, girl. Donovan will get them." The large placard on the front of the house read: SASHA'S ON THE BEACH.

The room was not what I expected. The Jacuzzi, double vanity, extravagant décor, mini-bar, and other trappings that usually went along with an Alaysia vacation were missing. Two twin-size bamboo beds, a simple rack to hang our clothes on, and a hand woven floor rug gave the room a rustic feel. I gasped at the huge open windows that framed a perfect view of the ocean.

The sight of the beautiful, white sand and the clearest blue water stole my breath. Down the beach a short walk, water crashed off huge rocks with an upward spray that looked like God hand-painted it.

"This is beautiful, Laysia. It's so serene and natural."

"I figured it would be good for what ails you. Getting close to nature, feeling God, all that good stuff."

I raised my eyebrows. Alaysia mentioning God? Alaysia only ever acknowledged God to ask why I was so into Him.

As soon as I hung up the few clothes I brought, a young woman brought in a tray with two glasses. "Fresh tamarind juice? If you'd like to change into your robes, your masseuse will here in a few moments."

I turned to Alaysia. "Masseuse?"

"Yeah, girl. We have daily massages, yoga in the morning, tai chi in the evening, and sunrise meditation."

This was different. I was used to Alaysia the party animal. I studied her new look and figured this was yet another "Alaysia transformation." Alaysia had reinvented herself so many times, I could hardly count the different facets of her I lived with in college.

A tall woman with jet-black skin, wearing a flowing white dress sauntered in. In a thick Jamaican accent, she said, "I'll be setting up the table in the gazebo overlooking the beach. Meet you out there in a few, dear?"

I nodded. A massage on the beach? Life was starting to look up.

*   *   *

Must have been the combination of the cool breeze across my body, the sound of the waves crashing against the reef, and the strong, but gentle hands kneading my muscles. I was crying again. This time it was different. More of a release. Like she was massaging out the misery and releasing it to the water, where the rhythmic tide carried it further and further away. I was being washed. Baptized into peace.

When she finished, she gave me a last rub on the shoulder and whispered, "Stay here as long as you like. Let the water speak to you. Your soul needs it."

Rest overtook me. I think it was the first time I really slept in weeks. When I opened my eyes again, it was dusky.

Alaysia sat on a beach chaise beside the massage table. "She's alive."

I smiled. "How long have I been 'sleep?"

"What difference does it make? You needed the rest."

"Guess so." I sat up and let my eyes adjust to the light. I let out a sigh. "Oh my God, I feel relaxed. I don't think I can move."

"Good. That was the point."

We sat there in silence, watching the sun set over the horizon.

"Hungry? Dinner won't be for another hour." Alaysia stretched out like a big cat.

"I can wait." I thought for a minute. "Tell me this isn't one of those places where all they have is health food."

The guilty smile on Alaysia's face told all. "Yeah, I sorta forgot to mention this place is vegetarian. I told Sasha you weren't a veggie, so she's gonna see if she can get Donovan to bring fresh fish from the market every day. That's the only animal flesh you get."

"Don't tell me you're a vegetarian."

"For two years now."

"What's that all about?"

"It's all about being healthy."

I sat down on the beach chaise beside hers. We stared out at the water for a while and allowed the waves to hypnotize us. I felt like I could go back to sleep again. A gorgeous, brown man, whose rippling chest muscles justified his lack of a shirt, walked by and smiled.

I looked over at Alaysia. "Uh-oh, hottie alert. I'm 'bout to get left."

In college, I hated to go to parties with Alaysia. We'd be sitting at a table, and all of a sudden she'd say "hottie alert!" Invariably, some guy had walked in who was finer than fine. Alaysia would go introduce herself, and I'd be left alone—for the next hour if he was "just okay," or for the rest of the evening if he was "all that." I'd sit at the table feeling self-conscious and fat, hardly ever being asked to dance.

Alaysia looked over the top of her sunglasses at the "hottie" I was referring to, and pushed them back up on her nose. "Go for it, girl."

"Chile, I ain't trying to get my groove back. He's all yours."

She didn't budge.

"You're gonna let him get away?"

"I've grown since you last saw me. I no longer feel the need to make up for my father's abandonment in every man I see. I'm celibate now."

I clutched my chest. "Celibate? Alaysia Zaid celibate? The world is coming to an end."

"No, girl, it's just beginning. I've finally learned to love myself."

"Yeah, we'll see how long this lasts."

"Two years, three months so far."

I wrinkled my eyebrows. "Okay, this is too much. I remember the time you gave up pork. Then there was the time you wore only black for three months, mourning the death of the innocence of America's children. Then there was boycotting tuna to save the dolphins, and then sleeping in the park to champion the cause of the homeless. But no meat and no men? Even for you, that's kinda drastic. Come clean, Laysia."

Alaysia took off her sunglasses. "Girl, I got tired. Tired of the partying, drinking, smoking, man after man after man. It might have seemed like I was having fun all the time, but my life wasn't about anything." She looked out over the water. "When you make bad choice after bad choice, eventually you have to take a look at yourself. Most of my bad choices just messed up my life. When I made a bad choice that affected someone else's life, I knew I needed to make a change."

"What happened?" I had never seen Alaysia so

serious before. She seemed to be wrestling with whether she wanted to tell me.

"We're best friends, right, Monnie?"

I gestured toward the water and the resort. "I think we've established that."

"So you'll love me no matter what I've done?"

"Laysia, I think I've seen you at your worst." I thought of all the times I had seen her drunk, high, sleeping with three different men in one week. What could she possibly tell me that would shock me?

"I made a bad choice that cost someone else their life."

"What?"

She traced circles in the sand. "Remember Khalil?"

"You killed Khalil?"

She laughed and smacked my arm. "No, silly head."

"How could I forget him? He practically lived with us in the condo for a while."

"Oh come on, it wasn't that bad." Alaysia's smile faded. She picked up a scoop of sand and let it fall through her fingers. "Remember how strict I used to be about my birth control pills and condoms?"

I nodded. It was like religion to Alaysia.

"Girl, Khalil really stole my heart. I loved him more than I thought it was possible to love any-body. He was the only man that ever made me want to be . . . exclusive. You know that was a huge step for me. We got tested for STDs, shared our negative results over dinner, and decided to be one-on-one. It was the first time I ever went without a condom."

I raised my eyebrows.

"We were serious, girl. He always wanted to be monogamous anyway. I was the one afraid of a committed relationship. He was taking more of a chance than I was.

"I got a sinus infection and was prescribed antibiotics, but the doctor didn't tell me they would mess up my birth control. I was still taking it every day, but when I got to the sugar pills, no period."

Alaysia's eyes followed a sand crab wandering toward her feet. "I wasn't ready for a child."

She didn't need to say anything else. I understood, and she didn't want to speak the words. I knew that must have been hard for Alaysia. Because of her childhood, she always talked about what a devoted mother she would be. How she'd drop everything to spend time with her children to let them know how much they were loved.

Back when she was caught up in her causes, one of her main fights was against abortion. Not for religious reasons. She said no child asked to be here, and if they got here—from the point of conception—it was the parents' responsibility to make sure they were loved. She said parents who didn't love and properly raise their children were guilty of the worst criminal offense.

"I know. I'm a hypocrite, right?" Tears streamed down her face. "Over two years later and I still cry about it. I hope God can forgive me one day."

"He can forgive you if you just ask. You have to be able to forgive yourself."

She rolled her eyes. "There you go with that Christianity stuff. You guys can commit any sin imaginable—rape, adultery, murder—and all you have to do is ask forgiveness and it's gone, forgiven, forgotten. It's like a license to do whatever you want. Commit any sin, then repent, say three *Hail Marys* and it never happened. Where's the remorse?"

"It's not like that. Anybody who has a real relationship with God doesn't want a license to sin. I love God with all my heart and would never do anything to offend Him. Even though I know He would forgive me, I don't want to mess up our relationship."

"How do you get rid of the guilt?"

"I feel guilty for a long time when I do something wrong. I think it's a matter of realizing how much God loves me, and that Jesus died to get rid of the sin and the guilt."

Alaysia shook her head. "I couldn't get rid of the guilt. It haunted me. I imagined what the baby would have looked like, dreamed about it, thought about it and talked to it. I decided it would have been a boy. I kept apologizing to him, but I would dream he was standing over me, pointing his finger at me, blaming me and accusing me for killing him. That's when things got bad. I lived drunk for weeks. Khalil couldn't understand what had happened. There was no way I could tell him. He had wanted to marry me. I finally had to tell him after he heard me calling the baby's name out in a dream."

She answered my questioning look. "I had named him." Her eyes went dreamy. "Savon. I always liked that name."

I placed a hand on her arm. I wanted to tell her to stop so she didn't have to relive it.

"Khalil heard me calling Savon's name in my sleep and accused me of cheating on him. I had to tell him."

We listened to the waves swelling and crashing toward us. Seagulls flying overhead called to each other.

"He left me. Left all his stuff—his clothes, furniture, television, computer, everything. As he was leaving, he said the abortion thing was hard enough to deal with, but the fact that I killed his baby without him ever knowing there was one . . . He couldn't handle the lying. Me not being honest with him made him realize we could never have the relationship he wanted."

I could definitely relate, but I wasn't about to tell her that.

"I haven't heard from him since. I didn't realize how much I loved him until he was gone. I sank to a dark place I didn't know existed. I did everything I could do to help me escape my guilt and losing Khalil; drank, smoked pot, did acid, cocaine, heroin, everything."

My eyes widened. Alaysia had always been against anything stronger than pot.

"Then one day, I woke up and decided I either needed to go ahead and kill myself all at once, or stop and try to find some absolution. So I quit. Everything. That same day. I haven't touched a drop of liquor or even a cigarette since. I felt so good I started really caring for my body. Started exercising, doing yoga, meditating, gave up unhealthy foods, even caffeine. What is it you Christians say about the body being a temple? I realized there's so much truth in that."

She sighed. "I'm discovering who I am and what I want. I haven't quite gotten there yet, but I'm seeking inner peace."

I wanted to tell her there was no true peace outside of Jesus Christ, but I hadn't been the glaring example of that.

"I know, Monnie, I need Jesus if I want true peace." She rolled her eyes. "You don't have to say it."

"I wasn't going to say anything of the sort."

"Yeah, but you were thinking it. You just didn't want to say it because you feel like a hypocrite because you let a few curse words slip today and haven't been to church in a month."

I laughed. "You got me."

Donovan walked up with two trays. "You ladies didn't come to dinner, so I brought it to you." He put the trays down beside us. "For you, my dear, grilled Tilapia, steamed vegetables, and saffron rice. For you, my dear," he nodded at Alaysia, "black bean pate with corn fritters, vegetables and saffron rice. Enjoy your meal. Let me know if there's anything you need."

We ate in silence for a few minutes. The food tasted vibrant and exotic—the spices awakened every taste bud in my mouth.

Alaysia said, "I've been thinking about God lately. I've become a more spiritual person. I'm not ready for the whole church and rules thing, but I do want to try to find God for myself. I've always believed in a higher power. Now I need to know more about Him to decide what I believe."

I winced when she said "higher power." I didn't know what was worse, the partying Alaysia or New Age Alaysia. "I can respect that. No pressure, no preaching. Maybe we can try to figure it out together."

"What do you mean, Miss Model Christian? I thought you had God all figured out."

"I've been thinking a lot lately. I'll always believe in Jesus, but I'm having some challenges as far as church is concerned. I'm cool with God, but I don't understand some of His people."

"You're hurt because of what's happened. You'll come through this stronger than ever. Everything is for a reason. What was it you used to say all the time about all things working out for good?"

I sat up on the side of my chaise lounge. Alaysia had quoted, or at least referred to, more scripture than I had today.

"Yeah, I read the Bible. I also read the Koran, and stuff on Tibetan and Zen Buddhism, Hinduism, Taoism, New Age religions—all sorts of fascinating stuff. I guess you could say I'm on a quest for truth."

"Be careful with that stuff. You don't want to end up in anything crazy."

"I figure whatever the truth is will win out, and nothing else has any power, so it can't affect me."

"Oh, some of it has power all right—the wrong kind of power. You don't want to dabble in the wrong stuff and end up with some spirits you don't know how to deal with."

She waved her hand flippantly. "There you go with that demon stuff. I tell you what. Just pray God has me end up where I'm supposed to be. Tell Him to protect me from that demon stuff and guide me to the truth. If there is an objective truth."

She didn't have to ask me to pray that prayer.

15

When I woke up the next morning, Alaysia was missing from her bed. I put on a T-shirt and stretch pants and went outside to find her. I noticed some of the other guests sitting on the beach, up on the rocks, and on the beanbags and futons on the large granite back patio. Was this sunrise meditation?

I spotted Alaysia on the beach. She sat in that cross-legged yoga position with her eyes closed. I didn't want to disturb her, so I sat down on the sand not too close to her. What was I supposed to do for this meditation thing? Close my eyes and go "Ohmmm, ohmmm"?

Alaysia opened her eyes and motioned for me to come closer. "Isn't it beautiful?"

The ocean rippled toward us. I couldn't count the myriad of colors in the sky.

I took a deep breath and stretched. "Awesome."

A little bell tinkled.

"Yoga time." Alaysia got up and brushed the sand off her shorts.

"I think I'll stay out here on the beach."

"Come on, Monnie, just try it. It'll help you relax."

I followed Alaysia. Everyone pulled mats out of a bin and sat in a circle. There were only five other guests. I was glad Alaysia picked somewhere small.

"I am Milana, your yoga instructor for the week. Do we have any beginners?"

No one raised their hand but me.

Great. Fat girl does yoga with a group of experienced contortionists.

Milana smiled at me. "Welcome. The most important thing to remember is only do what you're comfortable with. Don't do anything that causes pain or stretches your muscles too much."

She proceeded to go through an explanation of what Hatha yoga was about. She talked about breath and energy and chakras and a lot of other babble that didn't make much sense to me. She told us to get into the rest position, sitting on our heels with our knees bent and our legs under us. After ten seconds, I realized if this was rest position, I was in big trouble. I kept shifting from side to side or lifting my body up to take the pressure off my legs.

Milana said, "If this is too uncomfortable for you, you can stretch your legs out in front of you."

I felt my face turn red, but it was too late to quit. I scowled at Alaysia, but it only made her laugh.

We went through a variety of poses and stances with funny names like warrior pose, cat pose, and downward facing dog. Most of the positions I couldn't do, so Milana showed me a modified version. She made me hold them, and it took a lot of strength from my legs and butt. I guess she figured I held the positions long enough when my legs quivered. By the time we finished, my face was flushed and I felt tingly all over, like I had electrified my body.

Milana bowed when the class was over. "Namaste."

"Namaste," the group said back collectively and bowed.

"Nama what?" I whispered to Alaysia.

"Namaste. It means 'I bow to the divine in you'."

I rolled my eyes. "Lovely."

"It's also like greeting, like peace, welcome, good day. Well, what'd ya think?"

"It wasn't bad. Actually, it was pretty cool. I feel kinda . . . zingy."

"Zingy? I hope that's a good thing."

"Yeah. I think it is."

After breakfast, everyone dispersed to their separate space to read or write in journals. The last thing I needed was a lot of quiet time to be alone with my thoughts. Alaysia beckoned for me to walk with her down to the beach.

We walked in silence for a while with the water tickling our feet. Finally Alaysia said, "Ready to talk?"

I let out a deep breath and nodded. "You were right about Kevin."

She nodded. Didn't say anything else.

"I walked right in on them."

"Oooooh, not good."

We kept walking.

"What are you gonna do?" she asked me.

I shrugged. "What can I do?"

She nodded.

We waded out to our ankles.

Alaysia said, "Sorry. I didn't want to be right."

"I know." I kicked sand and water in the air.

"You're gonna be fine."

"I know. It just hurts right now. A lot." I picked up a shell and examined it.

"If you need to get away, you've always got a home in Atlanta."

I smiled. "Thanks."

That was it.

The rest of the week was pure bliss. I got better at the yoga thing. The tai chi relaxed me. The food tasted great. I could see why Alaysia had gotten into the whole natural, holistic, organic, yoga, energy thing. It felt good to take care of myself. I didn't like the sunrise meditation. It gave me too much time to think about the mess of a life I had to go back to.

The long walks and talks on the beach with Alaysia were therapeutic. It was just like old times. Alaysia had wonderful, exciting stories to tell of her new life in Atlanta, her new business, new friends.

I needed a new life, but I didn't know where to start. During one of the reflective times where people meditated and wrote in their journals, I decided to start one of my own. I divided my life up into compartments to see what I needed to change.

For one, I had to proceed with a divorce. It was going to be painful, but what choice did I have?

I also needed to stop eating myself to death. I enjoyed the food I ate here in Jamaica, and needed to eat like this when I got home. I vowed to get some healthy cookbooks and check out the health food store not too far from my house.

And I had to start some sort of exercise program. I could walk every day. That's how I lost weight before. Give me a Walkman and a bright sunny day, and I could power-walk at least two miles.

I had to find me a yoga class. I wasn't into the whole spiritual babble, but I liked the way it made me feel. The electric, zingy sensation was addictive.

I also needed to find another church. Fellowshipping with other saints and hearing some good Word would help the healing process. There was no way I could go back to Love and Faith Christian Center.

Then there was my career. Did I want to go back to Nurse Practitioner school? Did I want to stay in the health field at all? If I didn't, what else would I do?

On our last night in Jamaica, Alaysia and I took one last walk on the beach. "Promise me we'll stay in touch."

I nodded. "Of course, silly. Best friends are forever, remember?"

She put her hands on her hips. "I mean it, Monnie. Your friendship means the world to me. You're like the family I don't have. I need you."

"And I need you, girl. I feel much better after this week. I think I can at least try to put the pieces back together now."

"Okay, we have to call at least once a week and email at least every other day, even if it's only to say hi. Promise?"

I nodded. "Promise. Cross my heart, all that good stuff."

Alaysia patted my back. "You're gonna make it through this just fine. You're stronger than you think."

"I hope so."

Alaysia's last words to me when she dropped me off at the airport were, "Remember, if things get too bad, you have a home in Atlanta. All it takes is a phone call."

I hugged her good-bye, wondering if I would need to take her up on that offer.

16

When I stepped off out of the airport, the contrast between the sunny, breezy air in Jamaica, and the gray, freezing cold in D.C. depressed me. The clouds were pregnant and angry, as if it might even snow. *God, couldn't You have at least had the sun shining when I got back here?*

It was as if I was being welcomed back to my life. Glad you had a great time in Jamaica, but let's get back to reality. I refused to be moved. I took a deep yoga breath, flexed my thigh and butt muscles and felt a tinge of zing. *I will not be discouraged.*

When I got to the house, I went straight to my bedroom. I dug in my dresser and pulled out my exercise clothes. If I kept them lined up on the chaise at the foot of the bed, I would be reminded every day I needed to walk. I put my tennis shoes right by them. Where was my Walkman?

I went down to the kitchen, got a big trash bag, and threw away all the fattening food: potato chips, toaster pastries, cookies, mixed nuts, cupcakes. God, did I really buy this stuff? What was I thinking? I braced myself and opened the freezer. Thank God there were only two pints of Tom & Larry's to throw out. I shut out my thoughts of the starving children dying in Africa and dropped the bag in the trashcan. *Sorry, Tom and Larry. I can't hang wit' y'all no more. I know you guys have been there for me through some rough times, but I gotta let you go. Try to understand, 'kay?*

I felt empowered. I was going to take control of my health and my life and turn things around. I decided I would give myself a week before I contacted Kevin or called a lawyer.

Alaysia and I kept our promise. We emailed or called each other every few days. Two weeks went by, and I still hadn't called Kevin. I didn't want to mess up my flow.

I decided to go ahead and find a lawyer. I wasn't quite sure how to do that, so I searched the Internet. Most of them had fancy web pages with articles explaining important facts about divorce. It was more information than I ever wanted to know.

I settled on Attorney Renee Hart. She'd graduated from Howard's law school about the same time I graduated from nursing school. I thought she would be able to relate to me better. Her picture looked like she could be a friend of mine.

My hands shook as I dialed the phone number listed for her.

"Attorney Hart's office," a soft, pleasant voice answered.

"Yes, I'd like to talk to someone, to a lawyer about, uh, I need some information about getting, uh . . . I need to get a divorce."

"Of course, ma'am. Ms. Hart is out of the office, but I'll direct you to her voice mail."

The lawyer's voice sounded calm and soothing on her message.

I tried to be calm when I left my message. "My name is Monica Harris-Day. I'd like to speak with you about starting divorce proceedings against my husband." Duh, who else would they be against? I left my contact information and hung up the phone.

After about a week of playing phone tag, I got an appointment with Attorney Hart. Her office wasn't too far from my job, and I took off early one afternoon to go.

When I pulled up to her office, I got the trembles. Walking through the door, I got the sweats. When her receptionist greeted me, I got the stutters. And when she led me back to Attorney Hart's office and introduced us, I got the goofies. I kept repeating everything she said.

"Hello, I'm Renee Hart." She stood and came around her desk to shake my hand.

"You're Renee Hart."

"And you're Monica Harris-Day?"

"I'm Monica Harris-Day."

"You called about a divorce?"

"I called about a divorce."

She smiled and gestured for me to have a seat. "Why don't you tell me what's going on."

I tried to make myself relax. I wondered if the soothing, pale blue walls and the plush armchair I was sitting in were designed to calm frazzled women like me.

"I've been married for two years, and I caught my husband cheating on me. I put him out, and now I want a divorce. That's about it." And then the stupid tears started falling. I had planned to be succinct and professional. Instead, I was bawling. "Excuse me, I—"

"Don't worry about it. Take your time." She passed me a box of tissue. "This will probably be one of the hardest things you'll ever have to go through in your life."

"Sorry. I didn't plan on doing that." I sniffed. "I think my husband will agree to an uncontested divorce and we should be able to come to a simple agreement about our property. We don't have any kids, and I don't want any alimony, so this should be about as straightforward as it gets."

"Wait a minute. Before we go into that, I want to make sure this is what you want to do. Have you two considered counseling? Not every couple that experiences adultery gets divorced."

Did I call a therapist or a lawyer? "I know this is what I want."

"I just want to be sure. Often, after the initial shock, there's a lot of pain and confusion. It's best to take some time to sort out your thoughts."

Did she want my business or not? "I'm sure."

"Have the two of you seen a marriage counselor?"

"No."

"Have you thought of seeing one before you

file for divorce? I don't mean to belabor the point, but divorce is final. Once you start the process, it's difficult to work things out. If there's any chance for reconciliation, it's best to try before you start divorce proceedings."

The tears started falling again. "No. There's no chance for reconciliation. I can't be in a relationship where there's no trust." If I told her the whole story, we would have skipped this part of the conversation, but I didn't think I should have to share all my dirt.

She nodded and handed me another tissue. "Okay, then. Sounds like you've made up your mind." She pulled a legal pad out of her desk drawer and picked up a pen.

We talked about the logistics and her fees, and then I left. I drove down the street and parked at the first gas station I saw. I sat in the parking lot and cried until I had no more tears.

Help me, God. This hurts so bad. Why did this have to happen? Why can't everything be normal and happy? Why, God, Why?

After feeling sorry for myself to God for a few minutes, I realized it wasn't going to do any good. I wiped my face and changed my prayer.

Father, my heart hurts so bad. Please, be with me right now. I need You close to me. Wrap Your arms around me and comfort me so I can make it through this. Give me the strength to do what I gotta do and move on. Help me, God. I need You . . .

After a few minutes, I felt okay enough to stop crying and drive home. I tried to focus on being proud of myself that I had made the first step. I only needed to call Kevin so we could discuss the terms of our divorce. The lawyer was one thing, but actually talking to him was going to be ten times worse.

God, give me strength.

17

When I finally called Kevin, he was eager to come over to talk. Too eager. He wanted to come over right away. I figured it was best to go ahead and get it over with.

I appreciated him ringing the doorbell instead of using his key. When I opened the door, he was standing there with a bouquet of lavender roses. My favorite.

I led him into the family room and didn't bother to take the flowers. I decided to keep it short and to the point. "I went to see a lawyer. I want to talk about a divorce."

He and the flowers wilted. "Why, Monica? I don't want a divorce. I know we can work things out."

"Kevin, I don't think so. I need to move forward with my life."

"No." He shook the flowers so hard petals fell

to the floor. "I can't believe you're saying this." He walked around the family room. "No. I won't give you a divorce. Why can't you forgive me? I love you."

I took the flowers out of his hand and laid them on the coffee table.

"Monnie, I want you back, and I'm willing to do whatever it takes to make that happen."

I looked at him like he was crazy.

"Why are you doing this to us?

"Why am *I* doing this to us?"

"Look me in the eye and tell me you don't love me anymore."

"Kevin—"

"You can't tell me you don't love me, can you? I know you love me. How can you throw our marriage away? I made a mistake. One mistake. Why can't you forgive me and we move on?"

"You know, you're asking a lot. I walk in on you having sex with another man and I'm supposed to get over it?"

"Not right away. I understand it takes time. I'll give you all the time you need. Just don't divorce me. I've been miserable all these weeks without you. I haven't written a song. Can't play right. My anointing is off. I'm nothing without you, baby. Can't you see that?"

"Why weren't you thinking about this on that day?"

"I've been over that day a million times in my mind. If I could take it back, God knows I would. If I could go back to when Trey first came back to D.C., I would've told him to go away and never contact me again. I was fooling myself to think I could be friends with him. Please, don't make me suffer the rest of my life for one mistake."

He stepped closer and I could feel his love like a magnet, drawing me to him. He stepped even closer and I laid my head on his chest. I closed my eyes for a second and inhaled his cologne. If I could just erase that day and have everything between us be like it was.

He slowly put his arms around me, moving carefully as if he was afraid he would break the spell he cast on me. I let him hold me for a second. I needed to feel him. I wanted to pretend nothing had happened.

But I couldn't.

I pulled myself away from him. He tried to hold me again, but I held up my arms.

"Please, don't push me away." Kevin's eyes pleaded louder than his voice.

I could feel my heart cracking in two. Like the life was being sucked right out of me. I went into the bathroom for a few minutes, hoping he would get his emotions under control.

Hoping I would get my emotions under control.

I was mad at myself for feeling anything for him. He was right. I couldn't look him in the eyes and tell him I didn't love him. I did love him. Would probably always love him.

Like my girl Tina Turner said, though, what's love got to do with it?

I came out of the bathroom, resuming my businesslike posture. "Perhaps I should give you some time to think about it."

"I don't need time to think about it. I don't want to talk about a divorce, not now or ever."

"You're being ridiculous. You cheated on me, but you won't give me a divorce? Does that make any sense? I really don't need your agreement. Based on what you did, any court in this country would grant me a divorce whether you wanted one or not."

Kevin paced around the family room, staring at the walls. I guess he just realized all the pictures of us were gone. He groaned, "Please, Monnie, don't do this to us."

"You did this to us. Not me." I could feel the tears rising. "Kevin, I need you to leave."

"Don't make me go. I'm sorry, but this is hard for me."

"You think it's easy for me?"

"Then why are you doing this?"

"Kevin. Just . . ." I held up my hand to let him know to give me a minute.

He sat down on the couch, rubbing his head.

I walked into the kitchen. Reflex action. Next thing I knew, I was standing in front of the freezer, cursing myself for throwing out Tom & Larry. I needed them to help me deal with Kevin. I walked back to the family room.

Kevin looked up at me. "I don't want a divorce, Monica. Take some time to think about it. Pray about it. I pray every day for God to help you forgive me."

I shook my head and stared at him. "You know what I don't understand? You knew how I grew up. You know about all the times my dad cheated on my mom and how much I hated it. And then you go and do the same thing he did. Only worse."

"I'm not your dad."

"And I'm not about to be my mom."

"It was one time. I only cheated on you one time. I swear it'll never happen again."

"I'm not willing to take that chance. How can I be sure?"

"You have my word."

"I thought I had your word when you said 'I do'."

He dropped his head.

I let out a deep breath. "Kevin, do you know how many kids my mom wanted when she and my dad got married?"

He wrinkled his eyebrows like he was trying to figure out where I was going with this.

"Four. She wanted four kids. She gained a whole lot of weight while she was pregnant with me. That was the first time my dad cheated on her. Long story short, the woman gave my dad something, my dad gave my mom something, and my mom got a bad infection. Spread through her tubes and made her sterile. I was an only child because my dad gave my mom a disease that stole her ability to have kids. His cheating made her infertile."

He looked shocked.

"I'm not going out like that, Kevin."

"I can't believe he did that. Why did your mom stay with your dad all these years?"

"Precisely." I nodded. "My point exactly."

Kevin looked like he wished he could take his question back.

"Do you know how humiliating it was to get tested for STDs? Do you know what it was like to wait all those days to find out if you gave me something? Would I catch something like my mom? Or worse still, did you give me HIV?"

"You got tested?"

"The real question is, did you? Did Trey?"

"It wasn't like I said, 'I'm gonna go cheat on Monica. Let's go get tested to make sure I don't give her anything.' It just happened."

"How did you know whether you would catch something and give it to me?"

He paused. "I didn't."

"You prove my point again. I'm not going out like that."

Kevin walked over to the fireplace and stared at the large empty spot where our wedding picture used to be. "I'm not the kind of man who could do that over and over. I love you. I love God. It was an enemy from my past that snuck up on me when I wasn't looking. I really believed God that I was delivered."

He turned to look at me with his soul-piercing eyes. "You don't have to decide now, but promise you'll take some time to pray about it. If God tells you to divorce me, I'll walk away and you'll never have to think about me again. But if God tells you how much I love you and how He's ordained for us to be together, you have to promise you'll try to forgive me and we'll work through this."

"I don't think—"

"Don't think. Talk to God. Please. That's all I ask."

Before I could stop him, he leaned over and kissed my cheek. He whispered, "I love you with all my heart," and then walked out the door.

18

Well, of course I didn't talk to God. I knew He was big on that forgiveness stuff. If He told me to forgive Kevin, I would have to do it, and I wasn't trying to.

I felt like Kevin had died tragically. The love of my life, the person I wanted to grow old with, had been snatched from me prematurely, only I didn't get to have a funeral for closure, and his ghost kept haunting me with phone calls, emails, and visits with flowers. I guess it wasn't as bad as him getting killed in a car crash, because I could still see him and talk to him. Maybe it was worse because I could see him, but couldn't have him in my life like I wanted to.

Was I wrong for not forgiving Kevin? Was it God's will for us to stay together? Maybe I needed to forgive him, but that didn't mean we were supposed to get back together. I got tired of thinking about it, so I stopped and went about escaping again.

My empowerment plan fell apart. My power walking dwindled down to nothing. I stopped writing in my journal, stopped doing yoga, stopped going to the health food store, and next thing I knew, I was cozying up with Tom & Larry again. I knew it was bad when I started avoiding Alaysia's phone calls.

At work one day, Tammy knocked on the bathroom door. "Monica, are you in there?"

I splashed my eyes with cold water then patted them dry so no one could tell I had been crying. "Yeah, be out in a second."

"You have an emergency phone call."

My heart jumped. Did something happen to Mommy? I ran out to get the phone. Tammy and Miss Odessa moved away from the nurses' station.

"Hello?" I could barely breathe.

"What is wrong with you? You don't answer my emails. You won't return my calls. What's going on?"

"Alaysia?"

"Who else do you think it is?"

"You scared me to death. Why'd you say it was an emergency?"

"'Cause *you* scared *me* to death. I dreamed you drowned in a vat of Tom & Larry's ice cream."

"Forget you, wench."

"Couldn't if you tried. What's the problem, Monnie?"

I lowered my voice. "I can't talk about it at work, Laysia."

"I can't get you at home."

"I'll call you tonight."

"You better."

"I will. I promise."

"If you don't, I'm on a plane tomorrow morning."

"I will. Gotta go."

"Don't make me come up there."

I laughed. "I promise. I'll call tonight."

Later that evening, Alaysia was quiet while I explained my recent encounter with Kevin over the phone. I was sprawled out on the couch in the dark family room, hoping my throbbing headache would ease up some.

"I don't know what to say. Sounds like he's really sorry, Monnie. I know how much you love Kevin, and sounds like he loves you. He made a mistake. You sure you don't want to try to work things out?"

I hung up.

She called right back. "I take that as a no."

I hung up again.

She called right back. "Okay, I get it."

"You're supposed to be on my side."

"I am. I want what's best for you. Maybe you should just think about—"

I hung up.

She called back. "Okay, Monnie, okay."

We sat in silence. The heater kicked on at a low hum. It was particularly chilly for February this year. I lay back on the couch.

Alaysia said, "Soooooooo, was my Tom & Larry's dream true?"

I didn't say anything.

"Hello?"

"I'm here. Did you call to harass me?"

"I'm not harassing you. I'm checking on you. That's what friends are for. To check on each other. Make sure everything's okay. Keep each other from gaining fifty pounds."

"In other words, you called to harass me."

"Harass is such a vile word. I'd prefer you not use it."

"Whatever, Laysia."

"Soooooooooo—"

"If you 'soooooo' me one more time, I'm hanging up this phone and I won't pick it up when you call me back."

"Wanna come to Atlanta?"

"For what? I still have to come back here. It's not gonna go away until I do something about it." I spread the blanket at the foot of the couch over my feet.

"I know. But maybe you need a break."

"I can't afford to do that right now. I need to save everything I have. I don't know what my lawyer bills might be."

"Ouch. Don't insult me. I didn't ask you to pay."

"I can't always let you pay for everything—"

Click. Wench hung up on me. I dialed her number.

"Stop playing, Laysia. I'm a grown woman. I can't be living off my—"

Click. I dialed her again.

"Laysia. Quit hanging up the daggone phone. I'm trying to tell you something."

"I'm not trying to hear it. We've been over this a million times."

"Fine. I can't come anytime soon, though. I just took a week off, remember?"

"Why don't you quit that slave labor and move to Atlanta? You'll love it here. You can get away from everything. Start over. You can help me with the financial part of my business. You know I'm no good at that stuff. I'm probably spending everything I'm making. Then you won't have this pride problem. You'll be working."

"Always got a plan, don't ya?"

"Pretty darn good one, if I do say so myself."

"I can't. Running away is not the answer. I have to face my issues, not escape them."

"Say that next time you hear Tom & Larry talking to you."

"Forget you, Laysia."

"Couldn't if you tried. And you did try, remember?"

"Ha, ha, ha."

"Don't go ghost on me again. Call a sista. Let her know how you're doing."

"I will. Thanks, girl."

"Forever and always. I mean it. Don't make me come up there."

"I'll call you in a week."

"You better."

"Bye."

19

I faded into autopilot mode again. A week turned into a month and a month into three months, and next thing I knew, it was May. My exercise clothes piled up in a heap in the corner. My tennis shoes taunted me every morning as I stepped over them. I couldn't bring myself to put them away. That would be to admit defeat and resign myself to being a fat slug.

One morning, I decided to get on the scale for a reality check. I stepped on with my eyes closed. Coulda swore the scale groaned. I opened my eyes. "OH MY GAAAWWWD." I kicked it, then jumped around the bathroom, holding my toe. "You filthy liar."

That was the problem with wearing scrubs to work every day. You couldn't tell if your clothes fit different. Okay, maybe the tie strings had gotten a little shorter. Okay, maybe my bras were getting too snug. Okay, maybe my underwear was cutting off the circulation in my thighs.

I went down to the kitchen and slung open the freezer. I yelled at a carton of Chocolate Brownie Walnut Crunch. "I thought you were my friends. Look what you did to me." Tom & Larry smiled at me from their perch on the carton. I could swear I heard them laughing.

"Bastards." I threw the pint in the trash. I pretended not to see the one on the top shelf. I knew Tom, Larry and I would make up later. I never stayed mad at them for long.

I didn't feel well when I got to work. I thought it was the tirade I went on that morning, but when the dizziness lasted into the lunch hour, I had to take a rest. I sneaked into one of the exam rooms and shut the door.

A few minutes later, Miss Odessa popped her head in the door. "You all right, baby? You been looking a little peaked this morning."

"Just feeling a little dizzy, Miss Odessa."

She hobbled over to me. Her bad knee must have been acting up. "You gettin' enough rest?"

"Yes, ma'am." Too much. All I did was sleep.

"You gettin' enough to eat?"

"Yes, ma'am." Too much. All I did was eat.

"You ain't pregnant, is you?"

"No, ma'am." Why did she have to go there?

"You sure? You never know these things."

"Yes, ma'am. I'm sure. I just had my cycle."

"That don't mean nothing. I 'member my cousin Greta had her cycle throughout all four of her pregnancies. We better check a test."

"I'm sure, Miss Odessa. I already checked one." Why she make me lie?

"Let me check your pressure."

"I've been under a little stress lately. I'm sure that's what it is."

"You done put on a little weight, and you know that can shoot your pressure up. You sure that pregnancy test was negative? Your hips done spread and your chest is bigger."

Miss Odessa was too sweet to cuss out, but she was taking me there. Maybe if I let her check my blood pressure, she would leave me alone.

She took the stethoscope out of her ears. "See, I told you. It's 160/100."

"It's just my nerves. Let me sit here for a few minutes and you can check it again."

The paper on the exam table rustled as I lay back. I did some deep breathing exercises and let her check it again. Even after I relaxed, my blood pressure was still 150/98—definitely high. I remembered it was elevated when I had my STD tests.

"Let me check your sugar."

Dr. Stewart walked in just as Miss Odessa pricked my finger. "What's wrong?"

"Monica wasn't feeling well. Her pressure is high, and I bet she got sugar, too. You know she been emptying the water cooler and living in the bathroom lately." Miss Odessa dabbed a drop of my blood on the glucose stick.

I frowned. Was that true? Come to think of it, I had been thirsty lately. I thought it was because it was getting hot outside.

The glucometer beeped.

"See, I told you. It's 182. Her sugar is high."

Dr. Stewart asked, "Did you eat breakfast this morning?"

I shook my head. I was too mad at the scale.

Dr. Stewart looked down at the reading, then looked up at me. "That's high for a fasting blood sugar. I know diabetes runs in your family. I've noticed you've put on a few pounds."

Did everybody notice my butt spreading but me?

My head was spinning. I didn't know if it was from my blood pressure or all the news. I really had gotten the Calvin curse.

Dr. Stewart insisted on doing a physical and labs on me. I could barely think. With my genes, I knew I'd end up with hypertension and diabetes. I just thought I'd be much older.

"Monica, you're going to have to make some serious lifestyle changes to avoid going on medication." Dr. Stewart said. "I'm going to send you to a dietician to put together a nutrition program for you, and you're going to need to start an exercise program. You'll have to get a glucometer and start monitoring your sugars. We'll see if we need to start you on some Glucophage."

Glucophage? My mother was on that diabetic medicine. No way in the world.

"I think if you're aggressive, you can stave this off for some years. But you have to get serious. You were losing weight there for a minute. What happened?" Dr. Stewart asked.

I opened my mouth to answer, but what could I tell her? My husband is gay and I caught him cheating on me? My pastor only cares about how this will affect his church and offering plate? My best friend is in the bush in Africa and I can't get in touch with her? My mom thinks I should stay with Kevin and have a messed up marriage like hers? Kevin broke my heart begging me not to divorce him?

I started crying instead.

"I know this is a lot at once. Why don't you go home and get some rest and we'll set you up with the dietician tomorrow." Dr. Stewart patted my shoulder then left the room so I could get dressed.

I nodded and got my stuff to go.

I could barely see the road as I drove home. How did I let this happen? I saw Tom & Larry's smiling faces in my head.

Bastards.

20

When I got home, first thing I did was call Alaysia. When her voice mail came on, I started crying and left a garbled message.

I went through the kitchen, crying and throwing away all the bad food. I couldn't blame God for this one. This was my fault. The trash can was full, but I felt no remorse. The poor, starving children in Africa didn't need high blood pressure or diabetes.

As I finished, the phone rang. I ignored it as usual. The answering machine clicked on, "Monnie, it's me, calling you back—"

I grabbed the phone. "Laysia, I'm here."

"What's wrong?"

"I don't want to hear 'I told you so'."

"Never."

I sat down at the breakfast table and told her about my doctor visit.

"Monnie, Monnie, Monnie. Okay, now it's serious. I'm not asking you this time. You're coming to Atlanta and we're going to get your health back together."

"I can't drop everything and pick up and move."

"Why not? Look, if you want to end up like your mom, your grandma, and your aunts, go right ahead. Naw. I ain't having it. I'll be there to get you tomorrow."

"Laysia."

"That wasn't a question. Check your email for my flight information tonight." *Click.*

I dialed her again. "Can we talk about this?"

"I'm listening."

"I can't just leave. I have a house here. I have a job. I have bills. I have a husband I need to divorce. I can't just fly into a fairytale life like yours."

"Fairytale life?"

"I didn't mean it like that. I'm just saying, I don't have a rich father I can lean on."

"I'm not living off my father anymore. I have my own business now. I support myself. I told you I need some help putting the financial part of my business together. I'm not asking you to live off me. I'm offering you a real job in a legitimate business while you focus on getting your life and your health together." Alaysia sucked her teeth. "Fairytale life. You 'bout to make me mad, Monnie."

"Sorry. You know I didn't mean it like that. My brain isn't working too good right now. It's the sugar and the pressure."

"A'ight. I'ma forgive you because of the pressure and the sugar, but don't come at me like that no more."

"Sorry, Laysia." I was crying again. "I didn't mean it."

"You gonna have to stop all that durn crying, too. It's starting to work my nerves."

I giggled and sniffled. I got up to get a napkin to blow my nose.

"I'm still coming up there. We can go over a diet plan and I'll put together an exercise regimen. You can let Dr. Stewart know you're leaving, hire somebody new and train them. Put your house on the market. Get your divorce. Do what you gotta do. I'm giving you three months."

"Why do I have to move?"

"Why not? What do you have there?"

"I—I . . ."

"I'm listening. What do you have in D.C. that's so great you can't leave? You've been in that area all your life. You've never done anything different or new. If you can give me one reason why you shouldn't move, I'll leave you alone."

I couldn't.

"Fine, three months it is. I'll be up there next weekend to go over your new health plan. I need to meet with my tenant anyway. I'm thinking about selling our old condo for some cash to build my business more."

"You're serious about this business thing, huh?"

"I know you think I'm a joke, but I really have found something I'm passionate about. I know I said I'd never work, but it's not work if it's something you love. I'll be there next Friday morning. Can you get off?"

"Might as well. I'll be giving my notice soon, right?"

"Now you're talking."

"I'll have the guest room ready."

"Nah, I'll get reservations at the Capital Hilton. We can do the spa thing again."

"All right. Let me know what time to pick you up from the airport."

After we hung up, I went into the living room and plopped down on the couch.

The phone rang again. "What now, Alaysia?" The line was staticky for a minute. "Hello, is anyone there?"

"Monica?"

I squealed. "Trina, oh my goodness, I can't believe it's you."

"Monnie, I miss you so much. I can't talk long, but I just had to hear your voice. Are you okay? What's going on there?"

"Girl, forget me. You're in Africa. Tell me all about it."

"I don't even know where to start." Trina talked a mile a minute about everything she had experienced since she left. I could picture her face glowing and her hands moving animatedly. I wanted to tell her to stop and breathe.

I could almost picture the village where she was living—the poverty, the begging children, the scarce living conditions. She also painted a picture of a strong, intertwined community of beautiful African people. She sounded excited about the school they were building and the numbers of people who had not only gotten saved, but were learning about the Bible and prayer. I was almost jealous. It made moving to Atlanta and starting all over sound even better.

"Enough about me. I could talk all day. What's going on with you? I pray for you every day. Are you, you know, doing okay?"

What could I tell her? She sounded happy and I didn't want to spoil it by telling her about my encounters with Kevin, the divorce, my health problems. I decided to keep things positive and told her about Jamaica, hooking up with Alaysia again, and my focusing on exercise and taking care of myself. I tried to make it sound like I wasn't alone, depressed, diabetic and hypertensive. I wasn't confident in my ability to fool Trina. She knew me too well. My only hope was to distract her.

"I think I'm moving to Atlanta." The line crackled for a second. "Trina?"

"I'm here. Gee. That's big news. Are you sure?"

Once again I tried to paint a great picture, telling her about Alaysia's business and how the change would do me good and I'd be in a place to focus on myself more.

"That all sounds good. I guess I'm being selfish. I can't imagine you not being there when I get back."

"Who knows, girl. I might be back by then. I just need to get away for now."

"Just make sure you pray about it, Monica. Make sure you hear from God, and if it's Him, then go for it. I'm behind you one hundred percent. Just make sure you're being led by Him rather than your circumstances."

She didn't have to say that twice. We said our goodbyes and made plans for our next phone call.

I stretched out on the couch and stared up at the ceiling.

God, I have no idea what to do with my life right now, and I really don't trust myself to hear from You. If this is Your will, cause everything to work together perfectly. Open every door and make a way. If this isn't Your will, slam every door in my face and don't let anything work out. Please order my steps according to Your perfect will for my life. In Jesus' name.

21

When I picked Alaysia up at the airport, she hugged me real hard and long. When she stepped back to take a look at me, I could tell she had to force herself not to say anything about how much weight I gained. We chit-chatted all the way to the hotel. We checked into our suite, and on the way up in the elevator, she said "I hope you brought some exercise clothes with you. They have a nice gym here."

Working out was the last thing on my mind. "Oh, I forgot. I guess I could exercise in my scrubs." I didn't tell her I couldn't fit any of my stretch pants.

"We can check out what they have in the gift shop. I'm gonna go meet with my tenant to get it out of the way so we can have the rest of the weekend to ourselves. Wanna go take a look at our old spot?"

"Nah, you can take the car. I think I'm gonna relax." I didn't want to take any trips down memory lane. I met and fell in love with Kevin while living in that condo. He first impressed me by cooking gourmet meals in that kitchen, and we had many an all-night movie session when Alaysia was on one of her many trips out of the country. I even slept in his arms in my bedroom several times. I remember thinking him such a gentleman for not trying anything.

That was the last place I needed to go right now.

After Alaysia left, I curled up in a ball on the bed and tried to take a nap, but ended up tossing and turning for an hour. I couldn't shut my mind down. Was I really going to pick up and move to Atlanta? I had never lived anywhere but the Baltimore/D.C. area. I didn't see my parents a lot, but I had never been so far away from them. It was nice knowing I could get to them when I wanted to. Was I really just gonna up and quit my job and have no reliable income? What if Alaysia's business didn't work? She could always call her dad, but what would I do? Would I be able to get the divorce finalized in three months? What if Kevin refused to do things easy and I had to go to court and fight a big legal battle?

My head throbbed. I wandered over to the mini-bar to find some water. It was filled with tiny bottles of alcohol. I hadn't really drunk since college, but something about the cuteness of the miniature bottles fascinated me. *Don't even think about it, Monica.*

I grabbed a bottle of water and lay back on the

bed. Scary thoughts about my future haunted me. Would I ever get married again? Would I ever have a baby? Or would I spend the rest of my life alone? Husbandless and childless.

God, am I going to have to sleep alone for the rest of my life?

I couldn't seem to shut down my mind. I walked back over to the mini-bar. I knew better, but I needed a momentary escape.

I screwed the top off a bottle of vodka and took a swig. My throat caught on fire and it tasted horrible. Nothing like the sweetness of Boone's Farm Strawberry Hill. I held my nose and finished it off. I made a mental note that I didn't like vodka.

Next, I tried some champagne. It tasted a lot better and went down a lot smoother. I pulled some snacks out of the mini-bar. Bad idea to drink on an empty stomach.

After emptying a lot more little bottles, my head went from throbbing to buzzing. I needed to get a nap before Alaysia got back. I went to the bathroom to wash my face and heard a click. Alaysia was trying to use the electronic key in the door.

I ran across the room and swept the empty bottles into the trashcan in one fell swoop. I ran back to the bathroom and rinsed my mouth out with some toothpaste. All the running made me dizzy.

Alaysia finally got the door open. She barged in, talking, face flushed and eyes glowing. "Hey, sorry it took so long. He wanted to buy the place, so we discussed some terms. I'm so excited. It'll give me a big chunk of change to invest in my business. I want to take it to a whole new level.

Wait 'til you—" She frowned and tilted her head. "What's wrong with you?"

"Nothing." I tried to look normal.

"Why do you have that idiotic grin on your face?"

"You know, uh, I'm excited about your business and the condo and all that, uh, good stuff." I deliberately enunciated my words to avoid slurring. Alaysia had always told me it was a good thing I was a good Christian 'cause I was a bad drunk.

She walked up on me and sniffed. "What have you been doing?" She walked over and picked up the trash can. "Monica Harris, have you lost your mind? Tell me the cleaning people did this."

"Nope."

She stood with her hands on her hips. "What's wrong?"

I shrugged. "Nothing's wrong, just trying to get away from my thoughts."

"What thoughts?" She sat down on her bed and took off her shoes.

"If I talk about them, I won't be getting away from them."

"You're not getting away from them anyway. They're still there and will be there in the morning when you sober up, only louder. You know that's not the answer. Tell me about the thoughts."

"One thought leads to another and they take on a life of their own, and then my brain starts to swirl in circles, trying to keep up with the thoughts. They keep swirling in my head." I was getting dizzy describing them.

"I'm putting on some coffee."

"I don't need any coffee. I want to go to sleep."

I lay back on my bed while Alaysia disappeared into the little kitchenette. I heard her clinking around for a while, then smelled coffee brewing. Smelled like she made it extra strong. My stomach didn't appreciate it and started swirling.

She brought me a steaming mug. "Here." The way she said it made me know not to object. I sat there and sipped the coffee like an obedient child.

She sat down on the bed across from me. "Tell me about the thoughts."

I frowned. "Who do you think came up with the word 'divorce'? It's such a mean little word. Do you think it sounds so bad because of what it means, or is there something inherent in the way the letters are put together that make it a bad-sounding word?"

"Oh, boy. Here we go on a perilous trip through the mind of Monica. A trip made all the more dangerous by the ingestion of noxious chemicals."

"Deevorce. Divorce. Deeeevvvvooooorrrrcc-ceeee. It starts with 'di' which has negative connotations to it. Then the 'vorce'. It's like something bad or painful, like force and vortex mixed together. I'm about to go through an industrial strength, high-speed blender. I'm going to be deeeeevorced."

I took a big slurp of the ultra strong coffee and winced as it singed the roof of my mouth. "Think I'll ever get married again?"

"You never know. You may walk out of this hotel and meet Mr. Wonderful. Make you forget all about Kevin."

"Oh, no. I need at least two years to flush this whole situation out of my system so I won't be carrying baggage into the next relationship. I can see it now. If he goes to play basketball with his friends, I'll be standing courtside, watching to make sure they're not gay. If he goes shopping for clothes too often or if he can cook, I'll suspect him. No, I need some time before another relationship."

"Mm-hmm. Drink your coffee."

"Would I ever *want* to get married again? I mean, maybe marriage is overrated. You give away too much power. You hand someone the key to your heart, the most delicate, yet most important part of your anatomy, and trust them to take good care of it. They rip it out of your chest and drop it on the ground and stomp on it, and when you scream and ask them how could they, they look at you and say, 'I'm sorry, it's not my fault. It's because of something that happened to me when I was ten.' Then they pick up your mutilated heart and press it back into your chest and try to fold your ribs and chest wall back over it and say, 'Okay, beat again, pump the blood, work like nothing ever happened'."

Alaysia grimaced. "Lovely. The rantings of a drunk nurse."

"Let's say I get through this two-year period and my heart heals and starts working again. You think I'd be dumb enough to give someone else the key to it and say, 'Here you go. It just got healed, but I give you permission to rip it out and mutilate it'? That, by definition, is insanity."

"I couldn't think of a better word to describe this conversation." Alaysia got up and pulled a T-shirt and shorts out of her suitcase.

"Then again, I can't be in a relationship without giving my heart away completely. What's the point? If I'm going to be in love, I'm going to be in love. I don't believe in doing it halfway. Which is what got me into this situation in the first place."

"Monnie, you can't blame yourself for loving Kevin, and you can't blame him for what happened. He didn't mean to hurt you."

"And that, my friend, is the scariest part of it. That someone can love you and not mean to hurt you, but destroy you anyway. And don't be defending him. You're supposed to be my friend."

"I am your friend."

"Then act like it. Either join the pity party or go home."

Alaysia laughed.

"What if I do decide to get married again? I mean what are the stats these days? When we first got to Howard, they told us ten women for every one man. You count all the brothers getting killed in the black man's war, then all the black men in prison, then the gay men . . . a sista ain't got much to work with. How many girlfriends do we have our age that ain't got no man and no prospects either? The only thing saving us is the lesbians. That's the only thing helping out the ratio."

I leaned forward, almost falling off my bed. "You're not gay, are you, Laysia? Is that what this celibacy thing is about? You got fed up with the brothas and switched over to the sistas? You could tell me. It'd make my chances better."

Alaysia laughed and shook her head. "I'm not gay. Just taking a break from black men."

I nodded and pointed a finger at her. "Now you got the revelation. I'ma find me a Latino man—a Puerto Rican hottie. They black anyway. Or maybe I'll find an Italian man. They're pretty dark. I could try an Asian, but they don't have much spice to them. Maybe I'll just get me a white man. Naw. I better stick with my Puerto Rican hottie."

"You know how people treat interracial couples. You sure you can handle that?"

"It ain't like that for black women. Think about it. When you're out in public, you see a black man with a white woman and pure hatred rises up in you. Why? The ratio. That's anotha brotha the sistas lost. When you see a black woman with a white man, it don't bother you. You say, 'I feel ya, girl. I ain't mad at ya. Do your thang.' You think you're okay with it because you sympathize with the fact that she wasn't able to find her a black man. But secretly, you're glad because that sista has tilted the ratio a tiny bit more in your favor."

"You are out of control."

I stood up and did a little salsa dance. "Yeah, man, a Puerto Rican hottie." My dance didn't last long because it made the room spin. "Next time, I'd have to get to know him for at least five years before I even think about marrying him. I'd have to know his high school friends, his neighborhood friends; I'd interview his parents, want to know about his past relationships. Maybe I'd make him take a lie detector test—question him under hypnosis or something. I would say he'd have to be a sincere man of God so I could be assured he was telling the truth, but so much for that."

Alaysia frowned.

"And I need a manly man next time. He'd have to be a mechanic or a construction worker, or a garbage man. Someone who comes home dirty and stinky every day. Yeah, that's safe. He'll have to have a garage full of tools, and will always be working on the car or fixing something in the house. And he will *never* talk about his feelings. He won't know his way around a kitchen, either. When I ask him how I look in an outfit, he won't turn away from football on television and will say 'Fine, babe,' then slap me on the butt and tell me to bring him a soda. When I bring it to him, he'll pull the top off with his teeth, drink it in one gulp and let out a loud belch and stuff his hand down his pants."

Alaysia was rolling on the bed, laughing at me.

"We haven't even gotten to the whole issue of kids. If I am 'blessed' to get married again, after the initial two-year 'Kevin wash-out', then the five-year 'new man investigation', we'd need to be married at least three years so I could be sure I wanted to stay, then I would *think* about having kids. Which would put me at the ripe old age of thirty-nine. I know too much about what kind of babies old eggs could make."

"A lot of women are having babies when they get older these days. It's a trend. The career woman of the new millennium, getting established in her career and having kids later." Alaysia scooted onto the floor and did some stretching exercises.

"Thanks for trying to make me feel better, but I ain't having no old-egg baby."

"No, come on, Monnie. One of my clients swears by it. She had one child with her first husband when she was twenty-four, then got divorced. She got remarried at the age of thirty-seven and had another daughter a year later. She said motherhood when she was more mature was much better than when she was twenty-four. She thinks all women should wait until they're older to have their children."

"Say what you wanna say. I don't want no old-egg babies." I slurped down the rest of my coffee. "The way I see it, Kevin wasted my time. He took my precious reproductive years. Six of them. Now I'm stuck never getting married again and having no babies, or at best, getting a late start and having some old-egg babies."

"Monica, you've been thinking about all this too much."

"Good old Kevin." I lifted up my coffee mug in a toast. "You know what I miss the most about him?"

"No, but I'm afraid you're gonna tell me."

"His warmth."

"Yeah, Kevin's a nice guy."

I shook my head. "Not his personality, silly. His warmth—his body heat. No amount of comforters or electric blankets can replace it. I don't care how many body length pillows I buy and snuggle up next to—there's nothing like a warm body wrapped around you at night. Kevin's a great snuggler. What if I never get married again? That means I spend the rest of my life alone, in a cold, empty bed with no one to keep me warm at night. No one to share my life with. No babies, no grandbabies. I'll be one of those old women who lives alone, mutters to herself all the time, and has fifty cats."

Alaysia laughed. "You're allergic to cats."

"Fifty dogs, then." I frowned. "They never have a bunch of dogs. You ever notice that? Why do they always have a houseful of cats?"

"It's definitely time to go to bed. No more mini-bar for you. I can see it's not safe to leave you unsupervised."

Must have been the alcohol. That night I dreamed about being in a huge bed with a bunch of rotten eggs and dogs. Alaysia was right. No more mini-bar for me.

22

Early the next morning, Alaysia opened the blinds and turned on the lights. She pulled my covers off. "Get up, Monnie. It's time to exercise."

Where did she get a megaphone? I groped for my covers. "Alaysia, leave me alone. My head is killing me. Stop talking so loud."

"Didn't nobody tell you to empty the mini-bar yesterday. It's time for a workout."

"Don't make me hurt you."

She pulled my covers back down and smacked my legs. "Come on. Up and at 'em."

"If I could get up without my brain exploding, you'd be in trouble."

"Come on. You want a piece of me?" She slapped my feet and did a little boxing dance.

"ALAYSIA!" Screaming her name nearly ripped my head open, but I hoped it would make my point.

It didn't. I felt her put something on my legs. "I picked you up some exercise clothes yesterday. I think I got them big enough to fit your big ol' butt."

I opened one eye and glared at her through it. "You really want a beat-down this morning, don't you?"

She laughed and did some kicks and punches. "You look like you already got a beat-down from Jack Daniel's. You don't need another one from me."

"Alaysia, let me sleep for another hour and I promise I'll do whatever you want." I didn't plan on exercising, but I would tell her anything to make her go away.

"One hour. That's all you get. I'm gonna go do my workout. That means when you're working out, I'll be able to give all my attention to make sure you get the best workout possible."

"Lovely. Looking forward to it." I flipped her the bird.

"I love you, too."

She must have decided to have mercy on me, because when I woke up on my own and looked at the clock, it was three hours later. I rolled over and she was sitting in one of her yoga positions.

"She's alive."

"Forget you, wench."

"You—"

"Couldn't if I tried. I know. Did you have a good workout?" I sat up and wiped the dried slob crust off my cheek.

"Yeah. I let you off the hook today, but tomorrow you don't get off so easy. You might want to avoid the mini-bar this evening."

"Trust me. I have no intention of going near it again."

"Get up and shower. We have to talk."

"This sounds serious."

"It is. Do you have any idea how many carbohydrate calories you consumed last night?"

I flopped back on the bed and pulled the covers up over my head. "No, but I'm sure you're gonna tell me."

"I'm serious. You can't do that stuff with a sugar problem."

"Sugar problem? You make it sound like I'm an alcoholic or something."

"Some of us do alcohol and drugs. Others of us do Tom & Larry's." Alaysia mimicked someone dipping a spoon into a carton, ate off the spoon, then nodded off like she'd just shot up some heroin. "We all have our different addictions."

"Ha, ha, ha."

"I'm not laughing. Get up and wash your tail so I can let you know the house rules."

"House rules?" I threw the covers back and scooted to the edge of the bed.

"Yeah, rules for living in my house."

"You trippin' now. I'm grown. My momma live in Baltimore, not Atlanta."

"I'm your momma now. Until you lose about thirty pounds and your sugar and pressure go back to normal, you live by my rules."

"Okay, I'ma let you have your little ego trip for a second. What do these rules entail?"

"For one, you have to follow my diet and exercise program to a tee. No whining, no complaining, and no excuses."

I rolled my eyes.

"I'm not playing. You can only eat what I cook and buy, or what I order for you if we go out to eat."

"What are you? The food police?"

"That's Lieutenant Food Police to you."

"So what can I not eat?"

"No meat, no—"

"No meat? Just because you're a vegetarian doesn't mean I want to be one. I can eat low fat chicken and fish and pork and—"

"Pork?" Alaysia wrinkled her face. "There will be no swine to enter my home."

"Fine. I'll eat meat when I eat out without you."

"Uh-uh. I don't even want any meat farts in my house. Only pure organic vegetarian farts are allowed in my sanctuary."

"Meat farts? What the heck is a meat fart?"

She looked at me like the meaning was obvious. "A meat fart is a fart emitted from the colon of someone who eats meat. I don't want you emitting any gaseous animal particles into the air in my abode."

I rolled my eyes. "What else can't I have?"

"No white flour, no white sugar—"

"No sugar? You know how much I love sweets. I thought the whole goal was moderation. I thought when you diet you're supposed to still eat foods you enjoy, but not as much."

"I didn't say you had to give up sweets. I said

they couldn't be sweetened with white sugar. There are other ways to make things sweet."

"Like what?"

"Fruit sugar, stevia, raw turbinado sugar—"

I held up my hand. "Stevia? Never mind. I don't want to know."

"I promise you're gonna love it. Oh yeah, no dairy either."

"No dairy? What am I supposed to have on my cereal, in my coffee, with my fruit-sweetened cookies?"

"Soy milk, almond milk or rice milk. Take your pick."

"What else, El Capitan?"

"A strenuous exercise regimen."

"I'm afraid to ask what that consists of."

"We'll start the day off with yoga, later do some cardio, then some light weights."

I shook my head. "Why don't you shoot me now and get it over with?"

"Come on. Don't you trust me?"

"Promise you won't kill me."

"Just the opposite. I'm gonna help you live."

"Yeah, right. Any other rules, Massa?"

"That's all for now, but if I come up with any others, I'll let you know."

"You get to make them up as you go?"

"Yep. You are mine."

I walked into the bathroom. I was supposed to check my blood sugar when I first woke up, which technically was right now, even though it was almost noon. I hated to check it in front of Alaysia, lest I set her off on another lecture about how many carbohydrate calories I consumed. If I didn't check it, though, I couldn't eat, and I needed something to take the edge off this headache. After my binge last night, I knew it would be high. What was the point?

I did need to take my medicine, though. After monitoring my blood sugar and blood pressure for a few days, Dr. Stewart started me on the Glucophage and a blood pressure medicine. She said I could probably stop them if I lost ten percent of my body weight.

I pulled out my pill dispenser. I closed the door because I didn't want Alaysia to see me taking the pills. I hadn't bothered to mention I was taking the medicine, and knew she'd have a fit if she found out.

It was embarrassing that I let my health get to this point because I couldn't control my eating. I felt enslaved to the little pillbox in my hands and knew I didn't want to be stuck on meds for the rest of my life. Even though Alaysia's plan sounded extreme, I had to do something.

I looked at myself in the mirror. *All right, Monnie girl. You gotta get yourself together. You are not gonna be on these durn pills for the rest of your life, and you are not going to die of a stroke. You are going to treat your body like the temple it is and get this stuff under control.*

I thought about Alaysia's regimen and it seemed as much bondage as being enslaved to the pills. I looked up at the ceiling. *God, you gon' have to help me.*

23

The next two months flew by. We had no problem finding and training a replacement for me at Dr. Stewart's office. They had a big party for me at work to wish me well in my new life. Dr. Stewart said she hated to see me go, but had gotten the feeling I was unhappy in my position and was glad to see me moving on to something bigger and better. I tried to explain that it wasn't her office I was unhappy with, and she was the best boss I could have ever asked for. I got teary-eyed and mumbley-mouthed, but I think she got the gist of it.

Saying goodbye to my parents was difficult. They took me out to dinner at Phillips Seafood at the harbor. Their salmon was my favorite. My dad had this sad look on his face the whole night and kept asking if I was sure I wanted to go that far from home. I didn't know what my mom told him, and didn't care to ask.

My mom kept wringing her hands, patting my cheeks, and smoothing down my hair. When my dad went to the bathroom, she kissed my cheek. "Monica, I just want what's best for you, baby. Sometimes it's better for a woman to start over than to let somebody know they can get away with whatever they want to for as long as they want to. I'm proud of you for doing what's best for you."

I bit back my tears. I felt sad for my mother and the life she chose. I had to make myself be nice to my dad for the rest of the evening. I really wanted to hit him over the head with a chair to knock some sense into him. If he only appreciated the jewel he had in my mother.

As we left, I kissed his bald head and tried to convince myself that whatever demons drove him to do what he did, over and over again, were a by-product of his childhood.

I didn't bother to call any of my friends to tell them goodbye. I hadn't talked to most of them in months anyway. They probably got tired of me never calling them back. How could I? They'd want to know what was going on, and it wasn't like I could tell them what happened between me and Kevin.

Kevin.

Every time I picked up the phone to tell him I was leaving, I ended up holding the receiver until the recording came on telling me something about hanging up if I'd like to make a call. I kept remembering him shaking rose petals all over the family room. I didn't want a repeat of that scene. Maybe I'd send him a post card or an email after I got to Atlanta.

I decided to meet him out in public. That way he couldn't make a scene. At least I hoped.

I arrived at Starbuck's early so I could get a Venti Calm tea. It was too hot outside to drink tea, but I hoped the chamomile would relax me so I could deal with Kevin.

When he got there, I could tell he took extra care to look good for me. His hair was in perfectly shaped comb twists. He wore the blue linen short set I had bought him last summer. I hoped I looked so fat and sloppy he would change his mind about wanting to stay married, and agree to a quick and quiet divorce.

I stood up to greet him. Before I could step back, he hugged me. I figured I'd at least give him that since I was about to skip town.

Bad idea. He smelled good and felt good. Brought back too many memories and stirred up too many feelings. I felt him sigh.

"Hey, Monnie." He kissed my cheek. "I'm glad you called. I been waiting to hear from you."

"Hey, Kevin." I sat down and picked up my tea. I took a big swallow and prayed for the Calm to take an immediate effect. I patted the chair next to me. "Have a seat."

I handed him the Caramel Frappucino I bought him. He had this goofy smile on his face like he knew I heard from God and was here to ask him to move back home. In a way, that was true. I was going to tell him he could move back home. The only glitch was, I wouldn't be there.

"How've you been?" He brushed his hand against my cheek.

I pulled away. He frowned.

"Good, I guess. I don't want to keep you long, Kevin. I need to tell you something."

"What?" He started that eye-blinking thing, and I knew this wasn't going to go well.

No sense in beating around the bush. "I'm moving to Atlanta."

His mouth dropped. He started to say something and stopped. He tried again. "When? Why? How did you decide that? Why Atlanta?"

I let out a deep breath and put my hand on his. "I'm leaving next week." I gave him a big smile as I offered a consolation prize. "You'll be able to move back into the house."

He shook his head. "Why, Monica? I thought you were taking some time to heal so we could get back together. I don't need to come back to the house. I'm fine at my mom's. You can take some more time if you need to."

"I don't think it's a matter of more time. Look at me, Kevin. I'm a mess. I can't live like this anymore. I need to start over, and I need to get away from here to do that."

"Why? I don't understand. Why can't you forgive me?"

"It's not that I can't forgive you. In my heart, I think I have. Just because I've forgiven you doesn't mean I want us to get back together. I need to move on with my life."

"Why?"

His "whys" were getting on my nerves. He sounded like a two-year-old.

I decided to be honest. "Kevin, I've been depressed for the past few months." I held out my arms. "Look at me. I've gained a ton of weight. Dr. Stewart diagnosed me with high blood pressure and diabetes, and I have to take all these pills and check my sugar twice a day. I have to do something drastic or I'll be doing that for the rest of my life. I'm going to this specialized spa program in Atlanta to get a handle on things."

Okay, sort of honest.

His facial expression said I wasn't making sense. "Spa program? You're quitting your job and going to a spa?"

When he put it that way, it didn't make much sense.

"Alaysia runs her own health business down there. I'm going to help out. In exchange, she's putting me on this intense program to help me get my health in order."

"Alaysia." Kevin made a sour lemons face. "I should've known."

"What's that supposed to mean?"

"Nothing. Now I understand."

"Understand what?"

"Nothing. I know she never liked me, that's all."

"It wasn't that she didn't like you. She just knew."

"Knew what?"

I rolled my eyes. "About your . . . history."

Kevin looked around at the tables near us and lowered his voice. "How?"

"I don't know. I guess from her extensive experience with men."

"Why did you go to her about it?"

"Who would you prefer me to go to? Tracey? Regina? Janae? Shavon?"

He blinked faster as I mentioned my friends from the choir.

"I didn't think so. Trina's gone. I needed somebody to lean on."

"What about me? I'm all alone in this."

"That's your choice, Kevin. Your choice to live with this big secret. Your choice to keep living a lie. Or should I say Bishop Walker's choice?"

I never saw his eyes blink that fast. He chewed his fingernails. I hadn't seen him do that in a while. He usually kept them perfectly manicured.

The whir of the espresso machine and the jazz playing overhead filled the silence hanging in the air between us. Kevin ran his fingers through his comb twists. "Are you coming back after you get your health together?"

"Not if I like it there." I hadn't given too much thought about it. All my life, I'd had a long-term plan. I decided to live in three-month chunks from now on.

"How are you going to live? Are you going to get a nursing job down there?"

"I'll be working for Alaysia. Helping to build her company."

"You don't have to live off her. You can take our savings if you want. It'll last until you find a job."

"I won't be living off her. I'll be working. I'm not gonna take our savings."

"It's half yours. I don't want you to be without. I want you to be able to take some time and focus on getting your health together. I don't want anything to happen to you." A lonely tear edged down his face.

I wiped it away. "Kevin, have you thought of seeing somebody?"

He frowned. "Seeing somebody?"

"Yeah, like a therapist or a counselor or something."

"No, just Bishop Walker. He's been counseling me."

I hated to imagine what those sessions were like. "What—on how to keep a secret? How to stay emotionally bound for the sake of his ministry?"

"It's not like that. Bishop Walker is like a father to me. He cares about me."

Was he trying to convince me or himself? "All I'm saying is you might benefit from some professional therapy. You had a very traumatic life event at a young age that shaped the rest of your life. I'm not sure Bishop Walker is trained to handle that." I really wanted to say I wasn't sure Bishop Walker was interested in truly helping him.

"No. I'm fine. I've been feeling much better since I've been talking to Bishop. I think if you would talk to him, he'd be able to help us through this much better."

No sense in trying to get him to see. I patted his hand and stood to leave.

"I'll be waiting for you, Monica. I'll be right

here when you get your health together and come back. By then, the album will be released and you won't have to go back to work."

He looked so sad. I decided to let him hold on to his little fantasy. He'd realize after a year or two I wasn't coming back, and would hopefully move on with his life.

I bent and kissed him on the cheek. "Okay. Take care, Kevin."

I walked out the Starbuck's door and didn't look back. All I wanted to do was think about my new life in Atlanta.

24

Alaysia pushed the door open. "Here we are. Home sweet home."

"This is absolutely beautiful." It was like walking into an upscale spa. The walls were a pale, sage green. A wall-length fountain had pretty, smooth rocks with water splashing off them, making peaceful, tinkling sounds. She had a large, beige couch with soft lavender and green throw pillows. There was a sunroom out back that let out onto a large patio. Plants covered both of them.

"This is your room in here."

"This is wonderful."

There was a beautiful mahogany sleigh bed with a matching dresser and mirror and a sitting area with a chaise lounge and throw pillows. The whole décor was done in earth tones. Reminded me of Trina's.

"You go ahead and get settled. I'm gonna put

the finishing touches on dinner. I've prepared a special meal for your first night here."

"Lovely. What is it? Curds and whey? Granola and tofu?"

"It is tofu, actually. Jerked tofu and stir-fried vegetables over rice, and a surprise for desert."

"Great. I'll lose weight from sheer starvation."

"Keep an open mind. You'll like it. I promise."

I changed into some scrubs and unpacked my clothes. I didn't have many that fit anymore. I'd have to go shopping.

When I finished hanging up everything, I wandered into the kitchen. Whatever Alaysia was cooking smelled too good to be healthy.

We sat down at the table. I looked down at my plate and frowned. There were big chunks of whitish brown stuff mixed with a lot of different kinds of vegetables over rice.

"So, this is tofu. What is tofu anyway?"

"Soybean curd."

"I really am eating curds and whey."

Alaysia laughed. "Just try it, silly."

I took a tentative bite with only vegetables and rice. I knew that was safe. Maybe she'd stop watching me after I ate a few forkfuls. Then I could spit the tofu into a napkin if I needed to. It was well seasoned, like the food we had in Jamaica.

"This is actually good. Go 'head girl."

"Try the tofu."

"What if I just do the vegetables? Do we have to do the whole fake meat thing?"

"You're gonna need the protein when we start your workout regimen. Just try it."

It was good. It tasted like the spices she seasoned it with.

"Well?"

"A'ight Laysia. It's good." I kept chewing. "It's really good."

When we finished our food, Alaysia cleared the table with this big grin on her face. "Ready for dessert?"

"Bring it on."

She opened the refrigerator and pulled out a pie plate. "Tada! It's your favorite. Strawberry cheesecake."

It looked like cheesecake, but how do you make a cheesecake without dairy and sugar? I didn't ask because I didn't want to know. Dinner was a pleasant surprise, so I decided to try it.

"Oh my God. How did you make this? This is so good." It had a little bit of a different taste to it, but was still rich and creamy. If I didn't know the house rules, I might have believed it was real cheesecake.

"Silken tofu. It's sweetened with fruit sugar."

I savored every bite of the generous piece of cheesecake. "Maybe this whole healthy thing isn't going to be so bad."

"I'm glad you feel that way. We start your workout program in the morning."

"Dag, Laysia. Don't I get time to settle in and get acclimated?"

"Sure. Do all the acclimating you need to. Tonight. And be ready to work out in the morning."

"Sir, yes, sir." I saluted.

"That's right. Act like ya know."

"What's this gym like?"

"State of the art. The latest and greatest equipment. Real upscale. You'll like it."

I didn't tell her how much I hated gyms. If working out was punishment for being fat, then working out in a gym was like getting a whipping outside in front of all the neighborhood kids.

The phone rang. Alaysia grabbed it. "Hello?" She smiled. "Hey, Kevin, how are you?" She paused. "Oh, I'm great. Yeah, the business is going good. I'm hoping your girl can dig me out of trouble here." She paused again. "Yeah, she's all brains. I know you didn't call to talk to me. Here she is."

Alaysia handed me the phone and went to her room.

I sunk into the couch. "Hey, Kevin," I said after taking a deep breath.

"Hey, Monica. I wanted to make sure you got settled in. How was your drive?"

Kevin had begged to drive me down. He didn't like the idea of me being on the road ten hours by myself. Whenever we went on trips, he did most of the driving because the little white lines on the road hypnotized me. I never could stay awake too long.

"The drive was a piece of cake. I didn't even get sleepy." I stretched out my legs. "I'm getting settled. Alaysia cooked a healthy meal for me, and she was telling me about the gym. My workouts start tomorrow morning."

He laughed. That soft, sexy laugh. Dangit, why'd he have to call?

"She's not wasting any time, is she?"

"No, she's a drill sergeant. It's good for me, though. I gotta get off this medicine." I could hear him playing this love song he wrote for me on his guitar. "Kevin?"

"Yeah?"

"What are you doing?"

"Nothing, just playing around with some tunes. You know how I do. I have to write a couple more songs for the album, so I've been messin' around with some stuff."

I felt like he was plucking my heartstrings instead of the guitar strings.

"Kevin?"

"Huh?"

"I need some time. Can you give me some time?"

He stopped playing. "What do you mean? You're in Atlanta, I'm in D.C. I'd say that's giving you time."

I blew out a long breath. "Kevin."

"You mean not calling?"

"Yeah. I need to be able to focus on me and not think about us right now."

He was quiet. Started strumming the guitar again. This time it was a few melancholy chords. "Okay, I'll give you all the time you need. Call me when you're ready."

"Yeah. Okay."

As I was about to hang up, he said, "Monnie?"

"Yeah?"

"Can I email you?"

I had to laugh. "You're not gonna make this easy, are you?"

"I ain't trying to make it hard. I want what's best for you. I . . . I just want—"

"You can email me, Kevin."

"Yeah?"

"Yeah."

"Okay. Talk to you soon. Well, not talk to you—email you soon. I love you, Monnie."

"Bye, Kevin."

I knew it hurt him for me to not say "I love you" back, but I couldn't. Not that it wasn't true. I just didn't need to be feeling that love right now. It was hazardous to my health.

25

The next morning, Alaysia and I pulled up in front of a large building with a sign on the front that read: JIM'S GYM.

"I wonder how long it took him to come up with that name."

Alaysia chuckled. "Not very creative, huh? Wait 'til you see it, though. It's the best facility in the city."

My eyes bugged out when I walked in. Talk about sensory overload. House music blared. Rows and rows of cardio machines made whirring noises. Televisions hanging in front of the cardio machines played all different channels. Real high-tech.

There were two separate areas with weight equipment, fully occupied. An aerobics studio had a packed-to-capacity step class going on. Alaysia showed me another room where they had yoga and Pilates classes. Then there was the jock room in the back with the heavy weights and a bunch of swollen men looking like they had steroids for breakfast, lunch, and dinner. Then there was the "ladies' area" with the multicolored free weights. I knew this would be my spot. The place where the big women like me hid from the fit people.

As Alaysia walked me through the gym, she introduced me to a lot of people. I didn't catch any of their names because I was too busy looking at their bodies. There was a honey-colored girl with natural twists in her hair and a perfectly toned, compact, muscular body. Then there was a tall, almond-colored guy with muscles so huge he couldn't rest his arms flat at his sides. Then there was a tall, thin, mustard-colored girl who was all legs. It was a blur of perfectly sculpted bodies.

I hated gyms. They were full of cute, skinny girls in skimpy exercise outfits and strong, muscular men covered in sweat, who were overly interested in the skinny girls in the skimpy outfits. Then there were the big girls like me, trying to hide their bodies in big sweatpants and T-shirts and working our butts off so we could look like the skinny girls in the skimpy outfits. Then there were the skinny guys who were trying to lift more than their body weight so they could be like the muscular guys and get the attention of the skinny girls in the skimpy outfits.

No matter what, it was all about the skinny girls in the skimpy outfits.

"All right, ready to get started?" Alaysia asked.

"Laysia, can't I walk outside in the neighborhood around the condo?"

"Are you crazy? Monnie, it's August in Atlanta. It's got to be over a hundred degrees with a hundred percent humidity outside. If you wanted to do that, you shoulda said something first thing this morning."

"I hate the machines. You run and run but don't go anywhere. I feel like a hamster on a wheel just spinning around and around."

"How 'bout a step class?"

"Please. I can't keep up with those crazy steps." I pulled my T-shirt over my butt and folded my arms across my breasts. I looked down at my chest. I had tried to fit into a stupid sports bra, but it was too small, and I had a big hump sticking up in the middle.

Great. The dreaded third-breast syndrome.

I shifted from side to side. "Can't I start tomorrow? I promise I'll walk a whole hour."

"What's wrong?"

"I don't feel comfortable here."

"Why not?"

"Because everybody here is perfectly in shape and I'm a fat slob."

"You're not a fat slob. And nobody is looking at you." She rubbed my arm. "You gotta start somewhere, Monnie. Don't worry about what anybody thinks. This is all about you. Come on, there's a walking track upstairs. You can do your cardio there."

She led me upstairs to a soft-surfaced track that circled the entire gym. I could look down on the people exercising.

"I'm gonna let you walk at your own pace to

warm up some, then I'll come back and get you and we'll do some weight training."

I nodded. I stretched and started walking. I pumped my arms and walked with long strides. I distracted myself by watching the people on the weights. When I came around the curve, Alaysia was waiting for me.

"Ready?"

"What took you so long? How long have I been going?"

"About fifteen minutes."

"That all?" It felt like thirty. This was going to be a slow road getting back in shape.

"Push. Come on, three more."

I wanted to slam Alaysia in the face with the free weight I was lifting. Lucky for her, my arm was too tired to get it anywhere near her head.

"Okay, Monnie, we finished chest, back, triceps, and biceps. We need to do a few shoulder exercises and you'll be done for this session. We can do abs later tonight."

"Later tonight? You better get out of me whatever you want now, 'cause this is it for today."

She laughed. Good thing one of us was enjoying this. "A'ight. We'll call it a day and pick up tomorrow with lower body. How do you feel?"

"Not too bad, actually. I thought I'd be sore, but I'm not."

"Wait 'til tomorrow."

We brought our clothes so we could shower and go to the mall afterward. If I was going to have to be in the gym all the time, I at least wanted some decent workout clothes.

When we walked into the women's locker room, I stopped in my tracks. There were no private stalls. Everybody changed out in the open. Naked, skinny bodies everywhere. No way was I going to undress in front of a bunch of skinny girls.

I tapped Alaysia. "I'm too tired to go to the mall. Why don't we go on home and we can shop before my workout tomorrow?"

"Okay, but I still need to run to the health food store and I don't want to do it funky."

She proceeded to take off her exercise top. I just stood there.

"What? Come on. Go 'head and shower and then I can make a quick run so we can take you home to get some rest. Maybe I made you do too much for a first day."

"Laysia, there is no way I'm showing my big butt in front of all these skinny girls."

"Monnie, what is wrong with you? Nobody is looking at you."

"Fine." There was no way I'd be able to explain it to her. She was a skinny girl.

Unfortunately, the towel I brought didn't fit all the way around me. The big, open space in the front where the edges of the towel didn't meet had my fat rolls hanging out. I walked to the shower as fast as I could and hid in a stall. I choked down a scream when the freezing cold water hit me. Common sense said stand outside until the water warmed up, but I wasn't about to stand there with people walking by looking at my rolls.

After I showered, I went back to the dressing area and stood staring at my underwear, trying to figure out how to get them on without dropping the towel. The towel wouldn't stay on by itself, so I had to hold it with one hand and try to get my panties on with the other.

I ended up hopping around the dressing room, trying to get my other leg in the underwear without dropping my towel. The bra was even harder. Should I fasten it and then put it on like a shirt? Alaysia came from the shower just in time to see me slipping the bra over my head.

"Monica, what are you doing?"

"Putting on my bra." I pretended I didn't look like a complete idiot with my DD cup stuck on my ear.

She shook her head.

I decided to go ahead and put my pants on, then I could drop the towel and turn my back and put my bra on real quick. When Alaysia saw me hopping around on one foot, trying to get my other pants leg on, she stopped and stared at me.

Alaysia said, "You're gonna break your stupid neck. Give me that durn towel."

Before I could protest, she snatched it. I would've tried to get it back, but I was standing there with my huge titties flopping everywhere, and one of my thunder thighs and half my butt exposed. I pulled the pants on as fast as I could.

"You make me sick, Laysia."

She laughed until she saw I was really upset. "I'm sorry." She watched me pulling on my bra at breakneck speed. "This fat thing goes a lot deeper than I thought, huh?"

"You have no clue."

I hurriedly put the rest of my clothes on and shoved my stuff in my bag. "I'll meet you at the car."

After we went to the health food store, Alaysia dropped me off and said she had to run some errands. I decided to catch a quick nap.

When I woke up later, a brand new gym bag sat at the foot of my bed. I opened it and found two larger sports bras, three huge beach towels, an extra-large terry-cloth robe and half a dozen long T-shirts with matching stretch pants.

Guess I didn't have an excuse not to go to the gym the next day.

26

When I woke up two mornings later, I started to sit up and swing my legs over the bed, but I couldn't move. The muscles in my arms I would normally push myself up with felt like knives stuck through them. I had to throw my legs to propel my body to sit up. I stumbled into the bathroom and screamed aloud when I tried to squat on the toilet. We did Alaysia's infamous leg workout the day before, and my thighs were on fire. I carefully lowered myself down to the toilet, but my butt muscles hurt so bad when I sat on them that I jumped back up again. I stood over the toilet for a while, wishing I was a man so I could pee standing up. I finally let out a little scream, braced myself, and sat on the toilet. I had to hold on to the bathtub to stand back up.

I decided to get a hot shower to ease the sore-ness. When I lifted my nightshirt halfway over my head, I couldn't get my arms any higher without excruciating pain in my back, chest, and arms. The shirt was stuck at my shoulders. How was I supposed to get it off?

The way I felt reminded me of my anatomy class. I could probably name every muscle in my body right now.

I was going to kill Alaysia. As soon as I could get the shirt off, get a shower and put my clothes on. Anticipating the amount of movement it would take to accomplish these small feats sent me back to bed.

After an hour, I heard a tap on the door. "Hey, we got yoga this morning."

"I can't move," I moaned.

"Stop making excuses and come on."

"No, I really mean it. I can't move."

She stuck her head in the door. "Monnie, my yoga class starts in twenty minutes. Stop fooling around."

"Alaysia, I know you probably can't hear it, but every muscle in my body is screaming cuss words at you. I have never been in so much pain in my life."

She walked over to the bed, frowning like she was considering the fact that I might be serious. "Sore, huh?" She pinched my arm.

"Oouuuch!" I screeched. "Are you crazy?"

"Get up. You can do some gentle stretches and some light cardio."

"Or I could stay in bed and recover from your torture."

"Uh-uh. If you stay in bed, you'll be worse tomorrow. The only way to feel better is to keep moving."

"Whatever."

"Trust me."

"Trust you? Now is not a good time to expect me to trust you."

She looked at her watch. "Five minutes or I'll be late for my class."

I wished I had the strength to throw my alarm clock at her.

I had to admit she was right. After yoga and a little time on the treadmill, my muscles warmed up a bit. After I finished, I got in the sauna, then the whirlpool and felt a whole lot better.

When we left the gym, we dropped by Sevanandah's health food store and got some food from their hot bar, and then went to Blockbusters. As we searched the stacks of movies, I realized how long it had been since I'd been to a movie theatre. I hadn't seen any of the new releases. Thinking about it, I realized it had been a long time since I'd done anything fun. I couldn't remember the last time I laughed. We picked out a few movies then walked back to the car.

Alaysia caught me staring into space. "What?"

I smiled at her. "Nothing. I'm just glad to be here." What I should have said was, "Thanks for coming to rescue me and bringing me to a place where I could think about having a good time again." I gave her a big hug, right in the middle of the sidewalk.

She raised an eyebrow. "Girl, you gotta watch those outward displays of affection in Atlanta. You thought D.C. was gay city."

"Really?"

"Girl, second only to San Francisco."

"Great. That means after the two-year Kevin wash-out period, I need to move someplace else before I start looking for a new man."

Alaysia laughed. "Naw, just choose well, that's all. Choose well."

"Been there, tried that. Didn't do such a good job."

"Don't worry. I'll pick you out a man." We got in the car and Alaysia drove the short distance back to the condo then parked the car in her designated spot. We decided to have lunch out on the patio to let the summer heat work the rest of the soreness out of my muscles.

"What about you, Alaysia? When you gon' pick you out a man? How long is this vow of celibacy gonna last?"

"Girl, I've had enough sex to last me *and* you a lifetime."

"I'm not talking about sex. What about true love? A real relationship?"

Alaysia looked sad all of a sudden. "I don't believe lightning strikes twice in the same place."

"What?"

"I believe we only get one soul mate. I messed that up, and I don't believe there's anyone I could love the way I loved Khalil or who could be perfect for me the way he was."

"Alaysia, there are plenty of people who get remarried or have serious relationships after a big break-up."

"Yeah, but what if they're not as happy with the second person? No one would ever admit that. They'd just be silently miserable for the rest of their life. Or maybe the first person wasn't their true soul mate and they got it right the second time around. I know I had the best I could get in Khalil. I'd hate to get in another relationship and be comparing him to my true love."

"You don't ever want kids?"

Alaysia shook her head. "I don't deserve them. I messed that up, too."

"Now who's gonna grow old with fifty cats?" I laughed.

She didn't.

"That was supposed to be a joke."

"Not funny."

Her eyes told me she was tormented at the thought of never getting married. Never having children. That's all she used to talk about. Her wonderful husband and house full of children.

"Never say never. You don't know what God might do."

Alaysia shook her head and wiped away a tear.

I put my arm around her shoulders. "Well, then we'll be two old maids together. And instead of fifty cats, we'll adopt children. We'll get foster kids, drug babies, and HIV babies and all those babies nobody else wants. We'll be the little old ladies who lived in a shoe."

Alaysia smiled and wiped her face. "Yeah, we'll be mommies to all those little girls without mommies." She nodded and smiled. "Yeah."

We relaxed and sunbathed for a while, letting our food digest. I thought about what Alaysia said about only having one soul mate. Was that true? If so, could I ever expect to find someone who was more of a soul mate to me than Kevin?

I had always marveled at how perfect we were for each other. I couldn't imagine anyone else being able to be so in my head—in my soul. We connected on a level that seemed surreal. What if I tried to start another relationship and the connection wasn't as deep? What if he didn't listen like Kevin did, or share himself like Kevin did?

My thoughts were swirling again. "We better get this movie marathon started or we'll be up all night."

"A'ight, what do you want to watch first?"

"The comedy. Definitely the comedy."

We made ourselves comfortable in the living room and Alaysia cued up the first DVD. *Nutty Professor II* was hilarious. Me not having laughed in so long made it even funnier. Alaysia kept pausing and rewinding because I had laughing fits and missed the dialogue. She shook her head and called me a goofball, but I think she understood I needed to laugh.

We should've stopped after the first movie because *Antwone Fisher* depressed the heck out of me. The last thing I needed was to watch a movie about an abused little black boy. Halfway through, I got up to grab a snack. I found a box of chocolate chip fruit-sweetened cookies in the pantry. I was starting to like Alaysia's healthy foods.

I plopped down on the sofa and tried to get back into the movie.

After the scene where the skank ho molests Antwone, I turned to see Alaysia staring at me.

"Why do you do that?'

"What?"

"You just ate half a box of those cookies."

I looked down at the box. I didn't realize I had eaten so many.

"You can't possibly be tasting them, but you keep eating more and more. Why?"

I shifted in my seat. "I don't know."

"Think about it. Try to figure it out."

I sat for a second, then shrugged. "I don't know. It's just a bad habit."

"What were you thinking when you went to get the box out of the pantry? Were you hungry?"

"No. I . . . I don't know. Why are you badgering me?"

"I'm not badgering you. I think if you figure it out, you'll be able to stop." She paused the movie. "Talk to me."

I put the cookies on the coffee table. "I guess the movie was making me sad, so I wanted some chocolate."

"Why?"

"I don't know. It makes me feel better. It tastes good." It sounded stupid to me, so I knew she wasn't getting it.

"But how can it make you feel better when you get mad at yourself the next day and then even madder at yourself when you get on the scale or try on your clothes?"

"Because I'm not thinking about the next day. I'm just enjoying the chocolate."

She raised an eyebrow.

"I can't explain it. I eat whenever I get emotional. Mad, sad, anxious, fearful, worried. I eat."

"Let's say you find something else to do when you get emotional."

"Like what?"

"I don't know. Pick something. Something that makes you feel as good as or better than chocolate."

As good as chocolate? What could make me feel as good as chocolate?

The few times Kevin relaxed and we got the sex thing right, I remember thinking it was better than chocolate. That obviously wasn't an option.

Spending time with God was the only other thing that made me feel better than chocolate. Getting into a deep place in worship when I lost all sense of place and time? Feeling His Spirit around me so strong I felt like I could reach out and touch it? Yeah. That was definitely better than chocolate.

When was the last time I had actually been in the secret place, though? I hadn't been to church in forever, and I hadn't spent any personal time with God other than to try to read my Bible every once in a while or quote some perfunctory prayer. How did that happen? How did I allow my breakup with Kevin and fallout with Bishop Walker to affect my personal relationship with God? Just because I walked away from Love and Faith Christian Center didn't mean I needed to walk away from God.

"Monica? Where'd you go?"

I shook myself. "Trying to think of something that makes me feel better than chocolate. I would have to say my quiet time with God." I braced myself for her sarcastic reply.

Instead, she nodded. "Yeah. I know what you mean. When I meditate and shut out the world and everything around me and connect with spirit, it makes me feel good."

I was glad she was feeling me on the whole connecting with God thing, but was a bit disturbed by her calling Him "spirit." That ranked right up there with "higher power". I decided to keep it to myself. I'd keep praying God would divinely intervene and show her the way to Him. The real Him.

"I need to get back to my place in God. Maybe if I reach for Him more, I won't be reaching for the chocolate so much."

"Sounds like a plan. If you want, you can use my meditation room."

Alaysia had a little room off her master suite filled with candles and crystals and all sorts of figurines. No way I was going to pray in there. No telling what kind of spirits lingered.

"You haven't bothered to find a church here. Atlanta has more churches than any place I've been. You should try one out."

"Alaysia telling me to go to church? You used to tell me I went to church too much."

"Yeah, I didn't understand the importance of spirituality then. And it seemed to work for you before, so you need to get back into it. Especially if it'll keep you away from chocolate."

I threw a pillow at her. "Forget you." I thought for a second. "Hey, why don't you come with me? We can find one we like together."

"Naw. I'm cool with my meditation and seeking. I ain't into the whole organized religion thing. I don't think God is in a church or in a Bible or any one book. I believe in more of a universal religion." Alaysia stretched out on the couch and stared into space. "Everything that exists is God, and God is everything that exists. We're all gods. Instead of needing a church, I just look for God in me, and in you, and in everything beautiful I see. In fact, I believe that as more enlightenment comes into the universe, people will see that there's no one true path to reach God. All paths eventually lead to Him. Even saying 'Him' sounds funny. I believe God is the life force, the energy, the divine in all of us."

"Alaysia, doesn't that sound a little hokey to you?"

"No more than a big fight between God and the devil, and Jesus dying on the cross and coming back to life again, and flying up to heaven and taking away people's sins. Or a bunch of demons prowling around us, trying to influence us to do wrong, or jumping in some people and possessing them. Or there being a heaven for all the Jesus people and a hell for the rest of us poor souls who decided not to believe in Him. Or—"

"I get your point."

"I mean, how do you know what you believe is real?"

"I just believe it. That's what faith is about."

"Yeah, and you have faith in one thing and I

have faith in another. What makes your faith right?"

I suddenly felt that if I was a good Christian who studied my Bible as I should, I could answer her questions. Instead, my weak response was, "It's just what I believe."

"Then let me believe what I believe and you believe what you believe."

"Yeah, but what if the real answer isn't subjective? What if I'm right?"

"If you're right, your God has the power to make sure I end up on the right path. You pray that He saves me, and if Jesus is the only real God, then He will. If He isn't, then He won't."

We decided to skip the rest of *Antwone Fisher* and moved on to *Man on Fire*. Nothing like some violence to make a person feel better. Drooling over Denzel didn't hurt either.

After the movie was over, we were both ready to go to sleep. As I lay in my bed, trying to fall asleep, I decided to pray. God and I had been issued a challenge.

All right, God, You heard her. I need You to do whatever it is You need to do to get Alaysia saved. You know what will draw her heart to You. Give me the words, create the circumstances, and show her the truth. In Jesus' name.

27

After two weeks of working out like a fiend, I studied my body in the mirror in the aerobics studio. I frowned as Alaysia walked up.

"What's wrong?"

"Seems like with all this working out, I should be seeing some difference. I shoulda brought my scale from home." Alaysia refused to have a scale at home, and I refused to get on the scale in the middle of the gym. I didn't want anyone to see how far I had to slide the little bar over.

"Monnie, you can't do that. That's why so many people don't stick to their exercise routines. You're not gonna get immediate results. Try to focus on becoming more fit and feeling good after you work out. If you worship the scale and try to see a difference, it'll never happen quick enough and you'll get discouraged."

"How will I know if it's working or not?"

"You have to trust me."

I rolled my eyes. "This relationship of ours requires absolutely too much trust."

I settled into a routine of workouts and healthy food. I got addicted to the endorphin coma that came after a good workout. If I missed a workout, I was tired and cranky and my body didn't feel right. I enjoyed our healthy diet. I never felt that yucky, heavy, about-to-burst feeling after a meal.

One thing Alaysia was right about, though. The farts. The pure, organic, vegetarian farts were a force to be reckoned with. I hated to be around my own self if one slipped out. And they definitely weren't the kind you could ease out in a crowd and hope nobody noticed. One of those jokers would clear a room. I had to be careful in the gym. The up and down pounding on the treadmill was enough to make things want to slip out. I didn't want a reputation in the gym as the fat girl with the wicked farts.

Even the whole fat girl/skinny girl thing didn't bother me anymore. I became one of the regulars in the gym, and we had a camaraderie of exercise addiction. People would see me on the track or pass by me on my favorite treadmill and say, "Do your thing, Monnie." Made me feel good.

When I finally got up the nerve to try one of the step classes, I was discouraged at first. I couldn't keep up. The class would be going one way, and I'd be going another. Zanetta, a friend of Alaysia's, was teaching the class. She saw me struggling and yelled out, "If you can't keep up, just do the basic up and down step."

That was easy enough, so I did it for the rest of the class.

Zanetta caught me before I left the aerobics studio. "Hey, maybe if we go over some of the basic steps, you'll do better in your next class."

Next class? She was making a big assumption.

She spent half an hour showing me the tricks to mastering her step class. After she seemed satisfied I had gotten it, she made me commit to at least three classes a week for the next month before I decided to never step again. Might as well try. It was more fun than running on the treadmill.

Alaysia made a gross understatement when she said she needed help with the financial management of her business. It was an absolute mess.

Luckily, I knew a little something about running a business. I joined Dr. Stewart's practice when she'd just opened. She hadn't built up a patient panel and was agonizing over needing to hire a practice manager to do her billing and budgeting. I was always good at math, and convinced her I could do the accounting and billing for her. The small raise I asked for didn't compare to what full-time salary and benefits for an office manger would cost her.

After a few months of hard work, I turned her

whole financial picture around. Dr. Stewart was so grateful, she gave me a huge bonus.

Alaysia was going to have to give me a huge bonus for all the work it would take to get her business in order. Three weeks after my arrival in Atlanta, I sat at my desk, looking at her numbers. After an hour of pulling my hair, I called Alaysia into my room.

"What are all these 'payment pendings' about? Alaysia, most of your clients owe you money." I pointed to the places in her book with the little smiley faces and red circles around them.

"Every once in a while, I extend a little credit."

"Every once in a while? Alaysia, this person, Hazel Hampton, hasn't paid you in two months, but you've given her a one-hour massage once a week?"

"She's having some hard times. Her husband is divorcing her and she's short on cash. I'm waiting 'til she gets back on her feet."

"Then she doesn't need to be getting massages." Was it me, or wasn't that a logical conclusion?

"I know, but she's been stressed out. She's lost everything, and I didn't want her to have to give up her massages."

I rolled my eyes. "Okay, what about this? Jim hasn't paid you for yoga classes in six weeks. According to your contract, he's supposed to pay you every two weeks."

"I've been giving him the invoices, but he keeps making excuses."

"Then stop giving the classes."

"What would they do for yoga classes?"

I threw up my hands. "Why are you calling this a business? You should call it Alaysia's Charity Fitness. At this rate, you'll be bankrupt before the year ends."

"See? That's what I need you for." She bounced out of the room.

I'd definitely be earning my keep. I decided to deal with the mess later, and put the books in the file cabinet drawer.

I turned on my computer to check my email. I was excited to see Trina's name in my inbox. We had been trading emails over the past few months. I kept her updated on my move to Atlanta, and she told me about their continual progress in Africa. They were reaching out to surrounding villages and making a difference everywhere they went. I typed a long message back to her. When I first started emailing her, my messages were short because I was so careful, trying to make it seem like I was okay. Now that I was okay and had exciting things to tell her about my new life, my messages were almost as long as hers. I smiled. Things still hurt, but life was getting better slowly but surely.

I sent off the message and perused through the Spam in my inbox. My hand froze on the mouse.

There were two messages from Kevin. Only two? I had expected him to write every day. I guessed he was being considerate of me needing time. I didn't want to read them because I didn't want to feel that sad Kevin feeling, but my finger clicked the mouse against my will.

Monnie,
I really want to give you the time you need, so
I won't fill your box with a lot of emails. Just
wanted to let you know how much I love you,
not that you don't know that already, but in
case you were wondering. I love you. I know
how Jesus felt because I love you so much I
would die for you. I love you so much I'm
dying without you. I'm not going to write
anymore because I want you to focus on get-
ting yourself healthy. I plan on us growing old
together, so do whatever Alaysia tells you to
do.

Love, Kevin.

Oh well. I was sad now. Might as well click on
the other email.

By the way, did I mention how much I love
you?

Kevin

I was glad he promised not to write anymore,
because I didn't know how many of those emails
I could take.

Next thing I knew, I was standing in front of
the pantry reaching for a box of cookies. I couldn't
even remember walking into the kitchen. I slowly
closed the pantry door and leaned against it. *Choc-*
olate is not your friend, Monica.

I went back to my room and lay down on the
chaise lounge and pulled the chenille throw over
me. I pretended it was God wrapping His arms

around me. I imagined Him wiping my tears and smoothing back my hair, telling me how much He loved me and how everything was gonna be okay. I closed my eyes and imagined myself snuggling into His chest and falling asleep in His arms.

Yeah. God was definitely better than chocolate.

28

After working out for three months straight, I was addicted and even went to the gym if Alaysia couldn't make it. I still hadn't gotten on the scale, but all the clothes I bought when I first got to Atlanta were falling off me. I looked forward to getting some winter fashions in a smaller size.

After keeping my commitment to Zanetta to continue her classes, I was the step queen. Not only did I do the regular steps, I threw in some extra steps of my own, double-time what the rest of the class did. I had graduated to the advanced class after two months.

One day, Zanetta came up to my treadmill. "Monica, I need a huge favor. My little boy's school called and he's sick. I gotta go pick him up. Can you take my beginners class for me?"

"Me?"

"Yeah. The tape is already in the deck. Just push play."

"Me?"

"Yes, you, silly. You know my whole routine backward and forward. Hurry up. It's supposed to start in seven minutes."

What's a fat girl gonna look like teaching an aerobics class full of skinny girls? I stopped the treadmill and got off. Zanetta pulled her keys out of her bag and put on a big wooly sweater, as if me saying no wasn't an option. I'd hate to leave her hanging if her son was sick. How hard could a beginner's class be?

After ten minutes of leading the class, I realized I did know Zanetta's routine by heart. I stepped and called out the instructions like I had been teaching forever. I noticed a rather large young lady in the back struggling to keep up. I instructed the rest of the class to continue and jogged back to her step.

"Come on, right, left, right, left, tap left, now turn. Three knee repeater, do the same leg, two, three, now left, right, turn step, left, right." I showed her the footing, and she got it with no problem. I stayed in the back with her and had the rest of the class to turn to face us. By the time the class was over, she looked proud that she kept up with the skinny girls.

After we cooled off, she came over. "Thanks for helping me out. I was about to put up the step and sneak out the back door."

"I feel you, girl. That's how I felt after my first class." I extended my hand. "I'm Monica."

She shook my hand. "Talinda. Nice to meet you. How long have you been working out?"

"Almost three months now."

"Wow, you're in really good shape."

"Thanks. If you come on a regular basis, you'll be keeping up in no time."

"Are you the regular teacher of the class?"

"No, my friend Zanetta is, but you'll like her."

She frowned. "I wish you were teaching."

"Tell you what. I'll meet you back here tomorrow and we'll do it together."

Her face brightened. "Cool. I'll see you then."

Later that evening, Alaysia popped her head in my door. "Hey, Zanetta called. Her son has a bad stomach virus and she wanted to know if you could take her class for the rest of the week. Did you teach today?"

"Yeah, she grabbed me off the treadmill and forced me into it."

"How'd it go?"

"Great, actually." I told her how I rescued a fellow fat girl from exercise despair.

She stood there thinking for a minute. "You know, that's a great idea. You should start a class for the fitnessly challenged."

"Fitnessly challenged?"

"You don't want to call it a fat girl class, do you?"

In four weeks, my Full-Figured Fitness Class was so popular, I added extra time slots.

I started each class by going over the basic steps slowly before doing the routine. For some of the women who were really out of shape, I showed a modified version so they would still get the sense of accomplishment that comes with finishing a whole class. I used the bomb house music mixes, and sang and called out the instructions to make it fun.

Talinda came almost every day. She brought a few of her friends, and after a while convinced her mother to come, too. She and her mother could pass for twins. They had the same pretty face and the same big hips and butts. Made me miss Mommy.

Talinda introduced me to her mother after class. "Gosh, Monica. You've lost weight since I started taking your class. Can you help me out with a diet?" Talinda asked.

Next thing I knew, I was doing dietary counseling with several of the women in my class. We sat on the floor in the aerobics studio after our workouts. Alaysia came in one day as we were finishing.

After everyone left, she said, "You know, you should start a formal class. You can put together a handout with nutrition information and recipes. Only don't do it for free. I'll talk to Jim and figure out a way to get you compensated. A lot of people have joined this gym that never would have if you weren't doing your classes. He needs to give us more money."

I was contracting with the gym through Alaysia's business. "I don't want to charge the women. I want to get them the information so they can live healthy."

"That's not the way you run a business," Alaysia said.

My eyes widened. "Oh, now you want to run it like a business."

She laughed. "For real, girl. I think you're on to something here. You should get your personal trainer certificate and start working one on one with some of these women."

"What's a fat girl gon' look like being a personal trainer?"

"The same thing she looks like teaching the most popular aerobics class in the gym."

She had a point. Even though my class was a full-figured class, I had skinny girls and quite a few men in it, too. The classes were so packed, they started a sign-up list half an hour before the class began.

"Besides, have you looked in the mirror lately? You ain't Twiggy, but I don't think you should call yourself a fat girl anymore."

"Whatever."

"Naw, for real, though. You're shaping up. In fact, why don't you get on the scale?"

"I thought I wasn't allowed to get on the scale."

"That was four months ago when you were studying yourself in the mirror every day to see if your thirty-minute workout made you lose an instant fifty pounds."

I smacked her arm. "Shut up, Alaysia."

I was nervous about getting on the scale. I

caught a glimpse of myself in the mirror. What could it hurt?

Everybody turned around when they heard me scream, "Oh my God! I've lost forty pounds."

They all stopped their workouts and clapped. "Go, Monnie. Go, Monnie. Go, Monnie . . ."

I did a little sexy dance to their chant and got back on the scale to make sure I read it right. I lost forty-two pounds in the last four months. Amazing.

The women from my class gathered around me at the scale, all talking at once. "Okay, Monica, we want the whole program. Whatever you're doing, we want to do."

One woman said, "We'll pay you whatever we need to if you help us lose forty pounds."

"Yeah, girl, name your price. I'm trying to get whatever you got. You taking Metabolife?" Talinda asked.

"No, I ain't taking no pills. Just hard work. Five aerobics classes a week, a love affair with treadmill number four, and weight training. Plus a healthy vegetarian diet."

I lost half of them there. I still had twelve who were willing to try my program. We decided to form a lifestyle support group and cooking class to meet on Saturday afternoons. Alaysia planned to talk to Jim about the business arrangement.

She came home later that evening, slamming the door and everything else in the house. "Jim is a greedy dog. Can you believe he thought you should do the class on a volunteer basis? He acted like he was doing you a favor, offering to let you 'use his space.' He really made me mad. We're already offering our services at below market rate. Do you know how much other yoga instructors and personal trainers in the area make? Even for the step classes and massages. I got half a mind to . . ."

Alaysia paced around the living room, muttering to herself. "It's robbery. He's making a mint off us. It's worse than robbery—it's slavery. And we're not taking it anymore."

She reminded me of the old Alaysia, getting fired up for one of her causes. I could almost hear "We Shall Overcome" playing in her mind.

"We're gonna open our own gym. Only we're not gonna call it a gym. We'll call it a . . . uh . . . we'll call it a Wellness Center. Or Life Center or New Life Center—no that sounds like a church. How 'bout Alternative Lifestyles Center? Naw, that don't sound quite right. We'll call it . . . something."

"Slow down, Alaysia. Do you know how much it would cost to start our own place?"

"It's your job to figure that out."

"I was afraid you'd say that."

Alaysia continued pacing and muttering, throwing out ideas for our new enterprise. "We'll put it right next door to his gym and take all his business."

I laughed. "He really made you mad, huh?"

The next few weeks, all we did was plan our new business. We scouted locations, priced exercise equipment, did a market analysis, and checked out the competition. It helped me not get depressed over the Christmas holidays.

One evening, I sat at the kitchen table, putting figures together to see how much money it would take to get started. I walked out to the living room where Alaysia was decorating a Christmas tree.

"Alaysia, where are we going to get all this money? With what you've let slip through your fingers, and the money Massa Jim has stolen from us, I don't know."

"I still have the money from my condo sale. And we can always call Daddy. I haven't hit him up in almost a year. He's probably drowning in a pool of guilt." She threw the last few strands of tinsel onto the tree and stood back to look at it.

I thought about Kevin offering me our savings. It was only $12,000, but I wanted to do my part. I suddenly realized I hadn't thought about Kevin in months. Hadn't thought about a divorce. Hadn't thought about anything about us. I had been enjoying my new life in Atlanta.

Alaysia adjusted the star on top of the tree. "Why so sad? Daddy won't mind."

I shook myself. "I know he won't. I was just thinking—"

"I know. It would be nice if we could do this on our own."

"No, I wasn't thinking that. I was thinking he could give us a loan that the business would pay back once we got up and running."

Alaysia nodded. "Yeah, that sounds perfect."

29

Even though I thought I did a good job of formulating a business plan, we decided to hire a business consultant to make sure we were on the right track. We met with him right after the New Year.

When his secretary led us back to his office, I was surprised by how young he was. And how fine he was. Alex Thompson was the color of molasses, had to be about six feet two, muscular and broad-shouldered, with a stunning smile.

We shook hands. "I'm Monica Harris, and this is Alaysia Zaid."

"Alex Thompson. It's a pleasure to meet you both. I'm excited to hear more about your business idea. Please have a seat." His office was decked out to impress with expensive contemporary furniture and black art on the walls.

We sat down on one side of his conference table with me in the middle. Alaysia let me do all the talking. I explained our overall goals then pulled out my tentative spreadsheets.

He looked over my figures for a while then sat back in his chair. "I'm not sure why you came to me. Looks like you've got this thing figured out. Who did all this?"

Alaysia spoke for the first time. "Monica. She's got quite a business mind."

Alex nodded. "I'd say. If you weren't working on starting your own business, I'd snatch you up and have you join mine."

I blushed. "We did it together. It was both of our idea."

Alaysia kept bragging. "Yeah, it was our idea, but you were the one who did all the paperwork."

Alex leaned closer to me. "Where'd you get these skills? You have a business degree?" The intensity of his eyes reminded me of Kevin.

I leaned back. He was approaching the edge of my personal space. "Yeah, from Barnes and Noble. I sat in there for a few hours reading business books."

Alex laughed. Way too much for my stupid little joke. "A sense of humor too. I like that."

I cleared my throat and shuffled through the papers. "Do you think my estimation of the start-up capital is accurate? We want to move forward as soon as possible."

We crunched numbers for a while and decided we could do things cheaper if we bought the equipment in phases as the business expanded.

We talked about possible locations, marketing options, and did a mock timeline for getting things going. I don't know if I was overreacting, but he seemed to keep staring at me, or leaning into me. Maybe he was one of those close people.

An hour and a half into the meeting, Alaysia started doodling on the notepad she'd brought with her. I figured I'd cut things short and plan to meet with Alex again soon and not drag her along. She had the attention span of a three-year-old when it came to the business aspects of the business.

I looked at my watch. "Look at the time. When can we set up our next meeting?"

"You can let my secretary know on the way out when's the best time for you." We stood and walked toward the door. When we shook hands, it seemed like he held my hand longer than was professional. "I almost hate to take your business because then I can't ask you to dinner. I have a strict rule about mixing pleasure and business." He smiled the overly confident smile of a gorgeous man who's used to getting the girl.

I didn't know what to say.

"Well, you know, eventually the business arrangement will end, and then your rule won't be a problem." Alaysia didn't have three words to say the whole meeting, and now she wanted to talk?

I silently made plans to murder her in her sleep while I smiled a gracious smile at Alex. "I appreciate your ideas and input today. No way you're going to weasel out of taking our business." I knew my face was red. "I think we can make this work with your help and expertise." *That's right, girl. Keep him on track and focused.*

Alaysia waited until we left his office, pulled out of the parking lot, and drove down the street before she let out a screech. "Girl, that man was fine, runs his own business, and was obviously interested in you. What's your problem?"

"Whatever, Alaysia. He was just being nice."

"Nice? Girl, get a clue. That man was hitting on you."

"Yeah, right. You're reading too much into it."

Alaysia gave me a strange look. "He asked you out. He didn't ask both of us to dinner. In fact, he completely ignored me and pretended you were the only one in the room."

"That's because you didn't say a word the whole meeting." I turned the heat on full blast to combat the January chill.

"Then he held your hand like he didn't want to let go. Read the signals, girl. Oooowee, he was a hottie."

"Not Miss Celibate calling someone a hottie. Could it be? Is she stepping out of the convent and into the real world again?"

"Not me, girl. He only had eyes for you."

"Yeah, he's probably a fat girl vulture."

"Fat girl vulture?"

"Yeah, those men who want a quick, easy piece, so they prey on the fat girls with low self-esteem. The fat girls are flattered by a man taking interest in them so they fall for it, and next thing you know, they're giving up the panties."

Alaysia shook her head. "Do all full-figured

women have these complexes or is this just your warped world?"

I shrugged.

"Did it ever occur to you he might be interested in you because you're beautiful and smart and can put together a business plan that rivals his just by reading some books?"

I shrugged again. "Not really. He's too fine to be interested in a fat girl."

"Would you stop calling yourself that? It's getting on my nerves. That's my best friend you're dogging out." Alaysia frowned. "You need to add a self-esteem class to our business plan, because if any of our full-figured clients think like you, they're gonna need it."

"Whatever." I turned the heat down a little.

"Seriously, though, if he asks you out again, are you gonna go out with him?"

"I doubt it."

"Why not?"

"Two-year Kevin wash-out period, remember? It's barely been a year."

"All right, two-year wash-out period. Tick tock, tick tock. I hear them eggs getting older by the minute."

"Shut up, Alaysia."

"Hey, let's go to Camelli's Vegan Vegetarian. I'm starving and I don't feel like cooking."

I knew every vegetarian restaurant in Atlanta. We went to all of them so much, the waitresses knew us by name.

I ordered the barbeque tofu sandwich and Alaysia got the vegan nachos. The whole time we ate, I talked a mile a minute about the business plan. Alaysia still wasn't interested.

"Just make sure I have a yoga studio and a massage table and a good weight room. You can do whatever else you want." She crunched into a blue chip.

"I was thinking about a demonstration kitchen where we could do healthy cooking classes. And I was also thinking about classrooms where we could teach people about chronic diseases and prevention."

Alaysia nodded, dipping a chip in her soy sour cream and salsa.

"And we could have a meditation room." What did I say that for?

Finally, something Alaysia was interested in. "Yeah, and I could do sessions and teach meditation, help people reach a state of higher consciousness. I wonder if we can find someone to do Reiki and past-life analysis."

Oh, no. Last thing I wanted was to turn this into a New Age haven.

As we left, Alaysia ranted on and on about higher powers and selling life crystals and all sorts of other babble that had the Holy Spirit screaming on the inside of me. I would have to tell her I didn't feel comfortable with all that stuff and I didn't want to do it as part of our business.

Alaysia was so busy talking, she didn't see a young man approaching us. He was staring at Alaysia and seemed to be walking right toward us. I was used to guys trying to kick game to Alaysia, but he had this strange look on his face. I held my purse a little tighter, although he didn't look like a criminal. He was pecan-colored with beautiful, long, thin dread locks and big, brown eyes. Something looked familiar about those eyes.

He got so close to us, I was scared until he said, "Alaysia?"

When she looked up at who was calling her name, she gasped as if he stabbed her through her heart.

"Khalil?"

30

After the shock registered, Alaysia took off down Glenwood Street, running as fast as her long legs could carry her. Khalil and I looked at each other, then took off after her.

"Alaysia, wait!" Khalil yelled.

I broke into my fastest run. Even though his eyes looked calm and he didn't seem angry, I needed to have my girl's back. I had taken enough kickboxing classes that I could tear a brotha up if he was trying to get some revenge.

Khalil stopped running and called out to Alaysia. "Please, stop. I just want to talk to you."

I ran past him and caught Alaysia and grabbed her arm. I spun her around and saw her face filled with tears, eyes filled with panic. "Alaysia?"

She opened her mouth but didn't speak. Her eyes begged me to save her, but I didn't know what to do. Khalil approached us slowly, his hands held up as if he feared Alaysia would take off running again.

"I can't believe it's you. Oh my God." Khalil reached out a hand to touch Alaysia's face.

He put his arms around her. "Oh my God, I prayed I would find you again." She didn't move.

I didn't know whether to give them a private moment or stay there to protect Alaysia. The decision was made for me when I started to step back and Alaysia death-gripped my arm.

Khalil let go of Alaysia and turned to me. "Hi, Monica. Good to see you again. Can I have a minute?"

I nodded and started to back away, but Alaysia's grip on my arm got tighter. Made me remember my bicep workout from earlier that day.

Khalil looked down at Alaysia's grip on my arm, then up at her fear-plastered face. He shook his head. "I don't want to hurt you. Alaysia, I—" He reached out to touch her face and she bristled.

He looked at me for help, and I looked at Alaysia to figure out what to do. She looked at me and I saw the twelve-year-old Alaysia who lost her mother and father in the same year, the fifteen-year-old Alaysia who lost her grandmother and grandfather the same year, and the Alaysia of a few years ago who lost her baby and lover at the same time.

"Take me home." She breathed the words out in a whisper.

I looked at her, then at Khalil, then back at her. "Alaysia, don't you want to—"

She gripped my arm tighter. "Monnie, take me home."

My eyes spoke an apology to Khalil, then I led Alaysia back to the car. He followed us at a distance. "Alaysia, please talk to me. I can't lose you again. All I've wanted to do for the past two years is find you. I know it was a shock seeing me. I know you might need some time, but give me some way of getting in touch with you. Please."

Alaysia kept walking fast, staring at the sidewalk. When we got to the car, I put her in the passenger's seat and walked around to the other side.

Khalil stopped me. "Monica, please, can you give me a number or something?"

I didn't know what to do. In his eyes, I saw nothing but pure love. I knew how much Alaysia loved him.

"Give me your number." I whispered it.

"Huh?" Khalil's face registered blank.

I leaned closer. "Your number. Give it to me."

"Oh." He stood there for a second as if he didn't know his number and didn't know where to find it. He finally fumbled in his wallet and pulled out a card. "Please, Monica. Make her call me. I love her. I prayed for God to bring us back together. I know this wasn't a coincidence. If she doesn't call me, will you call to let me know she's okay?"

I nodded and stuffed the card in my pocket.

31

I got in the car and looked over at Alaysia. "Laysia, are you—"

"Drive drive drive drive drive." She pounded on the dashboard each time she said it.

I started up the car and took off, leaving Khalil staring at us driving away.

Alaysia let out an eardrum-bursting scream and then a deep, gut-wrenching cry. She cried all the way to the house. I led her upstairs to her bedroom, took off her shoes, and laid her in the bed. I sat next to her, rubbing her back until she finally cried herself to sleep.

The next morning, I got dressed for yoga class, but didn't hear Alaysia bumping around in the kitchen, making our protein shakes. I knocked on her bedroom door. "Laysia, time for yoga."

"Can you take my class this morning? I didn't sleep well last night."

I pushed open the door. Alaysia lifted her head and peeked at me through her tangled hair. Her eyes looked like she had been in a fight.

I went over to hug her, but she rolled away from me.

"Can you give me some time alone?"

I stepped away from the bed. "Okay."

I quietly closed the door behind me.

When I got back from the gym, I poked my head into her room. Alaysia was still in the bed.

"Aren't you gonna get up?"

"No. I'm fine."

"You want something to eat?"

"No, I'm fine."

I closed the door. I wanted to stay and make her talk to me, but I decided to give her the space she wanted. I'd make her come out tomorrow.

The next two days, I did Alaysia's yoga class and took her training clients. She never came out of the room. Never ate. I couldn't stand seeing her like this.

God, what should I do? Help me to help her. Tell me what to do.

Almost as if propelled by an imaginary hand, I went to the jeans I had on the day we saw Khalil, and pulled his card out of the pocket. I looked down at the card. "Khalil Johnson, ministerial student, Atlanta Interfaith University."

Atlanta Interfaith University? Khalil was a Christian? Becoming a minister?

I peeked in to make sure Alaysia was asleep and went into my bedroom and closed the door. I dialed the number.

"Hello?"

"Khalil, it's Monica. Alaysia's friend."

"I'm glad you called." I heard him let out a deep breath. "Is she . . . is Alaysia okay?"

"No. Not at all. That's why I'm calling. I hope I'm doing the right thing. I don't know what to do. She's gone to this . . . other place."

We were silent for a minute.

"Can I come see her?"

"I don't know if that's the best idea."

"Please. Trust me. I don't want to hurt her. I never should have left her like I did. I want to make that right. I . . . I love her so much, Monica. You've got to believe me."

"I do. I believe you."

Should I give him the address? If he showed up, Alaysia would know I called him and might not forgive me. But why not? She needed to deal with this to move on with her life. It was time for her to do what she preached to me all the time.

"Monica?"

"Yeah, Khalil. I'm thinking."

"If it helps any, I'm a Christian now. I know Alaysia told you the whole story about what happened between us. I've forgiven her, and I just want her to forgive me for leaving her like that."

"I know, Khalil. She's never forgiven herself. It haunts her."

"I can understand. I was messed up for a while after I left. If I hadn't found Christ, it would have eaten me up. Since I got saved, I've been praying

God would bring us together again. Please, Monica, I want her to know I forgive her and love her and I want her to forgive me. Can you tell her that for me?"

I paused. "Why don't you come tell her yourself?"

32

I decided not to warn Alaysia before Khalil got there. I knocked on her door and peeked in. "Alaysia, let's go out and get you some fresh air. You've been in the house for three days. Put some clothes on."

She didn't even lift her head. "I don't feel like it."

"I wasn't asking. Come on. You can't stay like this."

"Please, Monica, leave me alone."

"I am. Just like you left me alone when I was drowning in misery with Tom and Larry."

The little chuckle she let out gave me hope that she wouldn't kill me for calling Khalil.

"Ten minutes. Wash your tail, brush your teeth and put some clothes on. We'll go for a walk."

I was relieved she got up. If she did decide to talk to Khalil, she'd kill me if he showed up while she was wearing three days of funk.

She came out of her bedroom looking fresh, wearing a lavender sweater, some jeans, and a sad little smile. "I'm ready. Can we go get some hot chocolate?"

I laughed. "Now who's drowning their sorrows in chocolate?" Where was Khalil? He told me he was only fifteen minutes away.

She sat on the couch while I puttered around in the kitchen, loading the dishwasher. The doorbell rang.

"You expecting somebody?"

"Yeah. I'll get it." I opened the door and Khalil stood there looking like a scared sixteen-year-old picking up his first date.

"I didn't tell her you were coming."

He nodded. I led him into the living room.

Alaysia gasped when she saw him. "What are you doing here?" She turned to me. "Monica?" She ran to her bedroom and slammed the door.

"Have a seat, Khalil. We'll be out in a minute." I walked to her bedroom and didn't bother to knock on her door.

She was pacing back and forth in the bedroom. "What did you do? Did you give him our address?"

"You need to talk to him, Alaysia."

"I don't need to talk to him. Why did you do this? I can't believe you, Monica." She sat down on the bed and glared at me.

I sat down next to her. "You need to talk to him. All that stuff you tell me about facing my issues? It's your turn."

She shook her head. "I can't face him."

"He's not mad at you. He wants to apologize to you and tell you how much he loves you."

"Apologize to *me*?" She shook her head. "How do you know?"

"I talked to him."

"When? How did—"

"Laysia, that's not important. Just talk to him. Trust me, okay?"

I took Alaysia by the hand and led her back into the living room to Khalil. He stood up and held his hands out to her. I put Alaysia's hands into his. *My* stomach fluttered at the love in his eyes when he looked down at her. He wiped the tears starting to flow down her cheeks. She finally looked up into his eyes, then really started crying. He pulled her into his chest and held her while she cried.

That was my cue to leave.

33

For the next few weeks, Alaysia and Khalil were completely inseparable. They went through the whole talking, crying, and forgiveness process and then were in love again, like they were never apart.

I felt like a third wheel. Watching them being lovey-dovey made me miss being in a relationship. A lot. I missed being held, being kissed, being cherished. Missed dreaming of a future together. The bed seemed much bigger and lonelier and colder at night. Made me think maybe a two-year wash-out period was too long. Especially with my eggs aging by the minute.

This made my business relationship with Alex Thompson even more difficult. I dragged Alaysia with me to the second meeting, but she looked bored for the first half, then made matchmaking hints the second half, so I knew I couldn't take her again. Which means I had to be alone with him.

Palms sweating, face flushed, stuttering a little. He was too doggone fine. Some poor man was walking around double ugly 'cause Alex had enough good looks for two men.

My meeting alone with Alex wasn't so bad. It was the grilling from Alaysia when I got home that was the problem.

She pounced on me almost as soon as I walked in the door. "So, how was your meeting?"

I walked by her and plopped down onto the couch. "Good. We got a lot of ground covered."

"And?" She plopped down next to me.

"And he thinks we have a great idea and a great plan. The most important thing is going to be location and marketing. He says—"

"You know good and well that's not what I'm talking about."

"You asked me about the meeting, right?"

"Monnie!" She bounced on the edge of the couch.

"What? He flirted, I refocused. He flirted some more, I redirected. He flirted some more and then it was time to go."

"Why are you giving him such a hard time? You should go out with him."

"I told you—"

"I don't want to hear about your two-year Kevin wash-out period. Who decided that anyway? Sometimes you have to let things flow."

"Just because you're floating on cloud nine doesn't mean I'm trying to fall in love."

"I'm not saying fall in love. I'm just saying go

out and have dinner with the man. All you do is sit around the house."

I wanted to say I sat around the house all the time because she was always with Khalil, but that would sound adolescent. I walked into the kitchen and came back with two glasses of carrot juice. I handed one to Alaysia and sat back down on the couch.

"I don't know anything about him. I don't even know if he's a Christian."

"So what? You'll only date him if he's a Christian?"

"Yeah. 'Be ye not unequally yoked.' It's hard enough when two Christians try to make a relationship work. It makes things harder when one of the people isn't saved."

"Who said anything about being yoked? I'm talkin' 'bout dinner. Anyway, me and Khalil are doing fine, and I'm not a Christian."

Yeah, but it's only a matter of time. Between me and Khalil praying, you'll be saved in no time. "You're different than the average. You're a spiritual person and you're seeking to know God. You guys have long spiritual discussions, and plus, you have a history together when you both weren't saved."

She pointed an accusing finger in my face. "Don't think I don't know you and Khalil are scheming to make me into a Christian."

I tried to look innocent. "What are you talking about?"

"Don't play dumb. You two probably pray for the Holy Spirit to catch me every day."

"Catch you?" I laughed.

"Yeah. Don't think I don't know."

"Is it working?"

She thought for a minute. "I must admit it's getting harder and harder to find a reason not to accept Christ or get saved or get born again or however you say it. I don't know. I never thought *I* would be a part of an organized religion. It's so . . . conformist."

"You're not going to accept Christ because you'd be following the crowd?"

"No. It's just . . . it seems like with all Khalil tells me about this whole Kingdom thing, the church would be doing more than it does. Let him tell it, you guys are supposed to be taking over the world, changing the course of history, and making a difference in people's lives. I don't see that anywhere. Everybody I've ever known who 'gets saved' just gets this churchy attitude and quotes a lot of scriptures, but everything else about them is the same. If your God is real, He should be able to make a bigger difference in people's lives and in the whole world."

Being around Alaysia was a constant challenge to my Christianity.

"Anyway, you've distracted me again. You're good at that when it's something you don't want to talk about."

"What?" I rearranged the books on the coffee table and pretended not to know what she was talking about.

"Alex. We were talking about you going out on a date with Mr. Gorgeous."

"Alaysia, give it a rest. I'm not ready to date anybody."

"I understand, Monnie. Too much man all at once, huh?"

"Girl, you know it. I would probably be too nervous to talk."

"Nervous? Why?"

"'Cause he looks so good."

"Why should the way his facial features are arranged make you nervous?"

"I don't know. Beautiful people make me nervous. They make me feel self-conscious about the way I look."

Alaysia shook her head. "More fat girl drama, huh?"

"Guess so."

"Then you should go out with him to get over it. Not because you like him or you're interested in him, but so you can overcome another facet of the fat girl syndrome. You'll be conquering for fat girls everywhere."

"Conquering?"

"Yeah, conquering your fears and this misconception that how a person looks is any indication of their worth. He'll probably bore you to death or do something to make you realize his looks don't mean a durn thing. I've had so many guys who look good who have absolutely no substance to them. Then I've had plenty of not so great-looking guys I really liked because they were so smart or so funny or so creative. It's not about looks."

"Oh yeah? What about Khalil?"

Alaysia's face broke into a broad grin. "He's the best of all worlds. Sheer perfection."

I shook my head. "You're hopeless."

"Naw, girl, just deep in love."

I rolled my eyes. "Oh, brother."

"Don't hate. Come on, you should be happy for me. I feel like everything is coming together in my life for the first time. My body is healthy, I don't have any bad habits, we're starting a business, and my relationship with Khalil is ten times better than before." She leaned back into the throw pillows and sighed. "Everything feels so good, I'm scared something bad is gonna happen."

"Like what?"

Alaysia stared into space. "Like Khalil is going to die or something. Seems like the people I love either die or go away. Like I don't deserve to have any happiness."

I rubbed her arm. "Don't say that, Laysia. Nothing is going to happen."

"How do you know? I hate when people say things just because it's the right thing to say. You don't know."

I knew with all the people she had lost, she had reason to feel the way she did. "I tell you what. We'll pray for God to protect and cover you and Khalil and that nothing will happen to you.

She sat up. "And you too. I don't want anything to happen to you either."

"Okay, me too."

"And pray for our business, too. I've never tried anything like this before, and I want it to work."

"Okay, Alaysia. I'll pray. I will."

"Promise me you'll pray every single day that nothing bad will happen. Every day, okay?" She looked like a scared little girl.

"I will. I promise."

"How do you know whether it will work or not?"

"Huh?"

"How do you know whether the prayer will work?"

"I just know. There's a scripture in the Bible that says whenever I pray, God hears me and when He hears me, I have whatever I ask."

"Then how come so many people have unanswered prayers? I know people who pray all the time for stuff and they don't get it."

"Maybe what they prayed wasn't in God's will."

"How do you know what's in God's will? If He only answers stuff that's in His will, it doesn't make any sense to pray anything else."

"You know what? I'm gonna stop faking the funk. I'm a raggedy Christian. I don't read my Bible the way I should, and there's a lot of stuff I don't understand. I don't know how to answer most of the questions you ask me. You make me feel like my Christianity is just a habit I've always had, but I don't know all the stuff I should know about it."

"Sorry. I didn't mean to make you feel that way."

"I know you didn't. It's my fault. I should know more about what I believe."

"Maybe we can learn together. Khalil is a great teacher. He knows a lot about the Bible. Maybe we can all get together and study."

"That sounds cool. Let me know when."

She smiled. "I will."

34

The idea sounded good, but we never made it happen. Alaysia continued to spend every waking moment with Khalil, and I spent every waking moment focusing on getting the business started and working out like a fiend. Alaysia kept telling me I was overdoing it, but I needed the physical outlet.

I was happy everything was coming together in her life, but I still felt this big, gaping hole in my soul. As much as I wanted to be happy being by myself, I still wanted someone to spend my time with. That whole revelation about being satisfied with my singleness was all fine and good, but it didn't keep a sista company on a Saturday night. I went out with some of my friends from the gym and that was cool, but when they had other plans, I was left out in the cold. It would have been nice to have a partner—a definite Saturday night guarantee.

One Saturday evening, Talinda and I decided to hang out. It was Valentine's Day and neither one of us had a date. She was trying vegetarian restaurants with me. We decided to go to Soul Vegetarian in Virginia Highlands. Talinda said she needed a taste of healthy soul food to keep her away from the chocolate. She made a real commitment to living healthy, and had lost eighteen pounds so far. I was a triumphant fifty-nine pounds lighter. Best part was, my new doctor had cut my blood pressure and diabetes meds in half.

Talinda finished off her barbeque seitan and greens, then sopped up the juice with some cornbread. "Girl, I think I'll be all right now. I needed a little fix."

I looked at my watch. "Hey, wanna ride out to Stonecrest Mall? I need some new clothes. Feel like shopping? We can catch a movie afterward."

"Naw, I want to wait 'til I lose more weight."

"Why, girl? You've lost a lot. You should at least get a pair of new jeans. You look like a li'l thug with your pants hanging off you like that."

Talinda laughed. "All right. Let's go."

When we got to the mall, Talinda asked, "Do you mind if we go to Lane Bryant first? I'll pick out a pair of jeans real quick and then we'll go to your stores."

"I shop in Lane Bryant."

Talinda stared at me. "Why?"

"What do you mean why?"

"Monica, what size do you wear?"

"Last time I went shopping, I was in a 14/16. I haven't been in a couple of months."

"Girl, you could probably get twelves. If I was your size, you wouldn't catch me in Lane Bryant. The minute I can squeeze these hips into a four-teen, I'll never cross their doorway again."

I hadn't shopped in anything but a fat girl store since . . . since I could remember. I looked down at my hips. Could I fit into a size 12?

Talinda tugged on my arm. "Come on, girl. We're going to Limited Express. You're going to the skinny girl store today."

I must have tried on every outfit in the store. I hadn't fit into a 12 since my wedding day, and that was only for a minute. After eating like a pig on the honeymoon, and then eating Kevin's gourmet cooking every day, I went back to my size 14/16.

After a while, the sales lady looked annoyed. Must have got tired of reshelving the clothes she knew I wasn't going to buy. I didn't care about her stank attitude. I was happy to be looking so good.

I refused to be ashamed when I finally did leave with four shopping bags full of clothes. It only took Talinda a minute to pick out a new pair of jeans in Lane Bryant. She had dropped into a size 22 and was very happy with herself. It was hard to believe I used to be her size. Then again, it was harder to believe I wasn't her size anymore.

As we were leaving, Talinda asked, "Hey, do you mind if we stop by the Christian bookstore real quick? There's a new gospel album I gotta get."

When we got into the bookstore, she pointed at

a poster on the wall. "There it is. Girl, that album is tearing up the charts. That choir is the bomb."

I stopped frozen with my mouth open, staring at the picture she was pointing to.

Talinda laughed. "Yeah, girl. He is fine, ain't he? Don't be lusting after no man of God, though. You go to hell for that."

I still didn't say anything.

"Monnie, what's wrong?"

I shook myself. "Nothing. That . . . that's my husband."

35

Now Talinda stood there with her mouth open. We both stared at a beautiful picture of Kevin, plastered on the wall of Called to Conquer Bookstore.

"Your husband? What do you mean? You wish that was your husband?"

"No, that's my husband, well, ex-husband, well, almost ex-husband. He won't give me a divorce."

"Are you crazy? Why would you want to divorce a man like him? Not only is he fine, but he's the hottest new thing in gospel music, and he's a man of God. Why in the world would you want to let him go?"

"Long story." I shook my head. "Long, sad story."

She backed off. "Oh, sorry. I shouldn't have said that. Things aren't always what they look like on the outside, huh?"

She had no idea.

"You wanna go?"

"No. I'm okay. We should get a copy. I want to hear it."

We both bought copies of the CD. Our great fun had gone sour, so we decided to call it a night.

When I got to my car, I put my keys in the ignition but didn't start it up. I opened the CD and slipped it in my CD player. I didn't realize the album had been released. I used to know everything about every artist in the gospel music industry, had most albums before they were released, and listened to gospel radio religiously. Now, anything having to do with gospel music reminded me of Kevin. I didn't even know what the gospel station was here in Atlanta.

I turned on the overhead car light and scanned the CD jacket. I recognized most of the songs, but there were a few new ones. I turned to the dedication. After he gave the usual thanks to God for his gift and anointing, Kevin's next words were, "To Monica, the love of my life. Forever."

I didn't know how to feel about that. It had been thirteen months since Kevin and I went our separate ways, and he was still talking forever.

As I listened to the first song, one of my favorites, I tried to evaluate my feelings for him. I knew I would always love him because we started out as best friends. Whether I could work through forgiveness and the whole sexual identity issue? That was the real question.

I had no frame of reference for this situation. It wasn't like there was anyone I could talk to or any book I knew of I could read. Could I trust him when he had kept a huge secret from me about who he was? Would he ever cheat on me again? Could a man really be delivered from homosexuality, and if so, how?

That familiar sadness crept in. Was I really better in my new life or had I taken escaping to a whole new level in a whole new city? Then again, what could I do but move forward?

I wondered how Kevin was doing. I appreciated him not contacting me, but I missed him. Missed his laugh. Missed his smile. Missed his eyes.

On the one hand, I hoped he was getting over me. Then there was this totally insane part of me that felt sad at the thought of him getting over me. I had long given up trying to control my emotions when it came to Kevin, and accepted the fact that they weren't going to make sense. I was stuck somewhere between "absence makes the heart grow fonder" and "time heals all wounds."

I flipped the jacket over and my stomach turned when I saw Bishop Walker's picture. He had a little blurb about how proud he was of Kevin and how God had blessed him and blah, blah, blah. I would never look at him the same.

I skipped to the last song, one I didn't recognize by name. It was just Kevin and his acoustic guitar, playing the melody to that little love song he wrote for me. As I listened to him sing the lyrics, I felt every word he sang. They cut down deep to the core of me and unlocked a place I thought I successfully closed off. The tears started falling. I stopped the song. Why torture myself?

When I got home, I was surprised to see Alaysia's car in the parking lot. I expected her to be out with Khalil on a Valentine's date. Khalil was probably here with her. She tried to respect my privacy by not having him at the house 24/7, which I appreciated. Not so much for privacy's sake, but because it was so hard seeing them in love. She probably invited him over because she thought I would be out late with Talinda.

When I got upstairs, they were sitting hugged up on the couch, watching a movie. Great. Just what I needed, to see the lovebirds after listening to Kevin's album. I carried my shopping bags straight to my room. I splashed my eyes in cold water because I knew Alaysia wouldn't be far behind me.

After a few seconds, she knocked on my door. "Hey, Monnie. I didn't know you were gonna be here. Sorry about—"

"It's no problem, Laysia. You and Khalil are fine."

"You okay?"

I tried to smile as I held up my Limited Express bags. "Look. I shopped in the skinny girl store today." I pulled out a pair of jeans and held up the tag.

Alaysia laughed and gave me a high five. "A twelve? You go, girl." She sat down on the bed, looking at me in that funny way she looked at me when she knew something was wrong.

"You sure you're okay?"

I pulled out my other bag and held up the CD. "My other purchase for today."

She looked at the CD, then her eyes widened. "Oh my." She looked at me then looked down at the CD again. "That's Kevin."

"Yeah, that's Kevin."

"Give me five minutes and I'll send Khalil home. I'll be right back."

"Alaysia, you don't have to do that. I'm fine."

"Five minutes. He was leaving soon anyway. We have church in the morning."

"Church? We?"

She smiled and slipped out the door. Ten minutes later, she came back. "Sorry 'bout that."

"You don't have to apologize and you didn't have to send him home."

"I know. I feel like I've been neglecting you lately. We haven't spent any time together in forever."

"Girl, you've been spending time with your man. Trust me, if I had a man in my life right now, I'd be kicking you to the curb, too."

"Yes, I do recall you becoming ghost on me when one certain fine musician came along." She sat down on my bed and picked up the CD. "Did you know the album was out?"

"No. I mean, I knew it was coming, I just didn't know when. They must have rushed it because the original plan was an April release date." I curled my lips. "Bishop Walker probably pushed him to do it sooner."

"Whew. Bitterness does not look good on you, girl."

"What?"

"You should see your face when you said his name. All crunched up and ugly. You need to forgive and release, girl. Hate and resentment aren't good for you."

"All right, Reverend Alaysia." I sat down on

the bed next to her. "What's this about you going to church tomorrow?"

"It's no big deal. Khalil's been inviting me, and I decided to give it a try. If his church's beliefs are anything like him, I think it'll be different from most churches. Wanna go?"

"Naw. Can't say I'm in much of a churchy mood right now."

She put an arm around my shoulders. "I'm sorry, Monnie. I don't know what to say."

"I know. Me either. I don't know how to feel about the album. Or about Kevin. All I know is right now I'm taking care of me. I feel like I'm a much stronger person now and that's what counts."

Alaysia nodded. "Yeah? Good, girl. I'm proud of you. I know this hasn't been easy. Who knows what will happen? Look at me and Khalil's happy ending."

I slipped off my shoes and stood to get my pajamas out of the chest of drawers. "Yeah, you guys are an inspiration to failed relationships everywhere." I walked toward the bathroom to change.

"I know you don't think you going to bed. I sent my man home to be with you? Naw, wench, you staying up with me."

I yawned. "Come on, man, I'm tired. All that shopping took it out of me." It was really the emotions that had drained me.

"I ain't trying to hear it. Meet me in the kitchen after you change into your jammies. I got some chocolate ice cream. Your favorite."

As she left, I tried to remember the last time I ate chocolate.

We sat up half the night at the kitchen table, giggling and gossiping over soy ice cream. It wasn't Tom & Larry's, but it was still good. I finally looked at the clock. It was two in the morning. "Girl, you ain't gon' make it to church tomorrow."

Alaysia's eyes widened when she looked at the clock. "Oh, my goodness. See, this is what I get for not spending any time with you. Trying to get it all in one evening. I gotta go to church. I promised Khalil."

"Thanks, Laysia. I needed some girl time."

She gave me a hug. "Sorry I been neglecting you."

When I got back to my bedroom, I stared at the phone a few minutes and wondered if Kevin was awake. I dialed the number before I lost my nerve.

"Hello?" He sounded a little groggy.

"Hey, Kevin."

"Monica?" I could hear the surprise in his voice.

"Yeah, Kevin, it's me. How are you?"

"I'm . . . I . . . wow . . . I can't believe you called."

"Yeah, I was, uh, shopping today, and I see this big picture of you posted in the Christian bookstore. I got the album."

"Yeah? What'd you think?"

"It's awesome, Kevin, just like I knew it would be. Congratulations. You guys did a really good job." I slipped into my bed.

"Thanks, Monnie. That means a lot coming from you."

There was an uncomfortable silence. I pulled the covers up around my neck, trying to get rid of a sudden case of the shivers.

"I was surprised to see it out so soon. I didn't think you were releasing it until April."

"Bishop wanted to push the date up some. He thought we were ready to go ahead and make it happen. I guess he was right. It just took a lot of late nights and a lot of extra work."

I wanted to ask what the rush was, but didn't bother. Probably part of Bishop Walker's plan for money for his new building. "You okay, Kevin? You don't sound right."

"I'm a little tired. We've been doing a lot of traveling and album release parties and guest appearances and all sorts of stuff I wasn't ready for. There's a lot more to releasing an album than just releasing an album."

At that moment, I wished I could give him a nice supportive hug and let him lay his head in my lap and fall asleep. It was weird because I had started to believe I was over him. Maybe it was just being concerned about someone I loved. It didn't have to mean I was still "in love" with him.

"Monica, you still there?"

"Yeah, just thinking. Don't overdo it, Kevin. You know how you catch colds real quick when you don't get enough rest. And you know how your stomach gets if you're not eating right. Make sure you're taking care of yourself."

"Nice to know you care, Monnie."

The smile in his voice let me know I needed to end this conversation.

"I just wanted to call to say congratulations. I hope the album and the tour are a great success." I turned off the lamp on the nightstand.

"Thanks. I really appreciate that."

As I was about to hang up, he said, "Hey, we're gonna be coming to Atlanta sometime this spring. I don't have the schedule in front of me, but is it okay if ... I mean, it might be a nice if ... if you're not too busy ..."

"I'd love to take you out to dinner when you come, Kevin. Just let me know when you'll be here."

I heard him let out a deep breath. "I will. As soon as I know. I can schedule a few extra days there so we can spend some time together."

I hesitated. "Sounds good, Kevin. Let me know when."

"Monnie?" he said as I was about to hang up again.

"Yeah?"

"Happy Valentine's Day."

Couldn't let me off the phone without sticking a knife through my heart. "Oh, yeah. Happy Valentine's Day to you, too, Kevin."

36

The next morning when Alaysia came in from church, I was sitting on the couch reading my Bible. I was making more of a concerted effort to spend time with God. I was beginning to understand what the phrase "intimacy with God" meant. He was becoming my best friend. I could talk to Him about anything and everything. I cried in His lap often, and felt like He was really with me and would never leave me. Slowly but surely, through time in His presence, reading my Bible and books on emotional healing, I was getting better. I wasn't ready for church yet, but my relationship with Him was stronger than it had ever been.

Alaysia tiptoed past me like she was trying not to disturb my quiet time.

"Hey, how was church?"

She turned and smiled, then dropped onto the

couch next to me like she was just waiting for me to ask. "It was the wildest thing. They spoke in tongues." She waited for me to react, but when I didn't say anything, she kept going at a mile a minute. "I had heard about it before, but I thought it was just for crazy, religious fanatic type people. But then I looked at Khalil to say 'These people are crazy. Let's get out of here,' and he was speaking in tongues too. Now, I know Khalil, and he's not a crazy religious fanatic, so then I started to wonder about the whole thing like, wow, is it really real? And if so, what does that say about your God? It sure makes Him seem realer than the rest, you know?"

Alaysia was talking so fast I almost stopped her to tell her to breathe. "Then they started singing in tongues, everybody all together. It was the most beautiful thing I've ever heard. It made me feel . . . I don't know, I guess like your yoga word, zingy. But much better. I closed my eyes and let it overtake me, and I felt like I could fly, like I could literally go straight to heaven and meet God for myself. I got goose bumps it was so real."

I smiled.

"What? You don't believe me? If it wasn't for Khalil doing it, I wouldn't have believed it either, but it's real. I promise you. I *felt* God today."

"I believe you."

Alaysia took off her shoes and flexed her feet. "You gotta come next Sunday. You gotta see it for yourself."

I laughed.

"What? You've heard it before?"

"I've done it before."

Alaysia's eyes widened. "You've done it before? When? How? Have you done it more than once? What did it feel like?"

"Slow down. One question at a time. I got filled with the Holy Spirit when I was fifteen. I grew up in a Pentecostal church, and it was almost a requirement to be a member. I used to pray in the Spirit almost every day when me and God were tight, but then, you know, all the drama happened and my prayer life slacked off. But lately, me and God are patching things up, and it's a part of my daily prayer life again."

"Why?"

"Why what?"

"Why do you speak in tongues? What does it do?"

"When you pray in the spirit, your spirit is communicating directly with God's spirit, and it doesn't give your mind a chance to get in the way. I like to open my prayer time that way. It gives me a chance to shut out the world and focus on God. And sometimes when I don't know exactly what to say, I pray in the spirit. Even if my mind doesn't know what to say, my spirit does."

"That sounds real cool. I can't believe you never told me about this. How could you know about something so spiritual and beautiful and not share it with me? I always share my spiritual discoveries with you."

"Gimme a break. When we were in college, if I even mentioned God's name, you didn't want to hear about it."

"I'm not talking about then. I'm talking about

now. I thought we were on a journey of spiritual discovery together."

"Yeah, but we're on different paths of spiritual discovery. You're talking about crystals and chakras and chi and moons in alignment and past lives."

"That's not the point. I was sharing stuff I thought was important and real. You have this . . . this supernatural experience on a *daily* basis and you don't even mention it."

"I guess you gave me a complex in the past. Whenever I tried to share anything about God with you, you didn't want to hear it."

"That was before. Never mind. Now that I know this secret, you have to tell me all about it. I want to know everything. How can I get it?"

I laughed. "Can we take this to the kitchen? I'm starving."

She slapped her forehead. "Oh yeah, Khalil's on his way over for brunch. I'm supposed to be cooking. Oops, I hope it's okay. I forgot to ask you first."

"Of course it's okay. As long as you don't start the evening symphonies, I'm cool."

Alaysia blushed. Back when we lived in the condo and she had "company," things got pretty loud at night. I guess she thought she was being discreet by bringing them in late and making sure they left by the time I got up, but all the noise ruined any pretense of discretion. One day, she asked me if I minded her having company, and I said I couldn't sleep too well with her symphony going on in the next room.

"With our bedrooms so far apart, I probably wouldn't hear anything," I said.

"What are you talking about? We're staying celibate. There won't be anything to hear."

"Yeah, right."

Alaysia looked insulted. "What? You don't think I can stay celibate in a relationship? You did it for two years."

"Yeah, and now we know why I was successful, don't we? Really, though, it'll be harder because you guys have been intimate before. Once you've crossed the line, it's hard to go back to just holding hands."

"Whatever, Monnie."

"All right, remember you've been warned. Be careful."

"I'm fine. The new me is like you. Pure as the driven snow."

The doorbell rang. Alaysia jumped. "Oh my God, he's here and we haven't cooked a thing."

"*We*? I don't remember making any commitments to cook."

"Please, Monnie, help me throw something together."

"You know what? You—"

"I love you, too." She pushed me toward the kitchen. "Just start slicing some fruit. I'll do the rest."

"You darn skippy you'll do the rest."

Alaysia went to open the door and came back to the kitchen hand in hand with Khalil. They both looked like school kids, happy to be "going together."

"Hey, Monica. Good to see you." Khalil bent to kiss my cheek.

"Hey, Khalil. I hope you're not too hungry. Your girl here was too busy going on and on about church to start cooking."

He gave Alaysia a full kiss on the lips. "I guess that means you enjoyed it."

"Yeah, I was telling her about the speaking in tongues part, and she knows all about it. She's even done it before.'

Khalil chuckled and kissed Alaysia on the nose. "You are so cute."

"I'm glad you guys are amused with me. Okay, you have to explain it to me. How do you do it?"

I stared as Alaysia plopped into one of the kitchen chairs. I raised my eyebrows and gestured with the knife at the cutting board to invite her to help me put together this brunch she scheduled. She either didn't notice or ignored me. Khalil sat down next to her. I figured I'd cut her some slack and be Martha while she sat like Mary at Jesus' feet.

Khalil helped Alaysia flip through the Bible he bought her. "First Corinthians is right here. Turn to chapter twelve. Put a finger there, and also turn to John chapter fourteen."

For every question Alaysia asked, Khalil answered with scripture. By the time we finished our three-hour brunch, I felt like Alaysia knew as much about Christianity as I did. There were things Khalil talked about that I had never seen in the Bible. I'd practically lived in church all my life, but sitting here listening to Khalil made me feel like I didn't know anything.

I had to repent for being jealous of Alaysia. It seemed like she had everything a saved woman could want in Khalil, and she wasn't saved.

Yet.

37

After weeks of meeting with Alex, I was finally satisfied with the business and marketing plan we put together. Alex and I had spent many hours together, and he didn't charge me anywhere near what he should have for all the time he put in.

It was fun working with him. We laughed and joked a lot. He stopped flirting and we relaxed into being friends. He was almost as excited about the business as Alaysia and I. He said the numbers looked great and if we did our marketing right, we'd be turning a healthy profit in no time.

The only problem was we couldn't find a building in the price range that fit our business plan. Alaysia said she would ask her dad for more money, but Alex was convinced if we waited, we'd find what we needed.

I awoke early one Saturday morning to the

phone ringing. I peeped at my nightstand clock and groaned. Saturday was the only morning I didn't get up early to go to the gym, so I was mad at whoever was calling. After four rings, I figured Alaysia wasn't going to answer it, so I rolled over to grab it.

"Hello?" I put on my groggiest voice to let this person know they woke me.

"Monica? It's Alex. Are you sitting down?"

"Actually, Alex, seeing that it's seven on a Saturday morning, I'm *lying* down. What's going on? This better be good."

"I have a huge surprise for you."

"What is it?"

"If I tell you, it won't be a surprise."

"It's too early to be playing games. You got two seconds, then I'm hanging up."

"Let's just say I found the building for your gym, and it will be available exactly when you're ready to move in, and it already has most of the equipment you'll need, and it's less than the price we planned for."

I sat straight up in bed. "What? Where? How did you find it? How much is it?"

"Uh-oh, my two seconds is up. Goodbye."

"Alex, stop playing! Give me the details."

"Nope, that's all you get. You have to leave me something for the surprise. Meet me at my office at nine."

"Wait! At least tell me where it is."

"Nope, see you in two hours." *Click.*

I screamed and jumped out of the bed and took off for Alaysia's room. She must have heard me scream because she met me in the living room.

"What's wrong?" She looked scared that something bad had happened.

"Alex found us a building." I jumped up and down.

"What?"

"That was Alex. He said he found the perfect building for us and it's already got a lot of the equipment we need. We're meeting him in two hours."

"Where is it and how much is it and—" Alaysia jumped up and down with me.

"He wouldn't tell me all that. He said it was a surprise."

Alaysia screamed. "I can't believe him."

"I know. Let's get dressed."

We both put on some jeans and sweaters and ate a light breakfast. It was still only eight o'clock. We sat around and fidgeted for a few minutes, then decided to leave early just in case Alex got there before nine.

When we pulled up at his office at eight-thirty, he was driving up. We jumped out of the car and bumrushed him with questions.

"Where is it? How did you find it? How much is it? When can we look at it?"

Alex laughed. "Ladies, calm down. First of all, you're early. I told you nine o'clock. Second of all—"

"Stop playing, Alex. You 'bout to get jumped. Give up the information." I held up a threatening fist and threw a few air jabs.

Alex held up his hands to block my imaginary blows. He looked at Alaysia. "Your friend is violent, isn't she?"

Alaysia held up her fists. "Yep, and she learned it from me. Come on, Alex. Tell us or we're gonna double-team you."

Alex smiled a mischievous smile. "Only in my wildest dreams."

I punched him for real. "Stop playing. Come on."

"Dang, that hurt." He rubbed his arm. "Okay. A friend of a friend of one of my boys from school knows of this gym that's going bankrupt. The owner is about to get foreclosed on, and unless he sells everything real quick, his property and the equipment will go to the highest bidder at an auction. If he sells, he can avoid the foreclosure and not lose too much money."

My excitement faded. "Why would we want to buy a business going bankrupt? If it didn't work for him and we'd be doing the exact same business, why would it work for us?"

"That's the thing. The business was very lucrative, but this idiot was taking all his profits and funneling them into another business he was trying to start and not paying the loan on this business. This business will work because it's been successful for the past five years. The owner can't afford to make the payments anymore. You'd get to keep all his current clients, and can probably keep the employees if you want to. It would be a seamless transition."

Alaysia said, "We wouldn't want his employees. Almost everybody from the gym we're working at now will be defecting with us when we leave. They're as sick of our boss as we are. They're taking Alaysia and Monica's underground railroad and leaving the plantation for freedom."

I was still skeptical. "How do you know this insider information?"

"I told you, my boy's friend's friend. It's all about the six degrees of separation, baby."

"How does this friend's friend know?" I asked. It sounded too good to be true.

"He's the gym's accountant."

My eyes widened. "When can we see it?"

"Right now. Let's roll."

We piled into Alex's Expedition to go take a look. When we turned onto Piedmont, Alaysia chuckled. "Looks like I might get my wish. We're gonna be in the same vicinity as Jim's Gym, and we get to take his business. Serves him right for being a slave master."

As we continued and turned on Ponce de Leon, Alaysia bounced in her seat. "We're getting close to his gym. We'll put him out of business. See, God don't like ugly."

When Alex pulled up in front of Jim's Gym, Alaysia and I looked at each other, then looked at Alex, then looked at each other again and screamed.

"Are you serious? We get to take over Jim's Gym? We get to keep all the equipment? We get to keep all our coworkers? We can actually afford it?" Alaysia and I asked questions at the same time.

Alex held up his hands. "Wait a minute. Slow down. Let me answer your questions. Let's see, yes, yes, ummm, yes, yes, and . . . yes."

We both sat for a second, thinking, then screamed again, bouncing in our seats.

"I can't believe it." I reached to give Alex a big hug and kiss on the cheek at the same time as Alaysia.

"Mmmmm, I should give you two good news more often."

Alaysia frowned. "Jim would never sell us his business. He'd rather foreclose than sell to us."

Alex smiled. "Trust me, I got this. I knew you guys had some bad blood, so I told him I had an overseas investor who would be purchasing the club and hiring managers to run it. That's partially true."

"Alex, you're brilliant," Alaysia said.

"I know." Alex wore a smug look on his face.

I said, "Let's get out of here. I don't want him to see you with us. You have to do the negotiations for us."

"Does he hate you guys that much?"

Alaysia said, "The slave master has no reason to hate the slave as long as he's under his control. But when the slave rises up and claims his freedom . . . It's the same mentality that kept our forefathers enslaved and continues to enslave—"

"All right, Sojourner Truth. We get the picture." I rolled my eyes at Alaysia.

We went back to Alex's office to look at the numbers and saw that between Alaysia's condo money, my savings, her dad's contribution, and a small business loan we had already been approved for, we could easily take over Jim's club. The best part was we could subtract what we planned to spend on new equipment. Jim's club already equipped cost less than we projected for a building alone.

This was the most interested Alaysia had been in looking at the numbers since we started the whole process. She scratched her head. "I want to be able to pay the employees more. I refuse to rob people like Jim has been robbing us. Can you guys calculate in market rate for everybody and a little more for our best employees?" She smiled. "Employees. Ooh, I like that. We have employees."

Alex frowned. "You guys didn't plan to open such a large establishment, so we didn't figure for as many people working there as he has now. We could fire a few people and give everybody the amount of money you want to pay."

I didn't like the idea of firing anybody. "Why don't we take the money we allotted for marketing? The gym is already packed, so the money we planned for advertising can go for salaries."

Alex nodded and smiled. "See, that's my girl. You sure you don't want to ditch this gym stuff and come work with me?"

Alaysia smacked his arm. "Stop trying to steal my partner."

We talked a little more then made plans for Alex to start the anonymous negotiations with Jim.

We got back into Alaysia's car to head home. Alaysia's eyes sparkled. "Wow."

"I know. It's exciting, huh?"

She nodded. "This prayer thing really works."

38

Alex got a taste of Jim's shrewdness first hand. The negotiations went on for weeks with Jim playing hardball. He didn't know Alex knew the position he was in, so he tried to make it sound like he wasn't willing to sell for the price his accountant told Alex about. Alex was patient because he knew the foreclosure date was fast approaching, and the accountant told him no one else was biting. Apparently, Jim had cheated his accountant too.

Alex finally got Jim down to the price we knew he'd take and scheduled the closing. The night before, Alaysia and I could barely sleep. Alex took us to a lawyer's office the next day. After we signed a huge stack of papers, Alex announced that we were the proud owners of the former Jim's Gym, now Synergeez Health and Fitness.

We remained professional until we got out to

the lawyer's parking lot, but once the door closed behind us, Alaysia and I jumped and screamed then hugged Alex.

"You did it. I can't believe it's ours. We own a gym," I said.

Alaysia started making plans. "I can't wait to hire painters and a decorator and—"

"Wait a minute, now. We budgeted for painters, but we didn't say nothing about no decorator. We will not go broke on this."

Alex laughed at us. "Monica's right, Alaysia. You have to stick to the plan."

Alaysia pouted, but then started jumping up and down again. "I have to call Khalil." She pulled out her cell phone and walked toward the car.

Alex turned to me. "Well, my work here is done. You guys are gonna do fine."

"Alex, thanks so much for all your help. I'll be sure to refer anyone I know looking to start or improve their business to you. I'll keep you updated, and you'll definitely have a seat of honor at the grand re-opening."

"So that's it?"

"What?"

"I do believe you promised me a dinner after we were no longer doing business together."

"I said nothing of the sort." I had to give it to him. That was smooth.

"Come on. One dinner. That's all I'm asking."

"My life is far too complicated for you to be dealing with me, Alex. Trust me, you should run while you can." I looked over at Alaysia, talking a mile a minute on her cell phone, and silently willed her to come rescue me.

"I didn't propose. I asked you to have dinner with me. What's wrong with you black women these days? A brotha asks for a simple dinner and you start rearranging your life. I could just use some intelligent company for a change."

"Give me a break, Alex. This is Atlanta. There's a plethora of intelligent black women here."

"Yeah, but they all have an agenda. I ain't trying to be a checkmark on nobody's to-do list."

I laughed. "What are you talking about?"

"You know how y'all do. Married by age twenty-six, first child by twenty-eight, last child by thirty-two, get the tubes tied. Have a nanny so you can run your own business. Dating is a part of a master plan for you women. Nobody hangs out to enjoy each other's company. I just want someone to eat with, see a movie with, have fun with every once in a while."

"No commitments, no strings, huh?"

"See, now you're trying to make me sound like one of those guys who won't commit. It's not like that. I—"

"I didn't say it was a bad thing." *Stop it, Monica!* Why was I flirting with him?

"It's not?"

"No." I pulled my wool coat a little tighter around me. "As a matter of fact, it may be a good thing. I'm not in a position for any entanglements either, but it would be nice to have a hanging buddy. That, however, begs the question of whether men and women can be just friends."

He nodded. "I think it's a matter of choice."

"Love is a matter of choice, huh?" If it were only true.

"It can be. If two rational, intelligent adults make a decision to just be friends, they can stick to their decision."

"Okay then, dinner. Name the place and time, and I'll meet you there."

"Really?"

"Yeah."

"Okay, tomorrow night. Seven o'clock. Houston's up at Perimeter."

I tried to remember whether they had any decent vegetarian dishes on the menu. "How 'bout P.F. Chang's instead?"

"Oh, yeah. I haven't been there in forever."

We finalized our plans to meet, and Alaysia and I left. I refused to listen to the voice of God on the inside telling me "no." It probably wasn't Him anyway. It was probably me being nervous.

I'm just going out with a friend. That's all.

39

I tried not to make a big deal of getting dressed for my non-date with Alex. I kept in mind what Alaysia said about conquering my fears about fine men. That's all I was doing. Conquering for the fat girls. I put on a pair of jeans and a burgundy turtleneck sweater. I dusted on some face powder, put on eyeliner, frosty mauve lipstick, and some silver hoop earrings. I wasn't trying to look like I made an effort.

I arrived fashionably late and scanned the restaurant. It had a contemporary Zen decorum with the pungent fragrance of lemongrass and Asian spices filling the air. A waitress led me to our table, where Alex was already nursing a mixed drink. Alcohol? I mentally subtracted a point from his perfect ten-ness.

He stood and gave me a kiss on the cheek. He smelled wonderful. Some sort of earthy, musky scent like the Muslims sold in those little oil bottles. I silently added back half a point. He looked great in a pair of jeans and a black sweater that hugged his chiseled chest. I added back another half point, and he was back to a ten.

As we chatted through dinner, he kept losing and gaining points. He lost a point for making a face when I ordered the curry tofu with vegetables and brown rice. He got the point back for agreeing to be open-minded and taste it. He lost two points for ordering pork, then got them back for his really cute laugh when I said something silly. He lost three points for cursing several times, but got four added when he told me how great I looked in my jeans. He lost three points for interrupting our conversation several times by answering his cell phone and staying on it for long periods of time. He got one point back when I reminded myself we were just hanging buddies. I added one more back for the cute way he held up his finger to let me know it would be one more minute, and another point when he made silly faces at the phone to let me know the person on the other end was droning on and on.

He got two points when he finally said, "Enough interruptions. I'm turning this thing off."

He leaned over and said, "So, tell me more about you. What made you decide to go into this whole health thing in the first place?"

Minus one for leaning too close into the personal space zone. Plus five for asking me about me. "Before I moved to Atlanta, I worked for about six years as a nurse."

"A nurse? You mean a real nurse?"

"Yep, a bonafide registered nurse."

"What made you walk away from that?" He propped his head in his hands and looked genuinely interested. Plus two.

"It just got old. It didn't feel like we were helping anybody. And it was the same thing over and over, every single day."

"What made you go into nursing in the first place?"

The spikey blond waitress brought Alex another mixed drink and set a teapot and cup in front of me. I dumped a couple of packages of Splenda into the pot and warmed my hands over the steam.

"My grandmother. She moved in with us when I was twelve. She was really sick—high blood pressure, diabetes, and she'd had a mild stroke and had real bad heart disease. I made sure she took all her pills several times a day and took care of her feet. Over the years, she got real bad ulcers from the diabetes and had to get her toes amputated, then part of her foot, then her lower leg. Then her other leg. Seemed like she was always going to the hospital and coming back with a little more of her body cut off. My mom had a weak stomach, so I did her dressing changes. She always said I was going to be the best nurse one day."

I took a sip of my ginger-peach tea. "I watched her die every single day. Every time she came home from the hospital, a little bit of the sparkle would be gone from her eye and a little bit of spunk from her spirit. Right before the last time she went into the hospital, she called me into her bedroom and pulled me real close. She said she loved me, was thankful for me taking care of her, and was proud of the nurse I was going to be. I was sixteen, so I didn't get what she was doing. She never came home from the hospital."

"Sorry. She was lucky to have you." Alex squeezed my hand. "I bet you were a great nurse. What made you quit? Didn't you enjoy helping people?"

I didn't pull my hand away from his. The strength of it around mine felt good. Six more points.

"That's just it. You never really help people. The people like my grandmother, with the multiple diseases on multiple medications? They never get better. You feed them pills and watch them deteriorate until they finally die. Most people aren't willing to make the lifestyle changes it would take for them to get better."

"Is that why you decided to do the alternative health thing?"

I shook my head. "I wish I could say that. Truth be told, when I first got here, I was becoming one of my patients. I was overweight and had just been diagnosed with diabetes and high blood pressure. If I hadn't made the changes I did, in about thirty years, I'd probably have started losing my toes and having heart attacks. Alaysia saved my life. After a few months on her program, my doctor stopped my meds."

Alex's eyes were huge. "I can't believe you didn't tell me this before."

"Why would I have told you all that personal stuff?"

"Monica, it's not personal stuff. Don't you see? What a huge marketing hook for your business.

Not only can you be a gym, but you can market yourself to local doctors' offices as a lifestyle program with a registered nurse who does health counseling that can cure high blood pressure and diabetes."

"I wouldn't say 'cure'."

"Maybe that's a bit strong, but . . ." I could see the wheels in his brain spinning. Being brilliant at business made him even more attractive. Four points.

"You could probably set it up so you can bill health insurance companies. That gives you a broader client base and much more income. Do you have your nurse's license here?"

"No, but it shouldn't be too hard to get."

"Great. Start working on it and we'll put together a database of medical practices and do a brochure specifically for patients with the diseases you mentioned."

I smiled. "You never stop working, do you?"

He shrugged. "It's who I am."

The waitress came and set our plates in front of us. Alex looked over at my tofu. "I promised to taste that, huh?"

"Yep."

We spent the rest of dinner mapping out our new business strategy. While Alex was writing, his arm kept brushing against mine, and he kept touching my hand when he got excited about ideas. His touches intoxicated me, and I had to remind myself we were just hanging buddies. I kept adding up the points and Alex, with his good-looking, good-smelling, brilliant, funny, sweet self, was up to about thirty by the time we finished eating. I had to stop myself from thinking about what kind of husband and father he would make. I was doing that "black woman with a plan" thing he talked about.

Finally, the waitress gave us the "get out of my section so I can serve someone else and get another big tip" look, so I tapped my watch and hinted that maybe we needed to bring our non-date to an end.

"Are you serious? We're just getting started. I thought we might go to the salsa club in Buckhead. That is, if you can dance."

"Is that a challenge, Mr. Thompson?"

"I do believe it is, Ms. Harris."

"In that case, you're on." It just so happened that the Latin dance class at the gym was my favorite. I had learned how to salsa, merengue, mambo, and cha-cha.

I followed him to the club and we parked. He took my hand and led me inside. It was getting harder and harder to think of him as a hanging buddy.

The club was packed to capacity, and the thick air pulsed with the infectious heartbeat of the conga drums. I knew I was the envy of every woman and a few men in the club. Alex was not only gorgeous, but he moved like he had some Cuban in his hips.

I should have known better. Latin dance was way too sensual for hanging buddies. We gyrated and twisted to the Latin rhythms. I rationalized that we were just dancing, but I felt the Holy Spirit tapping me on the shoulder saying, "Excuse me, Miss Thang. What do you think you're doing?" I figured with everything I had gone through the past year, I deserved to have some fun with a beautiful man, so I ignored Him.

After we worked up a sweat, we decided to get some drinks. I ordered iced tea, and Alex got a Long Island Iced Tea. I frowned at his drink order, but after the dancing, I stopped subtracting points. We sat at a table in the corner, hugged up, talking some more. I rationalized that we had to sit close so we could hear each other over the music. I couldn't rationalize his hand on my thigh. I could almost see the Holy Spirit sitting across the table from me, shaking His head, tsk-tsking my bad-girl behavior, but I didn't pay attention. He had to understand how much I needed this.

Alex was at a solid fifty points and counting. After we finished our drinks, Alex fanned himself and suggested we go get some air. He put an arm around my waist and led me outside. I felt like I was the one who had been drinking alcohol.

When we got outside, the March evening air chilled the sweat on my body. Alex held my hand and looked down at me. My heart pounded. Before I could blink, his full, sweet lips were on mine. We kissed until I couldn't breathe. I could hear the Holy Spirit telling me to stop, but I didn't care.

I'll be good tomorrow. I promise. Just let me have this right now.

I kissed Alex again, shocked at myself. He pulled back and smiled.

"What happened to rational adults making a conscious decision?" I asked.

"You're right. We should go back inside. One more dance and we'll call it a night."

Everything was going so well until . . .

This *person* approached Alex on the dance floor. He wore tight jeans and an even tighter muscle shirt, and I could swear he was wearing foundation and eyeliner. "Hey." He stared at Alex too intently.

I looked at Alex to see if he really knew this person. I was shocked when he gave him a hug and said, "Don't you look good."

Forty-nine, forty-eight, forty-seven . . . Alex's points were plunging by the second.

"Monica, this is Shawn, an old friend of mine."

Forty-six, forty-five, forty, thirty-five, thirty . . .

Shawn shook my hand, but looked at Alex. "Old friend? Is that what I am now?" He paused dramatically and looked at me. "Oh, I'm sorry. Shhhh, my bad."

Twenty-five, twenty, fifteen, ten . . .

Shawn slipped Alex a card. "Call me." He walked off.

I looked at Alex. "I'm ready to leave." I didn't wait for his response.

When we got into the parking lot, Alex grabbed my arm. "Whoa, you aren't on a treadmill. Slow down. Let me explain."

I turned around, sure I didn't want to hear his explanation. Last time a man said, "Let me explain," it changed my whole life.

Nineeightsevensixfivefourthree . . .

"I didn't tell you because we were supposed to just be hanging buddies. I didn't expect us to . . . you know, hit it off so well on our first outing. I guess now is a good time to tell you. I'm bisexual."

Negative 100, negative 1,000, negative a million . . .

I nodded and walked to my car, pulling my keys out of my purse.

He followed me. "Monica, wait. I didn't think you'd have such a problem with this. You seem so intelligent and open-minded."

Negative ten to the ninth power, tenth power, eleventh power . . .

I didn't look at him. "Sorry, Alex. I gotta go."

I slammed my car door and drove off before he could say another word.

When I came in the door, Alaysia came running to hear about my date. "Soooooooo?"

"Sooooooo much for you picking me out a man." I slammed the front door. I stormed into my bedroom. I took off my shoes and threw them into the closet. One of them missed and put a small black mark on the wall.

Alaysia's eyes widened. "What's wrong with you? Did he try something?"

I mimicked her voice. "Choose well, Monica. Just go out on a date and try him out, Monica. He's fine, he's smart, he's successful. Forget your two-year wash-out period, Monica." I threw my purse on the bed.

"Calm down. What happened?"

"What happened? I'll tell you what happened." I described our run-in with Shawn at the salsa club. "Mr. Gorgeous, Mr. Perfect, Mr. Brilliant is bisexual."

Alaysia's hands flew to cover her wide-open mouth. "Alex is bi? Who knew?"

"You certainly didn't. 'Let me pick out your next man, Monica'."

Alaysia laughed.

"Please, help me understand what's funny." I stomped into the bathroom and grabbed a wash-cloth and some soap and scrubbed my face and lips where he kissed me. "That's it. I'm swearing off men forever. I will never look at another man, never go out with another man, never marry an-other man. NO MORE MEN." I came back out and paced around the room. "How does this keep happening to me? Am I a gay magnet or some-thing?"

"Technically, Monica, Alex isn't gay. He's bi-sexual. When you think about it, Kevin—"

Alaysia jumped when I let out a loud scream. "This is not the time for a lecture on the different categories of sexual preferences."

"Sorry." Alaysia sat down on the bed. "It doesn't mean you should give up on men altogether. There are plenty of men at Khalil's church you might be interested in."

"Do I look like I'm interested in meeting anyone else?" I gave her the evilest face I could muster.

"Can't say that you do. Not at this minute any-way. I don't want you to give up. You just got the nerve to date again, and just because things didn't go well with Alex doesn't mean—"

"Out. Get out, Alaysia." I pulled Alaysia's arm to get her off my bed and pushed her out the door. "No more matchmaking, thank you. I'm going to the pet store tomorrow to start buying cats. Why wait 'til I get older?"

"Monnie, really, you don't—"

"Out." I closed the door firmly behind her. I let out a scream and pulled off my jeans and turtleneck and took a quick shower before jumping into bed.

I pulled the covers over my head. *God, I know I wasn't supposed to go out with him, so that's on me. I don't want to hear You say I told you so.*

I cried into my pillow. *Help me, God. I'm lonely. I'm trying to be happy with just me and You, but I really want babies and a husband. I know You're my Husband, but can't I have one down here I can hug and kiss, who hugs and kisses me back and keeps me warm at night? Not that You're not enough, but . . . please, God. Please.*

40

I was glad I had to focus on getting the business going. It kept me from thinking about what happened with Alex.

Alaysia and I hired painters to tone down the colors in the gym. We wanted to decrease some of the sensory overload. Alaysia wanted to take down the televisions in the cardio room because she wanted people to be able to focus on how their body felt while they worked out, but I argued that people needed the distraction to make it through their workout. We decided to decrease the levels on the house music some. Alaysia wanted to do smooth jazz and New Age music, but I argued that people came to work out, not sleep.

Our first staff meeting was great. Everyone was excited about Alaysia and I taking over. They were even more excited about their raises. We opened up the floor for suggestions on how people thought the gym could run better. About half of them were feasible, and Alaysia and I decided to incorporate them into our plan.

In six weeks, we were ready for our grand re-opening. I debated as to whether to invite Alex. I felt like he deserved to be there because of all of his help, but at the same time, I felt awkward about what had happened on our non-date. I decided to be a grown-up about it and called him. I went into our office in the gym and closed the door securely behind me.

"Alex? It's Monica."

"Oh, hey, Monica. Long time no hear from. How are things going with the gym?"

"Great. That's why I'm calling. I wanted to invite you to our grand re-opening. It's next Friday evening at eight. It wouldn't be the same without you."

"I wouldn't miss it for the world."

"Good. I'll see you there."

"Okay."

The pregnant silence let me know that he was waiting for me to explain myself.

"Alex, I'm really sorry about the whole episode at the salsa club. I shouldn't have left like that."

"I know I kinda shook you up. It's hard to know when to tell a person, and we were just supposed to be hanging buddies, and I didn't expect for things to, you know, go as good as they did, and . . . well, I'm sorry."

"It's okay, Alex. I'm glad I found out early on, before . . . things got any further."

"Now that you've had time to get used to the idea, I was wondering if you'd like to go out again."

Was he serious? "Alex, I don't know. I—"

"Come on, Monica. I really had a good time that night. I know you did, too. I know what we said about hanging buddies, but I felt like we connected. Like it could be more than that."

I fingered the loops in the telephone cord. "Alex, let me be honest. If I was gonna be with you, I might as well stay with my soon-to-be ex-husband."

"Oh." Silence. "Oh. I didn't know. No wonder you ran off like that. I'm sorry. Must have been traumatic for you."

"Traumatic is a good way to describe it."

We sat there, not saying anything.

"Alex, I still want you to come to the opening."

"I'll be there, Monica. I promise. Maybe we can still be friends. I enjoy your company."

"I don't know, Alex. We sorta proved men and women can't be friends. At least not with such a fine, sexy specimen of a man as yourself."

"You're the sexy one. Especially doing the salsa. Man, you really put it on me."

We laughed. "See you next Friday?"

"I'll be there."

41

The gym was packed to capacity with people wishing us well for our grand re-opening. It was funny seeing people I normally saw only in exercise gear dressed in fancy clothes. I bought a red cocktail dress with the whole upper back out. Alaysia said she had to watch me because I was starting to dress like a hoochie since I lost so much weight. I told her I liked showing my sculpted arms and back. I worked hard to get them that way and deserved to show them off.

Talinda came over with her mom to greet me.

"Talinda, you look great. I can't believe how much weight you've lost." I motioned for her to turn around in a circle.

She posed proudly. "Thanks to you, girl."

I gave her mom a kiss on the cheek. "And you look great, too, Ms. Gaines."

She put her hands on her hips. "Thank you,

baby. Y'all need to start a senior citizens program for me and my friends. If you do it right, I bet they'd all leave the Y and come here."

I nodded. "Sounds like something I need to look into."

Ms. Gaines said, "I ain't trying to waste y'all's catering money. Especially since this is healthy food." She sauntered off to the spread of food we had catered by Whole Foods Market.

Talinda shook her head. "She'd be losing a lot more weight if she'd stop eating so much. I tell her it's not enough to only exercise. She really has to . . . who is that fine brotha over there?"

I followed her eyes across the room and saw Alex. I smiled and waved.

"Girl, you know him? Is he your new man?"

"Naw, girl. I ain't tryin' to get with him. It's a long story."

"What's up with you and these fine men and the long stories? I'm trying to have your kinda drama in my life."

If she only knew.

Alex walked up and kissed me on the cheek and we exchanged a hug. Talinda gave a little wave and followed her mom to the food table.

"Monica, you know you ain't right for wearing that dress." Alex looked me up and down.

I turned slowly, model-style. "You like?"

"Yeah, a little too much. You sure we can't go out again? I promise, no more run-ins with old friends."

I laughed. "Alex, I thought we settled this."

"Can't blame me for trying. I did want to see if you wanted to grab some coffee afterward. I want to talk to you about what you mentioned on the phone."

"What?"

"Coffee. After the opening."

"Alex."

"I only want to talk. I promise. No dancing or anything else."

I hesitated. "Okay, I'll think about it."

"Let me introduce you to a couple of doctors I invited. I sent them your brochure and they're anxious to meet you."

Alex had designed a brochure specifically targeted for doctors' offices. On the front were my before and after pictures, and on the inside, I explained about the diabetes and high blood pressure with my before and after labs and blood pressure readings in there. I knew the doctors liked seeing the numbers on paper. It gave them proof our program worked.

Alex introduced me to the group of physicians he had invited.

"So, this is the nurse you were telling us could 'cure' diabetes and high blood pressure, huh?" A tall, cinnamon-colored doctor shook my hand a little too long.

"I wouldn't say 'cure'." I pulled my hand away and stepped closer to Alex.

I chatted with the doctors for a while then spent the rest of the evening mingling with the other guests. Every once in a while, I looked up to see Alex staring at me. He winked and waved then continued schmoozing. We had some high power clients at our gym, so I hoped he was making some good business contacts.

When the guests dwindled down to a few, Alaysia, Khalil and I started cleaning up. Some of the staff members and regular clients helped out. I noticed Alex talking to Eric, one of the personal trainers, in the corner. He caught my eye and winked. He handed Eric a business card and came over to me.

I raised my eyebrows. "New friend?"

"We were talking business. He wants to open his own gym out in the southeast part of town. Looks like you guys inspired him to strike out on his own."

"Hmmm. He ain't the brightest firefly in the forest. Know that it won't be as easy as working with me."

"Do I detect a hint of jealousy, Ms. Harris?"

"Not at all, Mr. Thompson. Just letting you know what you're getting into."

He smiled. "Ready for coffee?"

I looked around. Most of the guests were gone. Alaysia came over. "You heading out?"

"You guys okay here?" I asked.

"Yeah, we got it. You guys go ahead." She gave me this strange look like she couldn't believe I was leaving with Alex. She walked back over to the food table.

I turned back to Alex. "So, where are we getting this coffee?"

"Wanna go to Tarrazu?"

I shrugged. "Sounds good."

"You can ride with me and I'll bring you back here. No sense in taking two cars."

"No way, man. A girl never knows when she may have to make a quick exit."

He chuckled. "All right then. I'll meet you there in a few."

When I walked into the dimly lit environment, I wondered if Alex had more on his agenda than talking. The café was small, and the tables close and intimate. I followed him to a table in the corner. I purposely sat across the table from him instead of next to him.

He smiled. "Afraid I'll bite?"

"Maybe I'm afraid I'll bite. What's up, Alex? What did you want to talk about?"

"Relax a second. Order some coffee."

"Alex."

He took my hand. "I wanted to talk to you, or let you talk about what you mentioned on the phone."

I frowned. "What did I mention on the phone?"

"You said if you were gonna be with me, you might as well be with your ex-husband. The way you said it, and the way you took off so quick that night at the salsa club let me know something bad must have happened and you're still hurt behind it." Alex shrugged. "I thought you might want to talk about it."

I looked at him. He sat there and waited.

"There's nothing to talk about. I'm trying to put it behind me."

"Doesn't look like you're doing a good job of it."

"Why do you say that? I think I've done a very good job. In the eight months I've been in Atlanta, I've changed my lifestyle, lost a ton of weight, conquered diabetes and high blood pressure, and successfully started a business. I think I'm doing pretty darn good."

"That's not what your eyes say."

I let out a deep breath and picked up a coffee menu. "You buying?"

Alex flagged down the waiter and we ordered two lattes. He put his hand on mine. He wasn't giving off his sensual energy this time. He just felt like a friend.

The jazz playing overhead was soothing. I let it and the rich, robust aroma of gourmet coffee relax me as we sat there listening for a while.

"You remind me a lot of him. Of my husband," I finally said.

"How so?"

"Beautiful eyes that look down deep into my heart, great listener who makes me feel like you're genuinely interested in what I have to say, affectionate and touchy-feely."

"He's not as good-looking as me, though, right?"

"Sorry, Alex. He's better looking than you are."

"Oh, I'm crushed. That means I don't have a chance, huh?" He looked at me with those eyes I thought I could lose myself in. "You still love him a lot, huh?"

The waiter brought our drinks. I took a sip of my latte. Nodded. Took another sip and then picked up a napkin to catch the single tear that escaped my eye.

Alex rubbed my arm. "What happened?"

"I walked in on him and one of his old lovers." I bit my lip. Why was I talking about this?

"Did you know he was bi when you married him?"

I shook my head and wiped my eyes. I hadn't cried about this in months, but talking about it now, it felt as fresh as when it first happened. I guess Alex was right. I hadn't done a good job of putting it behind me. It was like my junk closet at home. I pushed all the feelings inside and closed the door as quickly as I could. As long as the door stayed closed, I was okay. The minute I turned the knob, all the stuff came pouring out.

"So he decided to go back with his old lover?"

"No. He said it was a one-time mistake and he loves me and wants to stay married. He loses it when I even bring up the subject of divorce." I briefly told him Kevin's story. I figured the two of them would never meet, and I felt like I could trust Alex.

Alex sipped his latte. "Sounds like you really love him and he really loves you. You don't think you can forgive him?"

"I have forgiven him."

"Then why aren't the two of you back together?"

"Have you heard anything I've said?" I rolled my eyes. "Why am I explaining this to you? You're okay with this whole mixed sexual preference couple thing."

Alex chuckled. "Your case is different. You said your husband wanted to be straight and he believed God had made him straight."

"Yeah, but obviously He didn't."

"I don't think that one-time event means He didn't."

"Are you telling me you believe God can make a gay man straight?"

"I lost my best . . . 'friend' that way, so yes, I believe it."

"What do you mean, you lost your best friend that way?"

"My partner from one of the best relationships I've ever been in started going to this church pastored by an ex-gay and his wife, and after a lot of church and therapy, he 'changed.' He's happily married now with three kids. His wife is one of the most beautiful people I've ever met."

I looked at him. I tried to suppress the seed of hope rising up in my soul. I was moving on with my life without Kevin, and I didn't want to go daydreaming about God delivering him and us getting back together again.

My heart wanted to believe it, though. Wanted to believe Kevin could be okay and that we could get back together and have babies and I wouldn't end up alone living with fifty cats or dogs or fish or whatever in a cold bed all by myself.

"Monica?"

"Yeah?" I shook myself out of my daze.

"You okay?"

"Just thinking. I don't know what to believe. They actually have churches where they make gay people straight?" I lowered my voice and leaned toward him. The couple at the next table was close enough to hear our conversation.

Alex nodded. "There's this whole national group of ministries of thousands of people who used to be "in the life," who've gone through whatever process they take the people through, and they say they're happily heterosexual now, in healthy relationships, married with kids, all that good stuff."

"How come you never went to one?"

Alex laughed. "Because I'm happy being who I am. I know there are a lot of homosexuals and bisexuals out there who are miserable with their lives—unhappy and gay, as they call them. I'm not one of them. I'm happy being bisexual, and I don't want to change." He leaned closer and spoke right into my ear. "I must admit, meeting you made me think about it, though."

I was too stunned by everything he was saying to respond to his flirting.

"That was a joke, Monica."

"I'm sorry. I'm thinking. After that day, I never considered me and my husband getting back together. I figured it was over and I had to move on. I never thought . . ." I shook my head. "So much for being a Christian with faith, huh?"

"Don't beat yourself up about it. Sounds like the way everything came out was pretty traumatic for you. I think most women would have responded the same way."

Alex put his hand on mine. "I have to get you a copy of the pastor's book. My 'friend' sent it to me a few years back. I guess he was so happy with his new life, he wanted to share it with me. I have to dig it out of a box somewhere."

"Thanks. I'd like to read it."

"I'll have to see if I can get you the pastor's contact information too. They're right here in Atlanta. If nothing else, you should talk to somebody. Whether you decide to stay with your husband or not, you still need to be able to get over this."

"Thanks, Alex." I kissed his cheek. "I might have to take back what I said about us not being able to be friends."

"We can be friends as long as you don't wear those sexy dresses. And you can't be kissing and touching all over me either. I'm still a man."

I laughed.

"Seriously, that's what friendship is all about. Me helping you get back together with your husband and ruining my chances of being able to get with you."

I laughed and punched his arm.

We finished our lattes and Alex walked me to my car. He hugged me. "I'll call you when I find the book. Remember, if it doesn't work out with you and your husband, I might be willing to look into this deliverance thing. You could make me want to change."

I shook my head. "You never stop trying, do you, Alex?"

"Would I be this successful if I did?"

Later that night, when I climbed into bed, Alex's words kept ringing in my head. Could God really make a gay man straight? I knew Kevin would be willing to do whatever it took. I couldn't wait to get the book and contact the pastor Alex mentioned.

Slow down, Monica. I didn't want to get too excited. Hope left too much room for disappointment, and I didn't need any more disappointment in my life right now, especially when it came to Kevin.

God, I don't even know what to pray about this. Don't let me get excited about this if it's not You. I want to believe You brought me and Alex together so he could tell me about this pastor and his wife. If it's just to help my healing process so I can move on with my life, then so be it. But if You really plan on delivering Kevin and . . .

Let your will be done, God. That's all I ask. Your perfect will be done.

42

The next day, I was spotting a client doing chest presses when Talinda came bouncing up.

"Girl, you just had a visitor." She looked like a kid with a big secret.

"Who?"

"Mr. Fine from last night. He left a package for you. That man is some kinda gorgeous. What's the deal with y'all? I wouldn't mind your leftovers in his case."

"Talinda, trust me. Everything's not what it looks like. What did he leave?"

"A big, brown envelope. It's in the office on your desk."

I couldn't think of any paperwork Alex had to drop off, so I hoped it was the book.

When I got to my office, I pulled the book out of a large envelope on my desk. *Touching a Dead*

Man: One Man's Explosive Story of Deliverance From Homosexuality by Pastor Derrick Ford. I stuffed it back into the envelope. I appreciated Alex's discretion. I didn't want anybody jumping to conclusions if they saw me with it. Thankfully, I was finished for the day, so I could go home and read.

I stretched out on the chaise lounge in my bedroom and looked over at the clock. It was almost one in the morning. I had been up the entire evening reading and was almost finished with the book. My head was spinning.

According to this guy, God not only *could* deliver homosexuals, He had. I felt guilty for not believing God was God. I saw how the spirit of homosexuality had preyed on Kevin, much like it had preyed on the pastor in the book. Life circumstances left an open door for the enemy to walk in and set up a stronghold in both of their lives.

I felt the most guilt for my prejudice against homosexuals. Being Alaysia's roommate in college, I had watched her sleep with more men than I could count. I hadn't thought much about her smoking and drinking, and even indulged with her on more than one occasion. I barely blinked when she told me about her hard drug use. I ministered to her about God's forgiveness when she told me about her abortion. I had watched Trina battle with her fornication demon and never condemned her. Why was the whole homosexuality thing the worst sin imaginable when I had easily forgiven other sins?

Of course, there was the fact that Kevin cheated on me, but if he had cheated with a woman, would I have been more ready to forgive him?

The last chapter explaining the title hit me the hardest. It was about Jesus resurrecting Lazarus from the dead and instructing the people to let him out of his grave clothes. In Jewish culture, touching a dead man was a sin and made one ceremonially unclean. For Jesus to tell them to touch him said to defy religious law and be willing to touch a stinking dead person to help them out of the grave and into new life. The church definitely wasn't that way toward homosexuals.

Could I be that person? I pulled up Pastor Ford's website on my computer. I looked at the picture of him and his beautiful wife, both with exuberant smiles. I studied his wife's face. She was gorgeous and obviously not hard up for a man. What allowed her to love her husband in spite of? What kind of woman was she? What did she do when she found out? Did she change up on him or did she love him so much it didn't matter? How did it feel for his ministry to be public?

I thought about Donnie McClurkin. Definitely one of my favorite gospel singers, ever since his first album with New York Restoration Choir came out. I didn't love him any less since he started giving his testimony. If anything, I loved him more for being transparent and willing to sacrifice his reputation for the sake of someone else's soul. Would Kevin want to do that when he got delivered? If he did, would I be able to smile like Dana Ford and support him one hundred percent?

It was too much to think about. I logged off and crawled into bed. Two last questions swam through my mind. Would Kevin be willing to seek help from these pastors? If so, would I be willing to take him back?

43

The next morning, there was a light knock at my bedroom door. "Yes, Alaysia."

She popped her head in the door. "How many Sundays do I have to invite you before you go to church with me?"

I sat up in bed. "Oh, I don't know. How many Sundays did I invite you when we were in college and you never ever went?"

"Is that what this is about? Revenge? I told you about walking in unforgiveness."

I laughed.

"Come on, if it wasn't the bomb, would I invite you?"

"My, how the tables have turned. This used to be me every Sunday."

"I'm through asking. You're going. Today. No excuses. Get dressed."

It wasn't like I had anything else to do. Alaysia

wore jeans to church every Sunday, so I figured I'd do the same, even though it felt weird.

Alaysia was waiting for me in the living room after I got dressed. "You're gonna love it. I promise."

"I'm going on one condition, Alaysia Zaid. You break this rule and I'll never go to church with you again."

"What?"

"No matchmaking allowed. I mean it. No pointing anyone out, no introducing me to anybody then running off and leaving me alone. If I see a hint of matchmaking, I'm out—never to return again."

Alaysia laughed. "Girl, I ain't trying to set you up with anybody but God. He's the only Man you need right now."

"Good. Now that we have an understanding, let's go."

Church was definitely different. For one, the congregation was mixed—all nationalities. Whites, Blacks, Hispanics, Indians, and Asians all worshiped together. The pastors were a mixed couple; she was black and he was white. I had never been to anything but a black church. It made me nervous about the music. That was one thing I was particular about. At Love and Faith Christian Center, Kevin had spoiled me with good worship.

The church was a transformed warehouse with a stage and a podium at the front. There were no pews, just folding chairs to seat about five hundred, much smaller than Love and Faith. The stage had a large keyboard, a guitar, bass and a big drum set. No organ. This definitely wasn't a black church.

The praise and worship was different, but I still enjoyed it. When the praise and worship leader began to usher us into the presence of God, I felt like I was home. He sang from the depths of his heart and took us into the throne room. It reminded me of Kevin, except that instead of a Bishop Walker cutting off the worship to move on with the program, neither of the pastors moved. They let the guy take us higher and higher until I thought my heart would explode. I knew what Alaysia meant about flying to heaven and feeling God. I felt like I was being raptured.

I enjoyed the pastor's teaching too. He sounded just like Khalil. He came at the Word in a different way that made me think outside my traditional Christian box. It made me want to study the Word more. I knew I would definitely be back. Throughout the whole service, Alaysia kept looking at me, I guess to see if I was enjoying myself. When the pastor directed the whole congregation to pray in the spirit, I opened one eye and caught her staring at my lips and had to laugh.

After service, Alaysia hugged a lot of people and introduced me to some friends she'd made. It was weird seeing her all into church. Everyone hugged and kissed her like she was a member.

Khalil came over and gave me a big hug. "Monica, glad to see you here. Got tired of Alaysia harassing you?"

"Yeah, you know how she can be. Sometimes it's easier to give in."

Khalil laughed. "Don't I know it. When she gets something in her mind she wants, I might as well forget it."

Alaysia put her hands on her hips. "Excuse me?"

He kissed her cheek. "Come on, baby, you know it's true." He waved to someone. "Monica, I'd like you to meet a friend of mine." Up walks the praise and worship leader. "Monica, this is David Harper. David, this is Alaysia's best friend and business partner, Monica Harris."

"Nice to meet you." I shook his hand. Oh my God, he was fine. Not pretty-boy fine like Kevin and Alex, but ruggedly handsome. "What a perfect name for a worship leader."

"Yeah, my moms was prophetic." David had the cutest smile.

Khalil said, "You guys wanna grab something to eat? We could catch brunch at The Flying Biscuit. It'll take forever to get a table, but you know we have to go somewhere vegetarian-friendly for Granola Sunshine and Sister Rabbit." Khalil rolled his eyes.

David laughed. "Sure, sounds good to me."

Alaysia looked at me. "Is that okay?"

"Sure. I don't feel like cooking anyway."

Khalil pulled out his keys. "David, you ride with me. You ladies can meet us there."

As we headed out of the building, I grabbed Alaysia's arm and whispered. "I can't believe you're breaking the rule already."

"What?"

"Don't 'what' me. Khalil just *happened* to invite

Mr. Fine Praise and Worship Leader out to lunch with us? This smells like a matchmaking ploy to me."

Alaysia laughed. "It's not like that. David's engaged, but his fiancée lives in Charlotte. He and Khalil are good friends. The four of us go out to eat after church when she comes to town."

Khalil and David followed Alaysia and me to the restaurant nestled at the end of a row of Candler Park specialty shops. We had expected to wait the usual hour for the Sunday brunch, but for some reason, it didn't take too long to get a table. The hostess led us into the big, sunny room with the sunflowers painted on the wall.

After we put our orders in, David turned to me and said, "How'd you enjoy church today, Monica?"

"I loved it. The praise and worship was great. Reminded me of my old church back home."

"Where's back home and what church did you go to?"

"I'm from D.C. I used to go to Love and Faith Christian Center."

"Kevin Day. I'm sure the music was awesome there. He's a great musician and a great worshipper. His new album is the bomb. I'm sure you've heard it."

I shifted in my seat.

"Do you know Kevin personally? I met him at a music workshop and he seemed like a nice guy. I'd love to do some music with him some day. We have a similar worship style."

Alaysia looked at David then looked at me. I could see her trying to think of something to say.

"Speaking of worship style, I've been meaning to ask you. When you say, 'We've entered the presence of God,' or 'We're in the throne room now,' or 'I see the armies of God arrayed against the enemy,' what do you mean? Can you literally see those things? Are you really in heaven while we're in praise and worship?"

David laughed. "The question monster strikes again. I swear, Alaysia, you ask more insightful questions than most Christians I know. I can tell you think about God a lot."

I unclenched my jaw and relaxed my shoulders.

David rubbed his chin. "Let's see. How I can explain this? I don't literally, physically see those things. I see them with my spirit."

"What do you mean? Your spirit has eyes?" Alaysia asked.

"Yes, not physical eyes, but . . ." David furrowed his eyebrows. "It's the spiritual counterpart to our physical sight and hearing. You shut down your physical senses and your spirit man sees what's going on. You connect with God on a plane outside of this natural realm. He gives images of spiritual things that have spiritual meaning."

Alaysia nodded. "Kinda like prophesying, but instead of God saying something into your spirit, He shows you a picture instead."

David said, "Exactly. Are you sure you aren't saved, Alaysia? You have an understanding of things most Christians don't have."

"Yeah, I don't know why she's still holding out. She can't really come up with a good reason." I sipped my water.

The waiter brought our food. The guys had ordered big breakfast platters, but Alaysia and I had gotten salads. The large, fluffy biscuits were the best.

Alaysia shrugged. "I still have a lot of unanswered questions."

Khalil said, "Like what?"

Alaysia thought for a minute. "Like, if God is so good, why does He allow so many bad things to happen in the world? Look at all the poverty, the sickness and disease, the people dying, bad things happening to good people. Why does a good, loving God let so much hurt happen to His people that He's supposed to love so much?"

David looked at Khalil as if to say, "I got it." "The real question is, why do His people allow it to happen?"

I frowned.

David continued, "If you look at God's original plan for man on earth, it wasn't for Him to rule us and govern everything that happens on earth. He put Man in the garden and said, 'Subdue the earth and have dominion over it.' God gave us authority and control on the earth and we were to rule in His name. Adam handed over that dominion to Satan when he rebelled against God in the garden. But Jesus won that legal right to dominion for us at Calvary when He destroyed the works of the enemy. We're supposed to be taking authority in His name and subduing the kingdoms of this world and establishing His Kingdom in the earth. We're looking at Him to fix it, but He's looking at us to fix it. He expects us to rise up and be the sons of God we're supposed to be."

Wow. I had never thought of it that way before.

"So you're saying all the bad things that happen are our fault, and not God's?" Alaysia asked.

"I'm sure He's more upset about it than we are. He gave us all this power and all this authority, and instead of doing something with it, we whine and pray and cry and beg Him to fix everything. Unless the sons of God stand up and act like we know, we'll always be victims of Satan's tools of bondage. We'll be sick, poor, depressed, and victim to every bit of hell he unleashes on us. Until we realize who we are in Christ and the power we have, the world will continue to grow darker and darker."

We all sat there and thought about it for a minute.

I looked at David and Khalil. "Is everyone in your church a Bible scholar?"

They laughed. David said, "The pastors are serious about their leadership having a strong foundation in the Word. Before we're licensed and ordained, we have to go through a very intensive study of the Bible. Either through Pastor's ministry course, or through seminary, like Khalil is doing."

I thought about Love and Faith, where being in leadership was more political than spiritual.

David finished off the last of his pancakes. "Monica, you never answered my question. Do you know Kevin Day personally? I got tickets for Friday's concert, but I would love some backstage passes."

"Friday? I didn't know he'd be here then." I hoped everyone at the table couldn't hear how loud my heart was beating.

"Yeah, Friday. You haven't kept up with him?"

"No. Can't say that I have." Kevin said he would call when he was coming to Atlanta. Had he decided he didn't want to see me? Did I want to see him? Alex's conversation came to mind. Should I give Kevin a copy of the book? I didn't want to give him any false hope of us getting back together. Was it false hope, though?

"Monica?" David was staring at me.

"Huh?"

"Do you think you can get the passes? Will Kevin remember you or have you been gone too long?"

"He remembers me, David." I looked around the table. Alaysia had this strained look on her face, probably upset that her attempt to rescue me from David's questions failed. Khalil was drumming on the table. I could tell he wanted to tell his boy to shut up, but didn't want to embarrass me.

I forced a smile. "I'll get tickets and backstage passes for everybody. We can all go together."

44

First thing I did when I got home was pick up the phone. I dialed my old number, but there was no answer. Kevin was probably out of town, touring somewhere.

I hung up and dialed his cell phone number. No answer. I left a quick message.

I sat on the bed. Maybe Kevin didn't want to see me now. Maybe he decided to go on with his life. Maybe he got tired of waiting for me and found somebody else. I'm sure plenty of women in the choir were glad to see me go, and were waiting to try to snatch Kevin up for themselves. Isn't that what I wanted?

Until I read the book.

I realized no matter how hard I'd tried, I hadn't been able to kill the hope inside of me. Was I too late? He hadn't called me since I called to congratulate him on the album. I tried to call him to tell him about the opening of the gym, but couldn't reach him then either.

The tears started falling. At that moment, I realized how much I missed Kevin.

The phone rang. I jumped to answer it. "Hello?"

"Monica, it's Kevin. I'm glad you called. I lost my cell phone with your number in it in L.A., and we've been on the road, and I lost my address book, and I tried directory assistance, but you guys are unlisted, and you haven't returned any of my emails, and we're gonna be in Atlanta next weekend, and I was afraid I wasn't going to see you, and—"

I laughed as I wiped my tears. I sat down on the bed. "Kevin, slow down. I haven't checked my email lately 'cause I've been so busy. My friend, David, told me about the concert at brunch today."

"Who's David?"

"He's the praise and worship leader at Alaysia's church. He really wants to meet you. He asked if I could get backstage passes. I told everybody I could. I hope it's okay."

"This David . . . is he a friend or is he a—"

"He's a friend. His fiancée will be at the concert, too."

"Oh." I heard him let out a deep breath. "Okay. So you're coming then."

"Of course I'm coming. When do you get to town? How long are you staying?"

"We're in Colombia, South Carolina on Thursday night then Atlanta on Friday night, then I have to do Nashville on Saturday night."

"Gosh, Kevin, don't you get tired?"

"Tired is not the word, Monnie. I'm living purely

off the anointing. Feels like all I do is sleep, eat, and perform."

"When's the tour over?"

"We have a few more stops after Nashville, but we were thinking about adding some cities. It's going better than I thought."

"Just don't overdo it, Kevin. When do you get to stop and get some rest?"

"Rest. What's that? We have a few days after Nashville when I'll probably sleep."

"I guess I won't get to spend any time with you then."

"You want to?"

"Yeah . . . I mean, I haven't seen you in forever, and I thought you said you'd be here a few days. I know you have the tour and all, so maybe I can catch up with you when you finish."

"Ummm, okay."

"What?"

"I'm surprised. You've treated me like I have the plague for the last sixteen months, and now you want to see me and spend time with me? I don't want to be excited about seeing you and then you push me away again. My heart can't take it. So when you say you want to see me, is it a 'Oh, it would be nice to see Kevin' or is it a 'I really want to see Kevin'?"

I held my breath. I walked over to my dresser and picked up Kevin's CD. I stared at the picture. Stared at his eyes.

"Monica?"

"It's a 'I really want to see Kevin'."

Silence.

"Is it a 'I really want to see Kevin because we

have some good memories together and it'd be good to see him for old time's sake,' or is it a 'I really want to see Kevin because I really want to see Kevin'?"

"Kevin, I—"

"I need to know, Monnie. I don't want to be hoping and wishing and then getting a knife through my heart. I finally got my feelings about you where I can deal with them. I don't need to open up my heart to get crushed again. This tour is taking all the energy I got. I can't be—"

"Kevin, I . . . I want to see you because I really want to see you."

Silence.

"Kevin?"

"Don't say that if you don't mean it. I can't—"

"I mean it."

"You do?"

"I do."

"Does this mean—"

"I don't know what it means yet. Can't it just mean I want to see you?"

"Yeah. I guess we can take it from there."

I took a deep breath. "A friend of mine was telling me about this ministry here. It's run by a pastor and his wife. They have a ministry for people dealing with sexual identity issues. A lot of people have been delivered from homosexuality through their ministry. I was thinking—"

"I can't talk about that right now, Monica. Can't it be okay for me just to see you and us enjoy some time together?"

"Okay, Kevin. We don't have to talk about it."

"You didn't talk to these people about me, did

you? Last thing I need right now is to have my face on some tabloid. I can just see it, 'Gay Gospel Artist?' That would ruin everything I've worked so hard for. Please—I don't want you talking to anyone about me. Let me deal with this in my own time."

"I haven't talked to them. You know I would never do anything to affect your career. I just think you need to deal with it, and I think they could help."

"Monica, please. Can we talk about it after the tour?"

"Of course." I tried to keep the disappointment out of my voice.

"You still want to see me?" He sounded like a scared little boy.

"Of course."

Did I? I was feeling that sad Kevin feeling again. I put a smile into my voice. "When do you get into town and where should we meet?"

45

I couldn't believe I was in an elevator going up to Kevin's hotel room. I wiped my palms on my jeans and put my hand on my stomach as if touching it could ease the waves of anxiety rippling through my colon. I found my way to room 1107 and knocked on the door.

"Just a second."

Oh my God, I was about to see Kevin.

He swung open the door. He stared at me for a second and then his mouth dropped. "Monica? You look like a totally different person. You . . . you look . . . great."

Kevin stared at my body, then stared at my face, then back at my body again like he couldn't believe it was me. He pulled me close to him.

I inhaled his scent, his touch, his aura, his love and was completely overwhelmed. The tears started falling. He stepped back into the room and closed the door, still holding on to me.

We stood holding each other for what seemed like forever, as if we could make up for the whole sixteen months we'd been separated with one hug. When we finally pulled apart, Kevin's T-shirt was wet from my tears.

"Oh, sorry." I wiped his shirt.

He took my hand and kissed my fingers. "It's okay. I can change." He stepped back to look at me. "I can't believe how great you look. It's like you're a whole different person."

"I am, Kevin. I really am."

"My goodness, how much weight have you lost?"

"I should be asking you the same thing. What happened to you? You're skin and bones."

He glanced down at his body as if he didn't know how he looked, and shrugged. "Working too hard, I guess." He shook his head and smiled. "Monnie, you look great."

"I wish I could say the same for you." I smoothed a hand across his cheek. "Look at the bags under your eyes. Look how thin you are." My heart pounded in my chest as I considered the unthinkable. "Are . . . are you sick?"

He laughed. "I don't have the dreaded disease if that's what you're asking. I told you about my tour schedule. It's been real tiring these last few months. And if I have to choose between getting some food or getting some sleep, I'd rather sleep. Stop fussing, Monnie. I'm fine."

He pulled me close and kissed my cheek. "It's good to see you."

I pulled back. "I wish I could say the same for you. This isn't good for you, Kevin. You can't keep this up. You're wasting away. How much longer is the tour? Can't you cancel any of the concerts? You need some rest and some food. Why can't you take a few days off? Could you—"

He pulled me into his chest again, I guess to shut my mouth. "Monnie, please—you're making me tired. I can't cancel. We're already sold out in the next few cities. I'm fine. I promise. Stop fussing and let me enjoy the little bit of time I have with you."

He motioned for me to take a seat on the couch. The suite had a king-sized bed, couch, and a small table with two chairs. The décor was fancier than the average hotel.

"Nice room."

"Yeah, they've been treating me pretty well on the tour."

"Where have you been so far?"

"All over the place—Houston, Dallas, Los Angeles, Detroit, New York, Philly, D.C., of course, Miami. You know, the usual spots."

"What's it like being on the road and doing the concerts?"

"I don't want to talk about me. I want to hear about you and your business and this dramatic change. How's your health? Is the diabetes gone?"

I smiled. "Yep. At least it's diet-controlled. I came off the meds not too long after I got here. My blood pressure is normal too."

"I'm glad to hear that. I was afraid you were

going to end up like your mother and aunts and grandmother."

"Yeah. Me, too."

"Tell me about this business. Did you guys open your gym?"

"I can't believe I haven't talked to you." I told Kevin about our "hostile takeover" of Jim's Gym. "I wish you had time to come see it."

"I can come back."

"Yeah. That would be good."

I told him about Alaysia's church, Bible study with Khalil, my Full-Figured Fitness Program, all the restaurants I had tried, all my new friends, and everything that had been going on for the nine months I had been in Atlanta. He listened, hanging on to every word until his eyelids got heavy.

"You must be exhausted, Kevin." I looked at my watch. "I should let you get some sleep before the concert." I stood up to leave.

"Wait. Please, don't leave. We haven't spent this much time together actually talking to each other in forever. I don't want you to go."

"Yeah, but you need a nap before the concert. I hate seeing you this tired. Why don't you lie down?"

He reached for my hand. "Will you lie down with me? Just for a nap. I just want to hold you."

"Kevin—"

He pulled me into his arms and kissed my cheek. "Come on, Monnie. It doesn't have to mean anything. You can walk out of here and never want to see me again. Just let me hold you right now. Let me fall asleep and be able to feel your breathing against my chest. Let me have that. Okay?"

"I guess I could use a few snuggles."

He smiled. We lay down on the bed, fully clothed. Kevin laid his head on my chest and put his arms around me. I rubbed his back.

"I miss you so much. I love you, Monica. God knows I do."

"I love you too, Kevin. Please get some rest, okay?"

He nodded. In a few seconds, his breathing was heavy. I knew he was tired because it usually took him a few tosses and turns to fall asleep. I drifted off myself after a while.

I awoke to the sound of the door opening. Someone flipped on the lights and said, "Come on, Kevin, man. It's almost show time. Get up."

I squinted at the bald-headed, brown man that had used a key card to get into Kevin's room.

"Oops, my bad. Sorry, ma'am. I didn't mean to disturb you." He backed toward the door.

"Ricky?" It was the drummer for Kevin's band.

He stopped. "Do I know you?"

I lifted Kevin's head off me and got up, smoothing out my shirt. "Ricky, it's Monica."

"Monica? Your voice sounds like you, but you don't look like you. "

He hugged me. "Girl, look at you. It's so good to see you. And so good to see you with Kevin. Maybe he can get back to himself now. Please tell me you're coming back to D.C. I don't know how much longer he's gonna make it without you. I feel like we're losing him. The only time he's himself is when he's ministering."

"What do you mean?"

"What's up, Ricky, man? Did I oversleep again?" Kevin sat up, wiping his mouth, reaching for the clock. "Where we at again?"

"Atlanta, man. You straight. We got about an hour before we need to go. We did the sound checks this afternoon without you."

"Oh yeah, Atlanta." Kevin squeezed his eyes shut and opened them again. He looked at me and smiled. "Ricky, man, you see my beautiful wife?"

"Yeah, I didn't recognize her at first. I thought one of the hotel groupies finally wore you down."

"Whatever, man. You know I ain't going out like that."

"Monica, you think you can get him together and have him down in the lobby in about half an hour? He needs some strong black coffee and his vitamins. Should be in his toiletry case. His eye drops are in there, too. Make sure he ain't blood-shot when he comes down. His clothes should be ironed already. I sent them down to the hotel laundry people. You got him?"

I nodded. "Yeah, I think I can handle it." I looked at Ricky then looked at Kevin.

Ricky backed toward the door. "Good to see you, girl. I'll see you back stage after the concert?"

I nodded.

After he left, I looked at Kevin.

"I know what you're thinking. Ricky makes sure I keep it together, 'cause when I get tired, I forget things. He only has a key because when we were in Dallas, I overslept and they were banging on my door and calling my phone, but I didn't answer. They finally had to get a key from the hotel people to get in to wake me up. That's all. There's nothing going on—"

"I wasn't thinking that, Kevin. I was thinking if you're so run down he has to do all that . . . I'm not gonna fuss. I just don't like what this is doing to you."

He smiled and kissed my cheek. "I'm fine. Now come on. Dress me." He held out his arms and flashed a mischievous grin.

I smacked him on the butt. "Dress yourself. I'll start the coffee."

He went into the bathroom and I started making coffee in the hotel coffee pot. I thought about what Ricky said about Kevin not being himself. I knew there was no way I could convince him to end the tour early, but maybe when he was finished I could convince him to come down for some rest. Give him the spa treatment and see if I could put some weight back on him. Was that a good idea, though?

He came out in some black slacks and an olive mock turtleneck with a black sports jacket. In spite of how much weight he had lost, he still looked good. Real good. I inhaled the familiar scent of his cologne. God, how I missed that smell.

He turned around. "How do I look?"

"You look good, Mr. Day. Very good. And you smell good, too. Did you take your vitamins?"

"Yes, ma'am." He dabbed some dark foundation on the bags under his eyes and then looked up at me. "It's just to make my eyes look better. I don't put it on my whole face."

"I didn't say anything and I wasn't thinking anything."

"I don't want you to think I go around wearing makeup."

"You're going on stage. People wear makeup on stage."

"That's the only time I wear it."

"Kevin, stop being paranoid. I'm not thinking anything bad about you."

"I . . . I don't want you to feel like I . . ."

"Don't worry about that. Just worry about getting ready. And put those eye drops in. You look like an ol' alcoholic."

He grinned. "A'ight." He dashed back to the bathroom.

There was a knock at the door. When I opened it, I heard a bunch of shrieks. "Monnie! It's you. Ricky told us you were up here. Oh my God, look at you. You're gorgeous."

I got a group hug from Shavon, Janae, Regina and Tracey. "Girl, it is so good to see you. Where you been? You live in Atlanta now? You coming back home?"

"Hey, you guys. It's good to see you, too." I hugged each one of them. "Tracey, you chopped all your hair off. You look good, girl."

"You the one. Look at you, Monnie. Look like you lost a hundred pounds." Tracey grabbed me around the waist.

"What's the story, Monnie? You went ghost on us and up and moved to Atlanta and left Kevin all jacked up. I thought we were friends. What happened?" Regina asked.

"Girl, shut your big mouth. If she wanted us all

up in her business, we'd be all up in her business." Shavon put her hands on her hips.

Kevin came out of the bathroom. "Hey, y'all. Time to go?"

"Yeah, Kevin. Ricky sent us up to let you know twenty minutes. You ready?" Regina was studying Kevin's eyes. "You take your vitamins and your eye drops? He said he'd have coffee downstairs."

"I made a pot of coffee," I said.

"Girl, we gotta get on the bus," Shavon said. "We can't be late to no more concerts. You're riding with us, right? Wait 'til everybody sees you."

"I drove. I'll meet you guys there."

"Come on, Monnie. We haven't seen you in forever. Hang out with us," Tracey said.

Kevin came up behind me and put an arm around my waist. "Yeah. You can ride with us. We'll bring you back to your car."

"But I have my friends' tickets. They won't be able to get in."

Kevin said, "I have five comp tickets for the front row. Their names are on the list."

I looked down at my jeans and T-shirt. "I can't wear this."

Tracey looked me up and down. "I got something you can wear."

I nodded. "Okay. I guess so."

"I'll be right back with the outfit." Tracey darted toward the elevator.

Kevin smiled. "Cool. We'll see you guys downstairs in a minute. I promise I won't be late. Monica's keeping me in line."

Regina raised her eyebrows. "I bet she is. Go 'head, girl. Keep your man in line then."

"There goes your mouth again. Come on here, girl." Shavon grabbed Regina's arm. "We'll see you guys downstairs in a minute."

46

When I stepped onto the bus behind Kevin, I heard my name being echoed all the way to the back.

"Oh my God, look at her . . . That ain't Monica . . . She looks great . . . Is that really her? . . . Is she going with us? . . . She lives in Atlanta now?"

I received a million hugs as I made my way down the aisle. I didn't know what Kevin told everybody when I left, but they seemed glad to see me. Except Janine. She scowled and gave me a fake hug and an air kiss. Skank ho was probably glad when I left and was probably planning her name change to Janine Day.

"Hey, Janine. It's good to see you." I gave her a big smile.

She pursed her lips. "Good to see you, too, Monica. Glad you lost some of that weight. You look much better." She scrunched up her face like she smelled something bad. I kept walking by.

"Monnie Monnie Monnie Monn-ie, Monnnieee." The horn section sang my name to the tune of the O'Jays "For the Love of Money."

"What's up, dawgs?" I hugged Tony, Eric, Raymond, and Jo Jo.

"Look at this foxy girl." Aaron, the bass player, came up and kissed me on the cheek. "Kevin, man, you better keep your girl under lock and key. If you wasn't standing right here, I might have tried to step to her."

"Aaron, you better step off, man." Kevin laughed.

We took our seats and the bus pulled off. Kevin squeezed my hand. "I'm glad you're here."

I smiled and squeezed his hand back. "Me too, Kevin." He kissed me on the cheek and laid his head on my shoulder. It wasn't two minutes before he was sleep.

When we pulled up at the Civic Center, I shook Kevin to try to wake him up. Ricky came over and stood him up. "Come on, dog. Show time."

"I'm straight, man. I'm straight." Kevin wiped his mouth. He gave me a sheepish smile. "Hey."

"Hey. You okay?"

"Yeah. I'm straight."

We followed everybody off the bus. I went in through the back entrance with them and then told Kevin, "I'm going to my seat. I'll see you afterward."

"Wait. Stay and have prayer with us."

Every time I tried to leave, Kevin kept telling me to wait—right up until it was time for them to go onstage. When I got to my seat, Alaysia, Khalil,

David, and his fiancée, Nakia, were already there. I figured Alaysia and Khalil had probably clued David and Nakia in on the fact that Kevin was my estranged husband because they all looked at me like they were trying to see if I was okay. I plopped in my seat beside Alaysia, but only for a second. When the band filed out onto the stage and started the music, it was on. I stayed on my feet for the rest of the evening.

I would never have guessed it was the same Kevin who couldn't sit still without falling asleep. He was on fire. He led the whole arena into such a place of praise, I thought it was going to explode. Kevin sang, played the guitar, played the keyboards—he was all over the place. When he got it to a certain peak, he switched gears and moved into worship. The whole auditorium was filled with the thick, tangible presence of the Lord. People were weeping with their hands raised, clapping and expressing their worship in all different ways. After two straight hours of singing with only a couple of breaks for water, Kevin signaled the band to start up his signature song. I hoped this was the last one. Kevin had to be tired.

When they finished the last song, Kevin waved and jetted off the stage. The audience kept clapping and started yelling "Encore." I wanted to scream and tell them to shut up. Kevin was too tired and didn't need to come back. They kept yelling, and Kevin came back, carrying his acoustic guitar. He sat on a stool and strummed his guitar, playing the chords to my love song. My heart jumped.

Kevin pulled the microphone closer to him.

"This is my favorite song on the album. I'm gonna do something special for you, Atlanta. This is a song I wrote for the love of my life." He strummed his guitar. "This is the first time I'm performing this anywhere but in the studio. This is for Monica." He started singing, and I felt like I was the only person in the whole auditorium.

Alaysia passed me some tissue to wipe the tears coursing down my face. Kevin winked and blew me a kiss before he left the stage.

I was no more good.

47

We went out to IHOP afterward. The choir packed into booths, and Kevin and I, Alaysia and Khalil, and David and Nakia sat at a table in the back.

"Kevin Day. Man, it's good to meet you." David's face had to be tired from smiling.

Kevin said, "Man, I hear you can put it down too. We gotta hang out when I come back to visit so I can hear some of your stuff. Monica tells me you're a serious worshipper."

David looked at me then back at Kevin. "I'm just trying to please God, man. Just trying to please God." They gave each other pounds.

"Alaysia, I'm glad I get a chance to thank you in person for what you've done for Monica. I still can't believe it's her," Kevin said.

"She did all the work. You should see her at the gym. She's relentless," Alaysia said.

Kevin leaned over and kissed my cheek. "I can't wait to come back and see that."

Alaysia watched Kevin's every move, breaking her stare only to watch me. I smiled and winked to let her know I was okay. She smiled back, but I could tell she wanted to know what was going on.

Kevin turned to Khalil. "Yo, man, Monica tells me you're quite the Bible scholar. I gotta hear some of the stuff you've been teaching her. Sounds like a whole different Bible from the one I've been reading."

"I hope that's a good thing." Khalil frowned.

"It is a good thing," Kevin said. "She's all excited about the Word. More than I've ever seen."

The waitress came and took our order.

I said, "Nakia, it's good to finally meet you. Are you back in town for good?"

"I wish. I live and work in Charlotte, so I can only come visit on weekends. I'm believing God for a good job here in Atlanta, so I can be with my sweetie." Nakia kissed David's cheek. She was cute. One of those petite girls with the fly short haircuts, perfect skin and sassy smile that I used to hate so much in the throes of my fat girl syndrome.

"How did you guys meet?" I was glad to be delivered from my skinny girl hateration. Nakia seemed nice, and I looked forward to getting to know her. She was one of those people you felt like you were close friends with within five minutes of meeting them.

"David and I met almost four years ago at church. I fell in love with him the first time I

heard him lead praise and worship, but I was trying to be a virtuous woman and let my husband
find me instead of me going after him. Everybody
was loving praise and worship, but it was painful
for me 'cause I was lovin' me some David Harper
and he was playing the "just friends" game. I ain't
one of those musician groupies. Something about
seeing a man functioning under the anointing does
something to me, especially a worshipper with a
heart after God. It was too much for Nakia." Nakia
fanned herself and leaned toward me. "Girl, I know
you know what I'm talking about if nobody else
does."

I smiled and glanced at Kevin. "I feel you, girl."

Nakia continued, "When I found out my job
was transferring me, I figured David wasn't God's
choice for me, so I decided that moving to Charlotte was the best way to get him out of my system. After my going away party by the singles'
ministry, two days before I was leaving, brotha
decides to profess his undying love for me. Says
he was shy, but God spoke to him when we first
met and said I was supposed to be his wife. He
was waiting for the right moment and figured
since I was leaving, he better make his move. We
didn't start our relationship until I was living
three hours away."

Everybody laughed.

"Better late than never." David squeezed Nakia's
hand. "I'm telling you, babe, God knew what He
was doing. My moms named me right. Yeah, I'm
David the worshipper, but I also have some of my
namesake's other characteristics. God wanted to

honor your desire to be a virtuous woman, so He knew I needed to court you from a different city."

"Court? David, you so old." Nakia laughed.

I really liked them together and said a silent prayer for God to open up an opportunity for Nakia in Atlanta soon.

"Kevin, how long have you had your Triton?" David asked.

"Monnie bought it for my birthday a couple of years ago. Best keyboard I ever played. I love it. You got a Triton?"

"Man, I wish. I'm trying to be like you when I grow up. I have a Trinity. Maybe Nakia will get me one for our wedding gift."

"I ain't buying you no wedding gift." Nakia held her arms out and winked. "I *am* your wedding gift, baby."

"See, that right there is what I'm talking 'bout," David said. "You don't need to live in Atlanta until the wedding day. Just drive from Charlotte in time to say I do."

Everybody laughed. We talked over pancakes and omelets for about an hour, then Kevin started nodding off.

Ricky came over to our table. "A'ight chief. Time to get you back to the hotel. We gotta do this all over again tomorrow night."

Kevin said his goodbyes to everyone and exchanged numbers with David. "Yo, man, maybe you can come up to D.C. some time soon and hang out with me in the studio."

David's smile looked like it was going to crack

his face. "That sounds great, man. Just let me know when."

Kevin grabbed my hand. "Ready?"

I nodded. Alaysia gave me a questioning look. "My car's back at the hotel. I'll be home in a little bit."

The bus trip back to the hotel was quiet. Kevin fell asleep before we even got comfortable in our seats. As we pulled up to the parking lot, I searched for my keys.

Kevin woke up. "Would it be too much to ask for you to stay with me tonight? I'm not ready to let you go yet."

"Kevin, I don't—"

"Please, Monnie. Like I said before. It doesn't have to mean anything. I just need a good night's sleep. I slept so good this afternoon." He smiled his crooked, little-boy grin. "If I get some good rest tonight, I think I can finish out this tour."

"You ain't slick, Kevin. Don't be trying to make me feel bad."

"Did it work?"

I laughed.

"Come on. Don't be skeered. I won't do nothing."

I shook my head. "You're trying to make this difficult, aren't you?"

"I promise I'm not. I don't know when I'll get to see you again."

I traveled with a stocked gym bag in my trunk, so I decided I could stay. When I got up to the room, I changed into a T-shirt and shorts to sleep in. Kevin wore his usual silk pajamas.

I climbed under the covers and Kevin got in

bed soon after. Being close to him, smelling his cologne, and being in bed together made the emotions well up. This was a bad idea.

Kevin's soft lips grazed my neck. My heart beat faster. *God, did I make a big mistake? What am I doing in bed with Kevin?* His lips moved up to my cheek. He snuggled closer and I felt him sigh. What if he didn't keep his promise? What if he tried something? Should I get up and leave?

Next thing I knew, he was snoring. I relaxed. I fingered his comb twists and thought about Dana Ford. Could I really do this?

Whoever made up the wedding vow "For better or for worse" must have gone through something. Was I willing to love Kevin through his broken state and walk with him through the healing process? That's what love would do. That's what God had done with me and every other person who accepted Christ as their Savior. Complete forgiveness and unconditional love—no matter what.

Could I really love like that?

48

The next day, after helping Kevin get packed and loaded onto the bus and after a difficult goodbye, I came home and crashed in my bed. The night was exhilarating and confusing, and I was worn out.

I woke up feeling much more rested, but anxious about the night before. Kevin said it didn't have to mean anything, but it meant everything. It meant he still wanted to get back together and I wanted to get back together, and somehow we had to make things work. He said after the tour was over, he'd be willing to look at the book and talk to the pastors to see how exactly one could get delivered from homosexuality.

Then, there was the whole logistical issue. He lived in D.C. I lived in Atlanta. I wasn't trying to go back to D.C. I liked my new life here and had just started a business. On the other hand, I knew it would take an act of God for Kevin to leave Love and Faith and Bishop Walker. Maybe I was getting ahead of myself. I decided not to try to figure out everything and just let God do whatever He planned to do.

I heard the front door close and a few minutes later, there was a light tap on my door.

"Come on in, Alaysia." She must have just finished her Saturday Yogaerobics class. After an in-depth discussion with Khalil about the spiritual ramifications of practicing a Hindu tradition, Alaysia decided to keep the yoga positions, but to forgo the chakras and other spiritual babble. I prepared myself for the interrogation.

She popped her head in. "Just wanted to make sure you were alive. Last time I saw you, you were on your way to pick up your car and you'd be home in a few minutes." She glanced down at her watch. "Those were some long minutes."

"I'm fine, Alaysia. Nice to know you care."

She came in and plopped down at the foot of my bed, kicking her shoes off onto the floor. "Soooooooo . . ."

I shook my head and laughed. "It's killing you, isn't it? You have to know what's going on."

"You have to admit your recent behavior has been a bit curious. You and Kevin hugged up at the table at IHOP and then you don't come home. I mean, technically you two are still married, so it wasn't like you were off committing some rampant acts of sin. I'm surprised, that's all. Not that I'm not happy for you. I think. If you want me to be happy for you then I am. If you're happy, that is. You certainly look happy, but then again—"

"Alaysia." I held up my hand to stop her rambling. "First of all, it wasn't like that. I didn't . . . you know, do anything. We just snuggled and fell asleep."

"I wasn't asking. It's not like it's any of my business. You don't have to tell me anything."

"Okay." I turned over and pulled the covers up around my shoulders. Ten, nine, eight, seven, six, five—

"Okay, Monnie. Stop playing. What's going on?"

I laughed and sat up in bed. "That's what I thought." I told her about my conversation with Alex and about the book. I told her about the pastor's past lifestyle and about his deliverance and happy marriage. I couldn't tell if she was nodding to be polite, or if she believed what I was saying.

"So?" As much as I didn't want it to matter, her opinion counted.

"So what?"

"So, what do you think, Alaysia? Am I totally crazy? Do you think God can make Kevin straight?"

"Monnie, I can't tell you if you're crazy or not. This is a decision you're going to have to make and live with, and my opinion is not gonna be enough to get you through it."

Alaysia shook her head. "That being said, this is another one of those things I don't understand about you Christians. You always talk about how great God is and how He can do anything and how with God, nothing's impossible. But when it comes right down to it—when it's time to put your heart where your mouth is, you guys flake out.

You talk about having faith, but when it's time to have faith, you get fearful. Either God is God and you believe Him, or He's not and you don't. Which is it?"

"Dang, Alaysia."

"I don't mean to make you feel bad, but there's so many inconsistencies. There's the God of the Bible, and then there's the God of the present day Christian. If God is the same yesterday, today, and forever, why are you guys so different from the people in the Bible? I mean, I sit around listening to Khalil and David and I feel like I could walk on water. Like I could become a Christian and we could take over the world and dominate for Christ. But then I look at the Christians I know, and it seems like all there is to Christianity is going to church on Sunday, Bible study on Wednesday night and then talking about how awesome God is, but living mediocre lives. Makes it seem like it's all words and no real power."

Alaysia pulled her knees into her chest and stared out the window. "But then I see how God brought me and you back together and brought me and Khalil back together, and how He miraculously gave us the club and how nothing bad has happened to anyone I love and I think maybe there is something to this God stuff. All I wanted was good friends and a man I could love and marry and have beautiful babies with, and to be able to help other people and make a difference in the world, and He's given me that and more. I guess I babbled all that to say God is God, Monnie. If He can create the whole world as we know it just by speaking a word, don't you think delivering Kevin and restoring your marriage is an easy thing?"

I couldn't even answer. I threw the covers off and reached over to hug Alaysia.

"What?"

"Nothing, Laysia. You're right. God is God and He definitely answers prayer."

49

Kevin and I talked almost every day for the next couple of weeks. We didn't stay on the phone long because he was either always resting from a show, resting for a show, or rehearsing for a show. He sounded more and more tired every time I talked to him. I was glad he only had a couple more cities before the tour was over.

He called late one night while I was in a deep sleep.

"Hey, Monnie. I got some great news." I could hear him strumming his guitar softly. I recognized the chords to my love song.

I sat up and looked over at the clock. It was after midnight. He must have just finished a concert.

"What is it?"

"Bishop Walker called to let me know we got

the extension contract. We're adding nine more cities to the tour."

I didn't say anything.

"Hello?"

"I'm here."

"Did you hear what I said? We got the extra tour dates. I'm gonna head for D.C. next weekend to do an anniversary concert for Bishop, then we'll be off to Cleveland."

I didn't say anything.

"Monnie, are you awake?"

"I'm awake. Just concerned about you. Can't they give you a few weeks to rest first?"

"We don't want to lose any momentum. And stop worrying. I'm loving every minute of it. I can rest later. We'll be in Savannah in three weeks. I was wondering if you wanted to come down and meet me. My next city won't be for four days, so I'd be able to come to Atlanta afterward for a few days."

"That sounds good, Kevin. Let me know the exact dates and I'll clear my schedule."

"I guess I should, uh . . . book a hotel or something?"

"Uh . . . I guess . . . I guess that would be best. I don't know, really."

Kevin laughed his deep, sexy laugh. "This is kinda weird, huh? I don't know either. Don't worry about it. A hotel is fine. Better if you'll come stay with me."

"Kevin, I don't know."

"It'll be like last time. I promise. We can keep things like before we got married until we figure out exactly what we're doing here."

I turned on the lamp on the nightstand. A warm glow filled the room. "Okay. That sounds good."

"What are you doing for your big day?"

"Huh?"

"Don't tell me you're getting senile already. Next Friday, your birthday."

"Don't remind me. I can't believe I'm gonna be thirty. It all goes downhill from there."

"Nonsense. You only get better as you get older."

"Good answer. I don't have any real plans. Knowing Alaysia, she'll try to throw a big surprise shindig together. She makes such a big deal of birthdays." I tried to sound nonchalant. "Why? Are you coming?" I was surprised at how much I wanted him to be there.

"Unfortunately, I can't make it. I'll be in San Francisco. I wish I'd known sooner that you'd actually want me to be there."

"I thought you guys already did California."

"We did L.A."

"Seems like you would have done all of Cali while you were out there. Doesn't make any sense for you to have to go back. I thought you had Bishop's anniversary concert Sunday."

"I do. I'll leave San Francisco Saturday morning and do Bishop's concert Sunday night."

"That doesn't make any sense, Kevin. It's too much flying all over the place."

"I know. How 'bout I let you plan my future tours?"

"I might have to. I'll make sure you only have

one concert a week, and you'll fly everywhere instead of riding that stupid bus."

"On second thought, I better stick with Bishop's manager. You'd ruin my career."

"Yeah, but I'd probably save your life."

"Okay, Monnie, I'm hanging up before you get on your soapbox."

"You know I'm right."

"'Night, Monnie. I love you."

"I . . . I love you too, Kevin."

50

On the morning of my birthday, I waited in bed as long as I could. I heard Alaysia banging around in the kitchen, making our protein shakes. I tipped into the kitchen, not wanting to spoil any potential surprise.

"I was wondering if you were getting up. You going to yoga?" Alaysia handed me my shake.

I looked around the kitchen. "I guess so."

"What's wrong with you?"

I shrugged. "Nothing. Just thought I'd be getting a special birthday breakfast or something. I only hit the big thirty once, ya know."

Alaysia slapped her forehead. "Oh, no!" She walked over to the fridge and flipped a page on the calendar. "It's May twenty-ninth. Your birthday. I am the world's worst friend." She walked over and gave me a hug. "I'm sorry. I've committed the worst breech of friendship. On your big thirty? Why didn't you remind me?"

My eyes widened. "Remind you? Miss Decorate For Every Holiday? Miss Never Forget a Birthday? I didn't think I had to remind you."

"You know how busy we've been with the business, and I've got these new massage clients, and you know I'm trying to do my billing right. And you know Khalil is—"

"Don't worry about it. It's not that big of a deal."

"It is that big of a deal. Let me make it up to you. I'll throw together something real special. We can go to whatever restaurant you pick. I'll call David. I don't think Nakia's coming this weekend, so he should be free, and I'll talk to some people at the gym today. Where do you want to go?"

"I said don't worry about it."

"Monnie, please don't be mad. I'm sorry."

"I'm not mad. It's cool."

I didn't bother to finish my shake and went back to my bedroom. Did she really forget or did she have something up her sleeve? I remembered when she threw my twentieth birthday surprise party at our condo. I knew weeks before because I heard her making plans and found the invitations stuffed in her bottom drawer, the presents hidden in the back of her closet, and the decorations in the trunk of her car.

I had snooped for the past two weeks and hadn't found any clues of her putting together a surprise party. No one at the gym had let anything slip, and Alaysia hadn't been acting suspicious. All signs pointed to the fact that she actually forgot my birthday.

She popped her head in the door. "Going to yoga?"

"Don't feel like it."

"Monnie, please don't be mad."

"I'm not mad." I wouldn't even look at her. "I just don't feel like it. Is that allowed?"

"Don't forget you agreed to take Zanetta's training clients this afternoon. She has a three, four, and a five. She's out of town with her hubby."

I sat up. "I didn't agree to take Zanetta's clients. Why would I agree to be stuck in the gym on my birthday? In fact, Zanetta was supposed to take my step classes this evening so I could be off."

"She didn't mention it to me. Is there anyone else that can take them?"

"At the last minute? I doubt it." I flopped over in the bed, giving Alaysia my butt to kiss. Great. Not only did she forget my birthday, but now I was going to be stuck in the gym all day.

"I'm sorry, Monnie. If you had reminded me, we could have planned and had you off."

"Forget you, Laysia. And right now, I really could if I tried."

She closed the door softly behind her.

I refused to cry. First Kevin, now Alaysia. I couldn't blame Kevin because his tour schedule had been planned way in advance, but Alaysia? My thirtieth birthday? She'd call some people and throw something together?

Unforgivable.

Fifteen minutes later, the doorbell rang. I wasn't about to answer it. Whoever it was at the door was persistent and kept ringing.

I stomped into the foyer and threw open the door. "What?"

The young man standing there dressed in a black suit with a hat jumped. "Sorry to disturb you, ma'am. I'm looking for Monica Harris-Day?"

"That's me."

He looked down at my pajamas. "I was instructed to pick you up at nine o'clock."

"There must be some mistake."

"I was supposed to give you this."

He held out a note. I snatched it from him and opened it. I recognized Alaysia's handwriting.

> *Ha, Ha, Ha, I got you. Happy 30th, Monnie. I would never forget your birthday. Hurry up and get dressed. Wear something comfortable. You have a full day planned and you can't be late.*
>
> *Love, your best friend forever,*
>
> *Alaysia*
>
> *P.S. My goodness! Turning thirty has made you snippy. Please treat the limo driver nicely.*

"Where did you get this?"

"The lady that hired me brought it down to the car five minutes ago as she was leaving." He looked down at his watch. "Will you be ready soon? We're supposed to be somewhere by nine-thirty."

"I'll be downstairs in fifteen minutes."

51

I couldn't have asked for a better day. The limo driver, Nathan, dropped me off at Spa Sydell in Midtown, where I got the full-day pampering treatment including a facial, manicure, pedicure, hot rocks massage, and seaweed wrap. I was nearly comatose when Nathan picked me up. He took me back to the condo and passed me another note.

> *I know you're in your post pampering high, but try to limit your nap to only an hour. Nathan will be back to pick you up at 7:30.*
> *P.S. Your outfit is in your closet.*

I couldn't get upstairs fast enough. When I threw open my closet door, I gasped at a gorgeous, black party dress with a halter-top and the back out. Alaysia was with me when I tried it on at Nordstrom's three weeks ago. I didn't buy it because I didn't have the nerve to go braless as the dress required. Not that I had a chest anymore. It was the first thing to go when I started working out. The DD queen was barely filling a C. I looked down and saw some black sling-back pumps and a little black beaded purse.

There was no way I could nap for an hour. I was too excited about where Nathan would be taking me.

At 7:30, Nathan picked me up in the limo and took me to Khalil's church. White tea lights and balloons decorated the front. A large banner in the window read: HAPPY 30TH, MONNIE!

My mouth fell open when they switched on the lights and I heard "Surprise!" The sanctuary was set up with a big buffet table and a bunch of tables and chairs. It was filled with my friends from the gym and new friends from the church.

Alaysia came up and gave me a hug. "How's this for throwing a little something together?"

I hugged her. "Laysia, you are the best. I'm sorry for this morning. I didn't—"

"Girl, you know best friends are no matter what. You was a trip this morning, though."

I laughed. "I'm sorry. I love you, girl."

I felt someone putting their hands over my eyes. The cologne smelled like . . .

"Kevin!"

He picked me up in a hug then planted a big kiss on my lips.

"I didn't think you could be here. What happened?"

"Come on, now. You didn't think I would miss this, did you? You almost found me out asking all those questions about California." He held me at arm's length. "It's a good thing I did come. I couldn't have you out here in this dress with all these men here. I need to mark my territory." He walked around me. "Baby, you look so good, it's a . . . you should . . . shoot, I can't even think straight. You just look good."

I laughed and kissed his cheek. "Thanks, Kevin. I'm glad you're here."

"Ahem." Alaysia put her hands on her hips. "You do have other guests here."

I turned around and there stood my parents. "Mommy! Daddy!" I grabbed them both and held them tight. "I can't believe you came. You guys actually got on a plane?"

"Monica, look at you. Look at that dress," Mommy whispered in my ear. "I told you Kevin would come back when you fixed yourself up."

I laughed and kissed her cheek. "I guess you were right, Mommy." Might as well let her believe her version of the truth.

"Hey, baby girl." Daddy held me tight. "Me and your momma miss you so much."

I kissed his cheek. "I miss you guys too, Daddy."

I really did. I felt bad that I hadn't seen them in so long. We talked on the phone at least once a week and they were real disappointed when I didn't come home for Thanksgiving and Christmas, but said they understood.

"How long are you guys staying?"

Daddy said, "I'm sorry, baby girl. We gotta get

back for church on Sunday. It's Pastor Clayton's anniversary, and all deacons have to be there."

I rubbed his bald head. "That's okay, Daddy. You being here tonight is more than enough. Where are you staying?"

"Miss Alaysia got us at this high falutin' hotel up the street. Had that boy pick us up in a limo. I tell you, that girl knows how to treat people. Everything been real nice. 'Cept the food here at the party. I see why you lost all that weight if that's how she feed you. Ain't a lick of meat in this place."

I laughed and kissed his cheek. Alaysia grabbed my arm and led me toward the buffet table. "Speaking of food, come check out your spread."

I walked the length of the table. Alaysia had all my favorite dishes from all my favorite restaurants.

"And there's plenty of chocolate soy ice cream in the freezer."

"Alaysia, you outdid yourself this time."

She wiped her forehead. "Whew, this was a lot to put together from the time you reminded me it was your birthday this morning."

Talinda came up and gave me a hug. "Happy birthday, Monnie. Boy, this almost killed me. I'm the worst at keeping secrets, but Alaysia threatened my life." She saw Kevin standing beside me. "Oh my God! It's you." She grabbed his hand. "I love your album. I'm glad you're here. With Monnie. That the two of you are here together. At least I think you're together. Well, you look like you're together, but I guess that doesn't mean you're together . . ."

Kevin laughed. "And you are?"

"Talinda Gaines. Your wife's most devoted client and your most devoted fan."

"Great to meet you, Talinda." Kevin kissed her hand.

Talinda whispered in my ear. "Since you guys are back together, that means you can hook me up with your boy over there." She nodded toward Alex. I smiled and waved him over.

He gave me a big hug and kiss on the cheek and then held me at arm's length. "Dang, girl. You look good. I told you about wearing those dresses."

Kevin took a step closer to me and put his arm around my waist.

"Kevin, this is Alex. Alex, this is my husband, Kevin."

Alex's eyes widened. "Your husband? Oh." He shook Kevin's hand. "Good to meet you." Alex looked at me with a mixture of surprise and joy and then back at Kevin. "Good to meet you."

I held Kevin's hand. "Alex is the business consultant I told you about that helped me and Alaysia get the gym going. He's also a good friend."

Kevin shook his hand warily as if he should worry about how good a friend Alex had been.

"Alex, this is my friend, Talinda. She's one of my clients at the gym."

Alex kissed her hand. "Nice to meet you, Talinda." Alex kissed Alaysia's cheek and hugged her. "And how have you been?"

"I'm good, Alex. It's good to see you."

"Thanks for inviting me." He winked at her.

Talinda linked her arm through Alex's. "Alex, Monica tells me you're a business consultant. I wanted to talk to you about an idea I've been tossing around." She led him off into the crowd. I wanted to warn her, but I knew Alex would disclose things soon enough.

Kevin leaned in close to me, looking around the room. "You got any more 'friends' I need to be worried about?"

I laughed and punched his arm. "No, Kevin."

David and Nakia walked up and gave me a hug.

"Nakia, you're here. I didn't think you were in town this weekend."

"I wouldn't miss your thirtieth."

David and Kevin gave each other pounds. David said, "Man, it's good to see you again. You gonna be in town long enough for us to do some music?"

"I wish. I gotta fly out first thing in the morning. Got a concert tomorrow night."

The crowd grew thinner as the night wore on. I kissed my parents goodnight as Nathan ushered them to the limo. Finally, it was just me and Kevin, Alaysia and Khalil, and David and Nakia. We sat around a table, nibbling on cake and ice cream, and talking.

Nakia took David's hand. "Not to steal the attention from Monica's birthday party, but I have some good news. I got a call today at work from the district manager here, and my transfer has been approved. I'll be starting here the end of next month."

David jumped up and swung Nakia around. She squealed.

"I guess you guys can set your wedding date now," Khalil said. "You should go ahead and put in for your dates here at the church. There's a lot of weddings coming up."

"I can't believe we actually get to set a date. I was starting to believe I was going to be engaged forever," Nakia said.

"A spring wedding would be great," Alaysia said.

"Spring of next year?" David frowned. "I can't wait that long to get married. Having you here in the same city every single day of the week? Naw, man, ain't no way I can make it a year."

Nakia laughed. "You so silly. How long do you think it takes to plan a wedding?"

David shrugged. "What's the big deal? You get a preacher, you get a dress, you rent a few tuxes, walk down the aisle and boom, that's it. You're married. I never understood why you women get all stressed out over a wedding."

I sighed. "Spoken like a true Y-chromosome bearer. Don't worry, Nakia. Men have no clue about these things. All they do is show up. They must think some magic wedding fairy does all the work."

"What are you trying to say?" Kevin frowned. "I helped with our wedding."

"Yes, dear, but you're not the average Y-chromosomer," I said.

Kevin clenched his jaw.

God, help me get my foot out of my mouth. I turned to Nakia. "I happen to have the most helpful, wonderful, thoughtful husband on the face of the earth. Not every woman can be so blessed." Kevin's jaw relaxed.

"Hey, I resent that. I think." David furrowed his eyebrows.

"Yes, think hard, David dear," I said. "Because if you resent it and say that you're equally wonderful, thoughtful and helpful, you're stuck planning a wedding. If you agree, then you've admitted that you're the average macho boob." I winked at Nakia.

"David, man, this is one of those situations where it's best not to answer. You can never outthink a woman. Learn that before the wedding and you'll have a much happier marriage." Kevin looked at his watch. "Yo, man. It's almost two in the morning. I gotta get some sleep."

David took Nakia's hand. "I better get you to your momma's house. I'm sure with you being out this late, she must think I got you somewhere 'having my way with you'."

Nakia giggled. "Yeah, you're right. We better go."

As they were leaving, I turned to Alaysia. "Do we need to clean up all this stuff?"

"Girl, you know me better than that. I'm gonna pack up whatever food is left and then I have a cleaning crew coming in first thing tomorrow."

"Wonderful. Leftover rabbit food. I'll start packing it up." Khalil walked over to the buffet table.

"I know Nathan is gone, so I guess I'm riding with you," I said to Alaysia.

Kevin took my hand. "I kinda thought you'd be going to the hotel with me. I wanted to spend more time with you before I fly out."

"Oh . . . yeah. That's cool, but what about clothes? I don't have my car, so I don't have my gym bag."

Alaysia pointed to the table filled with my birthday presents. "Somewhere in that stack over there is a box with some new exercise clothes in it. Be right back." She walked over to the table.

"Don't worry," Kevin said. Same rules as last time. I'll just hold you and we'll go to sleep. I won't try anything."

"Okay." I took off my pumps. They were cute, but my baby toes had enough.

Kevin looked around the room. "Great party. You have a really nice life here—your friends, your church, your business. I'm glad God worked things out for you. I was worried when you first left, but I guess He knew what He was doing."

"I know. Every day when I wake up, I thank Him for my life right now. I never thought I would be happy again."

Kevin's face fell.

"I didn't mean . . ."

"Yes, you did. It's okay. I'm sorry I ever made you feel that way."

"I know, Kevin. Let's not focus on that, though. Let's focus on moving forward."

"How, though? You have your life here. I can't

ask you to leave that. And I have my life at Love and Faith with the choir and Bishop and . . ."

I winced when he said "Bishop."

"I don't know, Kevin. But God knows. Let's let Him work it out."

52

Alaysia picked me and Kevin up at the hotel and we dropped Kevin off at the airport. He held on to me extra long and extra tight, like he wished he could squeeze away the pain he had caused me.

"I love you, Monnie. God's gonna have to work this thing out soon. I want to spend some more time with you."

I laid my head on his chest. "I know. He will."

We couldn't linger too long because a policeman came and told us we had to move the car.

Alaysia patted my arm when I got back in the car. "You okay?"

I nodded. "Yeah." I watched Kevin until he disappeared into the airport terminal.

"I'm gonna let you drop me off at the house and then you can go pick your parents up at the hotel. What are you guys doing today?"

"I'm taking them to brunch and then on a tour of Atlanta. They've never been here before and want to do the Coca Cola museum, the King Center and Underground, Stone Mountain, you know—the works. It's gonna be a long day."

"Girl, I haven't done most of that stuff, and I've been living here how long?"

"I know, right? Me either."

"Maybe me and Khalil should schedule a sight-seeing day. I don't think he's done the tourist thing either."

"Speaking of Khalil, he seemed all shifty and nervous during the marriage conversation last night. Are you guys talking about it?"

Alaysia looked over her shoulder to check for traffic and merged onto the freeway. "No. Not even in casual conversation. Do you think he doesn't want to marry me?"

"Dang, Alaysia, cut the man some slack. You guys have only been together for six months."

"This time. We were together before off and on for three years. We lived together for eight months. It's not like we're just getting to know each other. And he talked about marriage all the time then."

"Yeah, but you're a whole different person and he's a whole different person. Give him some time."

"You think he doesn't want to marry me because I'm not saved?"

"No, because if that was the case, he wouldn't be with you at all."

"Then what is it? Why hasn't he even mentioned it?"

"What's the rush? Why are you so anxious about it?"

"You're right. I guess I'm not walking in faith, huh? Are you supposed to have faith when it comes to love and matters of the heart, though? Does God get involved in that too?"

"Of course. He cares about every area of our life. Especially that one."

I was counting on it.

By the time my parents and I got through with the Coca Cola museum and the King Center, I was tired. When we got into the car, I asked them, "Are you sure you guys want to go all the way out to Stone Mountain? It's just a big rock with some men on horses carved in it."

Daddy pulled his souvenirs from the King Center out of his bag. "I don't know when we gon' get back down here. I want to see everything in one trip. I ain't gettin' on no more planes after today, and I can't drive that far with yo' mama. She got to stop and pee every three hours."

"We ain't been on a trip since your prostate started actin' up, Hershel. I bet you'd be the one having to stop all the time."

"Why you got to tell all my bidness?"

"Monica's a nurse. She understands all that stuff."

I had to laugh. It had been a long time since I'd seen Mommy and Daddy, and I missed these little interactions. "Stone Mountain it is. Then we'll go to the mall out at Stonecrest."

"Naw, now. I ain't trying to be shoppin' all day. You can drop me off after the mountain." Daddy folded his arms across his chest.

"But the mall is out there near the mountain. It doesn't make any sense for me to drive all the way back into the city."

"I ain't goin' to no mall wit' two women. I love y'all, but ain't that much love in the world."

"Okay, Daddy. Me and Mommy can go to a different mall."

"We don't have to go to the mall, Monica. You see one mall, you seen them all," Mommy conceded.

We drove in silence for a while.

"So you and Kevin back together?" Daddy asked.

I knew it was coming. I was surprised it took this long for one of them to ask.

"We're working on it, Daddy."

"Working on it? Does that mean you're moving back to D.C.? Y'all young folk don't make no durn sense these days. Working on it. What kind of—"

"Hershel, don't trouble Monica." My mother turned toward the back seat and undoubtedly cut her eyes at my dad.

"I ain't troublin' her. Just don't make no sense to me. Married woman up and move to another city and leave her husband. Y'all watch too much of that Oprah and that *Lifetime* TV. Give you all kinds of crazy ideas."

"Hershel," my mother said in her warning tone.

"Don't 'Hershel' me. I can talk to my daughter

if I want to. That's what parents supposed to do when they concerned. Leave your husband and move to a whole new city and starve yourself to death so you can look like those skinny women on television. Ain't nothing wrong with a black woman having some meat on her bones. Black men don't like no skinny women. They need some meat on them hips and them thighs. Then you wearing a dress with the back all out and split up the side, showing your tail. You done come down here and lost your good Christian upbringing. I hope you been remembering you married while you down here."

He muttered under his breath for while, probably realizing me and Mommy were ignoring him. Suddenly, my dad shouted out a spray of cuss words. "What the—?"

Mommy and I looked out the window to see what he was looking at.

"OhLawdJesus." Mommy obviously caught sight of what set him off.

Out of the corner of my eye, I saw two men holding hands at the corner of 10th and Piedmont. They leaned in to kiss one another on the lips.

Daddy yelled, "What is this? Sodom and Gomorrah? Where you done brought me? Two men kissing on the street? Outside? In broad daylight?"

I guess they were only supposed to kiss inside, at night.

Daddy continued to rant and rave in the back seat. "They better be glad I'm in this car. If one of them punks ever got close to me, I'd . . . I'd have to kill 'em. They better not ever come up to me."

"Daddy, they don't want you."

What'd I say that for? Daddy wasn't even making full sentences anymore. Mommy and I just got an earful of cuss words from the back seat. He cussed all the way out to Stone Mountain.

Even though I missed them, by the time I dropped them off at the airport, I was ready for them to go. Daddy swore he was never coming back to Atlanta. I didn't bother to remind him there were homosexuals in Baltimore.

When I got in the house, I plopped down on the couch.

Alaysia came bouncing into the living room. "Have fun with your parents?"

"Daddy drove me crazy, harassing me like I was some common whore, then I made the mistake of driving them through Midtown and he saw two men kissing. He was done. Cussed and fussed the whole rest of the day. My last nerve is long gone."

"At least you got parents you can see and spend time with."

That certainly put things in perspective. "You're right. I'm sorry. I guess what upset me more than anything was his anger and his attitude. Give him half a chance and he'd line up every homosexual in the city and have them executed. I'm not about to participate in the Gay Pride Parade, but I think he's extreme. Can you imagine if he ever found out about Kevin?"

Alaysia grimaced. "Oooh, that would be bad."

"If he ever said any of the stuff he said today around Kevin, it would kill him. He respects my father a lot."

"He's old school. This older generation isn't as tolerant of alternative lifestyles."

"Like I said, I ain't about to march, but the anger and hatred he has is a little over the top."

I took off my shoes and massaged my feet. "Girl, they had me all over Atlanta today."

"Why don't you soak and go to bed. I have some lavender bath salts."

"Sounds like a good idea."

Before I could sink into the tub good, Alaysia pounded on the door.

I sunk deeper into the water. "Go 'way. I'm trying to relax."

She threw open the door with a panicked look on her face, holding the phone. A look that could only mean bad news. Did something happen to Mommy and Daddy?

"It's Kevin's drummer, Ricky. Kevin was in a car accident."

53

I tapped my foot as the elevator made its slow as-
cent to the fourth floor. Seems like I'd spent the
evening waiting on airplanes, taxis and now this
stupid elevator. I was lucky enough to catch the
last flight to D.C.

I tried to make myself stay calm. Ricky said
Kevin's injuries were minor, and they expected to
release him from the hospital soon.

Kevin smiled when I walked into his room. "I
can't believe you flew all the way here for a concussion. Not that I'm complaining."

I walked over to the bed and threw my arms
around him, then stepped back to inspect him.
"What happened? Are you okay? Is it really just a
concussion? Did you break anything?"

Kevin held up his hands. "Slow down, Monnie. I'm fine. The only reason I'm in the hospital is
because I'm this big star now. If I was a regular

person, they would have sent me home from the ER."

"I still don't understand," a deep voice behind me said.

I turned around to see Ricky and Aaron sitting in the corner of the large private room.

"He should be dead," Ricky said. "No way he should have walked away from that kind of accident. Both the police and the ambulance people said there must have been an angel in the passenger seat because they'd never seen anything like it."

"Hey, guys." I walked over to hug them, crying tears of relief now that I knew Kevin was okay.

Aaron said, "I'm telling you, Monica. If I didn't believe it before, I believe it now. Kevin is a man of God with a serious purpose. The devil tried to kill him last night, but God must have some greater reason for him to be here. The car is completely totaled."

"Yo, man. Stop scaring my wife." Kevin frowned at Aaron. "It wasn't all that."

"Man, you need to quit lying and praise God. Don't act like He didn't work a miracle to keep your black behind on earth. If it was me, I'd be trying to hustle my way inside the pearly gates right about now," Ricky said.

I walked over to Kevin to examine him again.

"Don't listen to them, Monica. It wasn't that bad."

"What happened?"

"Monnie, it's no big deal. I—"

"Kevin, what happened?" I clicked the "off" button on the bedside remote to the large TV hanging over the bed.

"I was driving home from rehearsal and next thing I know, the paramedics were pulling me out of the car. I don't remember."

"Don't remember? Did you black out?"

"I bet he fell asleep. I told him not to drive. I even offered to drive him. He said—"

"Ricky, don't you two have somewhere y'all are 'sposed to be?"

"A'ight, man. You can throw us out, but we can talk to her later. We'll make sure she knows the whole story 'cause you ain't got the good sense God gave a frog." Aaron kissed my cheek and walked to the door.

Ricky hugged me and whispered, "Don't leave 'til he tells the whole truth." As they left, a waft of air carrying the smell of sickness came in the door. Reminded me how much I hated hospitals.

I sat on the edge of Kevin's bed. "Is there something you need to tell me?"

"They trippin'. The car is a little banged up, but it ain't as bad as they trying to make it out to be."

"Kevin, I can get a copy of the police report, and I can have a very intelligent conversation with your nurses and doctors. If there's something I need to know, you need to be the one to tell me."

Kevin's fidgeted with his sheet and looked past me out the window. "I fell asleep behind the wheel. I was driving and felt myself getting sleepy, but figured I could make it if I rolled the window down. I crashed into a median and flipped over three times. The car is totaled." He looked up at me. "You should be talking to a mortician instead of me. I don't know why God saved my life, but it couldn't have been nothing but Him." He waited for my reaction.

"Anything else?"

Kevin let out a deep breath. "They checked my blood. They found too high levels of the stuff I've been taking to help me sleep."

My mouth fell open. "Stuff you've been taking to sleep?"

"Monnie, it's no big deal—"

"It's a very big deal. What are you taking and why? Last time I saw you, you weren't having any trouble sleeping."

"That's 'cause you were there. I . . . I don't sleep at night. If I don't take the pills, I either lay in bed all night staring at the ceiling, or . . ."

"Or what?"

"Or have bad dreams." He let out a deep breath. "The nightmares are back."

"What nightmares?"

He shook his head and looked out the window.

I moved to block his view of the window. "What nightmares?"

"Nightmares of when Deacon . . . I mean, the deacon, you know, molested me. Nightmares of me and Trey, nightmares of you walking in on us and killing me. And some others."

"What others?" He wouldn't look at me. "Kevin?" I lifted his chin. "What others?"

"Monnie, I . . . I didn't quite tell you the whole story."

I waited. My heart was pounding. What else was there to tell? Could I take it?

He didn't say anything. Just sat there fingering the edges of his hospital gown.

"Kevin, the only way we can get back together is if I know we're completely honest about everything in our relationship. You have to be able to trust me enough to tell me everything, and I have to trust that you're telling me everything. No more secrets. I've grown a lot since we've been apart. Whatever you have to say, I can take it." *I hope I can take it.*

Kevin lay back on his pillow and stared at the ceiling. "Remember I told you about when I was ten and how confused I was afterward?"

I nodded.

"Well . . . when I was about thirteen, I was still dealing with all the . . . feelings. I didn't have anybody to talk to. I went to our youth pastor at the time. He was nice to us kids and would have sleepovers at his house and took us to the movies and out to eat sometimes." Kevin paused. "One day after service, he told my mom he was gonna take me out for dinner because he wanted to talk to me. I went with him, his wife, and two daughters. I went over his house afterward, and he asked me how I was doing. He said he had been watching me, and I seemed sad all the time. He said that God gave him a heart for young people, and it burdened him to see anybody as sad as me."

I took Kevin's hand. *God, please don't let him tell me what I think he's about to tell me.*

"So I told him everything. About what happened and all the thoughts I was battling with. I cried and he hugged me. He said he would take care of the deacon and make sure nothing like that ever happened again. He told me I could trust him. And then he started touching me. And then . . ."

Kevin put his head in his hands. "His wife and daughters were right upstairs. He had turned the game on real loud and told them men folk were watching football. I screamed a couple of times, but nobody heard."

I wanted to run screaming from the room. How could this have happened? Both times at the hands of leaders in the church. By men that a young Kevin should have been able to trust. I tried to keep my reaction to myself, but the flood of emotions was too much for me to handle.

"Why? Why would they do that to you? How could do that to you? They're supposed to be men of God." I hugged him tight, like I could squeeze away the memories and the pain. It was all I could do, but I knew that it wasn't enough. "Kevin, we've got to get you some help. You can't keep living like this."

"I will, Monnie, I promise. As soon as I finish the tour."

"Forget the tour!"

"Forget" wasn't the word I wanted to use, but I was trying not to let the cussing demon overtake me again.

"I can't forget the tour. I can't walk away from my career. It's all I've ever worked for. All I've ever wanted." He looked at me, his eyes full of passion. "Music saved my life. When I wanted to die, when I didn't have anyone to talk to, I always had my music. When I was sad, all I had to do was play my piano and I would feel better. When I woke up with nightmares, I would play my guitar until I could go back to sleep. Sometimes I'd fall asleep with the guitar in the bed with me."

His eyes pleaded with me. "If you take my music away from me, I won't have anything."

I ran my fingers across his cheeks. "I'm not trying to take it away from you. I'm trying to help you. Look at you, Kevin. You're in the hospital because you had to take pills to get to sleep. You fell asleep behind the wheel and wrecked your car. You said it yourself, you should be dead right now. Is that how you want to live?"

"No."

"I'm not asking you to give up anything. I'm just asking you to get some help."

"You don't know how it is. People in the church . . . they don't treat people well who are . . . who have my history."

"Forget them, Kevin. It's not about them. It's about you getting past the drama you went through so you can go on with your life."

"And what kind of life is that? Without music, without you? What else do I have?"

"Who said it would be without me?"

"What are you saying?"

"I'm saying we can get you some help. We can work through this together. I told you about the book I read and the ministry in Atlanta. They've been through it. The pastor's story was worse than yours. And he's delivered. And married. With four kids. Four babies, Kevin. Remember our babies we talked about?"

He nodded. "Yeah." He shook his head. "But I tried that before. I thought I was delivered and look what happened. What if I think I'm delivered and it happens again? I can't go through that again. I can't put *you* through that again."

"There's more to it than somebody praying for you and declaring you delivered. They take you through this intensive program where you deal with the heart of the issue. You buried it. The program is designed to uproot it. Completely destroy it at the core."

I could tell he was thinking about it because his eyes were blinking fast. "And you'll go through this with me? You'll stay with me?"

I nodded. *God help me to be able to do this.*

"And if I don't? Are you saying you'll only come back to me if I go through this program?"

"I can't watch you waste away to nothing and have nightmares and sing on stage night after night pretending nothing's wrong. I can't be worried every time you leave the house wondering if you're coming back or whether you'll wreck the car and not be as blessed as you were this time. I can't live a lie for the sake of the ministry'." I mimicked Bishop Walker's voice.

"Why do you hate him so much?"

"Because he's using you. He's building his ministry on your back and doesn't even care that you're almost killing yourself. He knew the struggle you were going through all those years. Did he ever do anything to help you? No, he swept it under the rug and let you build his church with your talent."

"He's not like that. After that second episode, when I finally trusted somebody again, he was there for me. He treated me like a son. He never hurt me, ever."

I put my hand on Kevin's. I didn't want to destroy his image of the only real father figure he ever had, but I wanted him to see the truth, as hard as it was to see. "Okay, Kevin."

I put my arms around him and kissed his forehead. We sat there until a thought hit me.

"Kevin?"

"Yeah?"

"What happened to those two men? The men that abused you."

He bit his upper lip. "Please, don't ask me that question."

"Why not?"

"Because you won't like the answer."

I pursed my lips.

"Aww, Monnie. I promise you don't want to hear this."

I wasn't letting him out of it. He looked up at the ceiling, his eyes blinking fast. "The youth pastor was Pastor Hines."

He sat for a minute, I guess to let it sink in.

My eyes widened. "Pastor Hines? As in the pastor who Bishop Walker ordained to be the pastor of our Alexandria Church? That Pastor Hines?"

Kevin nodded. "And Deacon Barnes."

I jumped off the bed. "Deacon Barnes? The head deacon at Love and Faith?"

Kevin nodded again.

I shook my head in disbelief. "How could you not tell?" I paced around the room. "What if you're not the only one? Think of how many other little boys they may have done the same thing to. Bishop Walker has put them in positions of leadership over other little boys."

Kevin's eyes widened. "I . . . I never thought of that."

"How could you never think of that? How could you not tell?"

"They told me . . . they said they'd hurt me. They said I'd destroy the ministry if I ever told."

"Destroy the ministry if you ever told what?" a deep voice boomed out.

I whipped around to see Bishop Walker's tall frame filling the doorway.

54

"Well, well, well. If it isn't the prodigal daughter."

I gave a polite nod. "Bishop."

He held out his arms. Last thing I felt like doing was hugging him. For Kevin's sake, I did, and tried to keep a smile plastered on my face.

"I see Atlanta's been good to you. You look absolutely beautiful. I heard the reports, but it's better than I imagined."

I didn't like the way he was looking at me. I don't know whether it was because I knew he was running an underground pedophile ring in his churches or because of the way he licked his lips as he looked me up and down. I walked over to the bed and held Kevin's hand.

"Hey, Bishop. Thanks for coming to see me," Kevin said.

"Had to come check on my son. You feeling okay?"

"I'm fine, Bishop. They should be discharging me soon."

"Good. I wanted to make sure I didn't need to call off the anniversary concert."

I cleared my throat. "You should call it off anyway. Kevin's going to need some rest."

"Monica, it's nice to know you're concerned about Kevin's well being all of a sudden."

I clenched my fists. *OhLawdJesus, help me to hold my tongue.*

He looked Kevin over. "Not a scratch. It's truly a miracle from God. What better way to thank Him but to do the concert? It'll show the enemy that even though he tried to kill you, he can't touch a man sold out for God. What a powerful testimony."

Kevin nodded. "Yeah, I do need to give God the glory for saving my life. The concert can go ahead as scheduled."

I stared at Kevin. Was he serious? "I thought we talked about you needing some time off to get some rest, Kevin."

"Monica, I'm not sure you're in a position to know what Kevin needs right now. You've haven't seen him in how long?"

I turned with my hand on my hip. "Bishop, I—"

"What she means is," Kevin slipped an arm around my waist and pulled me to him, "we've been talking about me taking some time off after the tour and going to Atlanta to recuperate."

Bishop glared at me like I was his archenemy.

He smiled at Kevin. "Sure, Kevin. Looks like God is finally answering our prayers." He smiled like he was responsible for bringing us back together. "Why do you need to go to Atlanta, though? I would think Monica would want to come back here. Spend some time with her parents, time at the church."

"I think Kevin needs to be where he can focus on relaxing." Did he really think I was coming anywhere near his church?

"And what about the choir? You know people are coming to Love and Faith just to hear you. Are you going to walk away from your ministry as it's getting off the ground?"

"He's not walking away. Just taking a break so when he comes back, he can be refreshed and rejuvenated," I said.

Kevin's eyes went back and forth between me and Bishop like he was watching a tennis match.

"Monica, when you left here, Kevin was a broken man. Through our time spent together, the Lord has begun to put the pieces back together. I know you're concerned about him because of this accident, but how do we know you won't hurt him all over again after the emotions have passed? I don't think he could survive that."

I clenched my teeth. "You don't know anything about the pieces coming back together. If anything, he's fallen more apart. You don't know—"

"Monica, please." Kevin pulled me to him and pressed his head into my stomach.

"Kevin." I ran my fingers over his hair.

"Please, Monnie. I promise I will. Just not yet." His voice was muffled against my shirt.

"Not yet, what?" Bishop Walker's voice boomed.

I sat on the bed next to Kevin and took his hands in mine. "You can do this. You have to do this. Think of all the little ten-year-old and thirteen year-old boys at Love and Faith. Do it for them."

Kevin gripped my hands tighter.

"I'm right here."

"Would somebody like to tell me what's going on?" Bishop crossed his arms and gave me a stern look.

Kevin let out a deep breath. "Bishop Walker, you might want to pull up a chair. I . . . I need to tell you something."

55

I never saw a black man turn gray. At least not one still living and breathing. Bishop Walker's jaw locked permanently open, and probably for the first time in his life, he was speechless. He stared at Kevin while he told the story of what happened in his childhood.

When Kevin finished talking, silence filled the room. I was afraid of what Bishop Walker would say, more for Kevin's sake than anything else. Bishop finally stood up and walked over to the window, rubbing his hands together. A few times, he lifted a finger like he was going to say something, but stopped and shook his head. He finally came back over to the chair and sat down. "Monica, can I talk to Kevin alone for a few minutes?"

I looked at Kevin. He shook his head. "Whatever you need to say, you can say with her in the room." Kevin squeezed my hand.

"All right, then. These are some very serious . . . um, allegations. I will have to . . . uh, look into the things you're saying and determine what actually happened."

"What do you mean?" Kevin started blinking fast.

Bishop Walker took a deep breath and leaned back in the chair. "I can't go accusing these men of the things you just said. I need to talk to them first and get their side of the story. You can't expect me to—"

"You think I made it up? Why would I do something like that?" Kevin squeezed my hand so hard, my fingers turned purple.

"I'm not saying you made it up. Sometimes, when you're young and vulnerable, you can misinterpret certain things people might say or do—"

"How could I misinterpret another man sticking his—"

"Kevin!" I wrestled my hand out of his grip. I couldn't feel my fingers.

He looked at me then looked down at me massaging my hand. "Sorry, Monnie."

"It's okay, Kevin."

"No, I'm really sorry. You . . . you were right."

He turned to Bishop Walker. "I want you to leave."

"Kevin. I'm not saying—"

"I want you to leave. Now."

"I can't believe you're letting her come between us. I've been there for you since you were a child and you let this—"

"Been there for me?" The vein in the middle of Kevin's forehead bulged. "Been there for me?"

I took Kevin's hands and looked into his eyes and said, "Bishop, I think it's time for you to leave. You can tell everyone that Kevin won't be able to do the anniversary concert because of the accident."

Kevin held my intense gaze. "I won't be extending the tour either."

Bishop Walker rubbed his hands together. "Okay . . . okay. I understand." He put on a smile. "It's probably best if you get away for a while and get some rest. I know this tour has been long and taxing. I'll let the choir and everybody know that you'll be back in a month or so. In the meantime, I'll see about these . . . uh, issues you mentioned."

Kevin never turned to look at Bishop. "I won't be back."

Bishop Walker let out a long breath. "Don't make any rash decisions. Take some time to think about it. You don't want to throw away your whole musical career. We've worked hard to get you—"

Kevin finally turned to look Bishop in the eye. "I—won't—be—back." He said it as if Bishop was deaf and just learning to read lips.

Bishop Walker's lips tightened into a thin line. His eyes got that fiery look they had when he preached. "I'll tell you this. If you make any of these allegations against me or these men of God, you'll have a big lawsuit on your hands. Not that you'd be stupid enough to do that. What do you think your precious fans would do if they found out you were a homosexual? How do you think they'd react if it was rumored you had several affairs with men in every city on this tour? Or worse still, if we were to suddenly discover you'd been molesting young boys under your charge in the youth choir? Not only would your lose your superstar gospel singer status that *I* made possible, you might even end up in jail."

The smile on Bishop Walker's face was so sinister, I thought I was looking at the devil himself.

"No, I think you're smart enough to keep this to yourself. We can say you decided to relocate to one of our affiliate churches in Atlanta to reconcile with your wife. That way, God is glorified and no one has to get hurt."

Bishop Walker stood and adjusted his tie. Neither Kevin nor I looked in his direction as he stormed out of the room.

56

There's nothing better than when God's hand is on something and He makes everything flow together perfectly. A few days after Kevin was released from the hospital, I flew back to Atlanta. When Kevin told the band he was moving to join me there, the trombone player, Jo-Jo, wanted to know if we'd consider selling him our house. He made us an offer that would give us a nice little profit, especially since we didn't have to pay a realtor.

When David found out Kevin was moving to Atlanta and that we were looking for an apartment for him while we worked on some marital issues, he said Kevin could move into his guest room until he and Nakia got married. We tried to say no, but David insisted. His only condition was that Kevin let him play the Triton every once in a while.

David's house was fully furnished, so we had to figure out what to do with our furniture. I wanted to get rid of it and start all over—there were too many memories associated with the house and our stuff. When we asked Jo-Jo if we could leave the furniture until we could move it into one of those monthly storage rental places, Jo-Jo asked if he could buy it. His fiancée had complained that he had to get rid of his bachelor pad décor, and he didn't feel like buying new furniture.

I flew back to help Kevin pack our personal stuff—books, instruments, pictures, and the kitchen stuff. We fit most of it in the Ford Excursion Kevin bought not long after the album was released. I thought it was excessive, but he said it was perfect when he and the band had to go somewhere, because most of them could fit in one vehicle. Every time he mentioned the band, he got this sad look in his eyes. I was glad he already had some friends in Atlanta to make the transition smoother.

When we had everything packed in the truck and were ready to leave, Kevin handed me the keys. "Feel like driving?"

"This big ol' bus? Not really. Why you want me to drive?"

He held up my copy of *Touching a Dead Man*. "Thought I might do some reading."

"Where'd you get that?"

"Come on, Monnie. You're not exactly subtle. You left it on my nightstand, then on the coffee table, and then in the bathroom. You telling me it walked to all those different places?"

"Maybe I was dropping little hints. I want you

to read it because you want to read it, not because I want you to read it."

"Yeah, right. That's why I finally found it on my keyboard yesterday, huh?"

I laughed. "You got me. I think it will help us. Just read the first chapter and tell me what you think. If you don't like it, you don't have to finish it, and I won't bring it up again," I lied.

He took my hand. "I'm going to read it cover to cover. I'm committed to doing whatever I have to do to make our marriage work."

I kissed him. "Thanks, baby. Me too."

We got in the truck and drove away from our life in D.C. to start our new life in Atlanta.

57

"Monica? Kevin? Nice to finally meet you. I'm Derrick Ford, and this is my wife, Dana. Please come on in."

I was nervous when I called to make an appointment with Pastor Ford, the author of *Touching a Dead Man.* I actually talked to his wife first. She was very gracious about offering help to me and Kevin. She made me feel at ease with discussing our situation. She told me she and her husband received many phone calls like ours, and always did whatever they could to help.

"Thank you for inviting us into your home." I wiped my sweaty hands on my jeans.

"Our pleasure. We're glad to meet you." Dana Ford led us into the living room. It was elegantly decorated in burgundy and green. The furniture looked like Dana was knowledgeable when it came to antiques.

We sat down facing each other on their couch and loveseat. A young boy came toddling in and almost tripped over Pastor Ford's feet. He scooped him up and threw him up in the air and kissed him.

"How's my big boy doing?" He kissed his fat cheeks over and over until the boy squealed in delight. "Where's Daddy's hug?"

The little boy threw his arms open and wrapped them around his father's head and squeezed. "Daddee, Daddee."

I watched Kevin watching the two of them. His eyes were filled with longing. I wondered if he had been as upset over the thought of not having kids as I was.

"Isaiah, come get your brother," Pastor Ford called out.

A pre-teen boy came bounding into the living room. "Come here, Josh. What's up, baby brotha?" He stopped when he saw us. "Oh, I'm sorry." He smoothed back his cornrows and looked at his father.

"Isaiah, this is Mr. and Mrs. Day." Pastor Ford put his hand on his son's shoulder.

Isaiah shook our hands. "Nice to meet you." He took his little brother in his arms and hoisted him up the stairs.

"Sorry about that." Dana sat back down on the claw-footed couch.

"No problem. Your children are beautiful." I smiled.

"Thank you. We have two more around here somewhere. Another son and one daughter." I could tell Pastor Ford was proud of his brood.

"Three boys and a girl? That's perfect," Kevin said.

"In your dreams, Kevin," I said. "We're having three girls and maybe a boy."

"Like you can control it."

The Fords laughed at us. We all relaxed.

"I know you guys didn't come to talk about our kids. Why don't we open up with prayer?" Pastor Ford said.

We stood in a circle and held hands.

Pastor Ford prayed. "Dear Father, Thank You for this precious couple You brought to us. God, we consider it an honor that You would entrust them to us. Help us to speak into their lives, to give them the help and the insight they need. Father, we trust You for the regeneration process. Bring light where the enemy sought to bring darkness, life where he sought to bring death, and love where he sought to sow hate. Heal this man, God. Make him whole in every area of his life—mentally, emotionally, spiritually, sexually . . . send your anointing, Lord, to destroy every yoke. Heal this woman, God. Heal the pain this situation has caused. We commit these things to You in Jesus' name."

I could tell from the prayer that I liked them already. It was drastically different from the prayer Bishop Walker prayed when we first went to see him.

Pastor Ford put his hands together. "Who wants to start?"

I looked at Kevin and he looked at me. We both started talking at the same time, then laughed nervously.

Dana smiled. "Monica, why don't you start?"

So I did. I talked about how I walked in on Kevin and Trey almost eighteen months ago, how it made me feel and how we split up. Kevin flinched and winced the entire time I talked. He took over and talked about what happened with Deacon Barnes and Pastor Hines. Not only were his eyes blinking fast, his leg bounced a mile a minute. Every once in a while, I squeezed his hand or put my hand on his knee to slow down his leg.

Pastor Ford said, "I don't know whether you read the book or not, but it sounds like our childhoods were very similar. Too similar. I want you to know I understand everything you've gone through. I know the damage that's been done to your heart and your mind. What I really want you to know is God has the power to heal you—completely. He can make you whole, and you can have a healthy relationship with your wife and your children-to-be. I'm a living example."

Kevin nodded and stared at the floor.

Pastor Ford continued, "That being said, it's going to take a lot of hard work on your part, and a lot of love and patience on your wife's part." He squeezed his wife's hand. "God had already brought me through a lot of the deliverance process by the time I met Dana, but her love completed my healing. I can tell you two love each other, just by watching you. Kevin, I know you love God because I've heard your music. Are you both willing to do what it takes to make this work?"

We looked at each other and nodded. Kevin reached for my hand.

Dana turned to me. "Monica, this will be a difficult process for you, too. I know you'll have a lot of questions and concerns. I've been through the process and have walked with other women as they've come through it. Anything you need to ask me, no matter how personal, even if it's about sex—especially if it's about sex—please ask me. I'm here for you."

I nodded. Made a mental note to definitely talk about the sex thing.

Kevin leaned forward. "What do we need to do? How do I get delivered?"

Pastor Ford answered, "The first thing you have to understand is deliverance is a process. I went through the same thing you went through. Everybody laid hands on me and prayed for me and drowned me in olive oil and said I was delivered. When I got the feelings and thoughts again, I figured it didn't work. That's not true. Deliverance does happen immediately spiritually, but in terms of renewing your mind and receiving healing in your soul, that's where the process comes in. It's like getting saved. Your spirit man is instantly saved, but for your mind, will, and emotions, you still have to work out your soul's salvation. All those times you thought you were delivered, you actually were. You just hadn't done the rest of the work to make sure you were able to walk it out."

Kevin nodded. It must have been a relief for someone to explain to him what he experienced all those years.

Pastor Ford said, "The first thing I'm going to recommend is that you enroll in my Lifelines class for men and women coming out of a lifestyle of homosexuality. Even though it's intense and grueling, you'll be a new man when you finish. It's once a week for six months."

"I thought maybe we could meet one on one." Kevin bit his lip.

"It's better meeting with others who are dealing with the same issues. You get to hear that you're not alone, and you may have the answer to someone else's deliverance and they may have the answer to yours. It's like a support group."

"Yeah, but I don't . . . I didn't . . ."

"I think Kevin is concerned about his being well-known as a gospel musician. It might be difficult for him to participate in such a class," Dana said.

Kevin nodded and looked at the floor again.

Pastor Ford rubbed his chin. "I understand your concern, Kevin. We try to create an atmosphere of trust, where everyone can feel like their life secrets are safe. You'd be surprised at who comes through the group—people in all spheres of society who also have a lot to lose if the truth about their past were to come out. Many have just as much to lose as you do."

Kevin didn't look convinced.

Pastor Ford continued, "When I first started this ministry, it was difficult for me to step up to this platform. When I thought about how many people suffered because of my silence, I realized how selfish it was for me not to share what God had done for me. I sacrificed my own reputation so others could be healed. That's what the true love of God on the inside will make you do."

Kevin's eyes widened like he was worried Pastor Ford was challenging him to do the same thing.

Pastor Ford smiled and held up his hands. "I'm not saying you have to do that. That's a personal decision you need to think long and hard about. A lot of Christians are particularly prejudiced against our past lives, and don't have the ability to love us in spite of, even though God does. They don't realize their judging us is just as much of a sin. Unfortunately, full healing in this area can't come until the church embraces us with the love of God, no matter what state we're in. Who knows how many souls have been lost to the kingdom of darkness because a saint wouldn't open their arms to someone struggling with their sexuality and love them whole?"

He squeezed Dana's hand and leaned closer to her. "That's why women like our wives are rare jewels. If we had more Danas and Monicas . . ."

I smiled. I didn't know if I was worthy to be placed in the same category as Dana, but at least I wanted to try.

Pastor Ford said, "The next class doesn't start for a few weeks. We can meet one-on-one for a while, and if you feel comfortable, you can join the class when it begins."

Kevin nodded. I could tell he was relieved.

Pastor Ford continued, "You also need to get in a church where they teach the Word—some serious Word—that will bring you into a deeper place of intimacy with God."

"The church we've found here is like that," I

said. I was glad Kevin enjoyed service when we went this past Sunday. He said he looked forward to sitting and being ministered to for a while.

"Also, you need some strong men of God in your life. Men who are willing to walk with you through this process. Who aren't threatened or afraid to be there for you. I'll be one of those men, but you need to be surrounded by them," Pastor Ford said.

I said, "We have Khalil, my best friend's boyfriend, who is a minister and a walking Bible, and then there's David, the worship leader at the church."

"Do they know about Kevin's struggle?" Pastor Ford asked.

Kevin looked at me.

"I didn't tell them anything." I didn't think Alaysia had either.

Kevin looked back at Pastor Ford. "Do I have to tell them?"

"You don't have to, but it may help them to help you. They can pray for you and support you. It's up to you."

"What if they . . ." Kevin shook his head. "What if David throws me out or if Khalil doesn't want to associate with me anymore?"

I squeezed his hand. "They won't."

He looked at me. "You did."

"Kevin, that was different. I walked in on you cheating on me. They're not married to you, and they won't be seeing what I saw."

Kevin's leg started bouncing again. "I don't know about this . . ."

"You don't have to decide right now. Just pray

about it and see what God says. He knows whether your friends can handle it and how they'll respond," Pastor Ford said.

He turned to me. "Monica, you're going to have to reach down and forgive Kevin for betraying your love and trust."

"I have forgiven him."

"That's not what your eyes said a minute ago. I know you've forgiven him to a large extent, otherwise you wouldn't be here. I'm just saying there might be a tiny bit of bitterness and resentment in a little crevice in your heart you haven't dealt with yet."

I nodded. I gave Kevin's hand an apologetic squeeze.

"Lastly, Kevin, you may want to consider seeing a psychotherapist," Pastor Ford said. "A lot happened to you at a young, vulnerable age that has molded the man you are today. It may hasten the process for you to augment everything else with some therapy. I can recommend a Christian therapist who's worked with a lot of the people who have gone through our class."

Kevin furrowed his eyebrows. "Did you see one?"

"I wish I had. I think it would have made my process a lot easier."

Kevin let out a deep breath. "Okay. If it'll help."

"Good. I'll get you the number before you go. Sounds like we have a plan here. Let me say one more time, God is faithful, and He's already answered your prayers. I see your marriage healed, your ministry prospering, and beautiful children on the way. God has honored your desire to live upright before Him, Kevin, and your willingness to stand by your man, Monica. You guys are going to be just fine."

As we stood and held hands in our closing prayer, I trusted God that his words were true.

58

After Kevin got settled at David's and Nakia got settled in her own apartment, we all spent every waking moment we weren't working having fun. We had picnics, went to concerts, to the movies, shopping, everywhere. After a few months, Alaysia decided to have a pool party for the six of us one Saturday afternoon in August. We all suited up, then went up to the rooftop pool.

We barely got up there good and the guys peeled off their shirts and jumped in the pool. Nakia, Alaysia, and I sat on the side, dangling our feet in the icy water.

"I can't believe we finally get to spend some time with our men. I move down here thinking I'm gonna get to spend more time with David, and he's always off with Khalil and Kevin." Nakia held her hands up to keep the water the guys splashed from getting on her hair.

"I know. Ever since Kevin moved here, I don't get any time with Khalil." Alaysia pouted. "If they're not playing basketball, they're working out in the gym, or going to the movies or something that doesn't include us."

"Oh, and don't forget men's Bible study." I splashed Kevin as he, David, and Khalil swam up.

"What are you guys looking so sour about?" Kevin splashed me back. I gave him a warning glare not to get my hair wet.

"We were talking about how you men are neglecting us." Alaysia pulled her feet away from Khalil, who was tickling her toes.

"Neglecting you? How you figure?" David said.

"When you guys should be spending time with us, y'all are always off doing something together. We feel left out," Nakia answered.

"Do we complain when you all go shopping or to your veggie restaurants or to get your spa treatments?" David shielded his eyes from the bright summer sun.

"And we invite you out to eat with us every Thursday night when we go," Khalil said.

Alaysia sucked her teeth. "Yeah, to eat steak. You know me and Monnie don't eat steak."

"Yeah, but we do, so y'all go eat y'all's little bean sprouts, and we men folk will go and eat steak," David said.

"And what's up with the men-only Bible study? Help me understand how that's fair," I said.

"We have to discuss men issues—sensitive issues you guys couldn't deal with. You better be glad we do or y'all virtuous women might be in trouble." David and Khalil slapped hands. "I know that's right."

Nakia kicked some water at David. "And when I call you in the afternoon, you're 'sleep. What's that about?"

"Me and Kevin are up all night playing and writing music. Wait 'til you hear the new stuff we're pumping out. It is divinely inspired. I have to get a nap after work otherwise I'll be no good." David taught music at a local high school to supplement the small salary he got from the church.

I wasn't going to complain about the late-night jam sessions. I got serenaded with phone calls on a regular basis so Kevin could show off his new music.

Kevin hooked his arms around my legs. He looked good. Real good. Between me feeding him, his going out to eat with his boys, and all the working out he was doing, he had gained some weight and his muscles were bulking up again. He saw a therapist and went to his Lifelines classes once a week, so he was sleeping much better. The bags under his eyes were almost completely gone.

His eyes . . . They held a calm sereneness I hadn't seen in them before. Ever. He seemed happier than he was when I first married him.

"Are y'all gonna swim or just sit by the side of the pool and look cute?" David tried to pull Nakia into the water.

"Don't even play, boy." Nakia edged away. "There's no way I can wash, blow dry, and curl my hair in time for church in the morning."

"I know that's right, girl. Don't nobody feel

like all that." I pulled my legs from Kevin, just in case he was getting any ideas about pulling me in.

"You two are such slaves to your hair. It's such bondage." Alaysia eased herself down into the water, flinching at the cold.

"Just 'cause we ain't got that wash-and-wear white girl hair you got. We got true African-American hair we can't just wash and shake," Nakia said, holding David at bay with her feet as he kept splashing her.

"Truth be told, my hair is more African-American than you two," Alaysia said.

"Whatever, girl. You ain't got no naps like this." Nakia turned and pointed to her kitchen, badly overdue for a perm.

"My dad was African, my mom was American. That makes me more African-American than anybody here. So there." Alaysia stuck out her tongue.

Khalil dunked her and held her down for a while.

"Hey!" she sputtered when she came up, wiping her face. "What are you doing?"

Khalil raised a hand up toward heaven. "In the name of Jesus, I baptize thee." He dunked her again.

She came up, lunged toward him, and dunked him. "Before you start manhandling me, remember I lift weights every day. And you can't baptize me yet. I'm not saved."

"And why *is* that?" Nakia hadn't been privy to the conversations we'd all had, answering Alaysia's multitudes of questions about God, Christianity, and the Bible.

"Oh, please don't get her started." Khalil rolled his eyes.

"What's that supposed to mean?" Alaysia splashed him.

"That means that question sends you on a tirade of mind-boggling questions that will take us the rest of the afternoon to answer," Khalil replied. "Today is Minister Khalil's day off."

"Day off? You're supposed to always be ready to preach the Word in season and out of season. You gets no day off," Alaysia said.

Nakia shook her head. "See, this is what I don't understand. You can quote scripture better than most Christians, go to church more than most Christians, live holier than most Christians . . . I don't understand why you're not a Christian."

Alaysia stood there, making waves with her arms. She started to say something then stopped, started again, then stopped, and finally said, "I don't either." She dove under the water, mermaid style, then took long strokes to the other end of the pool.

"Oops. I hope I didn't upset her," Nakia said.

Khalil watched Alaysia swimming away with a determined look in his eye. "No, she's okay. She's right there at the edge. We're all praying, and I know God is gonna do it in His perfect time. She has fewer and fewer questions, her prayer life is stronger and stronger, and she reads the Word almost as much as I do."

"And last month, she made this big ritual of cleaning out all her crystals and figurines and New Age books and stuff," I added. "She put it all in a big box and carried it out to the Dumpster."

"Yeah, she's almost there." Khalil pushed himself off the side of the pool and swam after Alaysia.

The rippling water parting as they both swam beckoned me. "Forget it. I'll wear a ponytail to church tomorrow." I dove in and swam toward the other end of the pool. When I flipped to do a lap, I saw Kevin swimming past me, back toward the shallow end. We swam laps for a while, leaving Nakia maintaining her straw set at the end of the pool, blocking David's splashes. I guess he figured if he got her hair wet, she'd relent and get in the pool.

When we got tired of swimming, we played in the water until we were two shades darker and wrinkled like raisins. Hunger hit me. We toweled off and went back down to the condo to change.

We all met at the dining table when we were dry and dressed. Alaysia had picked up food from Sevanandah's earlier.

"Okay, before we eat, what is this stuff? I swear I'm gonna sneak some meat in here one day." Khalil frowned at the food Alaysia put on the table.

"We have jerk tempeh and curry tofu, both with stir-fried vegetables. There's Moroccan couscous with raisins and almonds, brown rice, grilled spinach and wheat rolls, and a chocolate silk pie for dessert."

"You mean a tofu pie for dessert." Khalil grimaced.

"Don't act like you don't like this food." Alaysia twirled the towel she was holding and zapped Khalil's legs.

"I like your food better, baby." He rubbed his leg where she popped him.

"Good answer." Alaysia kissed his cheek.

We held hands and Kevin asked the blessing. We ate like we had just been starving on a deserted island rather than at the pool. After we finished eating, we took our pie to the living room.

"Nakia, how are the wedding plans going?" I asked.

Nakia crossed her eyes. "Driving me crazy. My mom is trying to run the show, and we can't agree on anything. She wants this huge wedding that neither David or I want. She wants a sit-down dinner when we'd prefer a simple reception. She wants me to have both my sisters, three of my cousins, and you guys as bridesmaids, and I'd rather keep it simple with you two. Worst part is, she doesn't have any money, so basically she's making plans she expects me and David to pay for. I refuse to go into a marriage bankrupt over a wedding."

David intertwined his fingers with hers. "I'm telling you the answer. We should elope. Get a license, grab up the crew here and go do it."

"I don't want no Justice of the Peace wedding. I want to say my vows before a man of God." Nakia poked her lips out.

David leaned over and kissed them. "I'm agreeing with you. Don't make no sense to me either to spend all that money for one day. They say the wedding is for the mother of the bride anyway."

"Then she needs to pay for it." Nakia curled her upper lip.

"Don't worry about it, babe." David squeezed

Nakia's knee. "The important thing is that you're here and we can finally get married."

"Yeah, but when?" Nakia lamented. "At this rate, it'll be another year. I don't think I can make it that long."

"Me either, baby."

David turned to Khalil. "What about y'all, man? When y'all gon' tie the knot?"

Khalil's cheeks turned red. "How you gon' call me out like that, man? In God's time."

Alaysia looked at her feet when Khalil said that. I guess we were all wondering about it—including Alaysia—but no one was bold enough to ask.

We sat around the living room, joking, laughing and eating pie. It was cool to see Kevin so close to David and Khalil. He seemed comfortable and at ease. I hadn't seen him like that before. Even with Aaron, Ricky, and the rest of the band, he was jovial, but still reserved.

"When do we get to hear the new music?" Nakia asked.

"Yeah, when do we get to hear it?" I pretended I hadn't heard most of the new songs on midnight phone calls.

Kevin winked at me. "We'll give you guys a little taste." He went to the front closet and pulled out his guitar.

"Do you take that thing everywhere?" Khalil asked.

Kevin said, "Pretty much. Me and my first love can't be separated." He kissed the case.

I feigned a look of jealousy.

Kevin sat in the armchair and started playing

some chords. He and David harmonized on a song.

They sang the chorus a few times and indicated for us to join in. Nakia added a sweet soprano, I added my alto, and Kevin jumped down to tenor. We would have been in perfect harmony if Khalil weren't completely tone deaf. Alaysia sat and watched us.

Khalil reached over to take her hand as tears slipped down her face. He pulled her closer to him, kissed her forehead, and whispered in her ear, wiping her tears. David and Kevin kept playing and singing, doing that thing they did that invoked the pure presence of God.

They finished the words, but Kevin kept playing softly.

Khalil tickled Alaysia's toes. "I take it you like the song?"

She nodded and mumbled something none of us could understand.

"What's that, baby?" Khalil asked.

"I . . . I want to get saved."

Khalil sat up and looked at her. He and I said it at the same time, "What?"

Kevin stopped playing.

Alaysia held her hands out to Khalil. "I want to get saved. I don't have to wait 'til church on Sunday, do I?"

Khalil kissed her hands. "No, baby, you can get saved right here, right now."

She nodded. "Okay, let's do it."

We all scooted closer in a circle and held hands. Khalil led Alaysia through the sinner's prayer, and she accepted Christ into her life. We cried with her and hugged her.

Alaysia wiped her eyes. "Do I have to get baptized at the church?"

"Where do you want to get baptized?" Khalil cupped Alaysia's face in his hands.

Alaysia's eyes sparkled. "At the beach. I want to go to Tybee Island and get baptized in the ocean."

59

A few nights later, I was in a good, deep sleep when the doorbell rang. I looked over at the clock. It was 11:52 PM—too late for someone to be coming over. I knew not to expect Alaysia to get it. That girl slept like the dead.

When I opened the door, Kevin was standing there, eyes bloodshot red. He grabbed me and held on to me real tight.

"Kevin, what's wrong?"

"Nothing, Monnie. I just needed to give you a big hug and kiss and tell you how much I love you."

"At midnight? What prompted this?"

He looked at his watch like he didn't realize what time it was. "I couldn't sleep. I needed to let you know I love you."

"Okay." I led him back to my room. "Did something special happen to bring on this sudden overwhelming love, or were you just thinking about how wonderful I am?"

My little joke was lost on Kevin.

He sat down on the chaise and I sat on the bed opposite him. "Me and David and Khalil had Bible study earlier. We opened with prayer, and before we got into the Word, Khalil said he felt like God knitted our hearts together for a purpose. That there was destiny in Him bringing us together. He went on and on about how he was grateful for having such strong men of God in his life, and how God had given him the brothers he never had, but in a better way than he ever imagined. Then he asked us to pray for him. He's been struggling in his relationship with Alaysia."

I must have looked worried because he said, "Not like that. I mean, they're happy and he wants to marry her."

I must have looked excited because he said, "And if you tell her, I'll have to kill you. I mean it, Monnie, this was said in confidence in our men's meeting, so I shouldn't have even told you."

"I won't tell, I promise." I clenched my fists like I was holding on to the secret.

"He said he's struggling because he's a broke grad student with only the promise of being a broke minister when he finishes school. He's afraid of not being able to provide for her like she's used to. Said it made him feel like less than a man, but at the same time, he can't deny the call of God on his life. He can't imagine doing anything other than preaching the Word of God, but doesn't know how he's going to support a family doing so. He said he hadn't been able to talk to anybody about it, but it was really getting him down, and he was glad he could come to us."

Kevin got up and paced around my bedroom. "Then David talked about how he had met so many brothers who weren't about anything, but he was glad God brought him true spiritual brothers he could trust and be honest and transparent with. He asked us to cover him in the Spirit because he and Nakia are really struggling with the whole sex thing. He said he was glad he had us to come to and be accountable to, and knew if we were praying for him, they'd be able to make it. He said he was glad God brought us together as covenant brothers.

"I felt like the biggest hypocrite. Here they were opening their hearts to me, talking about how great it was to have best friends they could be completely honest with, and I felt like a big fake. What could I do? I told them. Everything. Everything about my past, everything about what happened with our marriage. I told them about the classes and the therapist."

I leaned forward on the bed, hardly breathing. "What'd they say?"

"They were upset. Real upset."

My heart fell.

"They couldn't understand why I hadn't told them before. They said I had been carrying too much by myself all this time, and that God made us brothers so we could carry each other's spiritual burdens. They said I should have trusted them enough to tell them. I told 'em I was worried they'd change up on me."

Kevin stopped. His voice got choked up. "And

they said, 'Never that, dawg. We brothers for life, up or down, ride or die. We got your back, man. All the way.' I told them I was sorry for not trusting them, but I could never say how grateful I was for having friends like them in my life."

Kevin shook his head. "Then they both laid hands on me and prayed for me. Monnie, nobody's ever prayed for me like that in my life. They went back to my childhood and rebuked every spirit that had ever attacked my manhood. They prayed for our marriage and for our future together. They prayed I'd be able to stand as a healed, whole, complete man of God and be a leader to my family. I never felt anything so strong in my life."

"Oh, Kevin."

"And then they hugged me. Both of 'em. And they weren't scared of me. And for the first time in my life, I wasn't scared of them. And I didn't feel anything. I mean, I felt their friendship, but I didn't feel anything . . . you know, like I shouldn't have been feeling. I just felt washed and whole and strong and new and . . . I . . . I felt delivered."

"Wow, Kevin. I don't know what to say. Except God is more faithful than I could have ever imagined. I'm glad you were able to tell them and glad they were the men of God I knew them to be."

"Monnie, I . . . I can't thank you enough for believing in me and believing in God for me. When you left me, I thought my life was over. I thought Satan had beat me for good and I'd never be delivered. I felt like I woke up from the best dream back into the nightmare my life had always been and that things would never be good again. And now . . ."

"Now, what?"

"God is good. That's all I can say."

I smiled and took his hand. He pulled me into his arms and we held each other. I felt more love for Kevin than I ever felt before, and I felt more love coming from him than I ever felt before. I felt like God was standing there hugging both of us and melding our hearts even closer together.

Kevin pulled back and looked me in the eye. "There's one more thing. I need . . . I want you to go to my therapy appointment with me next week. Dr. Farley says I'm doing great, but there's one big issue I want to deal with, and I need you there to do it."

"What is it?"

"We'll talk about it when we get there. A'ight?"

"Okay, Kevin. Is everything all right?"

He grinned that crooked little-boy grin I so loved. "Yeah. Better than all right."

60

Kevin clasped my hand in his as we sat in Dr. Farley's waiting room. His leg was bouncing and his eyes were blinking.

The door opened and a tall, olive-toned man with a comforting smile gestured for us to come in. "Kevin." They shook hands. "And you must be Monica. You're right, Kevin, she is one of the most beautiful women I've ever seen."

I elbowed Kevin in the side. "You been talking about me?"

We followed Dr. Farley into his tastefully decorated office and sank into the plush armchairs facing his silver-framed glass desk.

"Monica, I'm glad you agreed to join us today. Let me start out by saying Kevin has made a considerable amount of progress over the past two months. If all my patients were as committed to the healing process as he is, my job would be much easier."

I smiled and nodded at Kevin.

Dr. Farley continued, "There are two issues Kevin is still dealing with, and I thought he needed you here to be able to work through them." He nodded at Kevin.

Kevin said, "Ever since that day in the hospital, I've been thinking about what you said. About all the little boys at Love and Faith in D.C. and Alexandria. How they're still in danger. How I have a responsibility to make sure the men who molested me don't have a chance to molest them."

I nodded.

"I've decided since Bishop Walker isn't going to address it, I need to go to his superiors. I've written letters to the Bishops' council governing Love and Faith."

I squeezed his hand. "That's great. I'm proud of you."

"One thing, though. I don't know what Bishop Walker is capable of and whether he'll do what he threatened to do. If he does, things could get ugly for me and our names and our marriage. Our whole life may be exposed. I need to know you're willing to risk that."

"I'll be right by your side, Kevin. I'm behind you one hundred percent." *God, please, don't let that happen. Haven't we been through enough?*

He smiled and nodded. "Thanks, Monnie. I feel like it's something I gotta do, no matter what the outcome. If I can prevent one little boy from having to live through what I've lived through, it'll be worth it."

Dr. Farley said, "Kevin and I drafted the letters last week, but he wanted to talk to you before he sent them out." Dr. Farley looked at Kevin. "The second issue is a bit more difficult."

Kevin grabbed my hand. His hand almost slid off mine, it was so sweaty. "I . . . I wanted us to talk about . . . I . . ." He looked at Dr. Farley. Kevin took a deep breath. "Monnie, I'm afraid I don't please you sexually."

I looked at Kevin, then looked at Dr. Farley, then looked at Kevin again. My silence said everything. I tried to fix it. "I wouldn't say that. I mean, it's not like I'm some big expert or anything. You're the only person I've been with, so I don't have anything to compare it to."

"Yeah, but you know whether you enjoy it or not. Come on, Monnie. In this room, we're honest about everything. That's the only way for things to get better."

I took a deep breath. "Okay, sometimes it seems like you're afraid or nervous or you don't want to do it. You're affectionate until it's time to make love, then you're an ice cube."

Dr. Farley leaned forward. "Monica, it's important for you to understand this is a very natural reaction for someone who's been molested. It's not so much the homosexual issue as it is that Kevin's first sexual experiences were traumatic, violating, and terrifying. Even worse, they were committed by supposedly spiritual men who Kevin should have been able to trust. Up until his relationship with you, all Kevin's sexual experiences were negative ones. Any pleasure he might have gotten from his relationship with Trey was overwhelmed by intense feelings of guilt, self-hatred, and fear of literally going to hell. Therefore, in Kevin's mind, sex is bad, sex is evil, sex is painful. Anytime he comes together with you, he brings all these thoughts with him. We've talked through the nightmares and have done some cognitive therapy to reshape his thoughts and attitudes about sex. Kevin still has some issues, and that's where you come in." He nodded at Kevin again.

"I want to make love to you," Kevin said. "But I'm afraid of what you think of me. I feel like you don't expect me to . . . perform well, and then I'm afraid you'll be thinking about whether I'm a real man or not."

I rubbed his hand. "It's not that I think you won't perform well. There have been times you've performed *very* well. It was one of the best feelings I've ever had. I felt like heaven and earth moved. Those were the times you were relaxed. Like when we went to Florida that time and had so much fun. And definitely when we went to Jamaica. But most of the time, you're so tense that it makes me tense, and I don't think either one of us gets anything out of it."

Dr. Farley stepped in. "Kevin wanted you to understand all this so that the two of you could work on this issue. Half of the battle is knowing what's going on inside each other."

I nodded.

Dr. Farley said, "Monica, is there anything you want to talk about?"

I shrugged. "Not really." It felt weird talking to a strange white guy about our sex life. Kevin seemed comfortable with him, but that's because they had talked about all sorts of deep and personal stuff for the last few months.

"Are you sure, Monica? This would be a good time to get it out." Dr. Farley's eyes probed into my heart.

"I guess my question is the obvious question. When we talked about what happened that day with Trey, Kevin just said it was a mistake. I still don't understand why. I've forgiven Kevin, but there's that question in the back of my mind. If I don't know why, how can I be sure it won't happen again? I thought we were happy. Why all of a sudden, out of nowhere, would he do that?"

"Ask him."

I turned to Kevin. "Why all of a sudden, out of nowhere, would you do that?"

Kevin stared at his shoes. "I've asked myself that same question every day for the past nineteen months. All those days I was without you, alone in a cold bed. Then, since we've been back together, I realize how much I love you and how much you love me. I keep asking myself, what made me do that?" Kevin rubbed his chin. "I didn't understand 'til Dr. Farley and I talked about it. To me, it still isn't a good enough reason. I don't feel like I can offer you a reason to explain breaking your heart."

"What did you come up with when you and Dr. Farley talked about it?"

Dr. Farley said, "I think it stemmed from the

exact issue we were talking about. Kevin was very uncomfortable in his sex life with you. He needed to express himself sexually, and along comes the only person he ever had a somewhat positive sexual experience with. It was almost inevitable. People naturally have a need for sexual intimacy. To be in a close relationship and not be able to express that is quite difficult. I think it's amazing that people of the Christian faith are able to maintain celibacy in intimate relationships."

I nodded, trying to process what he was saying. "So you're telling me Kevin needed to express himself sexually, but he wasn't comfortable with me, but he was comfortable with Trey. I guess I understand, but it doesn't make me feel any better. Just brings us back to the same point. What needs to happen for Kevin to be comfortable with me sexually?"

Kevin took my hand. "I think a lot of the work I've done with Dr. Farley has helped. Everything in my life right now has helped. The Lifelines classes. Just being in God's presence and being able to deal with the stuff I've kept inside all these years. All I need now is to know you forgive me and believe in me as a man."

"I've forgiven you the best I know how. This talk has helped. Seeing the new man you're becoming has helped a lot, too. I don't believe you're the same man you were when you cheated on me with Trey. I understand what your childhood did to you and everything you've been doing these past few months has brought healing. I just want you to be able to relax."

"I will relax. Once I know you forgive me, and you love me, and you know I'm a man and believe I can . . . you know . . . please you."

I nodded. "I do, but . . . now it's gonna be weird. The first time we try, I'm gonna be wondering if you're okay and you're gonna be wondering if I'm okay, and we'll both be nervous, and then if things don't work because we're nervous, the next time we try, we'll both remember the first time we tried and it didn't work that time, so we won't expect it to work the second time and then this vicious cycle. How do we keep that from happening?"

Kevin looked at Dr. Farley as if to second my question.

"Watching the two of you and your interactions, I can tell how much you love each other," Dr. Farley said. "The pain in your eyes, Monica, when we talk about Kevin's past. The way you instinctively rub his arm when he discusses difficult issues, the way he looks at you when he talks about making love to you. That's all you need. The love you already have inside and an understanding of what's going on inside each other's minds. Kevin, you now understand Monica does enjoy you when you're relaxed—that you do please her. Monica, you now understand the torment that went on inside of Kevin every time he approached you for intimacy. That knowledge will help you work through these issues. And time. If things don't go perfect the first time, that doesn't mean the second time won't 'shake heaven and earth'."

I blushed at Dr. Farley's use of my description.

"Just commit to keep trying until you guys get it right."

I took Kevin's hand and smiled. "I'm glad I understand now. It really wasn't my weight, huh?"

"No, it wasn't. And when it's time for us to come together again, I fully intend to show you how beautiful and sexy I think you are."

I didn't want to ask the unspoken question. When *would* it be time for us to come together again?

61

A laysia went through great pains planning her baptismal ceremony. While searching the Internet, she found what looked like a great beach house at Tybee Island. She made arrangements for Zanetta, Eric, and Talinda to teach our classes and clients at the gym for the weekend. She shopped for hours to find a beautiful, white, flowing linen dress.

"Why the dress?" I asked as she studied herself in the full-length mirror in her bedroom.

"Promise you won't laugh?"

"Of course not."

"I figure since the church is the bride of Christ, and I'm about to become a part of the church, it's sort of like marrying Jesus. I want to be a beautiful bride for him."

"That's sweet, Alaysia. I wouldn't laugh at that."

"I'm glad to be saved. When I think about all the things I've done in my life and the fact that He's willing to forgive me . . . it's hard to imagine. Just think—all my sins will be washed away in the ocean. The tide will carry them far away to the sea of forgetfulness, like I never did it."

I smiled.

"What? Are you laughing at me?"

"No, I think it's beautiful that you have more of an appreciation for your salvation than some people who've been saved all their life."

"I guess I'm like the woman with the alabaster box. I know I've been forgiven of many sins, so I appreciate Him saving me so much more."

"You spend too much time with Khalil. You're becoming a walking Bible like him."

"I found white bathing suits for you and Nakia with white bathing suit covers and sarongs. And the guys can wear white shirts and shorts."

"Now all we need is the bridesmaid flowers," I joked.

Alaysia's eye's brightened. "That's perfect. We should get some calla lilies for you guys to carry."

I smiled.

"You promised you wouldn't laugh."

"I'm not laughing. You a special person, you know that, Alaysia?"

The phone rang. Alaysia grabbed it. "Hello?" She smiled. "Hey, Kevin, how are you?" She paused. "I'm good. Here's Monica. Huh?" She frowned. "Oh, okay. What's up?" Her mouth flew open. "Oh, Kevin, that's a great idea. Of course." She turned her back to me. "Of course, that would be wonderful. I wouldn't mind at all. Oooh, that's so special."

She did a little happy dance. "Huh? Okay, I won't tell her." She listened. "Okay. Talk to you later." She hung up the phone and started walking out of her bedroom.

"Uummmm, excuse me?" I said.

She turned around with her innocent face on. "Huh?"

"You won't tell me what?"

"So you heard me tell him I wouldn't tell you. Why you asking then?"

"Don't even try it. You know I hate secrets."

"Are you asking me to betray the trust of a fellow Christian?"

"Stop playing, Laysia. What'd he say?" I put my hands together, pleading with her. "At least give me a little hint."

"Okay, here's a hint. Kevin loves you very much." She popped me on the arm and walked out of the room.

"No fair!" I decided to go to the source, and picked up her phone.

Kevin must have recognized my number on the caller ID. "Hello, Monnie. I know what you're calling for, and it's a surprise. You're gonna have to wait. Talk to you later. Bye." *Click.*

62

The six of us piled into Kevin's Excursion and headed for Tybee Island. We laughed and talked the whole ride down. Kevin drove and was quieter than usual.

I squeezed his knee. "You okay?"

He smiled and took a quick glance over at me. "I'm fine, just thinking."

"About what?"

"About your surprise."

"You mean I get it this weekend?"

"Yep."

"When?"

"What y'all whispering about up there?" Alaysia poked her face in between our seats.

"My surprise that you know about that I don't know about." I scowled at her.

"You'll get it soon enough. Be patient." Khalil patted me on the shoulder.

"You know about it, too? Everybody knows about it but me?" I poked Kevin in the side.

"Hey, don't bother the driver," Nakia called out from the back seat. She and David were hugged up back there like they hadn't seen each other in a week.

The beach house was great. There was a two-story great room furnished with a large, leather sectional couch, a big screen television, DVD, and full stereo. The kitchen was huge, with a breakfast table large enough for eight. There was a large master bedroom tucked away in a back corner on the first floor with a king-sized bed and sunken Jacuzzi tub. The upstairs had four bedrooms and two bathrooms. The sliding glass door in the great room opened out onto a deck with steps that led down onto the sand of the Atlantic Ocean. The deck had some comfortable beach chaises, a large umbrella, a table and chairs, and a large grill.

"My God, Alaysia, I hate to ask how much this place cost," I said.

"I got a good price through this vacation travel thingee on the Internet. It wasn't bad at all. Plus, I'm getting baptized. That's a big deal."

I think she was the only one who didn't notice Khalil shaking his head and muttering under his breath about the extravagance of the place.

Alaysia and I got dressed for a run on the beach. Nakia took one look at our running clothes, rolled her eyes and brushed the sand off a beach lounger on the deck. She pulled out a stack of books, fixed the beach umbrella and said, "If you need me, this is where I'll be. I gotta catch up on my reading."

I looked at her books. One said, *Heart of Devotion*, another *Joy*, and *For Love and Grace*.

"What are these about?" I turned the books over to look at the back covers.

"Girl, Christian fiction. I had to give up my secular novels when I moved here. Can't be reading no sex scenes living this close to David. Might get something stirred up I can't control."

I laughed at her. "Girl, you two just need to elope. I ain't seen nobody struggle this much with keeping it holy, and I been in church a long time."

"That's 'cause they ain't struggling. They doin' they thing and lying about it," Nakia said.

Alaysia put her hands on her hips. "That's not true. Me and Khalil are keeping it holy."

Nakia sucked her teeth. "Yeah, but Khalil is Jesus' first cousin, so that don't count."

We all laughed. I stretched my legs. "Come on, girl, let's do this thing before it gets too hot out here. Nakia, you going running?"

"Y'all go 'head. I don't believe it takes all that runnin' and carrying on." Nakia dismissed us by opening a book.

Alaysia and I ran for about an hour, until we were drenched with sweat. Even though it was early September, it was still hot and humid outside. Occasional breezes off the water cooled things off only slightly.

When we got back, Nakia had fallen asleep on her lounger, and David was curled up asleep in a lounger next to her. We walked into the house to find our men. Kevin was stretched out on one part of the sectional with a Myles Munroe book, *Understanding The Power and Purpose of a Man*, on his chest. Khalil was stretched out on the other end with *Rich Dad, Poor Dad* on his chest.

"Ain't this a sorry sight. We drive all the way down to the beach so these folks can sleep the day away?" Alaysia shook her head.

I stopped Alaysia as she was about to shake Khalil. "Let 'im rest. You picked such a perfect house that everyone is relaxed."

We both went to take a shower. Half an hour later, Alaysia was curled up on the ottoman beside Khalil, asleep. I grabbed one of Nakia's books, *Heart of Devotion*, and lay out on a beach lounger on the deck. It was relaxing sitting in the sunny, salty air with the wind whipping my cheeks. I was instantly engrossed in the book. It was contemporary, like a regular African American novel, but was based on Christian themes. I'd have to try this Christian fiction stuff. Nakia was right about not reading stuff that would keep me awake and smoldering all night.

Durned if them Negroes didn't stay 'sleep for almost three hours. I was almost halfway through the book by the time Nakia stirred.

"Well, good morning. Or afternoon, almost evening, I should say," I said.

Nakia squinted and shielded her eyes from the sun. "Where is everybody?"

"'Sleep, just like you." I closed the book and returned it to Nakia's stack.

Alaysia stumbled out onto the deck. "Why didn't you get me up?"

"For what? You were 'sleep," I said.

"Oh my God, I'm starving." Alaysia stretched her arms up in the air. Khalil came up behind her and grabbed her around the waist. She squealed.

He laughed. "Gotcha." He turned her around and held her close, kissing her on the nose and forehead.

"What did I do to deserve that?" She smiled up at him.

"It would take me forever to tell you."

She laid her head on his chest. "Love you."

"Love you, too."

Whoever thought Miss Alaysia—connoisseur of wine, weed, and as many men as she could get— would be saved, about to get baptized, and waiting for the man of her dreams to propose? God was truly a miracle worker.

Kevin came up behind them. "I hate to break up this moment, but if I don't get something to eat soon, I might have to hurt somebody."

Alaysia and Khalil said at the same time, "Me too."

Nakia looked at Alaysia. "You're the master chef. What bird food will we be dining on this afternoon?"

Alaysia had packed groceries for gourmet vegetarian meals for the whole weekend.

Khalil elbowed Kevin. "We'll cook, ladies. You have a seat and relax."

Alaysia said, "The veggie burgers are in the freezer. You don't have to thaw them before you put them on the grill."

"Who said we were cooking rabbit food?" Khalil said.

"That's all I brought, so that's all you get." Alaysia crossed her arms in front of her.

"We went to the market up the street while you were running." Khalil looked at Kevin. "Ready to fire up the grill, bruh?"

"I got you, man. I'm on it." Kevin lifted the bag next to the grill and poured some charcoal out. He drizzled some lighter fluid then looked around. "Anybody got some matches?"

Alaysia watched all this with her mouth wide open. "I can't believe you guys. What did you buy? Did you buy meat? You're actually gonna cook meat?"

"Y'all better be careful or lightning's gonna strike." Nakia smirked and tickled David's toes. He must have been really tired because he didn't move.

"Khalil, you bought meat?" Alaysia was pouting now.

"Alaysia, just because you love fake meat doesn't mean everybody else does. We usually humor you and eat that stuff—and it *is* good—but you gotta be fair. Sometimes we wanna eat what we wanna eat." He beat on his chest. "Me man. Me need meat."

Alaysia pushed her lips out further.

He leaned over and kissed them. "Come on, Laysia. Let us enjoy our weekend. You don't expect me to eat vegetarian for the rest of my life, do you?"

"The rest of your life?"

"Yeah, the rest of my life. I know you brainwashed Monica, but I ain't convertin'."

"Brainwashed? What's that supposed to mean?" I said.

"Means you've joined Alaysia's veggie cult. The rest of us will not be sucked in." Kevin disappeared into the kitchen.

Alaysia's ire must have been defused by Khalil's "rest of my life" comment. "I guess a little meat wouldn't hurt."

I stared at her. "You never said that to me. It was your way or no way."

Alaysia batted her eyelashes. "I know, but you're not him."

"Oh, it's like that, huh?"

"Yeah, girl. It's like that." Alaysia laughed.

Kevin emerged with a large pan piled high with thick steaks at one end and salmon fillets at the other.

Alaysia made a face. "Yuck. I'm cooking me and Monnie's veggie burgers on the grill inside. I don't want any of your meat juice getting on our food."

I gulped. "Salmon? That's my favorite."

"Be strong, girl. Don't give in to the carnivorous cravings of the flesh."

I bit my lip. "But it's salmon."

"After a whole year, you're going to slip back into the ranks of the animal flesh-eating beasts?" Alaysia's eyes were wide.

"Is that what we are?" Nakia asked.

"I'm sorry, Laysia. I got to have a piece of that salmon. It's high in omega fatty acids, so it's good for me." I licked my lips.

"Monnie! You traitor. Kevin, you did this on purpose. You knew that was her favorite."

Kevin grinned. "I ain't trying to eat tofu for the rest of my life either."

Alaysia shook her head. "First Eve and the serpent, now Kevin beguiles Monica. Oh, how the mighty have fallen."

We all laughed. David rolled over. "I'm trying to get some sleep here." He looked at the pan piled high with meat. "I'm awake. I'm awake."

Everybody laughed.

After we ate, we changed into our bathing suits. We splashed in the ocean, swam out to the buoys, and played beach volleyball until it was dusk. Then we showered and came back out to the deck. Alaysia lit a few citronella candles to keep the bugs away.

We laughed and talked and ate leftovers until Alaysia looked down at her watch. "We better turn in. We gotta get up early."

"Why are we doing this at sunrise again?" Nakia wrinkled her nose.

"Because it's the dawning of a new day in my life. Because the Son is rising with healing in His wings to make my life whole. Because the Lord is rising as a Sun and Shield in my life. Because—"

"Okay, okay, we get it." I rolled my eyes. "Man, you're worse than Khalil. What do you guys do? Have Bible study on all your dates?"

"Yep. Keeps us from doing other things God might not be as pleased with," Khalil said.

Kevin stood up. "Yeah, we better go on to bed. Tomorrow is a big day."

I stood up with him. "It is?"

"Yeah, and that's all the clue you get. Don't ask me no questions about no surprise 'cause I ain't telling." Kevin kissed my cheek.

I looked around at my friends.

"Don't look at us. We ain't telling you, either." Nakia waved a nanny-nanny-boo-boo finger in my face.

"Y'all make me sick."

"We love you too, Monnie," Alaysia said.

63

It was still dark outside when I woke up to Alaysia tapping me on my forehead. "Time to get up."

I peeked one eye open. "What time is it?"

"Six o'clock. On the news, it said sunrise is at six thirty-eight."

I knew there was no sense in asking for fifteen more minutes. Alaysia was acting like a kid waking her parents on Christmas morning, ready to open her presents.

After she seemed satisfied that I wasn't going back to sleep, she went knocking on the other doors. Nakia took the room next to us. David and Kevin were in the room across the hall, and Khalil in the room next to them. We agreed that no one would get the master bedroom because it wasn't fair to the rest of us for someone to have a king-sized bed and a Jacuzzi while the rest of us had twin beds and bathtubs.

I put on my white, one-piece bathing suit with the white sarong and cover-all. Alaysia already had her white linen dress on. Nakia came out of her room looking half asleep in an outfit that matched mine. We waited down in the living room until Khalil and David came out in their white trunks and T-shirts. Alaysia pulled the calla lilies out of the refrigerator and gave them to me and Nakia.

"Where's Kevin?" I didn't know why I was whispering.

"He's on his way down." David wiped the sleep out of his eyes. "We'll be outside. Why don't you wait for him to make sure he didn't go back to bed?"

The others filed out the door and walked down to the beach.

I heard a door open and Kevin walked out. Instead of his outfit matching Khalil's and David's, it was more like Alaysia's. He had on a white linen shirt with white linen pants.

"How come you got a special outfit?"

"I'm getting baptized again. I was gonna get an outfit like the other guys, but Miss Alaysia insisted that I wear this. Something about a wedding ceremony and being the bride of Christ."

"I don't understand."

He took my hand. "I want to celebrate being a completely new man in Christ. These last few months have been life changing, and even though I know I still have a ways to go, I feel like I'm finally becoming the man God originally intended me to be. At the risk of sounding like Alaysia, I want to let God wash the old man away into the ocean and solidify the new creature I've become."

"Kevin, that's wonderful." I kissed him. "What a beautiful surprise."

He looked past me out the glass door to the beach. "We better go. If the sun comes all the way up and we're not outside, Alaysia will kill us."

It was the most beautiful baptismal I had ever seen. Khalil officiated and David assisted. The sky glowed with the dazzling colors of the sunrise, and the cool breeze off the water kissed each of us awake. We gathered in a circle with Alaysia in the middle. She shivered, and I didn't know if she was cold or nervous.

Khalil held his hand up to heaven. "In the name of the Father, the Son, and the Holy Spirit."

He took Alaysia down under the water and I swear when she came up, she radiated like the woman on *Touched By An Angel*. She cried and said, "Jesus, thank you for making me new."

Her tears and glowing were contagious. As she hugged each one of us, she said, "I love you guys so much. I finally have a family."

When she was finished hugging everybody, Khalil held out his hand then pulled her to him. He cupped her face in his hands and said, "Alaysia, I love you with all my heart. I may not be able to give you the life you're used to, but I promise I can love you better than you've ever been loved. I want to protect you, take care of you and be with you . . . for the rest of my life." Out of nowhere, he pulled out a beautiful engagement ring. He slipped it onto her finger. "Alaysia Zaid, will you be my wife?"

If Khalil hadn't been holding on to Alaysia, I think she would have fallen over. She stared at him with her mouth wide open, then looked at me as if to say "Did he really say what I think he said?" I nodded and smiled and she turned back to Khalil. Fresh tears fell down her face as she put her arms around him and kissed him.

He pulled back. "I take that as a yes?"

She nodded. They kissed and held each other for a while.

Alaysia collected herself and we refocused. Kevin took his place in the middle of the circle.

Khalil held his hand up again and said, "In the name of the Father, the Son, and the Holy Spirit."

It took both David and Khalil to take Kevin down in the water and bring him up again. When he came up, he held his hands up to heaven as his tears mixed with the salt water streaming down his face. Khalil and David hugged him, and the three of them held on to each other for a while. Alaysia and Nakia joined in the group hug then stepped back as Kevin walked over to hug me. As we held each other, I felt Kevin's heart pounding against my chest. He brought his lips to my ear.

"Thanks for loving me and believing in me, Monnie. It was your love and God's love together that made me a new man."

I kissed him until David tapped him on the shoulder. "Yo, man, this is a baptism, not a wedding."

We all laughed and headed inside.

After we showered and changed, we came downstairs to cook breakfast together. We had a huge feast of fresh berries, pancakes, scrambled tofu, tofu sausage, wheat biscuits, leftover salmon, and steak and fried potatoes and onions. When we spread everything out on the table, Alaysia clapped her hands together. "Now this is what I call a wedding feast."

We sat down and heaped our plates.

David looked around at everybody. "How would you guys feel about coming back in a few months and doing this whole beach weekend thing again?"

"Why? You wanna get baptized?" Kevin asked.

David took Nakia's hand. "No, we're gonna go ahead and elope. We don't want to do it at the courthouse. We want to do it here at the beach, with the family God has given us."

"Aaaawww," Alaysia and I sing-songed together.

Nakia smiled. "We're gonna invite Pastor Ramsey and his wife down for the weekend so he can marry us. I'll tell my family after we get back. They'll be mad, but they'll get over it."

Alaysia clapped her hands together. "Shoot, girl, we might make it a double wedding. I'd love to get married here."

Khalil looked surprised. "You mean you don't want a big, fancy, downtown, expensive wedding and invite the whole city of Atlanta?"

Alaysia kissed Khalil's cheek. "I don't need all that stuff, baby. All I need to make me happy is you."

Khalil kissed her on the lips. "I love you."

David laughed. "Yeah, man, maybe y'all better get married in a few months with us."

When we finished eating, Khalil patted his belly and said, "After that kind of meal, I think we all need a run on the beach."

Alaysia said, "Yeah, I could use a few miles."

David nodded. "Yeah, man. Then after that, we can go back to that market. We're gonna need some more steaks for lunch."

"No more animal flesh." Alaysia made a face as she and Khalil went to get their running shoes.

Nakia shook her head. "I ain't runnin' on no beach. I'm going back out on the deck to read my book."

"Don't you mean read the back of your eyelids?" I teased.

Nakia threw her napkin at me.

"How 'bout we take a walk instead of a run on the beach?" David said to Nakia.

"I don't feel like that either." Nakia wrinkled up her nose. David elbowed her and she jumped. "Oh, yeah. A walk on the beach sounds good."

"Let me get these dishes and I'll change into my running clothes." I got up to take the dishes to the kitchen.

I put the fruit in a container and put it in the fridge. Kevin helped load the dishwasher. The others trooped back downstairs and walked to the patio door.

I wiped my hands. "Oh, shoot, you guys are ready. Let me get my shoes."

Kevin took my hand and said, "Why don't you stay here with me?" He kissed my fingers then took the keys out of his pocket and threw them to David. "Make sure y'all get plenty of steak, man. Take your time and pick out some good ones."

David caught them. "Yeah, man. We might drive back to Atlanta for the steaks. You know ain't nothing like steak from Atlanta."

Nakia popped his arm. "Shut up, boy. Come on here."

They closed the patio door behind them.

"Why do I feel like I've been set up?"

Kevin answered me with a kiss.

And then another.

And then another.

And then all the kisses ran together into one long kiss until I couldn't breathe. The intense look in his eyes was full of desire. "I told you I wanted to celebrate being a new man."

He scooped me up and carried me back to the master bedroom, the whole time kissing my face, my neck, my lips. I thought I would melt. He lay me down on the bed, covered with lavender rose petals, and slowly undressed me, kissing me the whole time. Everywhere.

My body was singing. And so were the birds, and the ocean, and the sun, and the trees and all of creation it seemed.

And heaven and earth moved.

All . . . day . . . long.

Reader's Group Guide

1) In deciding whether she should tell Bishop about Kevin's sexuality, Monica says that if God gives her a sign, she'll tell him. Trina tells her she's fleecing God and recommends that she learn to hear from the Holy Spirit. "Fleecing" refers to a passage in Judges where Gideon asks God for a sign to prove what He said was true (See Judges 6:37-40). Is fleecing wrong? What are ways of hearing from God and confirming His will for our lives?

2) Trina refers to Love and Faith as a gay-friendly church. What does she mean by this? What should be the approach to homosexuality in the church? Monica states that Bishop wouldn't want Kevin as his minister of music if he knew about Kevin's sexual orientation. Should known homosexuals be allowed to hold positions of leadership in the church?

3) Trina says on repeated occasions that sin is sin and that homosexuality shouldn't be treated any different than any other sin. She equates Kevin's problem with homosexuality with

her past problem with fornication. Is homosexuality a worse sin than others? Why are homosexuals treated differently than individuals with sin issues in other areas?

4) Through her conversations with Bishop Walker, Monica discovers that his motives are impure. She has to calm herself down and remind herself not to disrespect her pastor. How should one respond if they discover that their spiritual leader is wrong, has improper motives, or doesn't have their best interest at heart?

5) Monica stops going to church because of the incident with Kevin and her disappointment at Bishop Walker's response. She later tells Alaysia that she's fine with God, it's just His people she's not sure about. She later laments that she doesn't know how she allowed her fallout with Kevin and Bishop to cause her to fall out with God. How can being hurt in the church, especially by a spiritual leader, affect one's spiritual walk?

6) Monica's best friend in college, Alaysia, was unsaved and made bad lifestyle choices. Alaysia's habits affected Monica—she drank alcohol and smoked marijuana. Should Christians be friends with unsaved people? If so, how should they respond to their unsaved friend's ungodly lifestyle habits? Monica's friendship with Alaysia, in spite of causing her to sin, ultimately resulted in Alaysia's get-

ting saved. Does that justify Monica's drinking and smoking?

7) In referring to her abortion, Alaysia admits that she can't overcome the guilt of having done something so wrong. She sarcastically says that Christians can commit any sin and just have to ask forgiveness, but have no remorse when they do wrong. Does God's grace and forgiveness make it "okay" for Christians to sin?

8) Initially after the incident, whenever Monica feels stressed or sad, she reaches for food. When Alaysia comes to visit her in Atlanta, Monica reaches for alcohol from the mini-bar when she's dealing with upsetting thoughts. Later in the story, she admits to Alaysia that she's eating cookies to make her feel better, and Alaysia tells her to use something else. What other bad habits do individuals use to deal with negative emotions? How does Monica eventually learn to handle negative emotions?

9) Monica admits to Alaysia that her questions about the Bible and Christianity make her feel like a "raggedy Christian." After a brunch Bible study with Khalil, Monica feels as if Alaysia knows as much about Christianity as she does, even though she's spent her entire life in church. Why is this? Do you think the average Christian possess enough Biblical knowledge to minister to the unsaved?

10) While Alaysia is struggling with her decision to become a Christian, she mentions several obstacles that have blocked her. She doesn't understand why a good God would allow so many bad things to happen. She also says that present day Christianity is nothing like she would expect it to be based on the things she's read in the Word. She also says that Christians "flake out" when it's time to have faith. How can the attitudes and actions (or inaction) of Christians affect the unsaved around them?

11) Monica becomes frustrated with being single and cries out to God that she knows that she should be satisfied with Him being her husband, but she desires to have a husband "down here." What does it mean to be satisfied with one's singleness? Does it mean her love for God is any less if she desires a husband?

12) While reading the book, *Touching A Dead Man*, Monica feels convicted when she realizes that judging people struggling with homosexuality is just as much of a sin as homosexuality itself. Has this book at all caused you, the reader, to examine your ideas, thoughts, feelings and prejudices toward homosexuals? If so, how? How can a change in attitude in Christians affect the deliverance of individuals struggling with homosexuality?

Urban Christian His Glory Book Club!

Established January 2007, **UC His Glory Book Club** is another way by which to introduce **Urban Christian** and its authors. We are an online book club supporting Urban Christian authors by purchasing, reading, and providing written reviews of the authors' books. *UC His Glory Book Club* welcomes both men and women of the literary world who have a passion for reading Christian-based fiction.

UC His Glory Book Club is the brainchild of Joylynn Jossel, author and Executive Editor of Urban Christian and Kendra Norman-Bellamy, author and copy editor for Urban Christian. The book club will provide support, positive feedback, encouragement, and a forum whereby members can openly discuss and review the literary works of Urban Christian authors. In the future, we anticipate broadening our spectrum of services to include online author chats, author spotlights, interviews with your favorite Urban Christian author(s), special online groups for *UC His Glory Book Club* members, ability to post reviews on the website and amazon.com, membership ID cards, *UC His Glory* Yahoo! Group and much more.

Even though there will be no membership fees attached to becoming a member of *UC His Glory Book Club*, we do expect our members to be active, committed, and to follow the guidelines of the Book Club.

UC His Glory Book Club members pledge to:

- Follow the guidelines of *UC His Glory Book Club*.
- Provide input, opinions, and reviews that build up, rather than tear down.
- Commit to purchasing, reading and discussing featured book(s) of the month.
- Respect the Christian beliefs of *UC His Glory Book Club*.
- Believe that Jesus is the Christ, Son of the Living God

We look forward to the online fellowship.

Many Blessings to You!

Shelia E. Lipsey
President
UC His Glory Book Club

**Visit the official Urban Christian Book Club website at *www.uchisglorybookclub.net*